Typewriter Pub, an imprint of Blvnp Incorporated
A Nevada Corporation
1887 Whitney Mesa DR #2002
Henderson, NV 89014
www.typewriterpub.com/info@typewriterpub.com

ISBN: 978-1-64434-139-1

DISCLAIMER

This book is a work of fiction. The characters, incidents, and dialogue are drawn from the author's imagination and are not to be construed as real. While references might be made to actual historical events or existing locations, the names, characters, places, and incidents are either products of the author's imagination or are used fictitiously, and any resemblance to actual persons living or dead, business establishments, events or locales is entirely coincidental.

SUGARCOATED PAIN

SUMMER NAWAZ

*To everyone who read the entirety of this book on Tumblr
and had to wait days to weeks for me to update this story.
Thank you for seeing it all the way through—all the way to this.*

CHAPTER ONE

The feel of the hardcover in her hands and the smell of new books that greeted her every time she picked them up comforted Noelle Simon as she continued her work. She was currently fixing up the horror or thriller section of the store she helped run, replacing the sold out books with copies she picked up from the inventory earlier. Once she was satisfied with how a shelf looked, she moved on to the next one.

While she normally enjoyed doing this, her sister talking her ear off made it difficult for Noelle to work peacefully.

"Come on, Elle," her twenty-four-year-old sister, Beverly, whined to her left. "He just wants to take us out. You like Aiden. Why're you being so difficult?"

"Because I don't wanna be a third wheel," Noelle replied, putting up copies of Bram Stoker novels as she shot her blonde sister a pointed look. "I do like Aiden, but you two end up in your own little world. I don't wanna be sitting there all awkward and shit."

Beverly huffed, glossy lips forming a pout. "I promise we'll try to hold back on that," she insisted, shuffling forward as Noelle moved further down the aisle. "Andrea loves going out with us, and it's about time you come too. We're not that bad, I swear," she added with a laugh.

What Beverly said was true; Noelle liked Aiden. She had no reason not to. Knowing there was something special about him for her sister the day, almost a year ago, that Beverly called her up to gush about the absolutely divine—Beverly's exact words—instructor who worked at the new gym she went to. They met last summer, right after Beverly graduated from college and was getting ready to fully run Simon's Stories on her own. It was a miracle given that Beverly took a year off after high school to do some traveling. She was convinced she didn't want to go back to college until she finally gave in on her own accord. Aiden had been a lender of support when she took over the business, which sometimes overwhelmed Beverly, and Noelle was too busy finishing up her own last year of college to be of much help. He was a good guy.

Not only did he treat Beverly well but Aiden also had a soft spot to their seventeen-year-old sister Andrea, bringing her along to nice outings as well. Noelle only met Aiden a handful of times despite him being with Beverly for the past year, but that was because Noelle was living in New Jersey for college. Now that she was back in the city and having just graduated a few weeks ago, Aiden wanted to take them out for dinner. While that wasn't strange and Noelle adored Aiden, she genuinely didn't want to be a third wheel.

When Beverly wanted something, she would insist and persuade until she would get it. Noelle could already feel her fight leaving her. She knew she was a bit of a pushover, especially when it came to her sisters, but Noelle didn't really care about that unless she absolutely had to stand her ground on something. Unfortunately, this didn't qualify.

"Why do we have to go to Brooklyn though?" she finally complained.

A smile began spreading on Beverly's lips, knowing she had talked her sister into dinner. "Because one of Aiden's friends opened up a restaurant there, and he hasn't tried it out yet." She smiled excitedly. "We'll get free dessert!"

2

Noelle shot her a dry smile, raising an eyebrow as she pushed the almost empty cart with her hip. "But dinner isn't free?" She clicked her tongue teasingly. "Then what's the point?"

"It is for us. It's Aiden's treat." Beverly laughed, shaking her head and walking past Noelle to go to the front of the store. "He'll pick us up at home at seven-thirty!"

*   *   *

Despite her initial hesitance, Noelle would be lying if she said she wasn't enjoying her time. It was nearing 9 PM, and she's been seated in the restaurant for about an hour and a half, finding it difficult to swallow a sip of her wine as she laughed at yet another joke Aiden made. They were almost finished eating, and Noelle was savoring every taste of her Penne alla Vodka.

They were in an adorable and quaint Italian restaurant with sleek floors and dark walls that went nicely with the red chairs and white tables. The soft glow of the individual lamps hanging from the ceilings over each table provided a calming ambiance. The restaurant was right by the East River, and Aiden had gotten them a table on the upstairs patio that had fairy lights strung above their heads. The breeze was gentle against her skin, and the view of the Brooklyn Bridge kept demanding Noelle's attention.

"How much did you miss the city?" Aiden asked Noelle once they calmed down from their laughter, leaning back in his chair. "Or have you become a Jersey girl?"

Noelle snorted, picking up her almost empty glass of wine once more. "I'm always gonna be a city girl," she confirmed as Beverly smirked, "and I'm proud of it."

Aiden grinned, dimples in full view as he opened his mouth to say something, only to be cut off by the sound of his phone ringing. "Sorry." He shot Beverly and Noelle apologetic smiles as he answered the call, looking out over the railing they were sitting next to, towards the river.

3

"Hey, what's up?" The girls took this time to finish their food but didn't miss the sudden change of Aiden's tone as he practically hissed into the phone, "What?"

Noelle's eyes widened slightly at the harshness in Aiden's voice, drastically different than the usual excited, pleasant lilt his tone held whenever she talked to him. She glanced at Beverly, who didn't at all look fazed by his demeanor and instead had her eyebrows lowered in concern.

Am I missing something? Noelle thought.

"He's not scheduled for toni—" Aiden stopped, face contorted into a scowl as he listened to whoever was on the other end, still looking out towards the water. Noelle watched as Aiden clenched his jaw, his free hand running through his short curly hair, then he kept his fingers entangled at the back of his head. "Max, he's booked for the next two nights. He had tonight off for a goddamn reason."

Whatever Aiden was talking about sounded like some kind of work scheduling conflict to Noelle's ears. She knew Aiden was a fitness instructor at a gym in Manhattan, but the way he was speaking—the hard edge in his voice and severe frustration on his face—made whatever he was talking about sound like a really big deal. When she looked at Beverly, Noelle saw realization flitter across her sister's face, but there was still worry etched onto her features.

Aiden's hazel eyes glanced over the two girls quickly. "I can't. I'm in the middle of dinner," he said into the phone before letting out a sigh and rubbing his hand down his face. He looked both riled up and defeated at the same time. "Fuck. Okay, alright. I'll be there in ten."

Noelle's eyebrows shot up at that. *Is dinner over already?*

"I'm sorry to have to do this, girls," Aiden apologized, his expression softening as he looked at them with a sheepish smile while pocketing his phone and taking out his wallet. "I have to get to Astros. It's Car," he said as his gaze met Beverly's.

4

Beverly's lips parted, evidently understanding what Aiden was talking about as he raised his hand for the waiter and gestured for the check while Noelle sat there, staring at the two of them in confusion. *What the hell is Astros and who is Car?*

"Um, what's going on?" she questioned, letting her bewilderment be known as she shook her head slightly and persistently.

The check arrived promptly, and Aiden didn't even bother looking at it as he put his credit card in and gave the little black folder back to the waiter. Noelle stared at her sister with a questioning raise of her eyebrows because, apparently, she knew exactly what was going on. "Oh, um . . . it's just—"

"She'll see when we get there, Bev," Aiden cut her off, looking around impatiently for the waiter to return with his card. The muscle in his jaw was jumping, agitation practically radiating off of him. He looked so frantic, a complete deviation from his normal easy-going personality Noelle was used to.

Noelle watched as Beverly shot a wide-eyed look at the man. "Are you joking?" she demanded, her own tone taking a hard edge to it. Noelle blinked, not expecting her sister to suddenly get so disconcerted. Beverly leaned closer to Aiden. "Noelle isn't going there," she said, dropping her tone.

Aiden looked exasperated even as the waiter returned to give back the folder. Aiden quickly took out his card and shoved it back in his wallet. "I have to get there ASAP, Bev. I'm not about to let either of you take the subway or Uber back home, okay? We don't have a choice, doll," he said to Beverly as he signed the receipt.

Okay. What the hell is going on? Noelle thought.

Aiden quickly stood up from his chair, looking like he couldn't get out of here fast enough. Beverly's jaw was clenched tightly, and she looked irritated as soon as Aiden said that Noelle would be coming with them. Meanwhile, the brunette slowly rose from her seat, trying to catch her sister's eye as she wondered why Beverly didn't want her going to this "Astro" place.

Noelle followed in silent bewilderment, frowning at the backs of Beverly and Aiden as they had an intense yet whispered conversation right in front of her while making their way out of the building. She was growing irritated at their lack of communication towards her, leaving her in the dark as they stepped out onto the sidewalk and approached Aiden's car. From the bits and pieces Noelle could gather, Beverly was still arguing that she didn't want Noelle to go to Astros, and Aiden was apologizing that there was no other way.

Beverly didn't bother hiding her distaste in the situation as they got in the car. "I don't like this." She heard her sister mutter as she slid in the back.

Don't like what? Noelle wanted to scream, watching Aiden let out a sigh as he buckled his seatbelt. "I know, doll. I'm sorry, but I have to go for Car."

Noelle clenched her jaw. She didn't like being in the dark. *Who the hell is Car?*

CHAPTER TWO

All of Noelle's questions were answered as soon as they entered a pair of soundproof doors that led them inside an old building in Brooklyn. Her mouth felt dry and her eyes widened as she stepped into, what seemed to be, an unexpectedly rambunctious environment. The stench of alcohol mixed with cigarettes lingered in the air along with an unmistakable coppery smell of blood, reminding Noelle of a dirty man's locker room. Her hand that was clasped with Beverly's tightened its grip instinctively as she took in the roars of the people inside—people who mostly consisted of men either her age or older with only a handful of women sprinkled around the boisterous group, most of who were gripping bottles and cans of beers in their hand while some were holding little paper slips.

It wasn't just the people screaming that had Noelle's heart jumping in her throat; it was what they were screaming at. The large crowd was gathered around a square that was situated in the center of the room; its perimeter surrounded with thick ropes, which Noelle realized in astonishment was a boxing ring. Right in the middle of the chaos were two men who, to put it simply, were beating the shit out of each other.

Noelle's eyes widened at the violent sight, her feet frozen in place as she noticed that neither of the two fighters were wearing gloves nor protective gear. Instead, the two merely relied on their bare fists where each hit connected with skin echoed in the air as they tried to knock each other down.

The atmosphere surrounding her was laden with excitement and tension. Throughout the fight, Noelle could make out some excerpts of what the audience was shouting; there were some insults while others shouted praises towards the two fighters as well as a throng of cheers and jeers whenever one of them got hit.

What in the actual fuck?

Noelle stumbled slightly as Beverly pulled her along and tightened her grip on her younger sister's hand as her other one held Aiden's who was guiding them through the thick crowd. Noelle's gaze never wavered from the ring, staring at a tattooed brown-skinned man punching a darker-skinned man in the face. With eyes widened and lips parted in both shock and mild horror, Noelle did feel goose bumps.

She could feel shifty eyes belonging to the overzealous men on her, which, much to her chagrin, wasn't surprising because she was in the midst of a crowd full of uproarious men filled with testosterone. She was wearing a loose full-sleeved crop top and black leather shorts that exposed her legs. Some men looked away from the ring long enough to admire her legs, and Noelle let Beverly pull her along to get away from them as her gut twisted at the unwanted stares.

"Fucking shit." She heard Aiden curse from ahead and looked at his profile as he stared at the ring with brows drawn together in an exasperated glare. Suddenly, they were at the front of the crowd, approaching one corner of the ring where Noelle saw two guys leaning their chests on it.

"Why the hell didn't he wait for me?" Aiden demanded towards the guys who looked over at the sound of his voice over the exuberant crowd.

So much was happening at once; Noelle had no idea where to focus. The cheers of the men surrounding her rattled her bones, the gruff tones thundering in her ears. There were two guys beating each other up where she noticed drops of blood splattered on the floor of the white ring, and Aiden was staring at two other guys in frustration. Even though Noelle was no longer looking at the ring, she winced every time she heard the unmistakable sound of fist colliding with skin.

"He said you were taking too long," one of the men responded to Aiden with a casual shrug. Noelle noticed he was tall—taller than Aiden. The other guy had hair blonder, curlier, and slightly longer than Aiden's and had bright blue eyes. He was handsome, just like Aiden and the other guy who stood next to them in glasses. His blond hair swooped into a fringe as he hid it under a beanie. It was the middle of summer in the city.

Doesn't he feel hot in that beanie?

"It's not a set match, Aiden. Montgomery was ready to fight anyone if Carson didn't get in the ring, and he wasn't about to pass on the money people were betting. Besides, they're already on the last round."

Noelle felt all the air rush out of her lungs at the blue-eyed guy's words. She wasn't clueless, and it didn't take a genius to figure out what the hell she just walked into. The questionable setting, excitable men, the gloveless fight, and the betting. She had stepped into some kind of rendition of *Fight Club*—bloody, sweaty, and *illegal*.

"Holy shit," she breathed out, her whispered words falling onto deaf ears over the roar of everyone. Her hand was still secured in Beverly's grasp as she forced herself to bring her gaze towards the ring to her immediate right. She watched just in time to see the tattooed guy swing a right hook, his fist connecting to his opponent's side as he failed to block the hit. She could only see the tattooed guy's back, which was glistening with sweat yet surprisingly smooth looking, while the other man's face was marred with a scowl and sweat along with a cut lip and blood pouring from it as well as some smudged around his nose.

Her mind was a whirlwind of thoughts. She pressed her lips together as she swallowed a lump that had formed in her throat. *What the hell are we doing here?* Noelle deduced that Aiden knew one of the guys in the ring as he kept on bringing up someone named Carson and looking towards the two fighting men, which answered the question of why they were here. Noelle glanced at her sister, who was watching the fight in concentration. Noelle gaped at her.

How is Beverly not cringing with every hit that lands on either men? How many times has she witnessed this?

"He better not be burnt out for tomorrow's match," Aiden grumbled, crossing his arms over his chest as his left index finger and thumb worried his lower lip, his eyes on the ring as well. "I told him to take today off for a fucking reason."

Aiden's friend with glasses snorted, looking unworried. "Carson? Burnt out?" He rolled his green eyes as he watched the match. "You're freaking out over nothing, Aiden."

Noelle pulled her lower lip into her mouth, teeth sinking into it as she wondered which one was Carson as the two men moved around each other in the ring like a predator circling its prey and waiting for it to attack. In this situation, Noelle wasn't sure who was what. Her heart was pounding wildly in her chest in anticipation. She wasn't too much of a violent person—the most she could do was watch it on TV shows and movies—so the sight in front of her had her stomach twisting nervously and throat drying like she hadn't drank water in days.

As the guys stopped circling one another, Noelle finally took in the face of the tattooed man through the ropes of the ring. Her eyes widened and felt the air rush out of her lungs at the sight of a devastatingly handsome face. He had dark brown eyes narrowed in concentration, never once wavering from his opponent. What took Noelle by surprise—much like everything else in here did—was the subtle yet noticeable smirk curling at the corner of his plump lips. With somewhat curly black hair matted to his forehead in sweat, Noelle could see the utter cockiness pulling at his features despite never having seen him before in her life, like he knew something nobody else did. Noelle wasn't sure if the warmth she felt was because of this guy's looks or because of the hot atmosphere of the room.

But she was sure she had never seen someone so unbelievably good-looking in her life.

He also had tattoos on his collarbones, but Noelle had no time to decipher what they were because he was moving suddenly. His fists that were bandaged with white cloth delivered relentless punches to the other guy who failed to defend himself. A choked gasp escaped Noelle as she watched with wide eyes. The loud clamors of those around her intensified tenfold to the point where she winced more from the sheer volume than the violence happening in front of her.

She couldn't break her gaze away from it though, especially when the black-haired man's right fist connected with the other's jaw, immediately knocking him to the ground with a loud thud. There was a mixture of cheers and boos following the guy's fall before everyone began counting up from one. Noelle watched as the tattooed man stood over his fallen opponent's body, staring down at him with an expression that challenged him to get up. The guy wasn't even looking back at him. His were eyes shut, and his face that was turned towards her scrunched in pain.

"Eight . . . nine . . . ten!" The crowd suddenly broke out into deafening cheers. Noelle was shaken that these people could make that much noise but not more shaken than the fact that there was a guy lying on the ring in front of her, probably unconscious at this point, while another stood over him smugly. *Is that guy a referee?* He wasn't dressed like one, but he stepped onto the ring and lifted the winner's hand up in the air.

"The winner, Carson Hayes!"

Carson. Noelle's jaw dropped at the name, confirming that the fierce, handsome winner was who Aiden and the two others were talking about, which she would've realized if she had paid

11

attention to see Aiden and the others cheering when the other guy had fallen down. Noelle couldn't pull her gaze away from the ring, staring with a mixture of surprise and healthy dose of fear as Carson ran his likely bruised fingers through his thick black hair. He pushed it away from his forehead, his glistening chest heaving slightly as he caught his breath.

"Ow! Elle, you're crushing my hand!" Beverly's voice suddenly sounded, making Noelle blink as she finally looked at her sister who was staring at her in mild surprise.

"Sorry," Noelle said, releasing her tight grip before letting out a breath and turning to face her. "What the hell, Bev?" she hissed, eyes widening demandingly. "What're we doing here?"

Beverly, who was about three inches taller than Noelle, stared down at her with a questioning brow. She didn't look nearly as pressed about Noelle being here as she had before.

"Do you really need me to answer that?" When Noelle didn't look away, Beverly sighed. "Aiden is Carson's best friend, and he's also his trainer. This match wasn't planned, and he needs to be here whenever Car's in the ring. So, you know, dinner had to be cut short."

Noelle gaped at Beverly or, more so, at the casual way she delivered her words. She made it seem like this fighting—this illegal fighting—was a normal thing. Noelle, for one, was trying to wrap her head around the fact that Beverly had most definitely been here a number of times to appear so unaffected by the punches getting thrown around. She never would've thought that her sister would be seen in a place like this. Hell, she never would've thought that Aiden—adorable, giggly Aiden—would be a trainer for, let alone best friends with, someone who took part in something as dangerous as this.

Suddenly, Noelle wished she had drank more than just half a glass of wine at dinner.

"We agreed on a night off. Why can't you just listen to me?" The sound of Aiden's voice was clear to Noelle since the

12

screaming from the now dispersed crowd had ceased. She looked to her left to see Aiden standing with his arms crossed over his chest. Noelle took in a soft breath at the person standing in front of Aiden, wondering if it was normal for her heart to beat so erratically at the sight of someone she had never met before.

Carson stood there, wearing nothing but black gym shorts and sneakers with a small white towel hung around his neck. She noticed he was tall, taller than Aiden and the glasses boy but only slightly shorter than the blue-eyed guy.

I really need to find out these boys' names, she thought.

For now, her gaze was focused on Carson, who had apparently used the towel to dry off the sweat from his face and neck. Noelle was taken aback at the lack of blood or bruising on him. The other guy, who was taken away by his friends or whoever, had blood on his lips and bruises blooming on his face, but Noelle didn't even detect a scratch on Carson's body.

She finally saw the tattoos decorating his skin; a pirate's compass pointing north on his bicep, a skull with a crow right below the inside of his left elbow, five seven-point stars positioned specifically on his right clavicle, and she even caught a glimpse of what looked like a black spades tattoo on the inside of his right wrist. Noelle only noticed that one because she knew Aiden had a small red heart tattooed in the exact place. Suits from a deck of cards? There were some other pretty-looking ones on Carson's arm that she didn't stare at too long because he was speaking suddenly.

"If I'd listened to you, then I would have missed out on making the money I did tonight." Noelle's eyes widened at the unexpected hint of an accent, subtle but still present.

Is he Australian?

Her gaze flickered to his collarbone, the tattoos of the stars ringing bells. The stars on his skin matched perfectly to the ones on the Australian flag from what Noelle could recall.

His voice was deep, but it was also startlingly smooth, much like his movements in the ring. He had a cool expression on his face, looking unbothered by Aiden's exasperation as he kept his gaze on the hazel-eyed boy while unwrapping the bandage from his hands.

"And what if you lost?" Aiden retorted with a quirk of a brow.

Carson's response was immediate. "It's not in my nature."

Okay . . . Hot. Noelle was aware that she was nervously picking at her unpainted nails with her eyes on the boys yet she couldn't stop. Most of the crowd had cleared out. Only a few people lingered about and talked amongst themselves. Noelle stayed close to Beverly because there were still some older guys standing on the side, shamelessly checking out her legs. An uncomfortable shiver shot down her spine, feeling her skin crawl wherever they looked.

"Hey, Bev. You ever gonna introduce us to your friend?"

Noelle's eyes flickered to the curly-haired guy, who was looking at her with a kind smile that she couldn't help but return. It was comforting despite the nerves swimming in her belly.

"Oh!" Beverly sounded surprised. "Right, right. Guys, this is my sister Noelle. Elle, these are Max, Levi, and Carson."

She gestured to each boy with each name, pointing out the glasses boy first, then the blue-eyed surfer-looking one, and lastly the man of the hour. Noelle somewhat nervously returned the smiles Max and Levi offered her but then felt her breath stop in her throat as her hazel eyes met Carson's dark brown ones. His expression was unreadable. He lifted his chin slightly as he unwrapped the other hand and assessed the unfamiliar girl, who in turn tried hard not to bristle under his intense stare. Not even a trace of the smirk she had given to his friends.

Carson's gaze shifted, landing on Beverly as his expression turned into one of pointed irritation. "You know how I feel about strangers coming to my fights, Bev," he said to her, completely ignoring Noelle's presence as her eyebrows twitched into a frown at his words.

14

She understood that what Carson did was illegal, and he wouldn't want anyone around who couldn't be trusted or whatever. It was ironic for her to acknowledge those betting could be trusted more since they were taking part in the illegality but at least have the decency to not imply that to Noelle's face. He looked unapologetic for his words, for the implication that he trusted the sleazy-looking men around them more than her, which seemed fair enough. They all seemed like regulars at this place. Meanwhile, Beverly rolled her eyes, the hardened expression on the fighter's face not fazing her. "She's not a stranger, bro. She's Bev's sister, so she's cool. Don't be a dick," Aiden spoke up before Beverly could say anything.

A swell of gratitude briefly rushed through Noelle towards Aiden, tense shoulders relaxing only somewhat when Carson pursed his lips, still unsatisfied with her presence. Not being wanted was kind of embarrassing even though Noelle had no intention of being here in the first place. She would appreciate it if Carson didn't show his disapproval so obviously though, the clear disdain in his features igniting an embarrassed flush to her skin.

"Whatever," Carson finally huffed out. He took the bandages off and balled them up in his hands before he tossed them to Levi, who caught them easily. "I'm gonna shower," he added, walking past Aiden and Max as he headed towards the back of the spacious room.

Noelle noticed there were punching bags hung up around the area as well as mats to be practiced on and benches spread out here and there. Not much else was around, save for a few cabinets lined against the walls. She couldn't help but stare at Carson, the muscles on his back working as he walked towards a back door that led to a different area she couldn't see. The building had appeared old from the outside, and the bricked walls inside only accentuated the rustic features.

"Sorry about Car," Max's voice sounded, drawing Noelle's attention back to him. "He can be a bit intense after a fight."

Noelle just smiled and shook her head dismissively, not wanting to show that Carson's unwelcoming demeanor had intimidated her. She just saw what he could do; she really didn't wanna get on his bad side.

She stood by as her sister and the guys talked for a bit, awkwardly hugging herself as the rest of the people in the building cleared out, not really paying attention to what they were talking about.

"Alright. I'm gonna take these ladies home, and I'll meet you and Max's. Make sure Car's alright, okay?" Aiden said.

Levi and Max nodded as Aiden clapped their shoulders. The two boys bid Noelle and Beverly goodnight before they followed Aiden outside. Through the car ride back home, Noelle was quiet as she stared out the window at the dark streets of New York. She was still trying to wrap her head around tonight's turn of events. The concept of illegal fighting wasn't what totally floored her; it was the fact that her sister knew people involved in it and never mentioned it to her. Beverly had known Aiden for about a year, so Noelle assumed Beverly knew about Carson and what he did for just as long.

Maybe Beverly never mentioned it because of how Carson reacted, but it was still crazy to Noelle. Beverly's boyfriend trained his fighter of a best friend, a best friend who was—Noelle had no shame in admitting—one of the most attractive men she had ever laid eyes on.

What the fuck? Noelle cursed to herself.

Seemed like that was the only thought running through Noelle's mind since the moment she stepped into Astros.

"You okay?" Beverly asked her once they had returned home. Their mom was still working a shift at the hospital, and their younger sister was at another friend's house for a sleepover. "I really thought you'd break my hand back there," she added lightheartedly.

16

Noelle let out a huff as Beverly crawled onto her bed, both of them bare faced and in their pajamas.

"That was freaking intense," she said, her legs crossed and covered with her comforter. "How could . . . how long have you—" she cut herself off, unable to properly voice her thoughts as she dropped her hands to her lap and let an exasperated expression wash over her face. Beverly took notice of this, a small smile curling at her lips as she straightened her back.

"Aiden told me about it four months into our relationship," Beverly confessed. "I had met Car, Levi, and Max, then there was this one night where Carson had an important match, so Aiden told me everything just hours before it."

Noelle blinked. "Just like that?" She assumed Aiden wouldn't have told Beverly about Carson judging by how the former had reacted or maybe Carson was more lenient seeing as Aiden was his best friend and Beverly was dating him.

"Yeah." Beverly shrugged with an airy laugh, blowing a tendril of blonde hair out of her face that was too short to be tied into her bun. "Look, I know tonight was . . . unexpected, but those guys have been involved in it for years now. Carson's one of the best fighters there is. He rarely, if ever, loses a match. I mean, he works at the gym with Aiden but he's only working part-time. Fighting is how he makes most of his money, you know? That's more his livelihood than anything else."

Noelle's lips parted as she inhaled softly, raising her eyebrows at the information. *So fighting isn't just a hobby for Carson; it is basically his job.* Noelle shook her head in disbelief. *This is crazy.*

"I know he seemed kind of like an ass tonight," Beverly spoke up once more, "but he's not so bad once you get to know him."

Noelle let out a light scoff and rolled her eyes at that, instantly remembering the irritated expression that had pulled at his face when he looked at her. Carson may be stupidly attractive, but that wasn't going to prevent Noelle from being affronted by his obvious dislike of her. Which was unfortunate since Noelle had never felt her heart literally drop to the pit of her stomach at the sight of a man like it did for Carson. Whether it was out of fear from watching him knock someone out or because of how attractive he was, she wasn't quite sure.

CHAPTER THREE

"I still feel bad for leaving you here by yourself," Noelle said worriedly, willing herself not to chew on her lips so she didn't eat off the lipstick staining them.

Her seventeen-year-old sister rolled her eyes in exasperation. "I'm gonna be fine, Elle," Andrea insisted. "I just found out Amazon Prime has all the seasons of *Bones* on it, so I'm gonna binge watch the crap out of that and order food that I'm gonna eat until I pass out. It's gonna be a fun night."

Beverly descended the stairs that led right into the living room the other two were in. "Since when do you have an Amazon Prime account?"

Andrea grinned impishly. "Mom got sick of me begging for it and gave in. Perks of being the paraplegic child."

Both Beverly and Noelle scoffed and rolled their eyes, used to Andrea using her disability as a way of getting what she wanted though Andrea didn't even have to use that as an excuse because they all babied her anyway. Still, Noelle and Beverly couldn't help but shake their heads in amusement as Andrea giggled giddily. She had been paralyzed for three years, and at this point, she was fully capable of cracking jokes about her being confined to a wheelchair.

It was a terrifying accident, one involving Andrea and their father and a drunk driver in which Mr. Simon died on impact and the driver was imprisoned for driving under the influence. It was one of the toughest times for Noelle and her family. They tried to deal with their dad's death and helped the youngest of the family adjust to a life in a wheelchair. For the longest time, Andrea was angry at everything in the world—for the loss of their dad and for the loss of feeling below her waist. It wasn't until a year and a half after the accident when Andrea cracked the first joke in regards to her being a paraplegic.

"I can finally get pedicures and not get creeped out by people touching my feet. Thank God for paraplegia, huh?" she had said back then when she decided to join Noelle and Beverly to the nail salon. The joke had left the two older sisters stunned in incredulity, laughing only when they noticed the grin on Andrea's face. They quickly realized they needed to be able to joke about it with Andrea, who was finally coping with her lifestyle after so much trouble.

"Okay, but if you need anything, call either of us, alright?" Noelle told Andrea with a raise of her eyebrows, unplugging her phone from the charger by the couch.

The seventeen-year-old nodded before waving her sisters off, telling them to leave already. It wasn't often that the girls left Andrea alone at the house. Their mom worked long hours at the hospital, and while Andrea was fully capable of taking care of herself, they still worried over her. They couldn't help it; she was their baby sister. They had been taking care of her long before she was ever paralyzed.

"So what's Aiden throwing this party for?" Noelle asked once she and Beverly slid into the backseat of the Uber, leaning her back against the door as she faced her sister. She dropped her bag next to her, heavy with the book inside. Herman Melville's *The Blithedale Romance* sat inside, and Noelle was determined to enjoy the novel without the droning commentary of one of her literary professors from college. The man had been more interested in discussing Melville's personal life than his actual writing. Reading it on her own time was far more enjoyable for Noelle.

Beverly ran her fingers through her blonde hair to push it back. "Car won every match he had this week, and Aiden sometimes throws a little celebration type thing. Obviously, no one really knows the real reason for the parties because of what Car does but, you know, still fun," she explained with a shrug before grinning happily. "Now that you're back in town, I finally have someone to go with!"

Noelle smiled wryly, pulling her phone out to scroll through social media. "Joy," she responded dryly, though she was fine with accompanying Beverly.

Truly, Noelle was never opposed to a night out when she really wanted to go. From what Beverly had told her, Aiden's parties or get-togethers were always fun, so it was time Noelle attended one. Though the fact that this particular party was for Carson—meaning he would be there— had Noelle's gut twisting nervously. Obviously, she hadn't seen him since she met him the first time three nights ago, but Noelle wasn't going to forget the disgruntled way he looked at her. She could only hope he wouldn't be irritated by her presence and make her feel embarrassed once more.

If she was someone else, it would be enough for her to reject the invitation, but Carson was too handsome for Noelle to not want to just get a glimpse of him again. *Am I that desperate? Maybe*, she told herself.

They arrived at Aiden's apartment in SoHo within fifteen minutes, getting rung in through the front security desk by Aiden and using the elevator to go to the fourth floor. When they walked in through the door, Noelle couldn't help but notice how nice Aiden's apartment was—large windows, slanted ceilings with lights embedded in them, and sleek wood floors. Aiden was a general manager at a popular gym in Manhattan, and he earned a pretty penny. His residence showed that in the least obnoxious way possible.

21

There was music playing at an appropriate, non-deafening volume, and there were a bunch of people hanging around with drinks in their hands as they talked and mingled. Noelle was relieved to see it wasn't like a literal house party, many of which she attended during high school and college, and that everyone here seemed much more relaxed yet enjoying their time.

"They're in the kitchen," Beverly said, nodding towards the left of the apartment before leading her sister over. Noelle noticed Beverly waving and saying hi to a few people as they walked, already familiar with almost everyone there as they entered the kitchen.

"You're here!" Aiden's cheery voice sounded, and Noelle easily caught sight of the dirty-blonde-haired man as he moved his way around the center counter that was full of different types of liquor bottles and weaved past a few people that were lingering about. He reached them, hugging and kissing Beverly with a grin. "Hiya, Noelle. I'm happy you're here," he added genuinely, pulling the younger girl for a surprise hug.

Noelle couldn't help but smile as she returned the hug before pulling away. "I can never say no to free drinks, you know," she teased.

Aiden chuckled before nodding towards the counter. "What will you have?"

Before Noelle could answer, Beverly said to him, "Oh, make her a tequila sunrise." Shifting her gaze to Noelle, she said with a smile, "It's so good. He's an expert at making them."

Not one to say no to a good drink, Noelle merely nodded and smiled in agreement as Aiden moved towards the counter to make two of them for the girls.

"Where are the others?" she asked Aiden, leaning on the counter opposite Aiden.

"Max and Levi are around here somewhere, and Car stepped out for a smoke," Aiden hummed as he picked up a bottle of orange juice.

Noelle tilted her head slightly as Beverly quirked a brow. "Isn't he trying to quit?"

Aiden snorted. "'Trying being the key term. We all know Car's not one to quit easily."

"Stop talking shit about me behind my back, mate."

Noelle felt her back straighten at the deep voice sounding behind her, watching from the corner of her eye as Carson appeared next to Beverly on the side of the counter diagonal of Noelle. Her gaze remained on him, taking in his simple outfit of black jeans and a white shirt with a black leather jacket on top, her thoughts immediately consisting of how damn good he looked. She watched as Carson reached for the stack of cups before pouring in whatever drink was mixed in a glass bottle. Her eyes were going to the tattoos on his hands, the silver bracelets on each wrist, and the chunky rings on his fingers. A man's hands should not look as good as Carson's.

"I'm not talking shit!" Aiden defended with a high-pitched laugh before handing Noelle and Beverly their cups. "Just, you know . . . complimenting you on your determination."

Carson scoffed, looking away from Aiden to his left as he brought the cups to his lips. "Bullshit."

It was when he turned his head that Noelle spotted the bruise blooming on his cheek, her eyes widening slightly at the sight of it. Dark blue and purple yet not too big. It was right on the side of his face, near his jaw. She couldn't help but wince slightly, thinking of the punch that caused it. If almost everyone here didn't know about Carson's fighting, what did he tell them if they asked about his bruise?

"Oh, shit. Ouch." Beverly's eyes widened, leaning forward slightly as she looked at Carson's face. Apparently, she wasn't hesitant on bringing up the bruise like Noelle was. "That looks like it hurts."

Carson's eyes flickered over to her, swallowing his drink without complaint and lowering the cup. "Nothin' I'm not used to," he replied as the corner of his lips curled smugly. His gaze shifted over slightly, finally landing on Noelle as she took a sip of her delicious drink and caught the subtle recognition flicker in his eyes. "Noelle, right?"

Honestly, Noelle was surprised that she didn't choke on her drink as Carson addressed her, taking her by surprise as she swallowed a sip. Tequila always warmed her up easily despite it being mixed or not, but she was sure the warmth spreading up her neck had more to do with the pair of dark brown eyes staring at her rather than her drink.

"Um, yeah," she stumbled out, mentally cursing herself for sounding unsure. "Hi."

Carson merely nodded in return, making Noelle bristle slightly. *How could a subtle action make her feel so unwelcome, and why did she care so much?*

"Congrats on your win, Car." Beverly smiled, holding her cup up to him as she dramatically added, "You've made me proud."

He lifted his own cup, lightly touching it with Beverly's. "It's why I do it," he said while his gaze never left Noelle's.

*   *   *

Carson raised unimpressed eyebrows as he stared at his two best friends, who were singing a Queen song terribly and totally off-key. He sat on Aiden's couch with his legs spread and a red cup in his hand. Though they weren't singing all too well, Aiden and Levi were definitely entertaining everyone here with their rendition of "We Are The Champions." Carson knew getting Aiden that karaoke machine for Christmas had been a bad idea.

Levi and Aiden started the second verse with their arm wrapped around the other as Aiden held the mic in his right hand and Levi held his cup in his left. Carson couldn't help but let out a deep chuckle. Everyone around was laughing and recording the two of them, and Carson shook his head in amusement as Aiden and

Levi swayed while singing. The party started a few hours ago and his friends were a few drinks in. Carson was surprised either one of them was staying upright.

His gaze flickered around the room before ultimately landing on a face he had seen twice now. Noelle leaned against the wall that separated the kitchen and living room, a bottle of beer in hand after switching to it from the liquor. A wide grin spread on her face that showed off dimples Carson wasn't aware she had as her eyes remained on Aiden and Levi. Just like everyone else, she was wildly entertained by the show the two idiots were putting on, her mouth forming soundless words whenever she spoke to Beverly.

Carson's eyes trailed up her figure, taking in the exposure of her legs due to the blue shorts she wore and the way her form-fitting pale yellow tank top hugged her tightly. He attempted to ignore the tightening in his jeans at the sight of her slender neck, wondering what it would be like to have his hand wrapped around it and his lips pressed against the skin. Carson wasn't afraid to admit he had similar thoughts the moment he saw her after stepping off the ring, wondering who the hell she was and what she was doing at his match, but he wasn't going to voice his desires about Noelle after just meeting her, especially not to Beverly nor Aiden. He couldn't deny, at least to himself, that the attraction had been there the moment he met Noelle, blindsiding him with its sudden arrival, but he kept it to himself, locking away the thoughts he probably shouldn't be having in the first place.

"That was for my man Carson Hayes!" Aiden's voice rang through the house. Thanks to the karaoke machine speakers that drew the Australian's attention back to his friends who had apparently finished the song already and everyone broke out into cheers. Carson's eyebrows shot up once more in amusement as Aiden gestured to him with one hand and pressed his other to his chest. "The champion of my heart."

Despite himself, Carson couldn't help but let out a laugh at Aiden's words, shaking his head as he lifted his cup to his two laughing friends in cheers, then taking a sip of the hunch punch. He had gone from beer to whatever mixed drink Levi concocted, his mood for liquor nowhere to be found.

"You're ridiculous, bro," Carson announced after swallowing his drink. Still, he found the gesture nice.

About an hour or so later, Carson had finished sipping his first cup of mixed drink and was now nursing another one. He made his way towards the bathroom in the hallway. He may have taken small sips of his drinks as an attempt to uselessly stall the effect of the alcohol he was consuming, but he still had to pee.

It was frustrating because the bathroom door was locked.

"For fuck's sake," Carson cursed under his breath, wishing that Aiden had more than one bathroom in his place. Raising his free hand, Carson rapped sharply and impatiently on the door with his knuckles. "Others have to use the bathroom too!"

He was slightly tipsy and had raised his voice a bit louder than necessary, garnering the attention of the few people lingering in the hallway. He paid them no mind. He was too focused on making sure he wouldn't piss his damn pants right there. Carson let out a groan when no one on the other side responded, clenching his jaw and leaning his forehead against the wooden door with eyes shut in exasperation.

The door suddenly swung open, and Carson lost all sense of his fighting agility as he stumbled forward at the lack of support, eyes shooting wide open. His free hand shot out to grasp the doorframe, but not before the contents of his full cup sloshed and a good chunk of his beverage spilled out.

A startled gasp sounded in front of him. Carson looked up in surprise to see Noelle standing in the bathroom, her hazel eyes widened as she remained frozen. For a brief moment, he wondered if she looked so startled because he was standing there but then his

26

eyes trailed down and caught sight of her pale top and blue shorts darkened by the reddish-purple drink he had been consuming.

"Oh my god," Noelle breathed out, stunned at the sudden cold wetness on her front. She looked down, taking in the drink that had spilled right below her collarbone, effectively wetting her skin and staining her light-colored clothes. It was wet and sticky.

Carson, too, was staring at what he accidentally caused, his gaze lingering on the swell of her breasts that glistened with the drink he had spilled. His breathing quickened. He could just barely make out the lining of her bra underneath. Carson had to force himself to break his stare when he realized whose breasts he was openly staring at, tightening his jaw at the reminder.

"Give a guy a warning next time, will you?" he bit out, immediately defaulting to his usual cold demeanor.

Noelle's head snapped up, raising her eyebrows in surprise and dropping her mouth over with a scoff. She seemed taken aback at the sight of Carson and the colorful drink she was now drenched in, but by the narrowing of her eyes, he could tell she didn't appreciate his attitude. Not that he particularly cared.

"Are you kidding?" She let out a short disbelieving laugh. "You're the one who spilled your drink on me!"

Carson dropped his hand from the doorframe, straightening to stand at his full height and fighting the smug smirk that threatened to grow when he noticed Noelle's throat work nervously as her gaze flickered up to maintain eye contact.

"You're the one who opened the damn door out of nowhere."

His reasoning was shit, and they were both aware of it.

"Because you were knocking and yelling on the other side!" Noelle countered, bringing her fingers to the front of her tank top to pull the tight material away from her skin. Carson's eyes tracked the movement as she let out a groan, probably realizing the stain that would be left. She furrowed her eyebrows as she looked up at Carson, and he didn't see the usual look of intimidation he had received from her before. "What were you even doing, leaning against the door like that? This is your fault," she demanded.

He seriously didn't have time for this. Sure, Carson felt kind of bad for spilling his drink on Noelle, but that didn't come anywhere near as the urgency he felt for needing to use the damn bathroom. And, yeah, he knew it was his fault for leaning against the door and losing his balance, but apologizing wasn't in Carson's nature and he wasn't about to start now.

Grunting, Carson reached forward and placed his half empty cup on the sink right next to Noelle before shrugging off the leather jacket he wore. It was his favorite jacket with two white stripes running down the length of the sleeves, but he begrudgingly put that aside as he held it out to Noelle, who blinked at the piece of apparel in confusion.

"Just wear it over your clothes for now and get out of the damn bathroom for shit's sake. I have to piss," he said through gritted teeth while holding out the jacket impatiently.

Immediately, Noelle's face scrunched up in mild disgust, and Carson ignored the intrusive thought that admired how cute she looked with her nose wrinkled like that. He watched her gaze lift to meet his eyes. He knew she took one look at his impatient, hardened expression as the bruise on his cheek enhanced that effect, and clamped her mouth shut before taking the jacket with a somewhat shaky hand. No doubt she was surprised at the gesture. Carson didn't quite understand it himself, reasoning that he just wanted this conversation to be over.

When she took it, Carson stepped aside and waved his hand, raising his eyebrows as he silently gestured for her to get the hell out. Noelle's throat worked with an inaudible swallow while Carson's gaze involuntarily followed the delicate movement as she shuffled through the narrow doorway, allowing Carson to catch a whiff of whatever fruity perfume she wore under the pungent stench of alcohol. He didn't hesitate in slamming the door shut

28

once she was out, just barely missing her wince before the door could even close.

Carson let out a relieved sigh once he flushed and zipped up his pants, then he washed his hands as he stared at himself in the mirror. He turned his head to the left with hands still running under the cold water as he assessed the bruise on his cheek. It still hurt when his facial muscles moved a certain way, and every time Carson felt that sting of pain, he also felt a surge of anger for letting Underwood get that hit in the first place. It was a slip on Carson's part, lost in a thinking strategy during the fight a second too long and not seeing Underwood's left hook coming for him but managing to return the favor by knocking him the fuck out. It was a lucky shot on Underwood's part, and Carson was determined to not let it happen again.

Grunting, Carson grabbed his drink and drained the rest of it in the sink before dropping the cup in the trash. He shut off the faucet and dried his hands. When he left the bathroom, he realized Noelle wasn't in the hallway anymore and made his way back to the living room. When he did, Carson couldn't help the way he froze when his eyes somehow almost immediately landed on Noelle.

She was standing by the window talking to Max and their friend Dominique. Carson's Adam's apple bobbed in his throat at the sight of her wearing his jacket. The jacket enveloped her short frame, hiding the few dips and curves she had under the leathery material. The sleeves were too long, and the shoulders were hanging off her smaller ones, but what really had Carson taking in a sharp breath was the fact that the jacket was so long on Noelle that it made it seem like it was all she was wearing.

She should not be looking as good as she did in his jacket. Carson huffed.

I shouldn't have thrown away my drink.

CHAPTER FOUR

The jacket remained neatly folded, sitting on a shelf underneath the counter of the bookstore where Noelle's gaze kept dropping towards. She was manning the register today, but the mere presence of the jacket demanded attention. Noelle found herself often looking down at it, almost in disbelief that it was still there—that she still had it.

Truthfully, she was a bit surprised that Carson let her leave Aiden's house while still wearing it last night, though maybe it was the least Carson could do after spilling his drink on her and not even apologizing for it. Now here she was, the next morning, with the jacket still in her custody and waiting to be returned to Carson. Noelle pressed her lips together as she recalled the faint scenthis jacket carried when she put it on, enveloping her completely; it was a nice minty yet woodsy cologne with another smell that she just deemed as Carson, but it was just so delicious. She was practically swimming in the material yet she didn't want to take it off.

Beverly, too, had made sort of a big deal when she saw her little sister wearing the fighter's jacket.

"That's, like, his favorite piece of clothing ever," she said when she recognized the jacket last night. "I can't believe he's letting you wear it!"

Safe to say, Noelle felt her face heat up while a chill ran down her spine, but she wasn't going to think anything of it.

"Excuse me? I'm ready to pay." Noelle snapped out of her thoughts, blinking in startlement as she took notice of the woman standing in front of her with a few books placed on the counter.

"O-oh! I'm so sorry," Noelle rushed out, offering an apologetic smile as she began scanning the items. Fortunately, the customer didn't seem too annoyed as Noelle bagged the books and handed them over. "Have a good day," she chirped, smiling once the woman returned the sentiment and left the store.

Noelle hadn't noticed Beverly lingering near the register by one of the aisles until she walked over and stated, "That's, like, the fourth time you've spaced out on the register."

Noelle jumped slightly at the sound of her sister's voice and turned to look at Beverly, smirking slightly.

"Do I need to demote you to stocking duty?"

"You can't demote your co-owner, Bev," Noelle pointed out, rolling her eyes. Sitting down on the stool she kept behind the register, Noelle's shoulders slumped. "I don't mean to space out. Sorry."

Beverly waved her off, walking behind the counter to lean against it next to Noelle.

"What're you thinking about? Everything okay?"

"What? Oh, no, yeah. Everything's fine," Noelle assured with a laugh because it wasn't really a big deal at all. She was just lost in her thoughts about the stupid leather jacket and its owner, whom she would have to return it to. The only question was, Was she going to go herself or have Beverly or Aiden do it?

"I was just wondering . . . um, do you know where Carson would be today?" When Beverly's eyebrows shot up, Noelle quickly added, "I need to give him his jacket back."

"Mm-hmm," Beverly hummed with eyebrows still drawn together, unconvinced as she stared at her sister. Noelle, in turn, flushed slightly as she wondered what the hell Beverly could be thinking. "He's probably gonna be at Astros until eight tonight. I can just give the jacket to Aiden, and he can return it."

For some reason, Noelle wanted to protest that suggestion. Carson might have been kind of a jerk last night at the party and even when she had first met him, but he still did a nice thing by letting her borrow his jacket. It was only right if Noelle returned it herself and thanked him personally. Though, at the same time, she wasn't too sure how Carson would feel if she showed up at the place where he fought. Truthfully, she wasn't entirely comfortable going there either.

"Unless, you know, you wanna go see him?" Beverly slowly continued, easily picking up on Noelle's hesitance.

Noelle rolled her lips into her mouth, slightly widened eyes meeting Beverly's knowing light brown ones. The sisters could read each other like the books in their store, but Noelle felt a bit exasperated that Beverly could probably see Noelle's desire to see Carson again so clearly. Was that pathetic of Noelle to feel drawn to him without rhyme or reason? Carson was . . . intriguing, to put it simply, with or without his questionable career in the mix. Beverly had known Carson for almost as long as she had known Aiden, and as much as Noelle loved her sister, she didn't need any words of wisdom from Beverly. If Beverly's hesitation had more to do with Noelle venturing into Astros than actually seeing Carson, then Noelle could understand that. Still, though, she noted the curious glint in Beverly's eyes and had a feeling that sooner or later, she would be on the tiring end of one of Beverly's interrogations.

"Alright. Since we took my car, I'll drive you to Astros after work," Beverly conceded, arms crossed over her chest. "You can give Car his jacket then."

Noelle sat up slightly in the stool. "You sure?"

"Yeah." Beverly shrugged. "We'll pick up dinner on the way back."

For the next few hours until the store closed at six, Noelle did her job while trying not to think of the jacket under the counter or the fact that she was going to be seeing its owner later on. She found it kind of ridiculous how she couldn't stop thinking about

Carson after only meeting him twice, especially when her interactions with him weren't totally of the pleasant nature. It definitely had to do with the fact that Noelle found Carson wildly attractive, and maybe laying eyes on him as much as she could would quell her fantasies.

Fantasies which, Noelle was determined, would never leave the confines of her mind.

When six o'clock hit and the girls locked up the store, they got into one of the two cars their family had. The other was used by their mother and the girls shared the Prius that used to belong to their dad, which they had gotten fixed up after the accident. They didn't drive it much since they lived in the city and their house was pretty close to the store, but they kept two cars in case of emergencies, especially regarding Andrea.

They arrived at Astros twenty minutes later. Beverly pulled into one of the only available spots along the sidewalk, right by a sign that stated no parking allowed. Assuring her sister she would be out in a few minutes, Noelle got out of the car with the jacket in her hands as she approached the somewhat run-down building. Her stomach was fluttering nervously the closer she got. The sun hadn't set yet but the towering buildings provided a shadow on the street they were on, and while there wasn't anyone lingering outside, Noelle quickened her steps towards the heavy doors of the makeshift gym.

The door slammed shut behind her, making Noelle cringe slightly, but she let out a small relieved breath when she realized she hadn't caught the attention of the people in the gym. There were a few people around, all working out on equipment she hadn't seen lying around before and taking their aggression out on the punching bags. Loud music was playing throughout the area, deafening the sound of the door shutting. Noelle took in the men around, all burly in one way or another as they worked out either alone or together.

33

She pressed her lips together when she caught sight of Carson on the other side of the room wearing a pair of basketball shorts, sneakers, and a grey tank top as he delivered relentless, glove-covered punches to a punching bag while she saw Aiden holding on the other side.

Oh god, I'm gonna be interrupting, Noelle internally groaned as she slowly began making her way over, trying to relax her panic-stricken expression. Her eyes, though, couldn't help but appreciate Carson's prominent biceps even from the distance, the ink on his skin shifting with every move he made.

Some of the men looked over her way, either acknowledging the presence of a female briefly or taking their sweet time in taking her in, which only made Noelle quicken her pace. As she walked, though, her mind raced to think of ways to politely interrupt Carson's obvious training session, wondering why she couldn't have just given the jacket to Beverly who would give it to Aiden to return.

Why did my dumbass self just have to see Carson again?

When she neared, however, she was stripped of the duty of interrupting when Aiden's gaze just happened to land on her as he gripped the punching bag.

"Noelle," he said, eyebrows shooting up in surprise as he straightened.

Noelle smiled a nervous smile as she stopped once she was close enough, watching as Carson ceased his punches at Aiden's voice. His stance relaxed from the rigidness his shoulders showed as he turned around to catch sight of their visitor. He wasn't all too sweaty, the front of his black curls sticking slightly to his forehead as he gazed at Noelle with a subtle frown.

Oh boy. "Hey, um, I just came by to . . . uh, drop this," Noelle forced herself to stumble out, trying not to cringe at how she idiotically stuttered over her words.

Both men's gazes dropped to the black material she held.

34

"Did you come here by yourself?" Aiden asked before Carson could even reach for the jacket.

Noelle looked at him, seeing the slight concern on his features.

"No, uh, Bev's outside waiting in the car."

At the mention of her sister, Aiden's eyes lit up.

"I'll be right back," he said before taking off in the direction of the door Noelle had come through, leaving just her and Carson.

She returned her gaze to the tall, brown-skinned man who was now pulling off the gloves and letting them drop on the dark grey floor.

If they fight without gloves, why is he training with them?

Before losing any nerve she had left, Noelle held the jacket out. "Thanks for, um, letting me borrow this last night," she said gratefully, offering a small smile since that's all she was capable of, especially with Carson's dark eyes trained on her.

"Yeah," his low voice responded, taking the clothing from her as he lifted an eyebrow. "Did you get the stains out?"

"Oh yeah." Noelle nodded, thinking of the late night laundry load consisting of the two pieces of clothing she had done last night. "Good as new," she added with a light chuckle.

Carson nodded slightly but didn't bother saying anything else as he draped his jacket on the bench behind him. From the subtle way his eyebrows pulled together, Noelle realized his weariness over her presence, no doubt her appearance unexpected. She bit her tongue. He probably assumed she would hand off his jacket to Beverly or Aiden to return to him, which she probably should have done.

Instead, she decided to give in to some pathetic nature she didn't know she possessed and showed up like some kind of stalker. Noelle could practically feel the heat spreading through her skin, an embarrassed flush enveloping her especially when she noticed the way Carson's dark eyes narrowed suddenly in a lethal scowl that had her stomach dipping.

Just as quickly, Noelle realized the dangerous look on his face wasn't meant for her. Instead, Carson was directing it towards something behind her. She heard someone whistle, then followed by a guttural voice speaking up, "Who's your friend, Hayes? And why haven't you introduced us yet?"

Noelle straightened at that, turning around to catch sight of a man a few years older than her stop right by her. He was taller than her—though most men were—with a blond buzz cut and dark green eyes. The guy was dressed similarly to Carson, though the neck of his tee and his skin were damp with sweat. Noelle felt her throat dry at the sight of him, and not in the wow-he's-hot-kind of way it did when she first saw Carson. This was out of pure discomfort by the way his eyes were practically undressing her.

She could practically see the disgusting thoughts running through his head as he took her in.

Her gut twisted queasily, but suddenly her eyes widened when Carson stood in front of her, shielding Noelle from Boman with his tall figure. He was taller than Boman. She blinked up at his back, seeing the damp spot in the middle of his own shirt and the lean bulge of his biceps, wondering what he was doing.

"Get back to your corner, Boman," Carson's hard voice sounded, his accent suddenly thick at the warning in his tone that had Noelle trying to swallow down the lump in her throat. She glanced around, realizing in relief that nobody else was watching.

"Come on, Hayes," Boman chortled, trying and failing to get a look at Noelle around Carson's broad figure. "You can't keep all the pretty ones for yourself, bro. Sharing is caring and all that shit, huh?"

Noelle's face scrunched up in disgust, absolutely despising being compared to some kind of object to go around. What was with certain men thinking it was okay to talk about women like they were a possession to be used?

36

Noelle noted the way Carson's hands clenched into fists at his sides, the cords beneath his muscled arms tightening at the gesture. Her stomach tumbled anxiously, half afraid that a fight would break out right in front of her. The tension seemed to return to Carson's shoulders, and judging by the scowl he wore, Noelle deduced that this Boman guy wasn't a friend of Carson's. Not that it was any of her business but that kind of made her feel better knowing that Carson wasn't friendly with some man who eyed women the way Boman had been eyeing her—like she was a piece of meat who couldn't wait to get a bite of. She suppressed a shudder.

"Walk away before I break another one of your teeth," Carson returned, his tone a terrifying sort of calm. Still, he was successful in voicing the maliciousness his words had been wrapped in, his fingers still curled into fists as the veins of his arms remained prominent.

Noelle had to swallow the gasp threatening to slip, staring up at Carson's back in unexpected surprise. She couldn't see the fierce scowl on his face, but just by his voice alone, Noelle could practically feel the anger and danger radiating off of him. All because some creep was making suggestive comments towards her. Not to mention Carson's threat of breaking another one of Boman's teeth hadn't gone over her head. He may be defending her, but her intimidation of him just spiked.

Boman, apparently registering the threatening look on Carson's face, paled slightly. He scoffed sharply through his nose to play it off, deeming it not worth it to get into the face of the best fighter they had.

"Whatever," he grunted before turning to walk off towards the doorway that led to the back locker room.

Noelle blinked after him, mildly stunned yet relieved that he had given up so easily before looking back at Carson. The gross discomfort she felt under Boman's gaze immediately washed away. Noelle was about to thank Carson for putting him off when he

37

suddenly let out an annoyed grunt and, without sparing her a glance, reached back and grasped her wrist in his large hand before tugging her forward.

This time, a gasp escaped her as she stumbled forward. Her wide eyes were glued to Carson's hand that was holding her and practically burning her skin as she struggled to keep up with his long strides. His grip wasn't too tight. He let go once he brought her in front of him, placing his hand on her upper back as he led her towards the front door of the building. Noelle had no choice but to let him lead her as her heart hammered in her chest.

With his free hand, Carson roughly pushed open the door as the metal clang. "You shouldn't have come here," he snapped in annoyance.

Noelle gaped up at him, mouth drying at the sight of his jaw clenching tightly and the bruise on his face slightly faded. They stepped onto the sidewalk, and Carson still didn't let her go. She stupidly wondered if his hand print would be seared into her skin as he led her towards Beverly's car, where Aiden was leaning into the window to talk to his girlfriend.

The two of them hadn't noticed Noelle and Carson's arrival until Carson let go of her and demanded in a hard tone, "Stop flirting and get back inside. We're not done yet."

Noelle hoped Carson didn't notice the way she bristled at the unfriendly tone of his voice. She felt her throat tighten at the knowledge of her being the reason why he was so pissed off, though she doubted he would care. Clearly, showing up to Astros to return his jacket and thank him hadn't been a good idea.

Aiden didn't at all seem fazed by Carson's harsh voice, straightening as he bid goodbye to Beverly and offered Noelle a smile, who returned it meekly. This made Aiden frown slightly, taking in her slightly shaken demeanor as his hazel eyes flickered towards his best friend in question. Carson, in turn, merely rolled his eyes and turned around, storming back into the building and leaving behind the three of them.

38

"What crawled up his ass and died?" Aiden joked, snorting.

Noelle couldn't even bring herself to crack a smile at that. Instead, she crossed her arms over her chest in an attempt to hug herself. Did her presence really annoy Carson that much? She hoped something else had put him in such a bad mood but then realized he was normal-ish when she approached him and Aiden until that Boman guy showed up. She sighed, wishing she didn't care so much. Only she would manage to piss off a guy she found stupidly hot.

CHAPTER FIVE

"There are so many other gyms in the city. Why'd we have to come to this one?" Noelle grumbled as she stepped out of the Uber after thanking the driver.

Her best friend, Camille, rolled her blue eyes in mild exasperation. "Because it's the only one we have memberships to," she responded. It wasn't the first time that Noelle mentally cursed Beverly for giving her the gym's membership card after overhearing Camille beg Noelle to come with her to the gym over FaceTime.

The gym that Aiden and Carson worked at.

She wouldn't mind seeing Aiden, but the last time she saw Carson, which was two days ago, he was pretty ticked off at her. Noelle had the habit of staying away from people that she annoyed or vice versa.

Taking in the hesitation on her best friend's face, Camille sighed. "Come on, he might not even be working today." She grasped Noelle's arm and pulled her towards the front entrance.

Of course, Noelle had told Camille all about Carson, except for the fact that he, you know, dabbled in illegal fighting. All Noelle told her was that he was a friend of Aiden's, and she and Carson had gotten off on the wrong foot, so she didn't want to bother him anymore with her presence. Showing up at his place of work— again—was sure to do that. There was also a good chance Noelle was overthinking everything, that she was making her existence in Carson's life a far bigger deal than it was, but she couldn't help it.

Driving herself crazy by overanalyzing everything was Noelle's biggest vice.

Using their cards to swipe in at the front desk, Noelle followed Camille towards the stairs that led up to where the weight room was as well as the area that had all of the treadmills, ellipticals, and cycles. Placing their bags in the available lockers, the girls headed towards the treadmills. Noelle placed her water bottle in the cupholder before starting the machine up, pulling her long hair back into a high ponytail as the machine lightly whirred and started moving.

"You wanna go for drinks tonight? That one club in SoHo doesn't have queues outside, so we won't have to wait or anything," Camille piped up.

Noelle snorted, glancing at her friend as she felt her ponytail swing behind her. "What's the point of burning all these calories if we're gonna drink them back?"

"We drink to get drunk and we don't think about the calories," Camille responded instantly, earning a breathless laugh from Noelle due to the somewhat fast speed of her treadmill. "Besides, the store's closed tomorrow so you can't use work as an excuse."

"How about not wanting to fuck up my liver?"

"Tough."

*   *   *

Unsurprisingly, it was hot inside the club as it was packed with people dancing to EDM. Truthfully, it was too loud for Noelle to even make sense of it, only hearing the beats and bass. As soon as they had arrived, Noelle followed Camille, Beverly, and Camille's half-brother Benny towards the bar to down some drinks before hitting the dance floor. It was a pretty nice club. Noelle couldn't help but dazedly admire as they made their way to the center. She looked up at the giant chandelier hanging from the ceiling as well as the multiple oversized disco balls, the flashing neon lights that went with the beat of the songs the live DJ was playing up front, reflecting off of the decorations.

As she danced with her friends, Noelle couldn't help but revel in the warmth in the pit of her stomach and the way all the tension of her muscles seemed to have disappeared, the liquor coursing through her veins bringing a dazed smile to her face as she danced amongst the packed bodies. The drinks she had consumed and the amount of people that surrounded her only helped in making her skin feel hot; the shorts and mesh crop top she wore did as much as they could to keep her cool. At one point, she had to tie her hair up to prevent it from sticking to the back of her neck.

About an hour and a half into dancing, she noticed Beverly had her phone in her hand and, while dancing, kept on texting someone. After Beverly sent what Noelle thought was the tenth text, she was about to tell her sister to just dance before noticing a pair of hands slide around Beverly's hips and pull her back.

"You're here!" Beverly's excited exclamation sounded over the thrumming music, and Noelle's movements slowed slightly in surprise as she recognized Aiden's grin from behind her sister. It had taken Noelle a moment to react, the booze in her system making her responses a bit slower than usual. She blinked as her eyebrows shot up at the sight of the dimpled man, not expecting to see him as Beverly kissed him before turning to everyone else. "Aiden, this is Camille and Benny. Guys, this is my boyfriend, Aiden."

Benny greeted Aiden cheerfully, and Noelle didn't miss the approving wink he shot Beverly. Camille gasped over the sound of the music as she grinned at him.

"Oh shit! It's so great to finally meet you in person!" she chirped, still jumping slightly to the music. Her pale cheeks were flushed from the drinks.

"You too!" Aiden shouted over the music with his friendly grin as he stepped next to Beverly to pull Noelle into a quick hug. "I'm gonna head to the bar to get a drink. The rest of the guys are there too."

Noelle's eyes widened slightly against the bright flashing lights, knowing that when Aiden brought up the guys, it meant Max, Levi, and Carson.

Oh hell, Carson is here? she internally groaned.

"Oh, perfect!" Beverly grinned. "I wanna take a break. What about you guys?"

When she glanced at the rest of them, Noelle wanted to say that she was fine dancing some more. She was still keen on keeping her distance from Carson despite the fact that her stomach became a residence for butterflies and the blood in her veins was often replaced by electricity whenever he looked at her. Before she could protest, Camille and Benny were groaning in relief as one of them blindly grabbed Noelle's hand and led her through the lively crowd towards the bar.

Noelle wasn't sure if her heart was pounding because of the excited environment she was in or because she may be about to see Carson who, she figured at this point, she was harboring a crush for. It made her feel kind of stupid because she had only seen him three times, and each time, their interactions weren't of the friendly kind, except when he offered her his jacket . . . after spilling his drink on her.

What did that say about her then? The man hadn't at all been friendly towards her, seemed to tolerate her presence at best, and that in turn, resulted in Noelle being unable to stop thinking about him. She deeply hoped it was just a physical thing because, really, what else could it be? It wasn't like she knew him well enough to have a serious crush on the man; she knew nothing about him. Whatever reactions her body had around Carson was purely because of the way he looked and maybe a little of the way

43

he sounded. He was still an ass though. Noelle suppressed a sigh. Talk about being a masochist.

Breathing came a bit easier for Noelle once they broke out from the crowd and headed towards the plush couches near the bar. Aiden paused for a moment, getting himself a drink before leading them to where his friends were. It was almost pathetic how Noelle's eyes immediately landed on Carson when they were close enough.

"Hey, you found friends!" Levi's loud voice rang, raising his glass with a grin as Noelle smiled at him. He sat in between Carson and Max. The small couch was occupied by the three tall men, leaving Noelle to wonder if they were uncomfortable in the restricted space due to their broad shoulders.

Aiden made quick introductions as everyone tried to find a place to settle down. One of the wingback chairs diagonal of the couch the boys occupied became available. Camille immediately sat down, pulling Noelle down with her to squeeze her into the seat as she whispered, "I think you were light on the details of how fucking fine these guys are."

Noelle stifled a giggle, grateful to be sitting down now. Her head was beginning to feel a bit heavy from all the drinks she consumed. While she wasn't one who got drunk easily, she could still feel the alcohol beginning to take its effect on her.

"Sorry." She smiled, shifting slightly to drape her legs over Camille's lap. "You know I lose my senses around pretty boys."

Camille snickered while shaking her head, and Noelle watched as her eyes trailed over to the laughing boys. Well, all of them were laughing loudly except for Carson who leaned back on the couch and lightly twirled the liquid in his glass, the smallest of smirks on his lips as he listened to his friends. Noelle noticed, not for the first time, that Carson was never very bold with his reactions to his surroundings, always keeping his expressions subtle and barely there, like he was always prepared to wipe his face of all emotions within the blink of an eye. The way he just watched and

44

interacted only when he wanted to seemed to add onto Noelle's attraction towards him.

"I'm gonna get a drink!" Benny piped up, drumming his thighs before standing up. "Anyone want anything?"

"Cranberry vodka," Camille smiled sweetly at her brother.

"A marg for me!" Noelle added, blowing a kiss to the boy who had cheekbones people spent thousands of dollars on plastic surgery for. He shot her and Camille a thumbs-up before disappearing into the crowd in the direction of the bar.

Noelle definitely needed some more alcohol as a way of distracting herself from the man sitting to her left. The bright neon colors flashing throughout the club lit up Carson's golden skin, reflecting off of his dark eyes that were filled with mirth at whatever Max was talking about. Noelle had seen him smile back at Aiden's party, catching a glimpse of the wide grin that somehow softened his cheeks while giving way to the crinkles by his eyes. Her heart had stilled in her chest at the sight of it. Sharp lines that reminded her of the man she knew him to be in otherwise surprisingly soft features she was only now seeing. It was breathtaking, and Noelle really did want to see it again.

Thankfully, Camille began to unknowingly distract her by pulling out her phone to take pictures, always wanting to document nights out. Amidst indulging into it with Camille, Noelle forgot all about the dark-haired boy as she smiled at the camera. She definitely got distracted enough to not notice Carson's gaze that had flickered over to her, watching her from the corner of his eye.

About ten minutes later, Camille huffed, "Where the hell is Benny with our drinks?"

Noelle blinked, realizing Benny had been gone longer than necessary. She squinted slightly against the lights in search of her friend amidst the silhouettes of people in the club. For a moment, she felt worried at where he could've gone off to, so she lifted her legs from Camille's lap and stood up.

"I'll, uh, see if I can find him."

45

"Take your phone." Beverly nodded towards the couch, and Noelle looked down to see her purse before picking it up.

Noelle made her way towards the bar, gaze flickering back and forth in search of Benny with eyebrows furrowing in mild concentration. She felt slightly dizzy, the loud music not entirely helping in keeping her balance. When her eyes landed on one pillar, a scoff of a laugh escaped Noelle, grinning in amusement. Right there, against the wall, was Benny locked in a heated make out session with some guy Noelle had never seen before, though she was positive Benny hadn't ever seen him either . . . until then.

Way to go, Benny! she silently praised before turning towards the bar and forcing her way towards it as she called the attention of one of the bartenders and ordered her and Camille's drinks. Once she returned, everyone's eyes were on her as she handed Camille the beverage.

"Did you find him?"

Noelle giggled as she returned to her seat. "Yeah . . . all pressed up against some hot guy," she informed with a suggestive wiggle of her eyebrows. The guys blinked in surprise and sounded their approval while Camille snorted out a laugh. Leaning back next to Camille, Noelle grinned. "Gotta say, I'm kinda jealous," she mused as she brought the straw to her lips.

She wasn't blind to the knowing looks Beverly and Camille exchanged, feeling her cheeks flush as she shot them both warning looks while taking a long sip of her drink. They totally knew Noelle's own desire of being pressed up against somebody. Could they be any more obvious? Subtlety, in Noelle's expense, was not their strong suit. Camille giggled lightly as Noelle settled against her, shooting her best friend a look that only had Camille's grin widening. Noelle's gaze went past Camille, then the grip on her glass tightened when her eyes met Carson's. Her throat dried despite the drink she sipped on, breaking her gaze from the dark eyes staring at her so intently, though not before she wondered if his body burned with the same fire his gaze did.

46

*   *   *

They had been at the club for hours, and most of Noelle's time was spent on the dance floor with Camille and occasionally Levi and Max. Both guys had no idea how to dance, but it was entertaining for the girls all the same. When it was nearing two in the morning, Noelle could feel her heart pounding in her chest from her constant movements. The alcohol she had stopped drinking two hours ago was nothing but a warm buzz in her tummy since she switched to soda.

Around two-thirty, they decided to leave after being at the club for hours. It wasn't until they stepped outside into the air that wasn't any cooler than inside the club—though Noelle was grateful for the lack of packed bodies—when they noticed Benny was missing.

"Why does he always disappear?" Camille groaned, stomping her foot in exasperation as she swayed slightly. She definitely had more drink than Noelle and that could be seen in her sad pout.

"I'll call him," Noelle murmured, pulling out her phone to call Benny. The guys waited with them, not in any rush to get home. As Noelle went through her contacts, she caught sight of Carson from the corner of her eye. He was leaning against the lamppost as he pulled out a pack of cigarettes and a lighter, then he placed one stick between his plump lips as he lit the other end, the flame of the lighter illuminating his face briefly in a soft orange glow.

She took a soft breath, tearing her gaze from him as she focused on pressing her phone against her ear as she waited for Benny to pick up. When he didn't, Noelle sighed as she shook her head.

"No answer."

47

Max, who Noelle decided was a sleepy drunk as he leaned against the wall with his eyes droopy, asked, "You think he, like, left with that guy he was with?"

"Nooo," Camille said, stretching the word out as she shook her head more forcefully than necessary. "He never leaves without telling me."

Noelle pulled her lower lip into her mouth as she shot Beverly, who was pulled into Aiden' side, a worried look. The club was busy, and there was a good chance Benny was still lost somewhere inside, too loud for him to hear his phone, but that didn't mean Noelle wasn't concerned for his whereabouts. They couldn't leave without him or without knowing if he was alright.

Suddenly, the club's door thrashed open behind them, louder than the music that was filtering out into the streets. They all turned around to see Benny and Clark, the guy Noelle had seen him kissing and then was all later introduced to them, being violently pushed out of the club. Her eyes widened in high alert. She gasped as she saw both Benny's and Clark's shirts being fisted by two guys who looked beyond pissed.

Even Max looked suddenly awake as they watched the scene unfold a few feet away from them.

"What the—"

Camille tried to take a step forward. "Benny—"

They were cut off, however, when the guy gripping Benny spat at him, "When I tell you to cut the bullshit, you cut the fucking bullshit."

Much to Noelle's surprise and alarm, Benny didn't look too fazed. Or maybe he was too drunk to care. "It's the twenty-first century, pal. If I wanna kiss a guy, I'mma kiss a guy." He tilted his head and grinned slyly. Noelle inhaled sharply once she realized that Benny was definitely too drunk to care. "You should try it sometime. It'll help ya loosen up."

Oh no, Benny.

Noelle's eyes widened, her heart pounding when she saw the dude's face twist in affronted disgust and anger. Before another thought could process through her mind, she watched in horror as the guy's right fist swung up and collided with Benny's jaw, sending him sprawling to the floor with a grunt.

Immediately, defiant exclamations sounded from Noelle and her friends as Camille rushed to her brother's side, seemingly sobering up at the sight of him getting hit as a handful of passersby stopped to watch the scene unfold. Clark then sneered into the face of the jerk holding him.

"Why do you straights always have to ruin everything? Suck a dick and relax."

Noelle wanted to yell in exasperation.

Why is he instigating things?

Unfortunately, no one was close enough to them to protect Clark from also getting punched, sending him stumbling back and right into Levi's arms, who easily held up the shorter guy and straightened him out.

There were more shouts from Noelle's friends, a clamor among them as they rounded on the two aggressive men.

"You can't just punch people because they're gay, and you think dick on vag is better than dick on dick!" she yelled.

She might have not thought that one through because, suddenly, the guy who knocked down Benny was scowling at her, his hands clenched into fists as he began stalking towards her.

"The fuck did you just say to me?"

Noelle's eyes widened, frozen in place as the large man made his way over, not even averting her gaze to see the alarmed look on Beverly's face behind him. The man's face was contorted with unabashed anger. While Noelle thought that may be a slight overreaction on her part, she was all too focused on the way her stomach felt heavy with lead as she wondered if this homophobic asshole would actually punch a girl in the face.

What she didn't see coming, however, was the brief glint of silver catching the light from above before a fist barreled into the guy's jaw, earning a startled gasp from Noelle as she watched him slam into the brick wall to her left.

"Victor!" the guy's friend called out.

He was the one that hit the wall and yet somehow Noelle felt breathless, especially when her wide-eyed gaze went to her right and saw Carson standing there.

Her heart pounded, taking in the hardened expression that the Australian wore as his steady gaze remained on Victor and his right fist remained clenched on his side. When Noelle looked at it, her breath hitched when she realized the flash of silver she had seen were the rings that decorated his fingers. She stopped herself from cringing when she thought of the pain the punch and the rings must have caused.

The look on his face—the clenched jaw, drawn-together eyebrows, and pursed lips—was all kinds of scary, not to mention the way that one vein in his neck was exceedingly prominent.

"Don't tell me you were really about to raise your hand at a girl," Carson spoke to Victor, his voice a low baritone that held nothing but controlled anger as he took a step forward.

Noelle's mouth was dry as she watched him, faintly hearing Aiden's voice.

"Carson . . ." he warned. It went ignored by everyone as Victor finally pulled himself up. Noelle was too busy gaping at them to notice any of her other friends or the other guy that was present.

Victor pushed himself to his feet and away from the wall. Noelle noticed the cheek that had hit the wall scraped slightly from the brick, his face contorting into a fierce scowl that didn't frighten Noelle as much as the one Carson was wearing did. The dirty blond guy unlocked his jaw as if to comfort the pain.

"I wouldn't have to if that bitch just kept her mouth shut," he spat out.

Noelle frowned, involuntarily taking a step back as his looming figure drew closer. Her heart pounded in her chest, not liking at all how this night was turning out as she exchanged an alarmed look with Beverly, who was clenching Aiden's arm so tightly that it didn't give him any room to move.

For a moment, Noelle didn't know if Victor was coming towards her or Carson, but she didn't get a chance to find out because, suddenly, Carson met him halfway with his right hand shooting out and grasping Victor's throat. Noelle's hands slapped to cover her mouth, hearing the collective intake of everyone else's breaths as Carson used his grip on Victor's neck to push him towards the wall once more. Victor's eyes widened at the pressure to his throat, having to look up at Carson because of the latter's taller height. Noelle could see the fear in the stranger's eyes as she felt the blood in her veins freeze.

Holy fucking shit.

Nobody else dared to interfere as Carson's icy glare was focused on Victor, leaning towards him.

"I've got no tolerance for bullies, especially homophobic assholes, and I've got absolutely no problem breaking your neck for even *trying* to hit a girl," he seethed.

A shiver ran down Noelle's spine, her gut twisting at the sound of his hard voice where his accent seemed to be a bit thicker due to the anger that was mixed in. Oh god. If Noelle was Victor, she would be shitting her pants right then. Hell, she couldn't even see Carson's face, but she knew his expression probably screamed death.

"Car," Aiden's voice spoke up, the same warning tone in his voice as Noelle's eyes remained on the Australian's rigid broad shoulders. "This isn't the place, man. Let's just go."

He was right. Noelle didn't know him well, but Carson seemed to emit the potential of being able to kill someone at this moment. Noelle wasn't sure if she should feel guilty for having that thought.

51

At this point, Victor was gasping for air. Noelle feared her eyes would pop right out of their sockets.

Holy shit . . . is Carson actually about to choke this guy to death?

Victor was fruitlessly clawing at Carson's hand and wrist, trying to get him to let go but Carson wasn't at all fazed. The fighter in him was definitely coming out at this moment, and from the worried look on Aiden and the rest of the boys' faces, Noelle knew this was going to get terrible awfully fast.

Carson didn't let go of Victor. He tilted his head slightly as he gazed down at a panicking Victor.

"Not so tough now, are ya, mate? Why don't you try to talk shit now?" he taunted. Noelle could practically hear the smirk in Carson's voice.

Noelle swallowed, her gaze wavering slightly as she caught sight of Camille's stunned expression, which Noelle wasn't surprised by seeing as her best friend had no idea about what Carson did. Hell, Noelle saw him fight only for a few moments, and she was still freaking the fuck out at what was happening right now.

Suddenly, Noelle could hear the distant sound of sirens getting closer and closer despite the ringing of panic in her ears. For a moment, she just figured they were headed off somewhere else until someone's voice called out, "Cops!"

"Fucking hell!" Levi cursed under his breath, his blue eyes widening as he looked at Carson in alarm. No doubt Levi was thinking the same thing as Noelle—that New York cops were always itching to handcuff anyone who seemed to be causing trouble. It was a valid concern that their group could get into a whole lot of trouble. The bouncer of the club, who had been standing by the entrance this whole time, would do nothing to aid them. His only job was to make sure it didn't blowback to the club. Levi began backing away as the sirens grew louder.

"We need to go now!"

It wasn't until the flashing of blue and red lights neared that Carson shoved Victor against the wall roughly before letting go of his neck. Noelle's heart jumped in her throat when she heard Aiden shout, "Meet around the block!" With Beverly's hand in his, he suddenly took off down the opposite end of the sidewalk.

Noelle blinked, startled panic hammering her heart.

What?

CHAPTER SIX

Before Noelle could comprehend, everyone suddenly dispersed after Aiden's shout, taking off in different directions. Even Camille and Benny didn't have to think twice as they took off with Clark, running up behind Levi and Max towards the other end of the sidewalk and leaving the passersby that were lingering around staring after them in confusion and surprise.

"Wha—" Noelle choked out a gasp, her feet seemingly frozen as the sounds of the sirens grew louder and closer as she had no idea what to fucking do. She wasn't sure if she was frozen in shock or fear.

"For fuck's sake," Carson deeply grunted before making his way towards her and grabbing Noelle's hand. His grip was warm, and as her gaze snapped down, she noticed his hand was much larger than hers. "Let's go."

He didn't give her much of a choice as he took off to scatter away from everyone else, pulling a startled Noelle along. Her feet stumbled beneath her as she tried to keep up with Carson's fast pace. Her heart pounded in her ears as Carson's grip on her hand tightened. She felt his cool metal rings against her skin as he led them down the sidewalk to put distance from the police sirens behind them.

Oh my god. We're running from the police. Oh my god.

Carson's curls bounced slightly as they ran, the wind ruffling both of their hair as their feet slammed against the pavement while they ran.

Is this a wrong moment for me to notice how warm Carson's hand felt in mine, especially when it is the same hand that was just wrapped around some guy's throat only moments before? God, something really is wrong with me.

Her lungs were burning from the unforeseen exercise, though Noelle was sure it only felt so intense because of her heart threatening to burst out of her chest in overwhelming anxiety.

To further send her into a frenzy, the sirens seemed louder. She heard Carson curse before they took a sudden change in direction, and Noelle let out a startled yelp when she was yanked to the right and directly into a dark alley—the kind of New York alley Noelle refused to walk past alone at night.

She tripped over her feet as Carson pulled her halfway deep into the long pathway between buildings, the putrid stench of trash nearly making her eyes water, but that didn't seem like the issue anymore because, suddenly, she was pressed against the brick wall. Instead of smelling the garbage that was overflowing from the dumpsters, all Noelle could smell were cigarettes and Carson.

Noelle's chest deflated as she let out a sharp breath, feeling Carson's front against her own as her palms pressed on the brick. His lower arms were against the wall on either side of her head as he leaned into her. She wondered if Carson could hear the erratic beating of her heart because of how close he was, her eyes flickering up to meet his through her lashes. Despite the lack of light in the alley, she could still see his deep brown irises peering down at her.

Oh god, how in the hell did I end up in this situation?

Nothing good ever happened in dark alleys such as this— shit, nothing good ever came from running from the cops. Was Noelle crazy for being more afraid of being caught by them than by the fact that she was pressed against the man who, just moments before, held another man's throat with his own hand? Her breath

55

had stilled at their unexpected proximity, but when she inhaled softly, all she was aware of was Carson.

"Why are we here?" she whispered, quivering.

Carson's lips parted. His warm, faint breath that smelt of cigarettes, which she strangely happened to like since she grew up around men in her family who smoked, tickled her face before Carson turned his head to look towards the opening of the alley. Noelle's hand itched to brush back a stray curl that fell over his forehead.

"Wait for it," he murmured, his voice raspy. She suppressed the shudder that threatened to pass through her.

She hesitated before following his gaze, swallowing inaudibly at their closeness because, with every breath they took, their chests brushed up together. When she looked at the front of the alley, absolutely nothing lined up against the walls to block her view or them from the opening of the path. She saw the bright red and blue lights of the police car that was slowly cruising its way down the street until the vehicle finally came into view. Noelle took in a breath, grateful they were towards the back end of the alley because one of the cops in the car shined a flashlight into the alley, most likely looking for them.

Noelle's heart pounded wildly in her chest for two reasons. One, there were actual cops looking for them, which was a situation Noelle never thought she would find herself in. Frankly speaking, the most trouble she had ever gotten into was getting after-school detention once in sophomore year of high school, and that was only because her entire geometry class had gotten it.

And two, because when the flashlight blindly shone in, Carson pressed himself closer to Noelle as if to blend the two of them with the wall. This time, neither of them missed the sharp intake of her breath as Carson's hips met hers and his forehead brushed against her temple, forcing Noelle to bite the inside of her lower lip from the friction of their bodies meeting.

Oh god, he is so close.

56

Her skin was tingling and her heart was thundering at their unfamiliar proximity, not even trying to wonder if this was having a similar effect on Carson as her cheeks heated up. An urge to get rid of any distance between them overwhelmed Noelle without her permission. She held her breath in her lungs as she vaguely wondered when Carson became so capable of making her feel this way. His body was warm against hers, comforting and welcoming despite the impression he gave off, which fueled Noelle's desire of wanting to press closer to him. But she fought it. She had to. If only her heart would slow the hell down.

The flashlight was gone as the cops moved on, and Noelle bit her lower lip as Carson remained in the same position. At this, Noelle turned her head to look up at him, wondering why he hadn't moved back yet but not complaining though.

Her eyes trailed along his face, greedily taking in his plump lips and wondering how someone could have full cheeks and a sharp jawline. Carson was a kind of pretty that Noelle hadn't seen before. Their breathing was soft despite the adrenaline coursing through their veins from running and evading the police, yet something about sharing the air with Carson brought a kind of twinge in Noelle's stomach that wasn't at all helped by the lack of distance between them.

"We should—" *Oh god. Did my voice just crack?* His gaze on her wasn't helping. "We should, uh, find the others."

Oh, leaving this current position is the last thing I wanted, Noelle thought.

"Yeah," Carson rasped, his gaze dropping to her lips as his Adam's apple bobbed slightly.

Doesn't he want to move either?

Suddenly, his hips moved away from hers and Noelle's skin under her shorts was burning at the lack of contact. She watched as Carson stood straight, pushing himself away as his ring-clad fingers threaded through his hair, then Carson nodded as Noelle bit the inside of her cheek.

"Let's go."

He began making his way towards the opening of the alley, yet Noelle found herself unable to move, staring at his retreating back as she let out a long soft breath and grimace slightly as the sound echoed in the quiet alley—to her, anyway. Her senses were slightly in an overdrive, both from literally running from the cops and being pressed up against the wall by a man who had the potential of knocking someone out.

The crazy part? Being in that close proximity with Carson . . . there was no fear. Just excitement.

Noelle wanted to bang her head against the wall. She really was crazy.

*   *   *

"He's a what?"

Noelle rolled her lips into her mouth, guilt washing through her as she stared at Camille's stunned expression. The blue-eyed girl blinked her wide eyes as she tried to process what Noelle just spilled.

"I . . . he fights. He's, like, you know . . . a fighter."

"An illegal fighter," Camille hissed sharply, leaning forward on the small table that separated them. "Oh my god! No wonder he looked ready to fucking kill that guy at the club!"

"Hey! Keep your voice down." Noelle shot her a wide-eyed, begging look. They were having lunch at a bistro in Manhattan, but Noelle still didn't want Camille saying stuff like that out loud.

Shit, I never should've said anything in the first place. Why couldn't I just have kept my big mouth shut?

It could be a curse how close she was with Camille, telling her things without thinking twice about it.

"I mean, that guy kind of had it coming, didn't he?" she added meekly.

58

"The punch, yeah." Camille nodded, eyes still wide in incredulity. "But not getting nearly choked to death. Shit. Elle, do you have any idea how dangerous guys who take part in that kind of fighting are?"

Noelle tried to play dumb. "Do you?"

"No, but I can imagine they're pretty fucking dangerous," she scoffed, leaning back in her seat to take a sip of her Sprite. "He probably fights at some run-down shithole with creepy men who stare at women like they're meat and won't care if anyone in the ring drops dead."

Noelle smiled wryly, the words slipping out without any of her control. "He does."

Camille nearly choked on air. "Wh—how do you know?" she demanded, sitting up once more as she stared at her best friend with a look of stunned suspicion. "Oh my god! Noelle, have you been there?"

When Noelle clamped her lips shut, the guilty expression washing over her face had Camille's eyes widening and her jaw dropping in shock.

"Are you kidding me? That's, like, the last place a girl should go! What if you got hurt or something?"

While Noelle loved Camille and knew her words were coming from a place of concern, she did think her best friend was being slightly melodramatic.

"It was fine! Bev and I were with Aiden and his friends. Nothing happened."

Well, except for the last time she went to the ring and a guy said some crude remarks until Carson stepped in, but Noelle wasn't going to tell Camille that, not when it would just prove her right. Unfortunately, Camille didn't seem to be done with this conversation.

"Look, Elle. I know you find him hot and all, but I honestly think you should keep your distance from him."

59

Noelle furrowed her eyebrows, staring at Camille in confusion. "What?"

She let out a sharp breath, glancing around briefly before her blue eyes settled on Noelle's hazel ones. "Elle, everyone knows how illegal fighting works. Those guys make a living off of beating the crap out of others with no sorts of rules or anything. The people who attend that stuff aren't any better. It's just a bad idea to get mixed up with those kinds of people. Hell, I'm surprised Beverly's even with Aiden just because he's Carson's friend."

Aiden might be the only one out of the four guys that Noelle was the closest to, being her sister's boyfriend and all, but Noelle felt a powerful urge to defend the other three as well. Sure, she had only hung out with Carson, Levi, and Max less than a handful of times, but Levi and Max were two of the sweetest guys. Besides, even if Carson wasn't the most openly friendly man, he had defended her twice—particularly with his own body. That had to count for something, and in Noelle's book, it sure as hell did.

For a moment, Noelle's mind flashed back to them hiding in the alley, reminiscing the barely-there pressure of Carson's hips against hers that had her yearning for more and his warm breath fanning her skin. It was like she could smell him over the aroma of her pasta, reveling in the cigarettes and piney scent she had inhaled with him so close. It was exciting and terrifying and nerve-racking altogether.

"Aiden's a good guy, Cami," Noelle said instead, settling to defend the guy she knew the most instead of the other three she hadn't known for long. "He wouldn't let anything happen to Beverly."

Camille raised an eyebrow. "And Carson?"

Noelle could feel herself getting flustered under Camille's scrutinizing glare, so she shrugged exasperatedly. "I mean . . . I don't know? I've only been around him a couple of times, Cami, so it's not like I know the guy that well. I only ever end up seeing him when Bev drags me places. We're not friends." *God, how I wish we are though.*

"You sound pretty disappointed by that."

Noelle didn't want to talk about this anymore. There was nothing to talk about anyway.

"Eat your damn sandwich."

CHAPTER SEVEN

"You know I shouldn't be here, Bev."

"Don't care! You have no plans for tonight, except maybe to watch old nineties flicks with Andy and her friends."

"What if I wanted to do that? Besides, you didn't even want me to come here the first time!"

"Well, things change. The boys are your friends now, and friends support each other. Besides, I'm sick of being surrounded by testosterone. Now that you know about this place, I could use the company."

An incredulous breath escaped Noelle at that, shaking her head in disbelief as she wrapped her arms around herself. Sure, her outfit was more modest this time consisting of boyfriend jeans and a loose shirt tucked in, but that didn't stop the shifty eyes from leering at Noelle and making her skin crawl. She wondered how many times she would have to come to Astros to get used to the stale smell of sweat mixed with alcohol, cigarette smoke, and the coppery tang of blood in the air.

Astros was full of the same kind of men Noelle saw before. Their voices were mixed in a deep rumble as they chatted while waiting for the match to start. She shouldn't be here—something both Camille and Carson had said to her—but Beverly practically pulled her out of the house to bring her here despite Noelle telling her what Carson said about her not belonging in Astros. Noelle most definitely could have put up a fight but then that irritating, nagging feeling of getting to see Carson won out.

"Here they come," Levi's voice broke into her thoughts, his words followed by the crowd breaking out into cheers and boos alike. Noelle blinked and noticed the entire crowd was looking to her right. When she craned her neck slightly, she caught sight of the guy who Carson would be fighting tonight. Max said his name was Jerry Sanderson. When Noelle took the guy in, her eyes widened in astonishment because if this whole fighting thing wasn't illegal and followed the rules of opponents being in the same weight class, then Carson wouldn't be fighting Jerry.

Her throat dried as Jerry made his way through the rambunctious crowd, ignoring the ringing in her ears as she took in the size of him; this guy was huge. He could most definitely be as tall as Carson, but in the sense of muscle mass, Jerry was ripped to a point where Noelle wouldn't be surprised that anyone would be able to tell that his bicep was probably bigger than her head if she ever stood next to him. The determined scowl on his face didn't make him appear any more approachable. The guy he was with stepped up to the ring and pulled apart the black ropes, allowing Jerry to climb inside.

"Holy . . . Carson's gonna fight *him*?" Noelle choked out. Her jaw dropped open as she glanced at Beverly to her left and Levi and Max to her right. The three of them didn't look as disturbed as Noelle felt, leading her to assume that such a drastic difference in opponents wasn't unusual in these fights, yet the ball of unease still knotted in her stomach, settling heavily and weighing her down.

She watched Jerry, who was wearing nothing but athletic shorts and sneakers, bouncing on his feet slightly on the other end of the ring as he talked to the guy with him and nodding along as he made punching gestures with his taped fists. That determined expression never seemed to waver from his face.

"Don't look so worried, Noelle." Max chuckled, hands shoved into the pocket of his windbreaker with an easy expression on his face. "Carson's fought guys much bigger than Sanderson."

"And won," Levi added helpfully over the sounds of everyone's shouting.

Noelle rolled her lips into her mouth, not entirely convinced as she glanced around. Everyone seemed way too hyped to watch two men beat each other up in her opinion. She caught sight of pieces of paper in multiple people's hands.

"What are the slips they're holding?" she asked Beverly as she leaned towards her.

"Betting slips," Beverly answered, gathering her short blonde hair to tie into a ponytail. "They get them after placing their bets on which fighter's gonna win and then get paid accordingly by the end of the matches." With a small chuckle, Beverly shrugged. "This place isn't that sophisticated, but they've got their own system. There's more money involved than you think. Everyone's just trying to make some. At the end, people who win their bets get their money, the winning fighter gets a nice payday, and the owner has enough to keep this place going."

Noelle's gaze briefly wandered around Astros, suppressing a snort. Clearly, the owner either wasn't making enough money to handle the upkeep of this place, or he simply didn't care. It was run-down and, although it seemed slightly cleaner in the daytime, didn't seem like the type of place that desired to look pretty. As long as the fighters had some place to throw punches and these people had some place to spend their money on, Noelle figured it didn't matter what it looked like.

Levi, having heard Beverly's explanation, decided to add in as well. "Carson's always the one who ends up with the heavy cut. Most of these guys that are here have been coming for a long time, so they know who to bet on." He snickered, looking smug on behalf of his friend. "Sucks for the first-timers though."

64

Noelle nodded along slowly as she wrapped her head around all of this. "So, basically, people just come here to watch some bloodshed and spend money on it?" she surmised dryly, earning a laugh from Beverly. "What, they couldn't head down to Atlantic City and gamble like regular people?" Noelle added, raising her eyebrow.

Max snorted in amusement. "It's not the prettiest place with the perfect system, but anything goes in the ring except, y'know, weapons, so no one really questions the shit that goes down out of their need to be entertained in this way. Plus, it's been working for years." He shrugged. "And so long as Carson gets his due, who are we to argue?"

That's fair enough.

The thought disappeared from Noelle's head just as quickly as it came as the crowd's volume increased once more, and Noelle looked back to see everyone's shouts being directed to someone making their way through.

Carson.

Noelle bit the inside of her lower lip, watching Carson's figure emerge through the crowd with Aiden behind him. She noted the former's expression remained one of concentration—locked jaw and hard, focused eyes. The rumbling roar of the crowd and words, mostly of support but some taunts as well, went completely ignored by Carson.

She felt strange thinking about it, but Noelle couldn't help but admire how under the harshness of his features, Carson looked calm in his approach to the ring. His hands were wrapped in white cloth, no jewelry on him, but his bronze and tattooed skin was in full view. Not a single blemish marked his body from what she could see, which Noelle found remarkable given his career. Max's point of no weapons being allowed during fights rang through her head, so she figured that was understandable. Still, Noelle couldn't keep her gaze off Carson, admiring the movements of his muscles

65

and feeling a dull ache to touch them, to be as close to him as they were in that alleyway again.

The crowd was abuzz with adrenaline and enthusiasm while Noelle cringed slightly, the noisiness almost hurting her ears as she watched Carson and Aiden step into the ring. Noelle recalled Beverly telling her that the guy who was in charge of this little fight club had gotten a soundproof front door as well as soundproof walls, so she didn't fear cops busting in all too much. Her ears ringing from the yells of those around her was better than her nose inhaling the stench of stale beer, sweat, and ever present metallic tinge of blood that lingered in the air.

She didn't miss the nasty glares Carson and Jerry were sending each other, eager to knock the other one down. When Aiden and the other guy stepped out of the ring and the commentator announced the start of the match, Noelle wished she hadn't eaten dinner before coming because of the nerves that were running rampant inside her.

There was a loud clanging of a bell that indicated the start of the round, and Noelle barely noticed Aiden come to stand on Beverly's other side because Jerry had immediately launched towards Carson. The roaring of the crowd never ceased as Carson effortlessly dodged the attack, ducking under Jerry's right hook and delivering one of his own to his back. Jerry jerked forward with the hit as she heard the mixture of cheers and boos, though the clapping that emitted from her friends was the most prominent to her ears.

Noelle paid no attention to how hot it was in Astros; all of her focus was on the ring and Carson's movements. She chewed on her lower lip, watching him move around the ring so smoothly, dodging and blocking hits naturally before delivering his own that Jerry could partly keep up with. Noelle figured that for all of that muscle mass he possessed, it also made it hard for him to move as quickly as Carson did. The Australian was muscular but in the lean sense, and he was pretty quick on his feet too.

The sweat glistened against the fighters' skin under the lights of the club, the energetic buzzing of the atmosphere never once dimming and then charging to life whenever someone threw a punch or tried to deliver a kick. Noelle could literally feel her heart jump every time Jerry threw his fists out, hoping it wouldn't come in contact with Carson in any way. She only felt a brief reprieve when Carson blocked or missed it. Much to her panicked delight, Carson hadn't gotten hit yet.

She couldn't help but admire Carson's movements. Like a dancer on stage, he knew exactly where and when to step. He was light on his feet, so he never gave his opponent an advantage. She watched as Carson ducked under Jerry's left hook while simultaneously putting his right leg out, tripping Jerry over and causing him to land on the floor of the ring with a warbling thud under his weight. Noelle heard everyone cheer as Jerry fell, clasping her hands in front of her mouth in anticipation and surprising herself by how into the fight she was.

"Yes, Carson!" Beverly cheered, bouncing slightly as she clapped her hands.

The only rule, besides no weapons being allowed, was that fighters couldn't assault an opponent while they were down, but that didn't mean Carson gave Jerry any room to move because as soon as he shuffled to his feet, Carson launched forward with a series of relentless punches. Noelle inhaled sharply, eyes widening at the sight of Carson delivering punch after punch, forcing Jerry towards the corner. His face twisted into determined anger with narrowed eyes, furrowed brows, and bared teeth. Carson wore his intent to win on his face, dark eyes ablaze with the victory that was no doubt in his grasp, his hits landing exactly where he wanted them to.

"Oh my god!" Noelle gasped, freezing in place as the pounding of her heart overpowered the overzealous spectators yet, somehow, she could hear the sickening sound of Carson's fist colliding with Jerry's skin. Her face scrunched up in incredulity as her lips parted.

Oh god, it is like watching a car accident happen. She knew it was horrible, yet she couldn't look away.

One last punch to Jerry's jaw and he went down once more. Noelle did not miss the blood that splattered from his mouth as he fell. The crowd rumbled excitedly as the commentator began counting up from one, everyone else joining in. Noelle was too frozen, wide eyes on Carson as he stepped away from Jerry's lying, bloody figure. Carson's eyes were glued on him as he wiped some sweat off his forehead with the back of his left hand. Noelle wondered if the knuckles of his other hand were raw. She wondered if Carson broke any of Jerry's teeth.

"Nine . . . Ten!" The bell rang, signaling the end. Some groaned and others cheered, shouting words of appraisal or utter profanities at both Carson and Jerry.

Aiden immediately went towards the ring, snatching up a water bottle.

"Is it over?" Noelle asked meekly. The desperation in her voice went unnoticed.

"Two more rounds left."

Noelle felt a kind of buzz she couldn't decipher, one she hadn't expected. She was definitely shaken, even a little bit horrified by what had happened in front of her, but she couldn't look away. Anxious anticipation swam in her blood over the next two rounds to come. She wanted this to be over, yet she was in awe of Carson—in awe of the way he almost seemed like some kind of god when he stepped foot onto the ring. Her teeth pressed together as Aiden offered Carson the water, and Levi folded his arms on top of the ring to speak to him. Her gaze remained on Carson, on the way his throat worked as he drank the water, at the small smirk curling at the corner of his lips as he took these moments to breathe easily. She knew she shouldn't be attracted to a man who was so obviously

68

capable of beating the shit out of another, but she also knew, in an almost twisted way, that the Australian was an exception.

*   *   *

Carson was down.

It was the end of the second round, and Jerry, bloodied and bruised, had managed to bury his left fist into Carson's side. Noelle could practically see the breath escape Carson as he stumbled. He tried to regain his footing for one heart pounding moment, but Jerry was keen on getting his revenge from the last round and delivered a roundhouse kick right into Carson's back, sending him to the floor.

She didn't know him well. They weren't friends, but Noelle could feel the panic tighten her throat and lead fill her stomach as Carson fell on his. She wanted to tell the entire crowd to shut the fuck up as they began the countdown to knock out. On either side of her, the boys and Beverly were silent while Aiden went up to the ring. He peered at Carson from under the lower rope as he repeatedly slammed his hands on the ring, yelling at the fighter to get up.

His head was turned away from Noelle, so all she could see was his black tousled hair and his back slick with sweat as well as a bruise or two that were beginning to form. Jerry had managed to get a few hits in, though not nearly as many as Carson got on him . . . fortunately.

Carson was still down and hadn't gotten up. Not even when the countdown finished and the bell rang, signaling the end of the round.

Noelle couldn't keep the panic in her voice at bay even if she tried. "Is he okay?" she said worriedly. She watched with wide eyes as Aiden slid into the ring to help Carson, then Levi running out as well. Max remained with the girls, though the worried expression on his face was enough to freak Noelle out even more.

69

"Yeah, yeah," Beverly breathed out, her eyes on the ring. Noelle couldn't help but notice that even Beverly looked a bit on edge. "It's . . . it's rare but this isn't the first time this has happened. Car will be up in no time."

Noelle wanted to believe her, trying to tune out the roar of the crowd. "Then why do you look so worried?"

Beverly forced a wry smile. "Not exactly a fan of watching my friends get knocked down, Ellie."

He'll get up, right? Noelle swallowed, her question being answered when she finally looked back at the ring. She let out a heavy breath of relief when she saw Carson on his feet, back against the corner post as Levi and Aiden stood in front of him, helping him out. He drank water and used the towel Levi offered to wipe off the blood from his mouth. Noelle winced when he turned his head and spat some of the crimson liquid on the ring. She may be used to seeing blood on her favorite TV shows, but in real life was a whole other story.

"Okay, okay. He's alright." She heard Max mutter to her right, glancing at him to see the glasses-wearing blond nod his head in approval, lips quirking in a small smile.

Noelle's stomach churned. Everyone around her was shouting different things as they waited for the final round to start.

"Knock him on his ass, Hayes!"

"Make Sanderson bleed!"

"C'mon, Sanderson! Break his fucking arms!"

"Fucking destroy him, Sanderson!"

The last one had Noelle swallowing inaudibly, wanting to tell whoever yelled that to shut up but knowing it was probably a guy twice her size. She didn't need to draw anymore attention to herself than she already was by her mere presence. Aiden and Levi gave Carson encouraging pats before bending out of the ring, landing on their feet and then making their way over.

"He'll be fine," Aiden assured once they reached the others, right when the bell rang once more.

70

Blood rushed to Noelle's ears, deafening her to the shouting of the spectators as she watched Carson and Jerry circle each other on the ring, both bruised and bloodied in some way or another. This was the last of the three rounds and Noelle just wanted it to be over. Her body was warm from the heat and the anxiousness running thick with her blood. Did Carson's friends feel like this whenever he was in the ring? Or was Noelle like this because this was her first time witnessing a full fight?

As if the universe was on her side for once, the match seemed to come to an end pretty soon because after dodged hits and kicks,Carson's right fist pulled back before launching forward, his knuckles coming in contact right under Jerry's chin in a fierce uppercut that had him bending back and blood once again showering out of his mouth. Noelle cringed, though she didn't dare look away as Jerry fell on his back. The ring groaned under his weight as the crowd began clamouring once more as the countdown started.

And then it was over. The cheering intensified, almost drowning out the few boos scattered around. Carson stood in the middle of the ring, his hair disheveled and chest heaving. His sweat coated his golden skin as blood was smeared under his mouth and slightly around his nose. The commentator stepped into the ring, holding up one of Carson's hands as he announced him the winner. Noelle wasn't sure if she should be surprised or not at the sight of the smug smirk curling at the corners of Carson's lips.

"Fuck yeah, bro!" Levi cheered, clapping his hands as the Australian jumped out of the ring, nodding at whoever threw appraisals his way as he made his way over to his friends. There was still lots of noise in Astros, but at this moment, Noelle didn't care about it. "You did it!"

Carson came to stop in front of them, which was when Noelle really took in his appearance. He wasn't gushing blood or anything, but his lips were stained with the crimson color as well as the skin under his nose and mouth. A bruise was forming right

71

along his jaw on the right as well as a few on his side, but other than that, there weren't any other injuries that Noelle could see.

"Did you think I wouldn't?" he retorted almost playfully, quirking a brow.

He seemed so calm and cool now, Noelle observed while she was still trying to calm her racing heart down. After what she witnessed, she was surprised she hadn't gone into cardiac arrest or something. Watching violence like that firsthand wasn't something she was used to, obviously.

"Excuse us for getting freaked out after the second round." Beverly snorted, the tension leaving her.

In fact, it seemed like everyone wasn't as tense as they were during the matches, and why should they be? Carson won after all. Noelle was still trying to process everything, trying to come to terms with the fact that Carson did this on a regular basis. She was only in a state of shock because this was her first time witnessing this. If Beverly was going to drag her to more of these, then Noelle would need to grow thicker skin.

Carson waved Beverly off before beginning to untape his hands.

"So, Noelle, what'd you think of your first fight?" Max piped up.

At the mention of her name, Carson's head snapped up. His dark eyes landed on her as he frowned slightly in confusion as if he hadn't realized she was there until that moment, which he wasn't at fault for. When he had been approaching them, Noelle had somehow subtly managed to push herself behind Beverly and Levi, obscured from Carson's view even if she could see him clearly. She hadn't even realized she had done it until she noticed Carson's dark eyes searching for her.

"It was, um . . ." Noelle started, eyes landing on Carson who was back to looking like his unreadable self as her mouth dried at the sight of him. "Pretty intense." Kind of a lame response, but Noelle was proud of herself for being able to utter that much.

72

She hadn't expected the small smirk to reappear on Carson's lips, gaze trained on hers as he unwrapped the rest of the tape on his hands. Noelle felt a thrill run down her spine at his intense stare, chewing on the inside of her lower lip as Carson lifted his chin slightly, his face a picture of smug coolness.

"Alright. My place for celebratory drinks?" Max asked, rubbing his hands together as he looked at everyone for approval. It wasn't new for Carson to win a fight, but the guys were always looking for an excuse to drink.

Beverly glanced at Noelle, knowing of her sister's initial reluctance to come to Astros in the first place. "You down?" she quietly asked her. "Or do you wanna go back home?"

Noelle looked at her sister, chewing the inside of her cheek as her body heated up once more; this time because of the weight of the dark-eyed gaze from the man standing right by her.

"I'm down."

CHAPTER EIGHT

The cool metal of his rings sent a pleasant shiver up Carson's arms as he slid the jewelry on, decorating almost every finger to serve as a distraction from the redness of his raw knuckles. The numbness wasn't anything new; it was a mere occupational hazard he had accepted long ago, much like the occasional metallic taste of blood that would dance on his tongue after every other fight. With a sigh, Carson tossed the balled-up napkin that was stained red into the trash and threw the ice pack Aiden insisted he use into the freezer in the corner of the locker room. As he slammed the door of his locker shut, rattling the makeshift wall of it, Carson frowned to himself.

He was normally overrun with adrenaline after a victorious match, his pride energizing him through a job well done that made him pay no mind to the bruises and cuts he acquired. He only reminded himself to make sure it didn't happen next time. For some reason, while still proud he won, Carson felt his gut twisting into a knot, and he was pretty sure it was because of the hazel-eyed girl that was currently laughing animatedly at whatever Levi said.

Carson's grip on his duffel bag tightened as he neared the group with his eyes glued on Noelle. This wasn't a place for her. She stuck out like a beacon amongst the usual group of stingy men that attended the fights. Her heart-shaped face and dimples and delicate features that he believed would break on touch. She wasn't at all like the other girls that came by, the ones in clothes that left

74

little to the imagination and whose eyes were enough to lure any guy in for the night of his damn life. Carson should know; he's been in bed with women like that. One look at Noelle and Carson could tell she wasn't like any of them.

The other night in the alley, with her flush against him and her flowery scent that somehow still clung to her after being in the club for hours, had Carson yearning for them to being so much more than just hiding in there, but that wasn't the time or place. Carson had to fight the practical primal urges to take Noelle right then and there. He didn't want her to think he was some kind of animal, especially after knocking that asshole at the club, not that Carson regretted any of it.

"Good to go." Carson gruffed, clearing his throat as an attempt to hide his somewhat down mood. He didn't need his friends asking questions why he was anything other than the smug bastard he normally acted like after a win. Glancing around, Carson noticed most of Astros had cleared out with the exception of a few drunks lingering about.

Their group left the gym, stepping out onto the sidewalk in the surprisingly cool night. New York weather was always unreliable.

"Oh, wait, um . . ." Beverly spoke up, glancing at Carson with that innocent smile on her face that he knew meant she needed something from him. He let out a knowing sigh as she widened her grin. "Aiden rode with Max and Levi, so can Noelle ride with you?"

Keeping my distance from the pretty girl with hazel eyes just isn't something the universe is allowing me, isn't it? Carson thought.

"You know, the way you speak for me makes me feel like I'm two years old instead of twenty-two," Noelle's voice cut in before Carson could even think of a response.

Her comment prompted snickers from Carson's friends while he felt his lips twitching into a slight smirk. Beverly merely fluttered her lashes sweetly at her sister. "Just looking out for you, sis."

Noelle rolled her eyes as she pressed her lips together before looking at Carson. He couldn't help but notice the way her throat worked nervously as a questioning look accompanied by an almost apologetic smile crossed over her face. She was silently asking him if he minded giving her ride, apologizing if it was any trouble.

"It's fine," he said, shrugging indifferently.

They were headed to the same place anyway, though that didn't mean Carson didn't curse Aiden for not bringing his own car, so they could have avoided this. Or cursing at Max for having that damn Nissan that could only fit two people in the back. Just Carson's luck.

The last time he was in a limited space with Noelle, Carson had her pressed against the wall in an alley to hide from the cops. He was well aware that he could have just leaned against the wall right next to her—hell, it would've been smarter to do that—but he had done it without thinking. When Noelle's hand was in his, her skin burned against his own and Carson just needed more. Even through the darkness of the alley, Carson could see the gleam of light in her eyes and the curve of her parted lips; the amount of restraint straining his muscles in that moment was astounding. The thoughts that ran through his head, with her pressed between him and the wall, would've downright terrified Noelle had she had any clue. Maybe he would have better luck in the car.

They dispersed, the rest of them getting into Max's car before Carson nodded his head across the street. "We gotta cross," Carson said to Noelle.

His car was an old BMW 3 Series Sedan, one that belonged to his dad who gave it to Carson after getting a newer model, which Carson happily took. After saving some of the cash he made through his job at the gym and at the ring, he got the interior leather replaced in black to match the exterior of his car, further making the vehicle his own.

The only thing that wasn't his was the girl sitting in the passenger seat, who was nervously chewing her lower lip as if she had never been in a car with a guy before. Or maybe it was just because it was him.

Carson clenched his jaw, revving the engine to life before maneuvering out of the parking spot and driving to where Max lived. While Carson enjoyed the occasional silence, he knew he wouldn't be able to tolerate it at this moment, so he switched on the radio, not bothering with the aux as The Weeknd's voice sounded through the speakers.

He wasn't much of a talker; everyone who knew him knew that. The only time Carson was talkative was around the boys, his family, or if there was enough alcohol making its way through his system. So right there, in the car with an equally quiet Noelle who he could hear was picking at her nails even over the music, surprisingly discomforted him. Carson didn't care who he was with; silence was his friend. So why was the silence making him painfully tighten his grip on the steering wheel and making his knuckles ache in protest?

"Congrats on your match," Noelle's soft, almost hesitant voice broke through the music out of nowhere.

Her taking the first step in starting a conversation came as a bit of a surprise to Carson, his eyebrows raising slightly as he couldn't stop himself from glancing over. Noelle was looking straight ahead, still chewing on her lower lip. Carson fought the urge to reach a hand over and free her lips with his fingers.

When her unexpected words registered in his head, Carson returned his attention to the mostly empty Brooklyn roads. "Thanks," he muttered. He may have only spoken one word, but he knew he came off as completely uninterested, and that's not what Carson meant. He was hopeless in properly articulating himself through spoken words. "Didn't expect to see you there."

"I didn't expect to be there," Noelle responded with a slight airy chuckle, the nervous tilt still present. Did he make her skittish? Carson wasn't too sure how he felt about that. "But Bev doesn't really take no for an answer."

Carson clenched his teeth as he made a right turn, ignoring the sharp pain the action caused in his jaw. He knew well of Beverly's habit of bossing people around; it made her and Aiden an interesting couple since Carson knew his best friend could be just as authoritative, but in this situation, it was a trait he wished Noelle's older sister didn't have. The frustration made itself known in Carson in the way his shoulders tensed. Astros was no place for a girl like Noelle. Sure, he didn't know her well, but one look at her in a place like that and it was obvious she didn't belong. Carson knew the people and the kind of people that frequented that place, and that brief incident with Boman was enough for Carson to conclude that Noelle shouldn't be hanging around a place as shady as Astros.

"If me being there makes you uncomfortable, then I won't come," Noelle spoke up once more, making Carson realize that Noelle took notice of his rigidness.

There was a brief silence in the car following Noelle's words, which, yet again, caught Carson off guard. He didn't like being taken by surprise, and Noelle seemed to be good at doing that to him.

That's what he wanted, wasn't it? For Noelle to stop showing up at Astros so she wouldn't be subjected to the gazes of the kind of men Carson wanted to put his fist through? It aggravated him to no end for being so damn concerned over this girl he had only been around a handful of times, bewildered by this sense of protection he tried to chalk off as disinterest in this stranger. But he was failing at that already. What was so goddamn special about her?

He quickly smothered that thought, not wanting to open that potential can of worms that would only serve to drive him crazier. Carson didn't understand what was going through his mind where Noelle was concerned, and he wasn't sure if he wanted to. It was frustrating because Carson was always aware of what he wanted, what he was after, so why was he second guessing himself when it came to Noelle? Why was his mind going blank? He had made it clear he didn't want Noelle to come around Astros, so why did the thought of not seeing her there selfishly made him want to tell her the opposite of what his brain was screaming at him? Why was he putting his selfish desire over the matter of her safety?

Carson pulled into Max's street, jaw painfully tightening when he felt Noelle's curious gaze on him as he searched for a parking spot. When he found one, it was like he had no say in his words. "I don't care," he practically bit out words he uncomfortably realized couldn't be the furthest thing from the truth.

His tone made her wince slightly, Carson noticed, but Noelle didn't say anything else as Carson parked the car. Was it his goal to make her hate him or something? Carson didn't care what people thought of him, which only played into him being so picky with who his friends were, but the unease that stiffened Noelle as they got out of the car made him think twice about being even the slightest bit harsh towards her, a seed of regret planting within him.

Didn't mean he apologized for it.

*   *   *

"Don't be stubborn. Just keep it there for a while," Beverly instructed, pressing the freezing ice pack in Carson's hand as she shot him a pointed look. He would be annoyed if he wasn't already used to his friends mothering him after every match. It used to just be the guys, but now, he's accepted Beverly's role in it too.

Carson rolled his eyes, not even wincing as he pressed the cool pack against his jaw. His gaze subsequently landed on Noelle through the open space in the wall that separated Max's kitchen and living room. She was sitting on the floor, having a conversation with the others while absently rubbing Rosie's, Levi's dog, belly.

Noelle had taken an instant liking to the bulldog-terrier, who seemed to return the feelings as she lay right in front of the brunette.

"Hey, wait a second," Carson quietly said, effectively catching Beverly's attention and stopping her from exiting the kitchen as she turned to Carson with a questioning look. A frown twitched at his brows. "What were you thinkin', bringing your sister out tonight? You know how crazy things can get."

Honestly, tonight was one of the tamer nights of a match. There were often times when the crowd got too rowdy, drunk off of liquor, and the thrill of the fight they witnessed or were about to. People have gotten injured by getting caught in the midst of the excited bunch, instead of just watching others get hurt in the ring.

Confusion pulled at Beverly's features, tilting her head slightly. "Noelle's a big girl, Carson," she spoke slowly, trying to figure out where this conversation had sprung from. "She was with me and the guys. Nothing's gonna happen to her." Beverly didn't miss the way he exhaled sharply through his nose, narrowing her eyes slightly. "I know you've got a thing about unfamiliar faces showing up at your matches, but Noelle's my sister. If I say she's good, she's good. So what's the issue?" she prodded.

Carson didn't like the knowing tone in Beverly's voice, like she was aware of something Carson didn't want her to be aware of. He didn't like that sparkle in her eyes; he wasn't going to let Beverly try to squeeze out whatever it was she was looking for. He was never one to play anyone else's games.

"D'you really want your sister to be stared at like a piece of meat by all the creeps that come to Astros?" he shot back, making sure his voice was low so the others wouldn't be able to hear. Though they were all engaged in conversation and the TV served as background noise, he doubted they would hear anyway.

Beverly scoffed as she grabbed Carson's wrist, dragging the ice pack away from his jaw and using her grip on him to get him to put the cool pack on the knuckles of his right hand. "If Elle was really uncomfortable—if she really didn't want to come along—she would've stayed home. She wanted to come, Car, and unless you tell her not to, I'm still gonna bring her. Besides, she's made friends with the others and she likes hanging out with them."

Pursing his lips, Carson ignored the urge to frown at the knowledge of Noelle befriending the boys. He had no issue with her being friends with his friends; it just reminded Carson that he wasn't the most approachable of the bunch. While, on a regular basis, he was perfectly okay with that, but for some reason, that particular trait of his rubbed him the wrong way.

He could feel Beverly's curious, questioning gaze on him, but Carson ignored it as he glanced to his left once more, watching as Noelle laughed along with the boys. Her dimples appeared as she took a picture of Rosie on her phone. This time, the frown knitted at his brows, and the only reason he tore his gaze away from them was because of Beverly's low tone.

"I seriously hope your issue with Noelle is because of your normal antisocial behavior and not because you, like, actually don't like my sister or something, Carson. Because I swear to—" she said.

His head snapped back over to the blonde, irritation spiking his blood as his face scrunched into a glare.

"Did I fucking say I didn't like your sister?" Carson all but snapped, forcing his voice to stay low despite his annoyance. Beverly pressed her lips together. She wasn't too fazed by Carson's sudden burst of anger, knowing he had a short fuse. He was done with this conversation. "If you're okay with her being ogled at by a bunch of drunks, then whatever," he hissed. "I couldn't give a fuck."

With an aggravated huff, Carson tossed the ice pack on the counter behind him. He heard it clatter against the marble top as he shouldered his way around Beverly and went to the hallway bathroom. The fire escape was outside the living room where everyone else was and the bathroom had a window Carson could easily open and let the smoke escape. A good smoke always calmed him down.

CHAPTER NINE

Carson shook hands with Darryl, keeping his expression one of polite neutrality as his other hand grasped an envelope he was handed. Darryl Gibson was probably the least sleazy guy in Astros, which was saying something since he owned the damn place. He was in charge of the illegal fighting ring, the one who got a cut out of everyone's earnings yet he did everything with an air of confidence and sophistication. Darryl was straightforward about what he wanted, which was something Carson liked about him. He never beat around the bush, didn't have any kind of ulterior motive that Carson could see, at least. Carson was good at reading people, which was why he was grateful that he got to deal with someone like Darryl when it came to doing what he enjoyed.

"Ya did me proud, Hayes," Darryl praised, his free hand clapping Carson on the shoulder once. "Over nine hundred in there and that's after I've taken my cut."

A smug smirk curled at Carson's lips as he dropped Darryl's hand, reveling in the feel of the envelope in his other hand. Darryl took ten percent of whatever a fighter won, no matter the amount, and used the money earned to keep Astros running. Carson was the top fighter who brought in the most. It wasn't the first time, but he was grateful to the spectators who came with deep pockets ready to place their bets. He didn't care who the money came from, as long as it ended up in his pockets. Satisfaction always ran through his veins when he felt a heavy envelope stuffed with cash in his hand. Whatever he made used to be Carson's sole income, and while he made quite a lot, it sometimes wasn't enough. There were times when Carson fell behind on his rent and bills.

That was why Aiden had hooked him up with a job at the gym he works at—being the general manager had its perks—and now, Carson had two sources of income that had him living in his comfortable lifestyle in his Brooklyn apartment with his dog. He had been doing this whole fighting thing for a few years now, and once he started becoming known as the best fighter in Astros, he never made lower than six hundred dollars. There were times where Carson lost a fight, but even the winner of those matches didn't earn his money without a number of broken bones or seeping blood.

"People needa find better ways to spend their money," Carson mused, chuckling deeply as he placed the envelope on the inside pocket of his leather jacket.

Darryl smirked. "Don't say that. It's how some of us make our living," he reminded just as his phone went off. "Gotta take this. Good job, Hayes, keep up the good work," he said to Carson as he pulled out his phone.

Carson gave him a nod before turning to make his way towards the front doors, walking past the few fighters currently training before stepping out onto the sidewalk. He barely made it two steps when his phone began ringing, pulling it out to see that it was Levi calling.

"What's—"

"I need you to go to Beverly's store before she throws my book out!" Levi's loud voice cut him off, making Carson move his phone away from his ear in mild annoyance.

Carson kept walking to the nearest subway entrance, mingling with the light flow of pedestrians. "What?"

Levi whined impatiently on the other end. "I had Bev hold a book for me for a while now, and I never went to pick it up. Now, she's threatening to sell it when the reason I asked her is because she's giving it to me for half the price," he rushed out, taking a breath once all the words were spoken.

Stopping at the curb and waiting for the 'walk' sign to glow, Carson snorted. "Since when do you read?"

"Fuck off. I read," Levi retorted. "It's for that master's course, and I need the book for my summer credits. Please, Car. Aiden and Max are busy with work and I can't get out either."

Carson rolled his eyes, not really needing to hear Levi's explanation. He would get the book for him regardless. Levi was the youngest of their friend group—with Carson only being older than him by a year—and was also going to school to get his master's degree in music. He admired that about Levi. Carson graduated college with a major in business and a minor in physical education and, obviously, didn't do much with those, so if he could make his friend's life slightly less hectic, he was willing to help.

He assured the blond before hanging up and going down the steps leading into the subway, his nose numb to the various scents of New York's underground wonders as he pulled out his Metrocard.

It wasn't long until Carson stepped off the busy subway once arriving in Chelsea, walking down a familiar sidewalk until he reached Simon's Stories. He had been to the store a number of times before, buying the books he knew his older sister would like to be sent to her and getting a journal for himself when his previous one ran out of pages. The shelves and the books and the cozily clustered atmosphere was familiar—except for the girl behind the counter bagging up books for a customer.

Of course, Carson wasn't surprised to see Noelle here; it was her family's store for fuck's sake. He just, strangely enough, wasn't prepared for it. Not seeing Beverly anywhere, he stood off on the side as he waited for Noelle to finish helping the two other customers waiting in line. Both of which, Carson noticed, were not-so-subtly eyeing him. Or, to be more specific, eyeing the bruise that had bloomed on his jaw and the noticeable cut on the corner of his lower lip. Nothing he wasn't used to.

Conveniently, he was near the shelf that held all types of journals. Carson couldn't help himself but lightly sift through some, seeing if any caught his eye. He wasn't done with the journal he currently was writing in, but it didn't hurt to have a new one ready to go.

"Carson?"

He looked away from the shelf, realizing the two customers had left, and now, it was just Noelle behind the counter, raising her eyebrows at Carson in surprise. Clearly, she hadn't expected to see him there. Walking over, he shoved his hands in the pockets of his jacket and watched Noelle straighten slightly.

"I'm pickin' up a book for Levi. He said Beverly was holding onto it for him."

"Um . . ." Noelle hummed, stepping away from the counter as she looked at the shelves under it. She ran her fingers through her hair, pushing it back. It looked incredibly soft; Carson couldn't help but notice as it fell around her shoulders. He lifted his chin slightly. Noelle pulled something from the shelf under the counter before standing up straight and pulling off a post-it note on a book about musical theory.

"Here we go. It's paid for."

Carson nodded, taking the book from her. He was about to thank her as he received it, but was cut off.

"Hey! Knock it off and get the hell out of here!" Noelle shouted.

He blinked, her raised voice taking him off guard. Noelle was looking past Carson with an irritated scowl on her face, and he looked over his shoulder to see what exactly got her so pissed. He could hear a collection of laughter sound from a distance, his eyes landing towards the opposite end of the store where the chalkboard wall was. Where, he realized, a bunch of guys that looked to be in their late teens were immaturely drawing crude cartoons and illustrations on the wall meant for people to write their favorite quotes or book recommendations.

Carson wanted to scoff. *Are all high schoolers of this generation that childish?* Sure, he and his mates enjoyed a good dick joke here and there, but they knew the line was drawn when it came to public settings.

Noelle huffed behind him, and from his peripheral, he saw her move around the counter.

"I will throw you out on your asses if you don't leave now," she warned, the agitation clear in her voice as she arrived in front of the counter.

One of the three guys grinned wolfishly at her from across the store. Other customers watched on, all wearing looks of disgruntlement and annoyance towards the boys.

"Why don't you come over here and show us what your 'lil ass can do and then we'll leave?"

Noelle froze, gaping as if she couldn't believe some high school kid had the nerve to speak to her—or any woman—that way. Her cheeks tinged an embarrassed pink, meanwhile, next to her, Carson's face darkened with the scowl that angered his features. For the sake of the kid, Carson hoped he had heard him wrong, but the uncomfortable look on Noelle's face confirmed otherwise.

Impulse took over and, without thinking, Carson tossed the book on the counter behind him. The thud of the weight wasn't even registering as he took just a few long strides to get to the other side of the small store. The three guys were snickering amongst themselves, chalks in hand, and didn't even notice the six-foot-one tattooed man stalking over to them until Carson's right ring-clad fingers shot out and fisted the front of the shirt of the kid who had made the leering comment.

"Wha—Hey!" The kid thrashed and the laughter instantly died, especially when he and his two friends noticed the dark, dangerous expression that the much taller, much broader man wore.

The way Carson's eyebrows were lowered and his bruised jaw was clenched—the tension in his neck obvious—was enough to send anyone running scared. His entire demeanor screamed menacing. He yanked the kid closer, making him look up at Carson with eyes widened in unrestrained fear and knees practically buckling under him. His two friends were no better.

"I dare you to repeat those words," Carson growled, his deep rasp making the kid swallow in terror.

The younger boy started stuttering, his friends doing nothing to help him because when a man of Carson's size who looked so fucking terrifying had your friend in his grasp, you don't interfere. Carson, for one, didn't care for any of the eyes that were watching in shock. He didn't even care that these were just teenagers. He didn't focus on anything, except for the irritating kids who he noticed smugly were looking like they were about to shit their pants.

"Carson," Noelle's voice sounded from behind him. He hadn't realized she had come at their side until he felt her hand wrap around his left bicep, gripping the leather as some kind of tropical fruity scent began making itself known in his nose. *It smelled good.* "Carson, it's okay. Let him go," she said, trying to pull him back. To pull him out of the fiery anger he sometimes lost himself in a bit too easily.

The mild urgency undertoning her soft voice had Carson clenching his jaw, his grip on the kid still firm yet his shoulders relaxed slightly, but he was still pissed. He had no tolerance for guys who had no issue speaking to women so degradingly, and while he could feel his body relaxing under Noelle's touch, his eyes were still narrowed into a glare at the kid.

"If you and your friends show up here again," he began, dropping his voice into a deep, threatening dare, "you'll have trouble writing anything on that wall with broken fingers. Got it?"

88

He ignored the soft gasp he heard Noelle let out, most likely taken aback at his threat, especially because she knew that Carson was more than capable of delivering his promise; never mind the fact that they were kids. Instead, he kept his gaze locked onto the boy's, tightening his grip and pulling him closer, not missing him wince.

"Got it?" he repeated roughly.

"Y-yes, sir," the kid stammered out, looking ready to piss his pants as his friends nodded their heads vehemently in agreement. "W-we got it."

"Good." Carson loosened his grip and pushed the kid back, refraining from smirking when he stumbled and his back lightly thudded against the chalkboard wall. "Now, get the fuck out."

In a blink of an eye, the three high schoolers were gone. They left behind nothing but their crude drawings and a gust of wind. Carson let out a breath, calming down as the angry heat on his face cooled as well. With the kids gone, he noticed the lack of pressure on his arm. He realized that Noelle had let go as he turned his gaze to her, taking in her wide eyes and parted lips as she stared at him in surprise, awe, and what he realized in irritating disappointment, fear. It was small and barely present, but Carson picked up on it easily.

Since when did Carson care if he scared someone? He usually enjoyed putting the fear of God in people.

"That was . . . you didn't have to do that," Noelle finally spoke, her wavering voice only intensifying Carson's irritation as he took a quiet breath. He bit his tongue, fighting the urge to tell her there was no need for her to be afraid of him. "But, um, thank you." He did his best to keep his expression neutral, not trying to so much as hint at the mild surprise he felt. "I've been trying to deal with those kids for weeks," Noelle added with an airy chuckle.

Carson returned his hands to the pockets of his jacket. "They won't be bothering you again," he gruffed, glaring after the door the little shits had run out of.

"I appreciate it." He dragged his eyes back to her, noticing the nervous tilt behind her smile, hinting at the dimples in her cheeks. "I really do."

Then why do you look so nervous? Carson wanted to ask, but he knew the answer. Anyone who knew him, knew what he did, was right to have some healthy doses of nerves around him, and he reveled in the intimidation he had, the power of inflicting. So second guessing it in Noelle's expense prompted his stomach to sink, the bewilderment of it forcing an annoyed furrow on his eyebrows. He figured the best thing he could do, in that moment, was to get the hell out of there.

Carson nodded, unsurprisingly offering no verbal response as he watched Noelle's eyes flicker towards the wall, letting out a sigh as she stepped towards it and picked up one of the erasers. She began to get rid of the inappropriately phallic drawings those kids had left behind. Pulling his lower lip into his mouth, he watched her for a moment, spotting another eraser and knowing he was capable of helping her out.

Instead, Carson silently turned around, went over to the counter to pick up Levi's book, and exited the store.

CHAPTER TEN

"I'm gonna break the heels off and stick them in Beverly's fucking eyes for making me wear them," Noelle grumbled angrily, wincing as she took yet another step forward and felt the fronts of her stilettos pinch her toes.

Andrea snickered next to her. "Do it." She grinned. "We're in a room full of doctors. I'm sure she'll be fine."

Noelle huffed into her flute of champagne, taking a sip as she continued walking alongside her sister. She was sure both Beverly and her mother had something against her; the former for making her wear these shoes and the latter because she refused to let Noelle sit down instead of looking like she was enjoying the event. It was a charity auction held by the Board of Directors of the hospital their mother worked at. Instead of letting her daughters sit at their table, Malorie Simon wanted them to walk around and at least pretend they were interested in what was going on. Much to the chagrin of Noelle and her blistering feet.

Every step she took made Noelle wince in pain, mentally telling Beverly's 'beauty is pain' mantra to go to hell, until at one point, Andrea let out a huff. "Alright, sit down. You look like you're about to die."

Noelle watched as Andrea stopped, reaching down to untie the laces of her black Converse. Andrea managed to get away with wearing whatever kind of shoes she wanted, being confined to a wheelchair. Noelle always felt the biggest stab of guilt for being even the tiniest bit envious of her sister's feet being comfortable. Andrea couldn't even *feel* her feet.

She watched, confused as she slowly sat down on the seat behind her at an empty table as Andrea undid the laces. Noelle's lips parted in realization as Andrea took off her shoes and socks, gratitude immediately swelling up inside her.

"Gimme your shoes," Andrea said.

They wore the same shoe size fortunately, so it made Noelle slipping on Andrea's socks and Converse under her long dress easy as Andrea strapped on Noelle's heels. The relief Noelle felt from being free of the horrid shoes was instant, letting out a sigh as she leaned back in the chair.

"You're a lifesaver," she breathed out.

Andrea grinned, hands on the wheels on either side of her. "Pays to have a paraplegic sister, doesn't it?"

Noelle shot her a dry look, though she still felt the slight smile tug at her lips. Andrea had come a long way to be able to joke about her disability the way she did. Noelle fixed her dress, the long hem covering her feet just when their mother made her way over. Malorie Simon wasn't too tall of a woman, something Noelle inherited from her along with her hazel eyes. Her blonde hair barely brushed against her shoulders, and her high cheekbones were a trait she passed down to all three daughters.

"Noelle, I told you, no sitting," Dr. Simon reminded once nearing them, one hand holding a glass of wine while the index finger of her other made a standing up motion. "Up. Come with me. There's someone I'd like you to meet."

Stifling her sigh, Noelle stood up and gripped her own glass, watching as her mother smiled down at Andrea. "You okay, hon?"

"Yeah, Mom. Terrific." Andrea smiled back, the hint of sarcasm in her tone going completely over their mother's head while Noelle bit back a smile.

Dr. Simon then motioned for Noelle to follow her, and she obeyed, though not before shooting her younger sister a helpless look. One-on-one time with her mother wasn't something Noelle always looked forward to. Ever since their dad and Andrea's accident, their mother had become withdrawn, to say the least. She lost herself in her work, which was where she spent most of her time. It wasn't too unusual since she was a trauma surgeon, but when it came to her daughters and any attention they may need, Dr. Simon mostly focused on Andrea as if her two older ones didn't exist.

Which, while it sucked, wasn't too terrible for Noelle. Andrea did deserve any attention their mom may throw their way, and Noelle and Beverly were fine with that. It was sad, but Noelle was pretty stoked when her mother showed up to her university graduation last month. At least Dr. Simon was there for the big moments—if at all. Though that was still relative. After all, Noelle and her sisters had to spend the past three Christmases and Thanksgivings without their mother who always got called away to work. Although that may not be entirely her fault, her absence was still heavy. There was already an empty space at the dining table where their dad used to be. Did their mother even realize the impact of her own lack of attendance?

"I'm going to introduce you to the son of one of my colleagues, Dr. Grant. He's the new oncologist, and his son, Isaac, is your age," Noelle's mother said as they walked across the ballroom the event was being held at.

Noelle glanced at her mother, mildly confused. Since when did she care who Noelle was befriending?

"Um, okay . . .?"

"He's a nice boy. Handsome," Dr. Simon continued as they kept walking. "Studying environmental law, so you know he's one of the good ones."

The more her mother talked, the more Noelle couldn't help but think she sounded like the guy's Tinder profile. She raised her eyebrows as she hesitantly followed along. Eventually, they reached a man looking to be around Dr. Simon's age—tall and handsome with a headful of dirty blond hair slicked back and an expensive suit adorning his body. Next to him was a much younger man, practically a twin with a strong jaw, straight nose, and hazel eyes, except his hair was dark brown.

"Levi, this is my daughter Noelle," Dr. Simon spoke up once they reached them, catching the attention of the two men. "Noelle, this is Dr. Grant and Isaac."

"Hi." Noelle offered a smile, her lips dancing on the usual nervousness she felt when meeting new people. She shook hands with Dr. Grant and then his son who was, she noticed, pretty nice looking. "Nice to meet you."

Isaac returned her smile effortlessly. "You too." His eyes flickered down before his smile transformed into a smirk. "Gotta say, your shoes really go well with your dress."

Involuntarily, Noelle's gaze dropped down as if she had no idea what he was talking about. Her lips parted in mild sheepishness when she saw the toes of her Converse peeking out from under her dress. Maybe it wasn't as long as she had hoped.

"Where are your heels, honey?" Dr. Simon, who glanced down at her daughter's feet, asked through a strained smile to Noelle.

Yikes, Noelle couldn't help but think. Guess she's not a fan of the fashion change. "My feet were hurting, so Andy gave me her shoes," she answered truthfully, offering a polite smile to remind her mom that this wasn't a big deal and reprimanding her twenty-two-year-old daughter for wearing what she wanted was kind of ridiculous. And slightly embarrassing.

Dr. Simon pursed her lips, clearly displeased but let it go. "Come on, Malorie. I promised Thompson I'd listen to his European trekking story and I'd hate to see you not suffer through it with me," Dr. Grant spoke up, grinning. Noelle couldn't help but notice how his smile made him appear younger than he was. "Isaac, why don't you and Noelle get some dessert, huh?"

Noelle's mother immediately submitted, following after him as she shot Noelle a look over her shoulder and mouthed 'be nice,' as if Noelle would be anything unless given reason not to. Once they were gone, Noelle heard Isaac sigh next to her.

"They're not that subtle, are they?"

Blinking, Noelle turned to frown up at him as she brought her glass up to her lips. "What do you mean?" *Did I miss something?*

Isaac stared at her with a mildly incredulous expression before letting out an amused laugh. "My dad and your mom are trying to set us up," he told Noelle matter-of-factly with a shake of his head.

As much as his words were surprising, what wasn't surprising was the way Noelle choked on her drink. Her eyes widened in startlement as her free hand shot up to cover her mouth, keeping in the spray of beverage that threatened to spill out. Isaac blinked at her alarmingly, snatching up a folded napkin from a nearby table and handing it to her. She took it gratefully as she dabbed at her mouth once she finished her mini coughing fit.

"I'm sorry. What?" *My mother is trying to play matchmaker?* Heat spread up her neck and across her cheeks in embarrassment, genuinely not expecting this turn of events. *No fucking wonder my mom and his dad were so quick to leave us!* Only, Noelle most definitely wasn't expecting them to be cooking up something like this. How had that gone completely over her head?

Sure, Isaac was handsome, in an almost Ken-doll kind of way, but looking at him . . . didn't do anything for Noelle. Much to her helpless bewilderment, all Noelle could picture in her head was a pair of familiar dark eyes, curly hair, and plump lips that always left her wondering if they felt as soft as they looked. Her body flushed at the mere thought of Carson—at the hard lines of his jaw and the tattoos inked on his skin and the deep rumble of his voice—and Noelle wondered when exactly she had become someone whose body so easily reacted to a person she barely even knew.

Or maybe it was just because it was Carson.

"Yeah, don't worry. I'm pretty embarrassed about it too." Isaac chuckled awkwardly, bringing Noelle's attention back to him. *Oh. Right.* The situation at hand—ambushed into a set-up by her own mother.

As uneasy as this whole thing felt, Noelle figured it was best to nip this one in the bud as she swallowed uncomfortably. She offered Isaac a nervous smile. "Look, I'm sure you're a great guy, but like . . ." she paused, letting out a small huff of discontentment, incredulous her mother would put her in this position. "I'm just, you know. . . not interested?"

The last part came off as a question, and Noelle felt a spark of irritation at herself go off inside her. Saying no to boys who thought they had the right to ask her out until she said yes was no problem for Noelle, but this was different. Isaac was caught in this awkward situation just like her, and she genuinely had no idea how to get around it. It was no big deal, right? He would surely understand if he felt just as uncomfortable.

"Oh, don't worry. I'm not interested either," Isaac scoffed as he waved Noelle's words off with his hand but then his eyes widened when Noelle's eyebrows shot up, a bit affronted at the way he dismissed her so easily despite herself. He made it sound like having any interest in Noelle was the worst thing ever, and while Noelle was fine with people not liking her—even if she would silently torment over why—she didn't particularly like the way Isaac made it sound.

"Wait, no. I didn't mean it like that," Isaac immediately backtracked, looking mildly panic-stricken at the thought of insulting her. It almost made Noelle smile in amusement. "I just . . . I mean, I'm not *not* interested in you because you aren't pretty or anything, because you absolutely are. I just meant I'm not interested in you because I'm gay."

Oh.

Noelle's lips parted as she processed this information, lifting her eyebrows. She couldn't help the small sense of relief she felt but then she frowned, tilting her head in confusion as she looked up at Isaac.

"Wait, do . . . does your dad know?" *Because why else would he set his gay son up with a girl?*

Unless, Noelle realized in disgusted horror, if Dr. Grant was one of those homophobic people that figured if their gay kid got with someone of the opposite sex, then they magically weren't gay anymore. Suddenly, Noelle felt like wiping the hand she had shaken Dr. Grant's with on her dress. She didn't want to have shaken hands with a homophobic asshole.

"No, he doesn't," Isaac sheepishly answered, rubbing the back of his neck as he chuckled softly. "He's not too good with change, especially after losing my mom a few years back. I don't wanna, you know, overwhelm him with it. Not until both of us are ready."

A small, albeit sympathetic, smile tugged at Noelle's lips at his words. She understood the part about not adjusting to change; it's something her entire family had to deal with three years ago—an adjusting period that Noelle still felt was underway despite the time passed.

"I get it." She nodded along. "My dad passed too, so I know that change can seriously suck, especially when it comes to the parent we've got left."

Isaac returned her smile, two strangers confiding in the loss of a parent and the effect it had on them and their parents. Noelle's relationship with her mother had shifted a bit since her dad died, her mom more closed off and focused on her job and, if she was home, shifting it all to Andrea. That part Noelle didn't mind. She just wished it didn't feel like a stranger living with them whenever her mom was home from work.

"Come on." Isaac nodded, tilting his head towards the left where the dessert table was. "We can talk about how change sucks while we eat some cheesecake."

Noelle grinned. "A man after my own heart."

*   *   *

Within the few hours she had been talking to Isaac, Noelle decided she wanted to be his friend. He talked about what he was studying passionately and showed Noelle all of the pictures and videos he took on the various marches he had been on for pride, women's rights, education rights—all the events for causes Noelle supported and attended. The two of them ended up sitting at one of the empty tables, Andrea eventually joining them as they finally felt relief from being utterly bored at the event they were no longer paying any attention to.

The more Noelle got to know Isaac, the more she thought how perfect he would be for Benny. Maybe Noelle's mom passed down the matchmaking trait to her as well.

"Come on, kiddos. Let's blow this popsicle stand." Noelle glanced up to see Beverly making her way over to them, short blonde hair straightened to perfection. Noelle was kind of jealous; her previously straightened hair was back to its natural waves.

Andrea quirked an eyebrow, leaning back in her chair to look up at Beverly. "Where are we going, and is Mom gonna let us bail?" she asked.

"The dessert here sucks, and I want some ice cream," Beverly informed with a huff, an irritated expression crossing her face as she shot a sour look towards the dessert table. Noelle had to agree, the dessert wasn't good at all. "And yeah, she will. We've been here since two. Four hours of suffering is enough." Then her light brown eyes shifted to the guy sitting amongst her sisters. "You wanna come with, Isaac?"

He laughed when he noticed Noelle and Andrea's hopeful faces. "Let me ask my dad if he's cool with it," he said as he stood up.

"Aw, how cute. He asks for permission," Andrea cooed after him as he walked off, though not before scoffing at the younger girl's comment.

Noelle shot her sister a pointed look. "So do you when you gotta go somewhere."

"Because y'all treat me like I'm seven and not seventeen. It's exhausting."

Isaac returned moments later, saying how his dad was thrilled with the idea of him going off with Dr. Simon's daughters. The four left the hotel promptly, the entire time listening to Beverly.

"Time to get some motherfucking ice cream," she muttered.

*　　*　　*

Rolled ice cream wasn't something Carson indulged himself in. He would rather just eat regular ice cream like a normal damn human being, but he did enjoy the two roasted marshmallows he added to his cup. Those were the only toppings he got on his chocolate-rolled dessert, and while he would much rather enjoy his treat, his attention was unwittingly being pulled away by a certain giggly brunette.

A giggly brunette who was sitting with her right leg crossed over her left knee, the limb sticking out from the slit of her long dress and showing off the invitingly smooth skin that Carson couldn't keep his gaze away from. A giggly brunette was currently giggling at whatever the fuck the guy she came with said. Carson's grip on his cup of ice cream and plastic spoon tightened; he knew he was bothered by the sight of Noelle with some guy, and the sight of her with him and his own irritation just further annoyed

99

him. He knew he was jealous, but he didn't get jealous. So obviously, this new turn of events was all the more unsettling.

The way his blood heated up in his veins was hard to ignore. Carson suppressed a grunt. He should've stayed at Astros instead of letting Aiden drag him out, but when his friend got a text from Beverly asking if he wanted to get ice cream with her and her sisters, Aiden dragged Carson out by the back of his tank top and texted Levi and Max where to meet.

So here Carson was, sitting in some rolled ice cream joint in downtown Manhattan against his will. He had been annoyed that his training got interrupted, especially since he had Astros all to himself tonight, and he planned on using that to his advantage. When he walked in here and saw Noelle in a dress that hugged her in all the right places with a guy he had never seen before, Carson's irritation grew and then he got even more aggravated that he was annoyed over her in the first place.

"Can't take your anger out on a punching bag, so you're doing it to your ice cream?" Levi's voice sounded in his ear, pulling Carson out of whatever thoughts he lost himself in.

He glanced at Levi, noticing the way the blond was raising his eyebrows at Carson's cup before looking down at it himself. Levi was right; Carson had practically stabbed his ice cream rolls to death, making them look like something akin to sludge. Carson merely huffed and roughly ate another spoonful of the cold treat.

Levi sighed next to him. "I know you'd rather be training for your next match, but you gotta have a life outside Astros, man. I've been telling you that for years."

Carson's brows lowered in defiance, sitting back in his chair with his legs spread out under the round table he was sharing with Levi, Max, and Andrea. The ice cream parlor was busy with music playing and people chattering to deafen them to Levi and Carson's conversation.

"I can spend my time however the hell I like, Levi."

Rolling his blue eyes, Levi gestured to the table they were occupying and the one directly in front of them where everyone else sat with his spoon. "Wouldn't you rather spend some of it with us? Your friends?"

Carson's jaw clenched, having heard this spiel a dozen times before. He had been fighting at Astros for a few years, and it was no secret that Carson spent most of his time there than anywhere else. If he wasn't asleep or working at the gym, he would be at Astros either fighting or training for his next one, and if it was a particularly important match, his friends would be lucky to even get a text from him during the days leading up to the match since he would be busy perfecting his kicks and punches.

So, yeah, maybe Carson's life revolved around Astros, but it had developed into his routine and he couldn't just break away from that.

"You're making it sound like I never hang with you," he grumbled, shooting his curly-haired friend with a side-eyed glare.

Levi wasn't affected. "You're not a hundred percent there when you do," he scoffed out a laugh, though Carson could sense the hint of hurt Levi tried to hold back. It constricted Carson's chest uncomfortably. He was glad everyone was busy in their own conversations to hear Levi's words to him. "Hell, you didn't even acknowledge Bev's offer of going out for drinks tomorrow night. You even interested?"

If Levi was trying to make Carson feel guilty for getting lost in his thoughts to the point of losing all awareness of his surroundings, then he was succeeding. Carson knew it wasn't Levi's intention to make him feel bad, but guilt from the acknowledgment of getting annoyed by being brought to eat ice cream with everyone sparked both anger and shame. And angering Carson in any capacity wasn't good for anyone.

So before he told Levi he didn't give a fuck about going out for drinks and he would probably end up coming out with them anyway because of how persistent his friends were, Carson stood

101

up. The chair screeched as he did so, bringing everyone's eyes to him. Unfazed, Carson tossed his mostly full cup into the garbage—seven bucks down the trash—and gruffed.

"I need a smoke."

He distinctly heard Levi sigh behind him as he made his way around the tables and chairs, his shoulders square as he felt the weight of a pixie-like brunette's gaze burn on his back. He didn't dare look back at her because if he did, he wasn't sure if he would want to stay for her or just subject himself to more annoyance at the sight of that Isaac guy she was glued to. It wasn't long until Carson was leaning against the glass wall of the ice cream parlor, a cigarette hanging from his lips as the comforting taste of nicotine easily overpowered that of the ice cream.

The smoke puffed past his lips as his left hand remained in the front pocket of his jeans while fingers of the other hand held the cigarette, leaning his head back. The Manhattan streets were unsurprisingly busy, as was the foot traffic on the sidewalk he was on. Cars were honking and people were talking, but somehow, Carson could hear the chatter of his friends inside the parlor.

He could hear Noelle's giggles, forcing himself not to glance in to see if she was laughing at something Isaac was saying. Carson had absolutely no reason—no right—to feel as annoyed as he did when he saw Noelle sitting next to him, hanging onto every word he spoke. But he did, and the cigarette was just barely an anchor enough to keep him from throwing an unjustified punch at the dude Noelle seemed so taken with. He knew he would be in the wrong for it.

CHAPTER ELEVEN

Carson didn't flinch as his front door slammed shut, utterly indifferent to the sour mood he caused the girl he brought home last night. He didn't recall her name nor did he want to, having literally just kicked her out of his apartment the moment both of them woke up amidst his tangled sheets. After his smoke break at the ice cream parlor, Carson decided he didn't want to head back inside, so he messaged Max, Aiden, and Levi in their group chat and told them he was heading back to Astros—much to each of their chagrin.

They chastised him for being antisocial, and Carson didn't bother explaining that any other day he may have stayed, but this time, he didn't want to witness Noelle fawning over some guy that she—according to what she said—had just met that night.

Jealousy was a fickle thing, especially for a short-fused fighter who refused to believe that was what he was feeling.

After a few more hours of training, Carson treated himself to a couple of beers at the pub a couple of blocks down, catching the eye of some auburn-haired chick before he let her talk him into bringing her back to his place.

Morning came and Carson was forcing a girl out, who seemingly didn't understand the concept of just one night—or maybe she did, and the more likely reason for her bitter departure was his callous way of kicking her out. Carson was never too gentlemanly with the women he brought home the morning after, never one to let them misconstrue what happened the night before. It happened more often than not; sex was always an alternative for him to get his frustration out when Astros wasn't enough, which was rare. Although he enjoyed it like any other warm-blooded man, he wasn't one who went actively looking for it. If a girl approached him when he was in the mood, he was down. Otherwise, Carson couldn't give a damn. Astros would have to be enough and, for the most part, it was.

Except last night.

It also didn't help that he had the image of a certain brunette in his mind when some other girl was riding him. He felt like an asshole, but it is what it is. Carson also figured that was a big red flag in regards to his emotions towards Noelle. *Seriously, hooking up with some girl driven by unforeseen jealousy?* Sounded like a bad episode of *Friends*, and he wondered if this was some kind of sign that his attraction to Noelle was more than just physical attraction.

The jealous side of him would certainly argue saying, "Yeah, dumbass, it is more than just physical." But the rational side tried to reason that didn't have to mean he liked her in more than just wanting her body. Even if the small voice in the back of his head argued otherwise.

"Fuck," Carson muttered to himself, feeling the dull throb at the back of his head. He only had a few beers, which was not enough to make him suffer through a hangover but enough to warrant a hot cup of coffee as he leaned against his counter that separated the kitchen and living room. His eyes landed on the small ball of fluff on his grey couch. "You have a better night's sleep than I did?"

His dog, who was some kind of mixed breed of a husky and corgi and something else Carson didn't have a clue of, let out a small bark from where he nestled on the couch. A smile curled at Carson's lips. He took Oreo's response as a yes.

With no unwanted guests in his home, Carson continued his morning routine of eating breakfast and taking Oreo out for a walk before returning to get ready for the day and head to work at the gym. It was a job he acquired out of necessity than anything else; Carson earned most of his money through his fights, but having a second source of income didn't hurt. Besides, the job was part-time, and he got to work with one of his best friends, so it wasn't the worst thing in the world. Though Carson would be lying if he said he didn't look forward to clocking out at the gym to head to Astros.

"I'll see you later, buddy," Carson mumbled, hands rubbing Oreo's face and tilting his chin up slightly as he felt Oreo's tongue lick at his skin.

After petting his dog one last time, Carson grabbed his gym bag and headed towards the door, throwing one last longing look at his pet who was staring at Carson with big black eyes from where he leaned up on the arm of the couch. Carson sighed, exiting his apartment. If only he could bring the little guy with him.

*   *   *

The canvas floor of the ring collided with Carson's back as he fell, a grunt escaping him at the impact. He scowled up at the high ceiling of Astros, a growl of utter aggravation vibrating through his throat as he slammed his hands on the ring floor before pushing up to his feet, irritation crossing over his features.

Carson felt the bead of sweat running down his back under his tank top.

"You're not focusing as much on your feet as you are on your hands, Car," Aiden's voice came off from the side. Carson clenched his jaw, fisting his hands at his sides. "Keep that up, and kicks to your feet are gonna knock you on your ass."

Exhaling sharply through his nose, Carson circled his training opponent, Jonah Fraser. The blood in his veins pumped as it would during a proper match. Carson needed to remind himself that this was just training, but it was no secret he took it just as

105

seriously as he would the night of an actual fight. So not seeing Fraser's kick coming, which effectively knocked him on his back fueled an aggressive fire.

There was a dull ache in his teeth as he clenched them tightly, though Carson ignored this as he dodged a left hook and ducked under Fraser's arm while, in his semi-crouched form, simultaneously delivering a punch to his stomach. Carson felt the blond's muscles spasm under the hit, then heard him release a sharp gasp as Carson steadied himself on his feet and watched Fraser stumble back into the ropes.

Carson huffed out a satisfied breath, his right hand pushing through his hair to push it off his forehead. His curls were slightly damp, and his body was warm. His clothes stuck to his skin as he bounced subtly on his sneaker-clad feet.

"Come on," he impatiently piped at Fraser with a jut of his chin. "Get up."

Fraser shot him a frustrated glare as he pushed himself up, though Carson was not at all perturbed as he fisted his fingers once more. The raw skin of his knuckles stretched at the action as he readied himself to deliver more hits. His fingers were practically itching to come into fierce contact with Fraser. Carson would feel bad for the guy if he cared enough.

He was all riled up and, for the life of him, Carson's preexisting annoyance only grew because he knew the reason why. It was unfortunate he was practically perpetually angry, so the smallest of things set off his fuse alarmingly fast. So when Aiden reminded him about going to drinks tonight and Carson had made the mistake of asking who else was going—only to find out that along with the boys, Beverly, and Noelle, they would be joined by those two friends of Noelle along with Isaac—Carson felt an unwarranted and unjustified surge of anger he struggled to keep a lid on.

106

Which, at this point, he was using to punch Fraser with all his might, along with his knuckles until Aiden was yelling at him to stop.

Carson stumbled back as Aiden's hand wrapped around his bicep, hauling him away from Fraser who had been backed into a corner as he fruitlessly tried to protect himself from Carson's relentless assault. His chest heaved with his eyes on Carson as he sank to the floor with a groan. He squeezed his eyes shut as he gripped his right side, which had dealt with the brunt of Carson's attack.

"What the fuck, Car?" Aiden hissed in his ear, yanking him to the other end of the ring. His grip on Carson's arm was bone breaking. "Are you trying to piss Fraser off?"

Panting, Carson shrugged Aiden's grip off, turning around to grip the top rope of the ring as he caught his breath. His knuckles stung and his heart raced, feeling the stares of others in Astros after they just watched him lose his shit during training. Carson had made it a habit of being extra aggressive only towards punching bags, never towards the other fighters he would train with. It had the potential of starting unnecessary beef that Carson didn't have time for; it wouldn't do anyone good if he had trouble with anyone else in Astros.

Except all of that flew out the window the second he began beating the shit out of Fraser. Carson briefly wondered if he could show it off as an accident.

"Are you okay?" Aiden sighed when Carson didn't respond, coming up to his side as he bent his head slightly to catch Carson's gaze. "Is there something on your mind you wanna talk about?"

Before Carson could respond, Fraser's voice echoed throughout the area. "Yo, Hayes, what the fuck?" Carson straightened, turning around to see a pissed off scowl on the blond's face as he stormed over, the canvas of the ring shaking subtly beneath him. "You think you can get away with something like that during training?"

Carson's body tensed, preparing himself for an actual round of fighting rather than training as Fraser angrily made his way over. Carson was ready to knock him on his ass in five seconds flat. The music that was playing throughout Astros as the others trained was still going, but everyone's attention was on the ring. Carson could feel it.

"Whoa, whoa, whoa! Hey." Aiden stepped between Fraser and Carson, one hand on Carson's chest and the other against Fraser's, making sure to keep the distance between the two fighters and the tension they were radiating. "Car was out of line and he knows it, Fraser. Let's not try to start something no one wants to finish." Aiden treaded carefully with his wary eyes on Fraser.

Glare clashing with Fraser's, Carson silently dared him to push Aiden's arm off, to come charging at him who was prepared to deck him without hesitation. His body was still on fire from training and the ache in his knuckles told him he would definitely need to ice them, but he was willing to put them through a little bit more if Fraser challenged him.

The guy thought better of it; he took notice of the challenging narrow of Carson's eyes—dark and indignant. While Fraser didn't appreciate being treated like a punching bag, the last thing anyone in the ring wanted to do was start some kind of rivalry with Carson Hayes. They wouldn't win.

Fraser scoffed and stepped back, sending a glare towards Carson, who was indifferent to it, before shaking his head and sliding out of the ring. Carson watched him disappear towards the back room, eyebrows still lowered, especially when his gaze flickered towards the others that were staring. When each of them caught sight of his scowl, they promptly turned back to whatever they were doing.

When Carson turned to the rope to pick up his towel, pressing it against his neck and face to wipe off the sweat, he heard

108

Aiden sigh. "Wanna tell me what the hell that was about?" he repeated his previous sentiment before Fraser had interrupted. "Thought we agreed you wouldn't go off on someone else like that during training. That's how you piss people off."

Carson scoffed, hands pressing the towel on his face as he lowered it to shoot Aiden a flat look. "Funny that you assume I care about pissin' anyone off."

Aiden rolled his eyes as he followed Carson out of the ring, not missing the way the Australian winced slightly when forced to bend to get between the ropes. He had seen Fraser get one good hit on Carson's side before he had knocked him down on his legs and was forced to face the relentless strikes Carson threw his way.

"You already piss off the guys you beat. No point in making more people hate you," Aiden mused, falling into step with Carson as they headed to the back.

Opening his locker, Carson didn't bother responding as he unzipped his duffel bag. Off the ring, he already felt somewhat relaxed than he did going in, but the frown was still on his face, replaying the scene of Fraser effectively kicking Carson's legs from right under him that had sent him to the floor. Nothing distracted Carson, which made him all the more agitated at his lack of attention.

Or maybe something—or someone—had distracted Carson, and he just pushed that to the back of his mind and piled it up with irritation at the thought of seeing Noelle and Isaac tonight.

Carson all but slammed the locker shut once he pulled out the towel and clothes he needed, the sound echoing throughout the empty locker room as Aiden raised an eyebrow.

"The hell is going on, man?"

"Nothing," Carson gruffed, feeling Aiden's gaze on his back as he made his way towards the showers. He hoped that the water would calm him down and wash off his unreasonable chagrin towards two people who hadn't even done anything wrong.

*   *   *

The shower had burned his skin and relaxed him somewhat. Carson figured that was enough, until he was sitting at a dive bar in Chelsea around a large round table with a scowl on his face directed towards the pool table area straight ahead. He nursed a bottle of beer, not in the mood for hard liquor—much like the previous night—as he watched Noelle enjoy herself a round of pool with the guy she brought along.

Carson couldn't help but wonder what the hell was going on between them, drowning out the conversation the boys and Beverly were having. Why did he care so much? He had only met Noelle a short while ago. He saw her again and again because she was the sister of his best mate's girl, so he shrugged off the way she fit into his friend group instantly. Now, because she started to hang out with some guy, she was going to bring him with her too?

Carson's grip on the bottle of Corona tightened.

Why the fuck do I care?

He wasn't the most vocal about his feelings, but he was in tune with them. Carson wasn't that dense where he didn't figure out his disgruntlement with seeing Noelle with another guy had to do with how he felt about her. Carson took a long swig of his beer.

God, I hated feeling things, Carson thought.

It wasn't like Carson was emotionally stunted, incapable of feeling anything worthwhile. He made a big show of asserting that fighting at Astros was his one true love, but Carson had more than enough room for his love for his family and friends. That was all justified, wasn't it? To feel so strongly about those you care about? But with Noelle, everything seemed to be thrown into a loop, and he tried rationalizing that it was just physical at first, except his gaze would wander over to her when she was there. His mind would conjure up her image if she wasn't, and Carson couldn't hope to decipher his own damn thoughts.

110

The rings on his fingers clinked against the bottle as he tapped them against it, the sound drowning out over the music and chattering as well as the sound of a woman's voice.

"Hey, guys!" she greeted.

Eyes flickering to the right, Carson caught sight of two familiar faces walking in. He recognized them as Noelle's two friends, Camille and Benny. He had only met them twice, but they seemed decent enough. They came over to greet everyone. Camille placed her bag on an empty chair that was three chairs away from Carson, her warm smile turning slightly strained when her blue eyes landed on him.

He looked away, feeling his eyebrows twitch with the need to frown but refusing to allow that. Everyone else may be oblivious to it, but Carson knew in that instant that Camille wasn't all too comfortable around him, not that he cared; they weren't even friends. Had she confided this to Noelle? Carson's jaw clenched when he figured that she probably had.

"Hey, I wanna introduce you to someone," Noelle's voice called, capturing Benny and Camille's attention as they walked over. Carson's eyes narrowed, watching as Noelle animatedly introduced her friends to Isaac with a giddy grin on her face—the kind that showed off her teeth and dimples.

"Car? Carson!" Max's voice snapped the Australian's gaze away from the pool section, sliding over to his friend who sat on the opposite side to his left. Carson kept a cool expression on his face, hoping to give away nothing as Max raised his eyebrows. "You okay? Been tryna get your attention for a minute."

"Sorry," he gruffed, sitting up slightly as he realized all three of the guys and Beverly were looking at him. He felt the slight twinge of being unnerved, hoping no one noticed who exactly he was staring at. "What's up?"

Max leaned forward slightly, arms folded on the wooden table top. "Aiden just told us what happened at training, and you didn't even say anything. What happened?"

111

Carson blinked, mildly disconcerted that he was so lost in his thoughts and his stares that he hadn't even realized the people he was sitting with were talking about him. An unfamiliar rock song played throughout the bar as Carson shrugged nonchalantly, leaning back in his chair.

"Nothing," he responded indifferently. "Fraser can't seem to take a punch."

"You gotta be joking." Aiden let out a surprised laugh, leaning back in his chair with his left arm thrown over the back of Beverly's. He shot Carson a look from across the table. "You were treating it like a real fight. You know Fraser isn't one of the guys you can do that with."

Carson rolled his eyes, not too worried about any consequences. While Aiden advised Carson to only go hard on the punching bags during training, there were a few other guys in Astros that Carson could have a real-fight-simulation kind of training with that would try to hit back just as hard. Fraser wasn't one of them out of his own choice. Too bad Carson didn't give him much of one tonight.

He didn't get to respond to Aiden because suddenly the chair to his right was being pulled back, and Carson hadn't even realized Noelle had made her way over until she sat down next to him. From his peripheral, he noticed the triumphant smile on Noelle.

"Call me Cupid 'cause I think I just created a match made in heaven," she announced.

Everyone's expression turned confused, lowering or raising their eyebrows in question. Noelle merely grinned before jutting her chin forward, dragging everyone's attention towards the pool section. Carson raised his beer to take another sip. When his eyes landed on what they were meant to be looking at over the bottle, Carson all but nearly choked on his drink in disbelief. He most certainly had not expected to see Benny and Isaac standing by the pool table, cues in their hands as they stood remarkably close to

112

one another, almost no sense of personal space existing as they conversed with the kind of smiles on their faces that just screamed smitten.

"Wait." Levi's eyes widened, a startled grin spreading over his face as he returned his gaze to Noelle. "I thought Isaac was with you?"

So the fuck did I, Carson wanted to pipe in but, as usual, he kept his words to himself as he casted a sidelong glance towards the brunette by his side who let out a giggle at Levi's assumption.

"So does my mom," she said, earning a knowing snort from Beverly. "She and Isaac's dad are trying to, like, set us up but they don't know he's gay. And he seems like the perfect guy for Benny so I thought, why not?" She shrugged her shoulders, a proud smile on her face as she looked back at the two guys who were now enjoying a round of pool.

"That's pretty damn nice of you," Max praised, raising his glass of vodka on the rocks at Noelle who jokingly huffed modestly with a wave of her hand.

"I'm a nice person." She grinned, showing off a dimple as she leaned back in her chair. Carson, for the life of him, couldn't stop staring at Noelle as she ran her fingers through her long hair, pushing it away and letting it cascade down her back.

He wondered if she could feel his gaze on her, especially because Carson knew he had been staring at her the moment she had arrived at the bar. It was like she was a magnet, always drawing his eyes to her, forcing him to admire the dress she wore—which was more like a long T-shirt—that showed off her legs. The physical effect Noelle had on Carson, which she was oblivious to, was ridiculous—the way his jeans tightened at the mere sight of her and how his fingers itched to run up her smooth legs. He hadn't even felt that way about the girl he hooked up with last night or any other girl he had ever been with, come to think of it.

Carson was feeling way too much too fast for a girl he hadn't known for long, and he hadn't made up his mind if he wanted to act upon it or push it away to nonexistence. One thing was for sure, Noelle was definitely weaving her way into Carson's thoughts—and maybe heart—without even trying, and that was enough to leave Carson wondering just how deep this went.

CHAPTER TWELVE

"Okay! Mom's gone for the weekend, and y'all know what that means," Beverly announced excitedly just as the door slammed shut behind their mother's departure at six in the evening. She was going to D.C. for a conference, so the girls were left to their own devices—much to their delight. Beverly tossed her phone to Noelle, who caught it despite her surprise as she remained laying on the couch.

"Noelle, use both your phone and mine to send out a mass text, tweet, Snapchat, and whatever, but make sure you block the people we don't want here. You know who I'm talking about," she added when Noelle snorted. "We're having a party, and I don't wanna hear any complaints."

Noelle and Andrea exchanged bemused looks but didn't offer any protests as Noelle sighed and unlocked Beverly's phone.

"What time should everyone get here?"

"Eight!" Beverly replied from the kitchen. "You think Mom will care if we drink her Pinot?"

Andrea scoffed, twisting around in her wheelchair to look at their eldest sister, though Beverly was out of sight because of the wall next to the staircase.

"She'll murder all of us! Hide that so no one finds it."

Noelle snickered as Beverly groaned in annoyance, sending the texts and tweets and Snapchats off of Beverly's phone before doing the same with hers. She didn't mind throwing a party in their

115

house; it was a nice townhouse with two floors. It was spacious enough for a good house party where some people could even spill out on the back patio. The girls had thrown a few parties during their high school years, though Noelle and Beverly had to make sure Andrea wasn't around because she had been too young at the time.

"Alright, you guys mind putting away everything that might break and make Mom actually wanna kill us?" Beverly huffed as she reentered the living room, offering her sisters a hopeful expression. "I'm gonna go to the store with Aiden to get liquor and cups and anything else we might need."

Noelle and Andrea didn't mind doing so as Beverly took her phone back. Noelle could feel a twist of excitement in her gut. They weren't in high school or college anymore, save for Andrea, but Noelle still did enjoy a good house party where the music was loud and the potential for making liquor-induced mistakes was high.

When Beverly left with Aiden, Noelle and Andrea got to work by taking down and locking away their mother's certificates that hung on the wall and the picture frames decorated around the house along with anything else that may fall or break. Decorative pieces, smaller plants, and anything valuable went into locked cabinets and drawers or even spread throughout the girls' and their mom's rooms because those would be locked as well.

Beverly hadn't returned yet, but it was nearing seven o'clock, so Andrea and Noelle went to their respective rooms to get ready for the impromptu party they were throwing. Since she had already showered, Noelle started her makeup straight away as she listened to music.

As she applied highlighter to accentuate her cheekbones, admiring the way it glowed under the light, Noelle heard the flutter of a thought loud and clear in her head.

I wonder if Carson will show up.

She instantly pursed her lips and inhaled a sharp breath, attempting to push away any and all thoughts of Carson out of her

116

head. The last time she saw him was two days ago when they all went out for drinks; she wasn't able to go to his fight the night before with Beverly because she was out with some friends, but that didn't mean she didn't feel a sense of relief and even a bit of pride when she received Beverly's text when she was at dinner informing her of Carson's win.

When she was done with her makeup and let her hair fall into loose waves, Noelle put on her favorite navy blue off-shoulder romper with pink flowers on it, then paired it with slip-ons of the same color before heading down the stairs. Just in time, too, because the front door opened and in came Aiden and Beverly, both carrying in bags clinking with bottles.

"We found a bunch of stragglers outside." Beverly grinned. Noelle's gaze flitted past her to catch sight of Camille and Benny trailing in, who were also carrying bags.

Noelle helped take the items out on the kitchen counter, raising her eyebrows excitedly at the many bottles of liquor that were bought. Camille pulled out packs of red and blue solo cups while Benny smiled innocently at Noelle.

"Can I roll in your bathroom?"

She sighed as she rearranged the various flavors of the same vodka brand before nodding.

"Fine, but make sure the window is open and the exhaust fan is on." Benny was already halfway up the stairs when she shouted, "And keep the door closed!" The last thing she needed was the upstairs part of her house smelling weed. Noelle tolerated the smell, and she knew she would have to endure it later tonight, but it didn't hurt to warn Benny.

"You're looking extra cute," Camille commented with a quirk of an eyebrow as she put a case of beer in the fridge. Aiden was back at the car bringing the last of the bags in, and Beverly ran upstairs to get dressed. "Trying to impress someone?"

Noelle refrained from sighing as she pulled out a bottle of Fireball. When they were at the bar the other night, Camille had voiced her opinion on Carson when the others weren't around. She told Noelle something along the lines of just because Carson was hot, didn't mean Noelle should get herself involved with him. Ever since Noelle spilled about Carson's fighting, Camille hadn't been the most accepting of people. Noelle regretted telling her in the first place.

"And if I am?" Noelle dared. Okay, so yeah, she might have slipped on this outfit to catch Carson's attention, but that didn't mean she would act upon it. Sure, she was ridiculously attracted to him, but the guy was intimidating as hell. Noelle would be lucky to even remember to breathe around him.

To her surprise, Camille just shrugged. "Just be careful," she advised.

"Careful about what?" Aiden's voice sounded as he came back into the kitchen, setting one last bag on the center counter as he began pulling out the two bottles of tequila in there while shooting the two girls a curious look.

Noelle's eyes widened ever so slightly at Camille, giving a subtle shake of her head because she didn't want to be vocal about the crush on Carson she was harboring.

"Nothing. Elle's just planning on getting dumb drunk tonight." Camille smiled over at Aiden.

Aiden smirked slightly, raising his eyebrows in anticipation. "Just don't do some dumb shit."

*   *   *

Noelle was pretty damn tipsy—which, to be fair, was to be expected because before everyone had arrived, she had taken some pregame shots with her sisters, Aiden, and her two best friends. Unlike Beverly, though, Noelle could hold her alcohol, so while Beverly was already drunk, Noelle was merely giggly and warm and felt her head's heavy weight only slightly.

118

It was nearing ten and the party was in full swing. Music was playing through their in-house stereo system the girls' father had installed when Noelle was nine. The house smelled of nothing but alcohol and weed as expected. There were already so many people in her house enjoying themselves, but through slow blinking eyes, Noelle realized that the one guy she was searching for wasn't anywhere in sight.

She pouted as she stood by the stairs, Drake's voice filling her house. *Did Carson not come?* The music thrummed in her ears as it was mixed with everyone's chatter and laughter, and the pit of her belly had a perpetual warm fuzziness present as Noelle decided to get herself another drink.

After successfully pushing her way into the kitchen, she grabbed a glass from the now short stack of cups and made herself a mix of orange Fanta and vodka. She grinned when she caught sight of Isaac directly opposite of her picking up a can of Coke since he was on designated driver duty.

"Isaac!" she chirped happily, successfully catching his attention as he smiled at her. "Where's Benny? Did you lose him?"

He snorted and shook his head. "Nah, he's out on the patio. Smoking with that friend of yours actually. The one with the black hair."

Noelle froze when her cup was halfway up to her lips, eyes widening slightly as an excited thrill shot down her spine. "Carson?"

Isaac's eyes, which had narrowed as he tried to recall the name, widened as he snapped his fingers at her. "Yes, him! He bought a joint off of Benny, and now, they're having the time of their life."

So he is here, Noelle thought, not even questioning the relief she felt at that. When Isaac nodded his head towards the back door, telling her to come along, Noelle didn't hesitate to follow. She may have stumbled slightly, the drink sloshing in her cup, but that was definitely because of the alcohol running through her veins and not because she was pathetically desperate to see Carson.

They stepped through the door that led to the back patio, which was big enough for about fifteen or so people to be on. A couple were lingering around, though most were inside the house, so Noelle easily spotted Benny and Carson. Both of them were sitting leisurely on the white outdoor bench with joints between their fingers.

Her eyes were glued on Carson—the way he was slouched with his head leaned back to expose the smooth column of his neck as he gazed up at the sky, releasing a ring of smoke after taking a hit. Noelle bit the inside of her cheek as she followed Isaac towards them, taking in Carson's relaxed state, looking so damn good in black jeans and a fitted T-shirt of the same color, which ridiculously accentuated his biceps, especially the tattoos that inked his bronze skin.

Noelle would be lying if she said her mouth didn't water at the sight of him.

She was also surprised at herself when she stopped in front of the boys on the bench. "You know, it's just basic manners to greet the person whose house you came to instead of sneaking to the back to get high," she commented with the liquid courage in her system.

Carson lifted his head, the action slow as his dark eyes met her hazel ones. Noelle found herself not being as intimidated by the eye contact as she would be sober, her chest tightening in anything but apprehension. He looked unfairly attractive with one arm laying by his side and his right resting on the arm of the bench, the joint hanging between ring clad fingers.

"Couldn't find ya." Noelle refrained from shivering at the sound of his unusually raspy voice and at the fact that he potentially looked for her. He took another hit, pausing before speaking as the smoke curled out from his lips, "Figured you found some bloke to keep yourself busy."

She nearly coughed into the cup as she took a sip of her stinging drink. "Some bloke?" Noelle repeated, not even trying an attempt at his accent because, even while slightly inhibited, she knew she would sound ridiculous. "What? You think I find just any guy to pass my time with?"

The pout on her lips once she finished speaking was inevitable, a little quirk she had when she drank, her mouth always puckering just so. Carson insinuating that she was some kind of floozy wasn't helping the situation, not when some guy she wanted to pass her time with was sitting in front of her, smoking without a care in the world with his legs spread, almost begging Noelle to stand in between them or straddle his lap. Both options were inviting.

"Don't know," Carson responded, head tilting to the side as he regarded her. Post Malone's voice playing through the house merely served as background noise. She watched the gentle ruffle of his hair against the light breeze, absentmindedly wondering if it felt as soft as it looked under the warm glow of the light above the backdoor entrance. "Still tryin' to figure you out."

Noelle felt her face flush at that, attempting not to tighten her grip on her plastic cup because the last thing she needed was her drink exploding like a volcano. She hadn't even noticed Benny and Isaac sneak off, leaving just her and Carson—and others out on the patio—but they weren't even a blip in Noelle's thoughts.

She attempted to calm her quickening heart rate down by taking a long sip of her drink, the Fanta and vodka sharp in her throat as she swallowed and lightly cleared her throat.

"What's taking you so long?" Noelle quipped, her words only beginning to slur together slightly. "I'm not that hard to read, honestly." He, on the other hand, was nothing short of an enigma. No matter how many books she could fly through, he was one she couldn't yet decipher.

Carson, who had the joint in his mouth, raised his eyebrows before releasing it. The smell of weed was getting stronger as he released a cloud of smoke, and Noelle hoped the queasiness in her stomach that always occured when she smelt too much weed would stay at bay.

"Does that mean you're easy?"

His words and suggestive tone he said it in intensified the heat that spread across Noelle's cheeks, though this time it wasn't just from the usual fluster she felt because of Carson. If anything, she was a bit affronted at his words. Squaring her shoulders, Noelle tried to ignore the sway she felt in her head as she narrowed her eyes indignantly.

"Did you just call me easy?" she demanded.

Alcohol truly seemed to live up to being known as liquid courage when it came to Noelle because the harsh tone sounded her offense clearly. Carson was hot, and while she may have an embarrassingly huge crush on him, Noelle wasn't going to let anyone get away with insinuating she was *easy* the way Carson had because it was obvious in what way he was talking about.

"No," Carson responded coolly. He leaned forward with his arms resting on his thighs, slouching a bit as he peered up at her. The silver chains he wore glinted under the light as they hung around his neck, and some curls brushed against his forehead. Noelle fought the bizarre thought of how fluffy they looked and the urge to run her fingers through them. "Just wondering if that's what you meant, love."

Love. How was it possible that one little word caused all of Noelle's airways to constrict? Did Carson even realize he said it, or was it just a slip of the tongue? Something he didn't consider a big deal? Because if Noelle was being honest, that term falling past his lips in his accented deep voice was enough to send yet another excited thrill down her spine.

Before she could delve deeper into the dark abyss of overthinking, Noelle heard Max's voice. "Hey, there you two are!" he shouted. Carson's eyes flickered towards the door as Noelle glanced over her shoulder, catching sight of Max practically hanging off the door frame with a sloppy grin on his face. "C'mon, time for shots!"

* * *

Carson was most definitely failing at keeping the smile off of his face. Every time he felt his lips twitch upwards, he would force them down. He fought to keep the neutral expression, but that was proving to be difficult because while weed helped him relax and not give a shit about anything, the alcohol he was happily consuming was taking its own effects, meaning Carson was pretty close to losing any sober control he had on himself and his facial expressions.

The sight he was smirking at, at the moment was of Noelle staring at the four mini shot solo cups in front of her. They were filled to the brim and ready to be taken. Her hazel eyes widened almost comically and her jaw hung, an expression of regret crossing over her features over her drunken state.

"I hate this game," she whined with a miserable giggle.

Sitting next to her, Benny had his phone ready to record. "You can do this, Ellie. God and I believe in you," he cooed to Noelle.

Noelle let out a laugh, staring at her friend with glimmering eyes. "You don't believe in God, so your words mean jack shit," she pointed out.

Carson snorted as snickers sounded from everyone sitting in their circle. It was just their little group sitting on the floor in the patio as the party went on inside the house, the door open to let them hear the music. They were playing a game of drunk UNO, and Noelle had just been given the Draw 4 card by Levi, which meant that she not only had to pick up four cards, but she had to down four shots as well. She seemed to be able to handle her alcohol, but she was already drunk and those shots weren't going to help at all.

123

He watched, leaning back against the wall as Noelle giggled after taking a preparing breath. All eyes were on Noelle, eager to see if she would go through with it, Carson included, his own eyebrows raising in surprise when she reached for the first cup. Cheers erupted from everyone as Noelle downed every shot of vodka back to back like a champ.

"Oh my god," Noelle choked out over her friends' cheering, picking up her mixed drink as she chased away the burning vodka, her eyes squeezing shut. When she lowered the cup, Carson noticed the drink thinly trickle down the corner of her mouth. He bit his tongue between his teeth at the sight of it. The way her neck tensed, showing off every tendon and collarbone really had Carson swallowing his groan. He wondered when he was so fucking responsive to the mere sight of a girl. She pointed a threatening finger at Levi, who sat next to her, while her other hand pressed to her chest. "I hate you so much," Noelle breathed out.

Levi merely giggled drunkenly as the game went on, with whoever getting skipped or having to draw cards taking shots as they played a couple more rounds. By the time they were finished, it was nearing two in the morning. It was when Beverly stood to her feet though not too easily as she stumbled, only finding her balance when Aiden, who was still sitting, reached up and placed a steadying hand on her hip.

"Alright," she announced through a hiccup, clapping her hands together. Beverly's voice was a lot louder now that she was drunk, clearly heard over the music. "Time to kick everyone out." Then, smiling down giddily to the group, she mused, "Except you guys. You can stay. You're our favorites."

Carson was absently surprised how quickly Beverly managed to kick everyone out, though it wasn't too difficult after she cut off the music and though he suspected getting everyone to leave was mostly Aiden's doing since he was a lot more sober than his girlfriend as he got people to walk out the front door.

"Hey . . . Noelle?" Andrea's voice sounded from Carson's right. Aiden and Max had helpfully gotten her out of her wheelchair, so she could join the group on the floor. She sat next to Carson as she leaned against the wall. Her slightly wobbly voice caught her sister's attention, which also prompted Carson to look at the younger girl who had her head leaned back against the brick wall and eyes closed, a slight furrow in her brows. "I need to . . . I gotta get to the bathroom. Gotta throw up."

Carson's eyebrows lifted at that, having no time for any other reaction as he saw Noelle instantly stand up. He watched her sway for a moment, shutting her eyes briefly as she regained balance before walking around their circle.

"Okay, Andy. I'll get you in your chair, alright? It'll just be a few seconds," she said.

Noelle brought the wheelchair over from where they left it in the corner, ignoring everyone's gaze on her as she placed it next to Andrea. Carson remained where he sat, lips parting ever so slightly as he wondered how Noelle could do that—go from being completely drunk to appearing as if she was utterly sober. Her movements were kind of slowed down, which wasn't surprising seeing as how much she drank, but she seemed pretty coherent.

Carson knew he should've asked if she needed any help— he wasn't that much of an emotionless asshole who didn't care about the well-being of a seventeen-year-old paraplegic—but all words died in Carson's mouth as he watched Noelle crouch down to Andrea's side. His gaze remained on the two sisters as Noelle placed her left arm around Andrea's waist with her right arm hooking under her knees before expertly standing up with Andrea in her arms. Noelle took just one step over before lowering Andrea into the wheelchair.

He didn't understand why the sight tightened something in his chest, why watching Noelle help out her younger sister without hesitation made the unadulterated lust he so overwhelmingly felt for her turn into something a lot softer. A lot more . . . unfamiliar.

125

Carson could feel his heart pick up its pace but not in the rushed, adrenaline-filled way it did when he was in the ring; it was more like his heart was coming to some sort of conclusion his mind had yet to reach.

"I'll come with you," Camille sounded, standing up as well before following Noelle and Andrea inside the house.

It was silent since the music was off, but Carson could hear Beverly and Aiden attempting to clean up whatever they could inside.

"Yo! Stop sitting like a bunch of logs and help clean up a bit!" Aiden's voice sounded, which was followed by collective groans and whines from Max, Levi, Isaac, and Benny.

Nonetheless, they all stood up, each swaying or stumbling one way or another before they trudged inside while Carson remained where he sat. There were a few cups and bottles thrown about the small patio. Carson sighed as he leaned forward and picked up the cards that were still strewn about before stuffing them into the little box. He pocketed that before standing up, picking up three empty beer bottles by the neck in one hand and stacking the ten or so empty cups in the other and bringing them inside.

He frowned in irritation at the bright lights of the house, used to the single dull lamp out on the patio, though he was indifferent to the smell of weed and alcohol lingering. A droll snort escaped him at the sight of Max and Levi, both of whom were throwing ping-pong balls at each other from the messy game of beer pong. Giggles escaped them instead of helping out.

Lazily, taking his time, Carson picked up the trash and tossed it in a big garbage bag Beverly had brought out. He was grateful for the air-conditioner blasting to cool down his mildly cross-faded body. He was still very much aware of his senses, but everything just seemed to move slower around Carson, not to mention his own actions weren't as swift as they normally were.

Honestly, he was kind of surprised the world was still right side up for him.

"You guys are useless." Aiden sighed once he caught sight of what Max and Levi were doing, who in turn began pelting him with the little white balls. "Hey! Stop! Damn children, both of you!" He couldn't help but laugh as the two guys began giggling loudly.

The bottles clinked loudly as Carson dropped them in the trash bag. They continued for a while until Noelle and Camille appeared from down the hall, announcing that Andrea was okay and already in bed.

"Okay, I think I should take these two home," Isaac announced after dumping some cups in another bag, gesturing towards Benny and Camille.

Beverly pointed accusingly at him while on her knees in front of the couch, pulling out cups that had somehow ended up under it.

"You sober?"

Isaac smirked. "Yes, ma'am."

She nodded, satisfied. "Then goodnight."

Isaac snorted as Camille and Benny hugged Noelle goodbye. She giggled happily between her friends before bidding them goodnight. The three of them shouted their goodbyes to everyone else, voices drunkenly loud as Isaac pulled out his car keys and guided them outside. The door shut behind them. Huffing, Beverly stood up from where she was sitting on the ground with plastic cups in her hand and tossed them in the trash.

They had surprisingly cleaned up quite a bit, and Beverly seemed to be okay with that, then her gaze swung at the boys.

"Sleepover?" Before anyone could protest, Beverly pointed at Levi and Max. "Y'all are too drunk to drive." All the guys had come together in Max's car, save for Aiden who had already arrived in his. "And I wanted you to stay the night either way," she drawled and smiled at Aiden sweetly as she pointed to him.

The suggestive tilt in her voice made Aiden smirk and the others scrunch their face up in distaste. And so, it was decided then and there that the guys would sleepover. Beverly said she and Aiden would sleep in her mother's room, ignoring Noelle's jibe of "if Mom finds out you had sex on her bed, she's gonna kill you" while the other two boys could take her bed and one of them could take the living room couch since it surprisingly hadn't gotten fucked up during the party.

"I call Bev's room!" Both Max and Levi shouted simultaneously, startling everyone in the room as Carson shot them an exasperated glare—both because of their volume and because it meant he had to turn towards the couch.

Maybe I should just call an Uber, Carson thought. He wasn't too keen on taking the subways this late, and with the weed and alcohol in his system, he had no doubt the stuffy heat of the subway would nauseate him.

Beverly grasped Aiden's hand and took him up the stairs while Levi and Max shoved each other as they made their way past Noelle and down the hall to Beverly's room, their footsteps thundering on the wooden floor as they went. Carson's eyes went from them to Noelle, who was still standing near the entrance of the hallway right next to the staircase, head tilted slightly as her gaze remained on the TV facing the couch.

Carson raised an eyebrow when her hazel eyes met his dark ones.

"Are you sleepy?" she asked unexpectedly.

He was drunk and high and wanted to sit down but not sleepy.

"No."

Noelle grinned, showing off her dimples as she bounced slightly on her heels before swiping her hand on the wall to turn off the main lights. Only the stove light in the kitchen and the tall lamp next to the TV emitted a warm glow in the room. She then made her way towards the couch, dropping down on it as she grabbed the

128

remote. Throwing a look at Carson over her shoulder, she smiled sweetly.

"Do you mind if I watch the new episode of *Chicago Fire*? I- I recorded it and really wanna watch it. Please?"

Her speech was slightly slow and stuttering, and a small wry smirk curved Carson's lips. He found it amusing that she was asking him permission when this was her house but then his gaze took in her pleadingly widened eyes and the way her lower lip was jutted out. Carson all but shoved down the near animalistic desire to catch that very lip between his teeth.

Clenching his jaw, he tried to push those thoughts to the back of his hazy mind, realizing Noelle was still waiting for a response as he shrugged.

"Whatever you want."

She grinned brightly, the sight of her smile and dimple that winked into existence knocking the damn air from Carson's lungs. He needed a moment to recover from it as she reached the couch and sat with her legs crossed before leisurely making his way over. He sat down next to her at a respective distance on the other end, the space mostly for him. Being near her was enough to crackle his blood with electricity. He needed to be careful. So he leaned back on the couch with his eyes on the screen as Noelle went to the DVR to play the episode.

He wasn't at all paying attention to the show; Carson's eyes kept flickering over to Noelle without any thought as he relaxed back against the couch. He tilted his head towards her ever so slightly as his gaze lingered over her form. The little romper she had on showed off her legs, the skin looking smooth and soft to the touch, all the way up to her thighs as the hem of the clothing rode higher. Carson slouched on the couch and leaned his head against it as he wondered if he had some kind of fucking obsession with Noelle's legs. All he wanted was to sink his fingers into her skin, feel the softness under his touch. He gritted his teeth at the images flashing through his mind without much thought.

As the show went on, Carson felt the familiar heaviness in his head from what he drank and smoked. A wave of sleepiness washed over him as he sat with his arms loosely crossed and head tilted back. He was in no rush to fall asleep, wanting Noelle to finish her show, but the couch was comfortable enough to fall asleep sitting up. It sucked because he would much rather be admiring the girl sitting to his left.

The hour had passed before he realized it. The TV was bright as the episode ended with a white screen that caused him to squint, so he wouldn't be blinded. Fortunately, Noelle shut the TV off as she looked at Carson, taking in his obviously sleepy form. Her own buzz was beginning to wear off; she didn't get drunk easily and the alcohol would wear off too fast. She wasn't sure if that was a blessing or a curse. She didn't feel as giggly or loopy as she normally would.

Standing up, she noticed Carson peek with one eye, looking up at her through an adorably sleepy gaze that made her heart leap.

"I'll get you a pillow and blanket from upstairs."

Carson hummed in disagreement as he stood up as well, his height easily towering over Noelle's. She tilted her head back slightly to look up at him. The sleepy look in his slightly red eyes and the flush on his cheeks made her, for the first time, lose all sense of being intimidated by him.

"I'll come," he rasped.

Noelle ignored the shiver his voice elicited, nodding as she walked around him towards the stairs. All the lights in the house were off, save for the lamps. The staircase creaked quietly under their steps as she felt Carson's presence behind her. How could she not notice it? His mere existence demanded to be acknowledged.

They walked past Noelle's mom's room. The unmistakable sounds of the headboard faintly thudding against the wall and the soft yet gratified groans muffled through the door greeted Noelle and Carson as they went. She pressed her lips together to stifle a laugh, and Carson's lips curled into a smirk. Noelle hoped her sister would remember to change the sheets.

There was a big dresser in Noelle's room where the drawers were full of bedsheets and pillow cases along with extra towels and such. She knew she would be able to find something for Carson. Using the key that had somehow stayed in the pocket of her romper, she unlocked her door and stepped inside. Carson followed behind her as she glanced to see his gaze flicker around the room curiously once she turned on the lights.

The smirk on Carson's face widened when he noticed two bookshelves by the window across from them—each shelf filled with books. He wasn't at all surprised at the sight, taking in the fairy lights draped across the wall above her bed, a dresser decorated with makeup and perfumes, and pictures either taped to the wall or hung on frames. Carson noticed Noelle displayed her love for reading and the people she cared about clearly.

Opening the bottom drawer of the dresser, Noelle crouched down and pulled out a comfortable blanket—one that would keep him warm from the AC but not overheat him like the weather outside. She then walked over to her bed, picking up one of the four pillows she had before walking over to Carson. He met her halfway in the middle of her room, right in front of her bed with arms out, so she could put the items.

"There you go." She looked up at him with a warm smile, not at all paying mind to their proximity. The only thing separating them was what was in Carson's arms. "I hope the blanket keeps you warm."

The smirk that reappeared on Carson's face wasn't surprising, but his next few words were some that neither of them were prepared for.

"I'm a warm guy, 's why I make a good cuddler."

Fucking shit. Are you kidding me? Exasperation swelled inside Carson as his grip on the blanket tightened, completely blaming the fact that he wasn't totally sober when those words even slipped out of his mouth. *A good cuddler? Who said shit like that?*

His jaw was clenched, and he was a second away from turning and swiftly exiting Noelle's room when she spoke up, "A good cuddler, huh?" She regarded him for a moment with a thoughtful tilt of her head, and Carson could practically hear the gears running in her head behind her mischievously glinting eyes. He paused, sparking curious wonder as well as the fleeting thought of how pretty her eyes were. He could detect a hint of green in her hazel irises, a ring just around her pupils.

Then, she took him completely by surprise as the corner of her lips curved upwards. He was absolutely floored at how someone could look so mischievous yet deceptively innocent. Noelle motioned to her bed with a subtle jerk of her head, twisting Carson's insides in an unexpected excitement.

"Seems kinda rude for you to drop a secret like that and then leave me alone in my bed. How am I supposed to know if you're telling the truth?" she mused.

For the first time, Carson's throat dried at the challenging look in her eyes and the teasing lilt her voice took as her lips formed a slightly pouted smile. It was an expression. Carson decided, then and there, that would be his downfall. Her words registered in his mind, obviously inviting Carson into her bed. Unlike the many punches and kicks he was given in the ring, he hadn't seen this coming. He knew she didn't mean her invitation to be anything more than cuddling—an idea he still couldn't believe he put out there—and despite the wolfish urge to strip Noelle off her clothing, Carson was well aware he wasn't going to do a damn thing about it when neither of them weren't in the completely right state of mind. If he was truly going to get her into bed, it would be when she would remember every single moment of it.

Still, the notion of climbing into Noelle's bed was both exciting and dangerous. It was disturbingly obvious to Carson that he was attracted to Noelle more than he had ever been to any other girl, but he was too faded to even begin to acknowledge where the head spinning concept of feelings came into play in this situation. He was sure if he took Noelle up on her offer, he would spend God knows how long trying to frustratingly figure out just what the fuck he was doing or what he wanted.

That didn't stop him from dropping the load from his arms onto Noelle's bed. "Guess you can find out now."

Carson had absolutely no idea what he was doing as he climbed onto Noelle's plush mattress, sitting on the left side as he raised his eyebrows expectantly at the brunette who was still by the edge of the bed. Her eyes were alight giddily, a smile spreading on her face.

"Be right back," she chirped before exiting the room.

Carson took that moment to empty his pockets of what they contained. He set his phone, keys, wallet, pack of cigarettes, and his lighter along with Noelle's pack of UNO on the bedside table next to him. He waited for her quietly, his thoughts beginning to make themselves known.

What the hell am I doing? Carson couldn't help but wonder how he managed to get himself into this situation, but when Noelle returned to the room minutes later, face free of makeup and her romper replaced with a pair of night shorts and a *Harry Potter* shirt, Carson ignored every question that was plaguing his mind in regards to the turn this night had taken.

His eyes were trained on Noelle as she shut off the lights, blanketing the room in darkness. The only light was the sliver peeking through her curtain. As Carson toed off his shoes and moved to properly lay down, he saw her silhouette making way to the other side of the bed. The closer she got to the bed, the more Carson felt his throat tighten up as if he had never been in bed with a girl before. Noelle wasn't even doing anything, and she somehow overwhelmed him.

Carson felt the bed dip slightly under her weight as she settled on her side. He didn't mind his own pants and shirt, knowing it was just for tonight as Noelle silently shifted to bring the duvet over their bodies. Suddenly, the scent of alcohol and weed from downstairs was replaced by something pleasantly fruity and another scent he couldn't decipher but ultimately knew it as Noelle. He decided, in that moment, he quite liked it.

He laid his head down on the soft pillow, laying on his right side facing Noelle.

"Too far." He heard her murmur.

The half smile curling his lips came easily at the sound of her sleepy voice.

"Waiting on you, babe," Carson responded quietly as if to not disturb the silence.

Noelle let out a soft giggle as Carson felt her shift closer, already laying on his side and waiting for her to close the distance.

Shit, when was the last time I actually cuddled with a girl? Carson couldn't remember if there even was a last time. All he could think of was now. His body seemed to mold around hers, adjusting to the shape of her against him. Every single one of his muscles relaxed despite the unfamiliarity of the situation. This—she—felt right.

When Noelle turned to have her back face him and as Carson felt her press up against his chest, his mind blanked. All he could feel was his heart picking up its pace, unfamiliar when it came to a rare, intimate situation as this as his left arm draped across Noelle's waist under the covers. In the silence of the room, his thoughts were suddenly roaring to life, bringing his attention—as if it would be anywhere else—to how snugly she fit into him, how good she smelt despite them spending hours at the party, how the absolute last thing on Carson's mind was to let go of her, and the comforting warmth she provided.

He couldn't help but think about how the last time the distance between him and Noelle had been this minimal was in that alley that one night, with her pressed between the bricks behind her and Carson at her front. Carson had tried putting the image of her being right there out of his mind, but here and now, with her back against his chest, all he could think about was wanting Noelle close. How he was unsure how she had so easily, so effortlessly had him letting go of any hesitation he may have felt about anything.

Carson felt his eyes drift shut, contentment washing over him as he dipped his head slightly. Noelle's hair was unbelievably soft, and Carson had no issue in pressing his mouth against her clothed shoulder blade, the top half of his face resting comfortable in the crook of her neck as strands of her hair tickled his cheek welcomingly. He felt her legs shift slightly, surprising him as she tangled them with his, uncaring that he was still in jeans. Carson fought the content sigh threatening to pass his lips after building up in his chest.

He couldn't remember the last time he slept with someone without doing anything, but the way his heart was falling into an easy rhythm, especially after feeling Noelle's left hand lay on top of his that was against her stomach, had Carson thinking a very dangerous thought before falling into slumber.

I could get used to this. I could get used to her.

CHAPTER THIRTEEN

The second Noelle's eyes reluctantly opened the next morning was the second she instantly regretted drinking the night before. She had brushed her teeth before sleeping, but the stale taste of alcohol was still lingering at the back of her throat with a sharp pain behind her forehead. She felt dizzy despite still laying down. Noelle groaned softly as she shut her eyes, moving to bury her face into her pillow only for her nose to press against something significantly harder than the pillow.

She hummed sleepily, eyebrows furrowing as she absently slid her hand up next to her head. Her mind was slowly registering that whatever she was laying on wasn't a pillow and was definitely longer . . . and smelled wonderfully like a goddamn rain forest and something else she couldn't identify.

Then, her not-pillow let out a groan that rumbled right beneath her cheek. Noelle let out a startled gasp as she shot up. Her head pounded at the rapid movement, but she paid it no mind as her widened eyes took in the sight beneath her. She could hear her heart drum in her ears at the sight of Carson laying in her bed.

At that moment, Noelle genuinely wondered if it was possible for one's heart to literally jump out of their chest.

Her eyes looked over his still sleeping form, starting from where she could actually see his body, where the duvet had fallen by his thighs.

How could he sleep in those jeans? Trailing her gaze up, Noelle bit the inside of her cheek at the sight of the golden brown skin she could see. Thanks to his shirt riding up, the band of his Tommy Hilfiger underwear prompted her to swallow in an attempt to ease her drying throat.

How the hell did he end up here? She knew for a fact they hadn't done anything, not with her in her pajamas and Carson still in those jeans and shirt. Noelle would be lying if she said she wasn't both relieved and disappointed. The latter because apparently nothing happened, and relieved because she wanted to remember if it did. Her face flushed; she really needed to question the situation at hand rather than fantasize about having sex with Carson.

Noelle really needed to get the fuck out of bed instead of sitting there and drooling over the godlike man still fast asleep. She took in the way his chest rose and fell steadily with his even breaths as his plump lips parted only ever so slightly. The material of his shirt stretched across his body. Noelle really needed to get the fuck out of bed instead of sitting there and drooling over the godlike man sleeping in her bed.

"What the fuck," she whispered to herself while running her fingers through her hair to push it back. She winced slightly at the knots she felt as she reached up with her other hand to undo them as best as she could. Her attention was drawn to the tangled mess as she grunted when she tugged knotted strands the wrong way, sending a painful jab to her already hammering head and glaring at nothing in particular. "This can't be happening."

"Didn't think cuddling went that badly."

Noelle jumped at the unexpected deep rasp of Carson's voice, heavy with sleep as her upper half turned around. She shuffled back ever so slightly as she caught sight of the man. Her heart was in her throat, looking at him as he propped his upper half up by his arms and his sleep laden eyes observed her. His hair was a curly mess and his lips were deliciously plump. Noelle had a hard time controlling her breathing as she thought how unfair it was for someone to look so heartbreakingly gorgeous right when they wake up.

"I . . . uh, i-it didn't?" Noelle stammered, taken completely off guard, which only caused her statement to come out as a question. She was still trying to process that he was in her bed. That they had *cuddled*. Not only that, she had cuddled with Carson who was now raising his eyebrows at her unsure words. She was once again surprised to see the mirth dancing in his tired eyes.

Oh god. Now, without all the drinks in her system, it seemed like any courage and bravado she had last night slipped into nonexistence as she sat on her bed with Carson.

"It didn't." She cleared her throat, steadying her voice as her gaze locked with Carson's. "It was . . . nice. I, um, enjoyed it."

Her cheeks flamed as she said that, feeling pathetically flustered at the mental image of her and Carson in her bed, wrapped in each other's arms for the night. Noelle remembered bits of Carson admitting to being a good cuddler and her boldly suggesting he do so with her, and at the current moment, Noelle didn't know whether to praise her drunken self or slap her silly.

Now that she was sober, she had to deal with the aftermath, which was hard enough without Carson looking like a literal god in her bed.

As her mind desperately tried to wrap around what was going on, Carson threw her in for another loop as he sat up. His hands rested on his knees as he leaned towards Noelle. She remained frozen, watching with slightly widened eyes as he closed the distance until there were only a few inches between them. She saw the faint redness surrounding his dark eyes that had long lashes framing them and the way his plump lips curved slightly. Noelle wondered how someone could have such squishable cheeks yet a jawline sharp enough to cut glass.

"I did too," his low voice rasped. His accent slipped in and Noelle sucked in a quiet breath. It was then, at that moment, when Noelle's stomach let out a complaining growl, instantly flushing her

138

cheeks with an even more embarrassed heat as she broke away from Carson's gaze with a deep chuckle escaping him. It was a faint sound, his little chortle, but one that had Noelle's heart once again picking up. "Guessin' it's time for breakfast?"

"Yeah," Noelle breathed out, kicking off the rest of the covers as she scooted to get off the bed. She stood on her feet despite her wobbly knees. She swayed in dizziness, and even though she was hungry, she was also queasy, though she could tell she didn't have to throw up. *Thank God.* Returning her gaze to Carson, Noelle almost wanted to whine at how nice he looked in her bed. Fully clothed, sure, but such a sight. "The bathroom's across the hall if you, uh, wanna freshen up or whatever. I'm gonna, um, make coffee and waffles."

She didn't give Carson a chance to even say anything as she quickly turned around. She left her phone on her bedside table as she opened the door to her bedroom and left, quickly making her way towards the stairs. As she made her way to the kitchen, she prepared a pot of coffee and put a couple of frozen waffles in the toaster. Noelle bit down on her lip hard, enough to nearly draw blood.

Did I really get into bed with Carson last night? Yeah, they didn't do anything, but the fact that he voluntarily got in to just cuddle with her was beyond Noelle's understanding. Since the moment she met him, there was a nagging voice at the back of Noelle's head telling her that Carson found her annoying, but last night's event was proving her previous thoughts so terribly wrong.

She leaned back on the counter next to the fridge, her eyes absently lingering on some of the remaining unfinished liquor bottles on the center counter. She bit down on her lip to quell the smile growing on her face as the giddiness inside swelled. Who the hell would've thought she could get this badass, admittedly scary guy to crawl into bed and hold her while she slept?

The fact that it was Carson—big scary Carson who punched people for a living and who effortlessly managed to send her heart into overdrive—only served to intensify Noelle's disbelief of the situation.

Shit. She didn't even want to think about how close he had gotten just moments before because Noelle knew she would drive herself crazy by overthinking and overanalyzing everything, so it was better to just . . . let it be.

The waffles popping up from the toaster startled Noelle out of her Carson-infested thoughts. She brought out a plate to place all four of them on it and grabbed another one for Carson, silently hoping he liked waffles. But then again, who didn't?

The house still vaguely smelled of last night's party with a few forgotten bottles and cups laying about. Noelle placed the plates on the counter after moving aside a few bottles and then moved to grab some forks and syrup. The smell of waffles mixed with freshly brewed coffee replaced the stale smell of alcohol and weed. She hadn't realized her heart was pounding in anticipation of Carson coming down, feeling her breath still as she heard his footsteps on the stairs. She watched him enter the kitchen, all tall and broad shouldered and gorgeous.

Forcing her gaze away, Noelle turned back to the coffee pot and poured some in a cup for herself. "I don't know how you take your coffee."

She turned, blinking in surprise as she hadn't expected to see Carson standing right next to her as he reached for the empty cup.

"Black," he offered while pouring the drink.

Noelle curved her lips into a smile. "I'm not surprised."

Black coffee seemed like a Carson drink. Meanwhile, she put some cream and sugar to stir away the utter bitterness.

Carson moved to stand on the opposite side of the center counter, leaning his front against it as his gaze flickered to her mug and smirked.

"I'm not either," he said before reaching for a fork.

It was surprising to both of them how comfortably they stood across from each other with the counter between them as they enjoyed their waffles; Carson drenched his in syrup while Noelle only zigzagged it thinly across. Noelle ate hers and raised her eyebrow as Carson cut off a piece with his fork, stabbing it and lifting it to his mouth as copious amounts of excess syrup dripped to the plate.

"I have diabetes just by looking at that." She laughed airily. "That much syrup cannot be good for you."

Carson swallowed the bite, pointing at her with his fork. "Don't shit on it before you try it," he quipped. Carson surprised her by cutting off another piece, coated with syrup, and held it out to her. He reached his arm across the counter. Noelle blinked at the sweet treat, taken aback as Carson leaned forward slightly, his height not making it difficult for him to reach across. "C'mon, you never know what you're missing until you try."

Something about the way he said that, the suggestive lilt his hoarse morning voice took, had Noelle's gaze flickering up to meet his. The mirth dancing in Carson's dark eyes wasn't expected—much like this entire damn morning—but it gave Noelle the push to lean forward a bit. The edge of the counter bit into her stomach as she opened her mouth and kept her gaze locked with Carson's cool yet somewhat smug one, as if challenging her to take a bite. Noelle's heart lurched as he inched the fork forward just enough to allow her to pull off the piece with her teeth.

She dropped her gaze to his plate and didn't dare look at Carson as the overwhelmingly sweet syrup danced on her tongue. It was then that Noelle realized she may have misjudged just how much syrup was on that one piece because she could most definitely feel a small amount of it dribble from her bottom lip to her chin from the fork as Carson pulled it from her mouth.

Before the mere thought of finding a napkin to wipe it off could even flutter through Noelle's mind, the fork that had been reached out towards her was replaced by Carson's hand. Her mind blanked, breath stilling in her lungs as she felt the calloused pad of his thumb gently swipe right below her lower lip. The action was so soft; nothing you would expect from someone whose hands have been involved in violence.

Hell, this entire morning was just wild. Noelle stopped trying to make any sense of it.

Every nerve in her body was sparking within her skin; everything else was slipping away. Her eyes followed Carson's thumb's movement as he brought it to his own mouth, slipping it between his plump lips that were curling into an arrogant smirk because she knew he was watching her watch him, but fuck it if she cared.

How could I not stare? The sight before her felt unreal, especially as she stood frozen on the spot. The area right below her lip tingled from where Carson's thumb brushed against it.

Noelle tried to ignore that even though he only touched a miniscule part of her, but it felt as though her entire body was on fire.

"Not bad, huh?" Carson mused after releasing his thumb, the mischievousness in his tone indicating that he knew that the last thing on Noelle's mind currently was the damn waffle. Seeing this . . . this playful, flirtatious side of Carson was out of the blue, and Noelle couldn't help but revel in it.

Before she could even hope to respond, footsteps sounded until Beverly and Aiden came into view. Their hair looked like a mix of sex and bed head; that alone being enough to tell everyone how much they fooled around the night before.

Noelle shoved another piece of waffle into her mouth. As soon as it came, she squashed the wistfulness of her and Carson did the same damn thing, especially when her skin still tingled from where he touched it and the weight of his gaze continued to burn into her.

*　　*　　*

142

"You know . . . if you wanna go for it, there's nothing stopping you."

Noelle was startled, not expecting to hear Beverly's voice as her older sister appeared in the aisle she was in. Once again, Noelle was restocking books in the historical fiction aisle this time.

"What?" she asked, eyebrows lowering into a confused frown.

Beverly rolled her eyes. She approached Ken, who was a high school senior working during the summer, as he helped Noelle out on the shelf opposite of her in the same aisle.

"Take over the register, Ken. Zara's about to leave."

Ken nodded, leaving the cart as he left the aisle and Beverly took over. Her back was facing Noelle's as she worked.

"Carson. I'm surprised you haven't made a move yet," she clarified.

The copy of *War and Peace* almost slipped out of Noelle's hand. A startled laugh escaped her as she looked over her shoulder to Beverly, raising her eyebrows.

"What?" she repeated, feeling the heat creep up her neck.

"Come on, Ellie," Beverly scoffed, shooting her a flat look. "Since when have you been someone who shied away from the guys you're interested in? What's holding you back with Carson?"

"The fact that it's Carson," Noelle muttered under her breath, returning her attention to putting the books in the right spots. Was her sister seriously blindsiding her with this? Getting interrogated about her feelings for Carson, which she hadn't been the slickest in hiding, wasn't how Noelle wanted to spend her restocking time.

Unfortunately for her, Beverly heard Noelle's not-so-discreet words as she let out a groan. She turned away from the shelf she took over to come stand next to Noelle.

"Please don't tell me you're, like, scared of him."

"What? Of course not!" Noelle denied a bit too quickly, shoving one book between two. When she caught the exasperatedly suspicious look on Beverly's face, Noelle let out a conceding sigh. "Okay, maybe I was at first, but I'm not anymore. He's . . . intense, but he doesn't scare me," she confessed, hoping her sister realized she was telling the truth.

Noelle came to the conclusion that she wasn't necessarily afraid of Carson; he was just this guy who, to her, seemed larger than life. The way his mere presence demanded attention, which required to be noticed and acknowledged, was overwhelming, but she wasn't afraid of him, not after the party last Saturday night and then the morning after yesterday. There was a soft, playful side to Carson that she only got a glimpse of, but knowing it was there was enough to wash away any fright she might have felt towards Carson.

"Good." Beverly nodded after realizing Noelle was being honest. She dropped one shoulder, leaning against the shelf. "I'm only bringing this up because I see the way you look at him, Elle. You really like him, and I love Car, but I love you more so I'm gonna say this. . ." she continued. Noelle blinked at Beverly's tone taking a serious turn. "If you wanna take a chance with Carson, then do it. You don't wanna be someone who always asks themselves 'what if'. This might be a silly little crush or it might not be, but you won't find out until you do something about it. Even though I think this is something worth, like, pursuing, I'm also just gonna say that because this is Carson we're talking about, you just. . . you be careful."

Now, Noelle really was confused. Beverly either wasn't being clear about what she was saying or Noelle was just too dumb to understand. Was Beverly telling her to admit her feelings to Carson, or was she advising against it? What was that whole last bit about being careful about?

Noelle shook her head, drawing her eyebrows together. "You lost me, Bev," she voiced. "Be careful of what?"

144

Beverly let out a frustrated grunt because even she knew she was talking in circles as she shifted her weight from one foot to the other, thinking of how to get her point across.

"It's just . . . I don't wanna say that Car's not a relationship kind of guy because I honestly don't know. He kinda just hooks up with whoever but he's also not, like, a manwhore, you know?"

Noelle pressed her lips together, surprised to feel amused at Beverly's explanation.

"Aiden said something about how Carson hasn't been in a proper relationship since, like, junior year of high school, and I'm not saying there's anything wrong with that. It's just . . . I don't want you to be disappointed if, like, things don't go your way. I think he's the kind of guy who doesn't truly get with someone unless he knows it's absolutely worth it. And you are worth it. If Carson sees that, then that's great, but if he doesn't, then screw him, okay?"

Biting the inside of her cheek, Noelle felt gratitude towards her sister while also trying not to be stunned at the fact that Carson hadn't been with someone for nearly six years. She also understood not wanting to be with someone unless knowing it was going to go somewhere. Hell, Noelle's last relationship was in junior year of college, but it wasn't a serious relationship even though she thought it was worth it in the beginning. Matter of fact, none of Noelle's relationships lasted more than a couple of months. Carson not wanting to be with someone unless he truly thought it was worth it was understandable.

Was that what she wanted with Carson? Was it messed up that she wasn't totally aware if she was just physically attracted to him or if it was something deeper than that? How deep could it be though? She hadn't known Carson for too long, and she didn't know all that much about him.

Noelle wanted to use the book she was holding and smack herself upside her head, hoping a bit of jumbling in her mind would put her thoughts in order. She understood where Beverly was coming from; her sister was encouraging Noelle to not just sit around and wonder on the what ifs and actually do something about her growing feelings for Carson rather than sit around on her thumbs, but to do so, shouldn't she be sure of what exactly she wanted? Who was to say her physical attraction to him couldn't evolve into something more? Getting to know him more would help with that, but it also all obviously depended on what he felt too. *If* he felt anything towards her at all.

Besides, it seemed like she and Carson were finally moving forward from the very first, very cold look he had given her the night they met. He had defended her against some assholes twice now, cuddled with her, and Noelle couldn't even think about that tiny incident with the syrup without feeling as if someone set off a fire in her cheeks. She and Carson may be moving forward slowly, but where to?

That was the million dollar question.

CHAPTER FOURTEEN

Carson knew he should give it a rest, save his strength and his hands for tonight's actual fight instead of delivering unabating strikes to the punching bag. No doubt Aiden would kick his ass if he found out Carson was still training at Astros just a mere few hours before tonight's fight, but Carson wasn't afraid of Aiden, so he switched from right and left hooks and roundhouse kicks until he was satisfied with the speed of his movements. He made sure he was quick enough to avoid a hit from his nonexistent opponent.

Carson struck out his fisted hands, still thinking about his best friend with a small wry grin on his face and feeling the warm layer of sweat clinging to his skin. He didn't know why he still bothered.

Where the fuck else was I gonna be?

He spent as much part of his day with Oreo as possible before leaving the little pup with food and water at his apartment and then came to Astros to train for a bit. Aiden didn't like it when he did that before a match, but it had been almost three years and Carson still didn't listen. Hopefully, Aiden got the hint if he hadn't stopped by now, he wouldn't any time soon.

Carson grunted as he assaulted the punching bag with a particularly hard left hook, feeling his fist throb as the bag swung where it hung on its hook with the chains holding it up and squeaking in protest.

"Not letting Boman off the hook tonight, huh?" a familiar voice spoke, pulling Carson out of his thoughts.

Relaxing his stance, Carson glanced to his left to see one of the newer fighters approach him. Something Rickards was part of his name; Carson was unable to bring himself to try and recall the kid's first name. Carson wondered how quickly the kid's unadulterated excitement that lit up his blue eyes would disappear, replaced by the pure desire of taking out his aggression and desperation to earn some decent cash. That was what happened to Carson mostly since he still got pretty thrilled whenever he had a match. It gave him something to strive for.

"First rule of the ring, kid: you never let anyone off the hook during a fight," Carson advised absentmindedly, not focusing on the conversation as he stretched his fingers out once he uncurled his fists. He came to Astros to train, fight, win, and get paid. He wasn't here to form friendships.

Bending down, Carson rested his weight on his folded left leg as he tied the laces on his right shoe. He wasn't one for conversation, but that was until Rickards spoke up again with a nervous chuckle preceding his words.

"Yeah, I heard you are unforgiving in the ring. I don't expect tonight to be any different, especially with all the fucked up things Boman is saying about your friend."

That caught Carson's attention. He lifted his head as he tightened his laces. "Which friend?"

"Um, he didn't give a name but it was, uh, about a girl," Rickards responded, shifting slightly as Carson slowly rose to his feet. His height made Rickards stumble over his words. No doubt the new fighter was aware he was probably unintentionally about to piss Carson off. "Just said some . . . some pretty messed up things about a-a girl he saw you with."

Rickards was having a hard time getting the words out because Carson's dark eyes narrowed dangerously, hardened anger tightening his muscles. It wasn't difficult to discern that the girl

148

Boman was referring to was Noelle, and the knowledge of that washed-out sleazebag saying pretty messed up things about her had Carson's jaw clenching into a near teeth-shattering tightness. He could guess what lewd things Boman was saying about Noelle. Carson was sure if he found out, he would end up tracking him down and making good on his threat of breaking his teeth again.

The thought of anyone making comments about her sent a startling surge of anger through Carson, curling his fingers once again. He ignored the nagging voice at the back of his head, contemptuously teasing him for being so affected by this. He couldn't help it; the need to shield her from Boman's thoughts was almost primal since that wasn't where she belonged. Carson knew the kind of lewd man he was; he knew the kinds of disgusting thoughts he would cook up involving Noelle that ignited yet another fire under Carson's skin. He wasn't going to let that happen. He needed to keep her away from Boman's leering eyes. Noelle could not show up tonight.

*   *   *

When Noelle walked into Astros later that night, following behind Beverly and Levi as she conversed with Max, Carson inhaled a sharp breath of indignation while pursing his lips at Beverly. As if feeling the heat of his glare, Beverly's gaze flickered over to him as she and the others made their way to where he stood with Aiden. She listened to what Levi was saying, but her raised eyebrows at him meant she acknowledged the irritated look on his face.

The fight would start in about ten minutes. Astros was already filled with the gruff murmur of spectators waiting for things to get going. Carson caught sight of Davey Boman amongst the crowd, taking him all his willpower to not say a big fuck you to the match and bury his fist in Boman's stomach.

149

He snapped out of his thoughts once the others reached them, only giving Beverly a brief moment to greet Aiden before Carson cut in. "Can I talk to you?"

He didn't bother greeting Max and Levi; he didn't even look at Noelle as he watched Beverly press her lips together knowingly before nodding. Ignoring the confused stares of the others, Carson turned and walked a good distance away from them, making sure they were out of earshot before scowling once again at Beverly.

"What part of don't bring Noelle did you not get?" he practically snapped, his dark eyes clashing with her lighter ones. His tone was harsh, but to Carson's credit, he was keeping his annoyance at bay. He had a short fuse, and while it didn't take much to set it off, Carson was mindful of letting it go off at his friends, but Beverly's blatant ignorance of what he asked of her got on his nerves.

"The part where my sister is a grown woman who can do whatever the hell she wants," Beverly responded coolly, unblinking at Carson's frustration. "If you really think that Elle is gonna stay home just because of some guy being a creep, then you better think again, Car."

That was a far cry from when he saw Noelle at Astros for the first time, like she had been trying to keep herself shielded from certain men's gazes by hiding herself amongst her friends. The Australian ignored the buzz of everyone around him, rubbing his hand down his face as his own stubble tickled his palm.

"Boman was specifically talking about Noelle, Bev. You get that, right?"

At that moment, Carson didn't care that Beverly could clearly detect the concern creeping into his exasperated tone, knowing she picked up on it by the small smile curving at her lips. He kind of wanted to throttle her at that moment for finding his anger over Boman even thinking about Noelle amusing. He kind of

150

hated that Beverly knew Carson wouldn't do shit even when he tightened his jaw in annoyance.

"Then make him eat his words," Beverly shrugged casually before adding, "with your fists."

Carson shot her a flat look, the playful smile on her face successfully making his own lips quirk up despite his irritation. The last thing he wanted was for Noelle to be here in Boman's line of sight. Carson couldn't do anything short of carrying her right out of Astros, but he wasn't one to manhandle women. He then heard Mick announce that it was time, so he straightened his shoulders.

Make him eat his words, Carson mused silently as a wicked smirk curled on his lips. *No fucking problem.*

*   *   *

"Gotta hand it to ya, Hayes. You really know how to pick 'em."

His expression hardened. Carson didn't give Boman the reaction he was hoping for. "Che," he merely let out before launching his right fist towards him, but Boman caught Carson's fist. He smirked in obvious pride for intercepting the dodge, but his expression fell when Carson's free hand, which had been grasping Boman's other wrist, used its grip to twist his arm to the point where he let go of Carson's fist amidst his pained groan.

Seeing his opening, Carson's fist finally connected with Boman's jaw. It sent him flying back onto the ropes of the ring. Carson was deaf to the cheers as he stalked towards Boman who was pushing himself up to his feet, then meeting Carson in the middle of the ring.

"Come on, man," Boman sneered. "Just complimenting you on your choice of fucks."

Carson was sure he would break his teeth by how hard he was clenching his jaw, fiery rage igniting his blood as if it was oil as

151

he decided then and there to end the first round. The taunting smirk on Boman's face only solidified his resolve.

Carson brought his fists up and let one fly towards Boman's face. Boman reached up to defend himself until, at the last second, Carson's right hand uncurled and slapped against Boman's neck and brought his knee up to bury it right in Boman's side, using the leverage on Boman's neck to pull him down.

He watched, lifting his chin in satisfaction as Boman fell onto the canvas with a thud while gripping his side with a groan and pressing his forehead and nose onto the floor where he lay. When those gathered around the ring began counting, Carson crouched down with his arms briefly resting on his knees.

"I'd stay down if I were you," he advised tautly.

Boman didn't even acknowledge him as the number ten roared from everyone's mouth, signaling the end of the first round. Carson stood up and went to his corner where Aiden was already leaning into the ring from where he stood down below.

"That didn't take too long," Aiden commented with a small grin, handing Carson a water bottle and a small towel.

Carson let out a droll snort, taking a long sip of the cold water before handing back the half empty bottle back to Aiden and then using the towel to wipe off the barely-there sweat that had gathered on his skin. Darryl should really invest in getting new air-conditioners for Astros.

"He kept saying something to you, didn't he?" Aiden questioned, furrowing his brows up at Carson. "What was it?"

Without a thought, Carson's gaze flickered a bit behind Aiden, where his small group of friends stood. They were in front of the rumbling crowd as usual, talking amongst themselves as everyone waited for the next round to start in just a few short moments. His eyes wandered towards her, and Carson resisted the urge to swallow.

How was it that after knocking someone to the ground, Carson didn't feel the quick beating of his heart until the moment

152

his eyes landed on Noelle? He didn't feel his adrenaline pumping until he saw her dimpled grin and didn't feel his stomach twisting indescribably at how comfortable she looked? It was a vast difference from when she first came to Astros, arms wrapped around her body to shield herself from unwanted stares. She hadn't been here nearly as long as Beverly had, and she would still stick out in the crowd, but she seemed so confident where she stood. It both comforted Carson and made him bristle.

She didn't belong here, but he selfishly wanted her to stay.

When her hazel eyes happened to lock with his, Carson saw the way her grin slowly dissipated at the sight of him already staring at her. It was replaced by lips parting in mild surprise before the corners of them tilted up slightly. Noelle offered him a small smile from where she stood, and Carson swore he didn't expect the pleasant tightness in his chest as a result.

"Just talking shit," Carson finally responded vaguely to Aiden's questions, right when the bell rang to signal the start of the second round.

Carson dropped the towel to Aiden as the older guy went back to stand with the others after calling out 'good luck' over the yelling of the crowd. Turning back to face the ring and ignoring the gazes that were directed his way yet feeling a particular girl's hazel-eyed one burn his back, Carson's own eyes landed on Boman who was back up on his feet.

When he smirked wolfishly, Carson raised an unimpressed eyebrow. He wondered what the hell had gotten him so smug when he lost the previous round.

"Honestly, Hayes, I didn't see you as a one-girl kinda guy," Boman quipped, sniffing as he rubbed the bottom of his nose with the back of his hand before fisting both of them and jutting his chin to the group standing behind Carson, deaf to Boman's words. "But if I had a pretty little thing like that around, I might consider it too."

Carson knew he was antagonizing him. Boman was all bark and no bite. He wasn't the best fighter in Astros but could hold his own if needed, but the more he spoke, the more irritated Carson grew. The ring was meant for fighting, not whatever the fuck Boman was doing. Carson was only just trying to discern what the fuck he felt when it came to Noelle; he didn't need Boman trying to throw him off with the shit he was spewing.

Carson's fist tightened, his eyebrows twitching. He had it with him.

*   *   *

Blood stained Carson's bruised knuckles, the liquid warm against his already heated skin. He hadn't meant to break Boman's nose, but he would be lying if he said there wasn't a swell of satisfaction that coursed through him when he heard the unmistakable crunch between Boman's face and Carson's knuckles. His own hand may be throbbing with pain, but he won.

After he was announced the winner, Carson didn't give Boman a chance to limp out of the ring. Instead, he grabbed the front of the guy's tank top. He felt everyone's curious gazes and heard their intrigued chatter like a hum in his ears as he pulled Boman closer. Boman's eyes were wide with blood coloring his nose as he meekly struggled against Carson's grip. The Australian wanted to smirk. *Isn't so tough now, is he?*

"Think twice before trying to piss me off, yeah?" Carson darkly advised, his face unapologetically getting into Boman's personal space who didn't even try to use his hands to break free. "Otherwise, next time, I'll stick by my promise and give you some broken teeth to go with that nose. Those won't be as easy to fix."

When Boman's Adam's apple bobbed viciously in his throat with alarmed eyes staring into Carson's glaring ones, the latter knew he got the message across. It was pathetic how Boman had been spitting out remarks here and there about Noelle during the fight, but now, here he was, nursing a broken nose for not being able to defend himself for the shit he said.

He let go of the dumbass, watching as Boman stumbled back a few steps before sliding out of the ring on the opposite side. Carson turned to do the same where he saw his group waiting for him. When his hand gripped the ropes to pull them apart so he could get through, Carson's jaw clenched at the sharp pain that spread from his knuckles, which were probably bruised under the blood smearing them.

"What the hell was that about?" Max questioned as soon as Carson's feet touched the ground. "What were you getting in Boman's face for?"

Carson took the towel from Aiden with his non-bloody hand, wiping at the sweat glistening his neck.

"Talked too much shit instead of fighting," he responded smoothly, still feeling that small spark of anger when he thought of Boman's words. Most of his aggression was taken out on the ring, but Carson would be lying if he said he had gotten rid of all of his frustration, that his muscles had completely eased from all the tightness locking them up instigated by Boman's stupid comments.

As she fluttered through his mind, Carson's gaze landed on Noelle almost instinctively. He was still rubbing his towel at the back of his neck as he peered at her. He wondered what she thought, if she was used to seeing him do what he did in the ring. Carson found himself indulging in on why Noelle's opinion would matter. She snuck up on him, and while Carson preferred to be prepared for any hit coming his way, he hadn't been ready for her.

Levi's amused snort pulled Carson out of his musings. "I thought you didn't care if people trash talked you?"

Carson's expression was cool as he looked at his blond friend. "I don't."

He wasn't going to expand on that because by the look on Beverly's face, Carson knew that she knew exactly what happened. The small smile quirking at her lips told him as much.

Half an hour later, he found himself in Aiden's apartment for a post-fight chill time as per usual. Carson was in the kitchen, pulling out a bottle of water for himself since he would be driving to go home when he heard footsteps enter the kitchen.

"Boman totally got under your skin about Noelle, didn't he?"

He turned around and caught sight of Beverly's knowing, triumphant smirk, which caused him to bristle ever so slightly.

"If you already know the answer, then why're you asking?"

"Because I wanna hear it from you." Beverly shrugged nonchalantly, crossing her arms over her chest. "Tell me, Car, do you like my sister?" she mused, leaning against the entryway frame.

Carson's grip on the water bottle tightened. The plastic crinkled as his eyes widened ever so slightly, not expecting Beverly to ask him so flat out—so boldly. He was good at reading people; he should've seen this coming from Beverly.

"I—" He stopped, clenching his jaw as he rushed through the very thoughts in his mind that had been plaguing him for countless days. Did he like Noelle? Was it just a physical attraction, or did he actually have feelings for her? He knew the answer to the first part was a definite yes; Noelle was gorgeous beyond belief, and Carson was a warm-blooded male after all, but to look for something deeper?

He might not be vocal about it, but Carson liked being in relationships. His last one was in high school—a relationship that lasted for about a year with his old chemistry lab partner, Violet, who was now engaged. Carson enjoyed being with someone; the level of intimacy that came with it rather than just a meaningless hook up, which he knew his friends sometimes found it hard to believe since he was more prone to participate in the former than the latter, but it wasn't his fault he hadn't met someone since high school who he genuinely had an interest in to pursue something more.

156

Then Noelle came along, and now, Carson wasn't so sure anymore.

Beverly walked further into the kitchen as she leveled him with a pointed look. "Come on, Carson," she began with a light, knowing laugh. He twitched, noticing the amusement dancing in her features. "I'm not forcing you to say you have feelings for Noelle or whatever, but I'm just saying, there's gotta be something there, right? I mean, you broke Boman's nose and nearly your hand because of the shit he was saying about her!" Beverly exclaimed, gesturing to Carson's right hand where the knuckles beneath his rings were an angry, purplish red from the ferocity of his punches tonight.

He glanced down at his hand, which truly didn't even hurt because if his knuckles still gave him hell after nearly three years of doing this, then that was pathetic.

When Carson looked back up to respond to Beverly, his thoughts stilled and words were lost because, instead of his gaze meeting Beverly's light brown eyes, it met Noelle's hazel ones—wide and startled and completely taken aback.

Carson squared his shoulders and pursed his lips into a thin line as his mildly alarmed gaze remained on Noelle lingering in the entryway, schooling his expression to not give away the brief wave of disconcert that passed through him at her presence.

How long has she been standing there? What did she hear? Carson didn't like the way his throat suddenly seemed so dry despite the water he was almost finished with.

Beverly frowned, realizing that Carson was looking behind her as she glanced over her shoulders. Her lips parted in surprise at the sight of her younger sister.

"Oh. Oh, geez, crap," she stumbled over her words, knowing that just by the look on Noelle's face, she heard what Carson did.

157

Noelle finding out the guy she liked broke some asshole's nose for talking shit about her, even if it was during a planned fight? Carson deemed Noelle's frozen reaction appropriate.

"I'm just—" Beverly started, turning back around to look at Carson, shooting him a sheepish grin when she noticed his glare was directed towards her. "I'm gonna, uh, go."

She exited swiftly, expertly avoiding Noelle's probing, slightly panicked eyes before disappearing down the hall, leaving a tensely awkward silence in her wake. Carson could hear his mates in the living room, but their mingling voices were distant as the sight of Noelle rendered him incapable of hearing anything but the annoyingly loud beating of his heart and the sharp intake of air Noelle just took.

"You didn't—" Carson kept his gaze on her as she spoke up, pausing as her eyebrows furrowed slightly while taking a few steps into the kitchen. The area wasn't too big, but Carson still couldn't help but notice that she seemed too far away. "You didn't actually break his nose because of me, did you? It . . . you did it because of the fight, right?"

He easily picked up on the hesitant, doubtful tone of Noelle's voice. She eyed him in genuine surprise and curiosity. Was she surprised that he would break someone's nose? Or that there was a chance he did it as a way of defending her? This wasn't the first time Carson had defended Noelle since meeting her. Hell, this wasn't even the first time he had defended her against Boman. Or was she afraid that Carson was capable of doing something like that for her? No . . . that wasn't it. There was no fear in her features or in her voice, and Carson immediately put that thought out of his head. She wasn't afraid of him.

At that moment, with her hazel eyes holding so many questions and her pretty lips parting in wonder, Carson decided this wasn't going to be the last time he would defend Noelle. Broken knuckles be damned.

Carson placed the water bottle on the counter behind him, crossing his arms over his chest as he met Noelle's gaze unapologetically.

"Both, but mostly for you."

CHAPTER FIFTEEN

She ran away.

Okay. Maybe saying she ran away was a bit of an exaggeration, but it was all the same in Noelle's ashamed, self-hating mind. In her defense, she didn't entirely know how to react when the guy she liked told her he broke someone else's nose for her. That . . . wasn't normal, was it? Maybe Carson breaking other people's bones wasn't a surprising occurrence, but Noelle being slammed with the fact that this particular time she might have been the motivation behind it was something she thought she deserved a moment to process. She spent her days mulling over her own feelings for Carson, that the second she was truly confronted with a hint of him reciprocating them instead of just showing physical attraction, Noelle didn't know what to do with herself. Or with him.

Evidently, that meant practically speeding out of Aiden's kitchen and demanding Beverly to go home with her. Sure, Noelle felt a bit selfish tearing her sister from her boyfriend's side and admittedly bad about leaving Carson in the kitchen, but she needed to get out of there. Thank God, they had been at Aiden's house for over an hour, so leaving didn't look too suspicious. Still, Noelle wouldn't be surprised if any of the boys could feel the urgency she left with.

"You can't avoid him forever," Beverly pointed out in a knowing, pointed tone that made Noelle want to throw her phone at her. She wondered when was the last time she was able to do work at work without Beverly somehow weaseling Carson into the conversation. "I'm telling you, Elle. He's been looking pretty bothered when you didn't show up the past few days."

The corners of Noelle's lips tilted into a frown, inhaling a sharp breath. Carson apparently being bothered by her lack of presence had been something Beverly kept telling her about, yet Noelle was somehow unsure if she should believe that. She and Carson rarely interacted when they were all together except as of late, but he couldn't be that pressed about her not being around for the past few days, right?

"I'm not avoiding him," Noelle defended, putting her phone away to return her attention to the computer. They were in the backroom of the store, taking inventory by themselves as their other employees worked the register and helped customers out. "I only see him when we go to Astros or one of the guys' place. And I've been too busy to go to either."

Which wasn't a lie. That night—the fight, Carson's bruised knuckles, and Boman's broken nose for Noelle—had been three nights ago. Noelle did get busy with other things such as shopping trips with Camille and hanging out with Andrea, not to mention spending some time with Isaac because, apparently, her mother and his father still thought they would be a perfect match and wanted them to spend time together.

The morning following the night at Aiden's house, Noelle's mother had asked her about Isaac and if she liked him. Noelle was about to ask her mom what the hell she was talking about because Isaac was gay. Then she remembered he hadn't told his dad yet, and she knew if she told her mom then she may let it slip to his dad, so Noelle just let her mother believe she and Isaac were interested in each other. She would take care of that situation when she wasn't freaking out over Carson.

Mostly for you.

161

Noelle's teeth dug into her lower lip, an embarrassed flush spreading on her cheeks as she recalled Carson's words from last night. She couldn't believe she left without saying anything, turning around as soon as his words slammed into her like a ton of bricks. His admittance of breaking another person's nose for her made her heart do so many things at once—skip a beat and stop all at once before picking up an erratic pace. She wasn't sure what took her more off guard; the fact that Carson actually did it, or that he so easily admitted that he had. She wasn't even sure what to do with the idea that him doing so was far more attractive than it was frightening. Because, while Carson was a guy meant to be feared, she wasn't scared of him. It only made what he said last night all the more thrilling and confusing.

What did he want?

"Fine." Beverly snorted, pulling out some books from one of the boxes to count them. "If you're not avoiding Carson, then you're hiding from him, especially since you're not coming to tonight's fight again." Noelle glanced over at her, huffing out a sharp breath as Beverly raised her eyebrows. "You're all anxious around him now because you found out he broke a guy's face because he talked shit about you, aren't you? We have six copies of *Grimms' Fairy Tales*," she added, referring to the books she just counted.

Noelle shot Beverly a helpless, exasperated look as she put it in the system. She had to admit, when Beverly told her in more detail after fleeing from Aiden's that Carson did what he did because he found out Boman had been saying some crude things about her, Noelle couldn't deny the flutter her heart gave. Was it odd to find it touching that Carson stood up for her like that despite the violence of it all?

It was unexpected how many times he came to her defense in one way or another, but Noelle was not at all complaining. She wondered if—and this was totally hypothetical—she would be able to handle that kind of aggression? Everyone she hung out with had

162

been around Carson and his fighting long before her. And while his fighting or apparent short fuse wasn't what was making Noelle hesitant on even dancing around with the thought of her and Carson, it was just a mere question of her being able to handle it. Don't get her wrong, there was no genuine fear in the matter when it came to him, personally. Despite knowing what Carson was capable of, he didn't frighten Noelle. The fear, she realized, lied in concern over him in the ring.

Watching Carson fight, the way he moved on the ring smooth and the looks of concentration and smugness almost arousing, was a thrilling experience but it still worried her whenever a fist or kick came his way. No doubt her worry, along with the excitement of watching him do what he did best, would increase if the two of them miraculously got into a relationship and she attended his fights. She already dreaded any hit landing on him when she went now; it would definitely multiply tenfold if she went as his girlfriend.

The thought of that alone had the butterflies erupting in her stomach, but Noelle quickly quelled them, reminding her too fast mind that it was boldly conjuring up scenarios that she didn't even know would come to fruition.

When Noelle didn't respond, Beverly sighed. Noelle knew her sister thought she wasn't going to say anything. Even though that wasn't the case, Noelle decided to stay quiet.

"Carson only goes around throwing punches for four reasons: when he's training, in a match, someone is pissing him off, or when someone he cares about is involved. Pretty sure the last three apply to the other night," Beverly said.

Noelle swallowed the small lump in her throat. "Weren't you the one telling me to be careful with him and this whole feelings mess?" she responded in an even tone, her grip on the computer mouse tightening.

"I also told you to take a chance," Beverly responded instantly, her next few words striking Noelle like a lightning bolt,

163

"especially when the possibility of him returning those feelings is there."

*   *   *

Imagine Dragon's music airily swept through the bookstore as Noelle hummed along over the sound of the rain pelting outside, using the rag in her hand to wipe the many shelves. It was after hours nearing 9:30 PM, and she was the only one left in the store. She took her time in sweeping and cleaning the thin layer of dust collected on the shelves over the course of the past few days while some nighttime summer rain wetted the city. It was quiet in the store, seeing as she was the only one there. The only sounds emitting were from the speaker of her phone, the rain and mild thunder, and the occasional honk of a car from the road outside.

Noelle liked being by herself, especially in the store. She enjoyed being there alone after hours, cleaning up after a busy day or week, surrounded by books and engulfed in her thoughts. Only this time, all she could think of was that she could be in a somewhat run-down building in Brooklyn right now, but her hesitation had her convincing an exasperated Beverly to go on without her as she cleaned up the store. She hadn't gone to the last two fights, though she knew Carson won because, of course, she was gonna ask Beverly; she had also seen the boys', minus Carson's, Snapchat stories celebrating, but right now, Noelle wasn't so sure if she was ready to face the music.

For God's sake, she practically ran from Carson. She felt incapable of manning up and looking at him after that embarrassing stunt. God, what did he think when she took off like that?

Sighing, Noelle fixed the cushions on the small couches by the chalkboard wall, her head snapping over to her phone when her music was interrupted by a text notification. When she checked the message, she saw that it was from Beverly. Noelle's eyes widened, brows drawing together in shock.

Noelle's jaw dropped slightly in disbelief as the music continued playing, thunder ironically sounding outside at the same time as she felt her mouth dry because Carson lost. She had only been to a number of his matches, and he hadn't lost a single one of those. From what she knew, it was a rare occurrence if he ever did. Noelle didn't bother replying as she put her phone back on the counter. Her movements were a bit slow as she picked up the rag to continue cleaning the shelves.

Her actions were thoughtless, her body moving on its own accord as she cleaned the shelves while her mind was once again filled with Carson. Only this time, she wasn't thinking of the two times his body was against hers—once in the alley a while back and then in her bed. She wasn't thinking about how he came to her aid, defended her more than once, which resulted in some asshole's broken nose.

All she could think of was that it was the first time since she met him. Carson lost a match, and although it wasn't Noelle's place, she wanted to be able to comfort him. Though she was sure that there wasn't anything she would be able to do to make him feel better about this. Noelle might have not known Carson for long, but he obviously took his fighting seriously, and a loss was most definitely not something he would take lightly. She pursed her lips as she absentmindedly cleaned one of the shelves.

He is probably pissed.

Noelle wasn't sure how long she was lost in her thoughts, thinking about the same guy who seemingly became a permanent resident in her mind. Suddenly, her heart was jumping in her throat at the sound of pounding on the glass door over the rain outside. She gasped, clutching the rag to her chest as she spun around, her wide eyes immediately going towards the door.

The windows looking out in the streets were shielded by drawn curtains, and Noelle's only view of outside was through the glass doors, which allowed her to catch sight of Carson standing right outside of the store.

"Carson—" She couldn't even hope to say anything else but his name, frozen in her spot as she noticed him standing with one hand on the handle. His dark-eyed gaze pierced through the glass and right at her, waiting for her to let him in.

Lightning struck, briefly shadowing him into nothing but a silhouette. Noelle was startled into action as she absentmindedly dropped the rag and moved forward, hurrying to the door. She didn't think—couldn't think. Her sole attention was on opening the door and getting Carson out of the rain, not even questioning what he was doing here until her hands were on the locks as she twisted them open.

She pushed the door open, feeling the light spray of rain and wind against her face and welcoming the smell of the outside world and Carson.

"What're you—"

Her words were cut off not by Carson's words but by his actions of pushing past her and inside the door. He was dripping wet as he unapologetically tracked water inside. She only got a brief look at his face as he moved past her, his features taut and jaw tight. Noelle swallowed her apprehension as she fumbled to swing the door shut and lock it before turning to face him.

Carson stood in the middle of the store in front of the shelves, facing the counter to his left with his hands on his hips and lifting his chin in agitation as if he was contemplating something. Noelle's heart was pounding, deafening her to the music still playing through her phone with the soft melody of Imagine Dragon's Dancing in the Dark just beginning to play and the rain outside.

What is Carson doing here? Why is he here?

Hesitatingly, Noelle took a few unsure steps further into the store she knew so well. Her eyes never left Carson's rigid stance. His dark hair was flat and wet atop his head, his black

166

leather jacket and everything under it clung to his skin as he finally turned to look at her. Noelle froze where she was under his sharp gaze, breath stilling in her lungs. There was a small cut on his right cheekbone, another one on his lower lip, and yellowish hintings of a bruise forming right along his left jaw.

Noelle wondered if there were any other marks, signs of a lost fight, marring his skin.

"This is all your goddamn fault."

Her eyes widened, brows drawing together incredulously. "I . . . Excuse me?"

Carson turned to face her as she noticed the way his grey shirt clung to his chest and torso invitingly.

Focus, Noelle, she chided herself, forcing her to pay attention to the fact that Carson was apparently angry at her—blamed her for something. "What's all my fault?" she continued, finally finding her voice with a disbelieving scoff.

He took a step towards her, his skin wet with rain as beads of water followed the path along his sharp jaw down to the side of his neck. Carson's dark eyes were narrowed in agitation, the mere look on his face igniting the tension in the room. Noelle figured the rain lightly thundering outside didn't help diffuse the thickness of the air.

"I lost tonight. Did you know that?" Carson responded to her question with his own, his head tilting to the side to accompany the rhetoric, sarcastic nature of his tone. Noelle pursed her lips, recognizing that he wasn't looking for an answer. One hand still on his hips, the other raised to rub at his stubbly jaw. Noelle noticed the familiar bruising of his knuckles. "Lost to a guy I should've had no problem knocking out in five seconds flat all because of you."

Okay, is he out of his mind or something? Noelle couldn't keep her jaw from dropping even if she wanted to, the scoff choking in her throat with her brows shot up in incredulity. What the fuck was he blaming her for?

167

"B-because of me?" she stuttered, her words jumbling out of shock as she reeled back slightly. "What're you talking about? I wasn't even there!"

"Yeah, I'm aware," Carson snapped, the irritation hardening his voice. Even his accent sounded thick. Noelle had to school her expression from recoiling. Why was he so angry? He took another few steps closer, running his fingers through his hair and effectively keeping it back due to it being soaked. Carson jutted his lower jaw out while his tongue was pressed to the floor of his mouth as his annoyed gaze remained on her. "You weren't there tonight. Or the past two nights."

Confusion overwhelmed Noelle, lips parted in bewilderment as she tried to make sense of Carson's words. So many questions were flying through her mind, trying to make sense of what was going on because she sure as hell wasn't sure. All she knew was that Carson was pissed off about losing. For some reason or another, the blame was on her. Had she missed something?

"But somehow it's my fault you lost?" Noelle found herself demanding, unable to stop the disbelieving laugh that escaped her. *He has to be joking, right?* "You're gonna blame someone that wasn't even there? Maybe take into consideration that you lost because you just weren't that good tonight."

She didn't mean for her words to come out so bitchy, almost to the point of antagonizing, but Noelle didn't appreciate Carson finding some way of blaming her for his loss. He was angry about losing, and she guessed he had the right to be annoyed with her for running out on him a few days ago, but assigning fault to her for something out of her control was overstepping it a bit, wasn't it?

Obviously, her words didn't settle well with Carson. His jaw snapped shut and tightened, his shoulders rigid as he took the final few dominating steps closer to her. At this point, he was basically toe to toe with her, forcing Noelle to reluctantly tilt her head back to maintain their gaze. She didn't even want to

168

acknowledge the wild beating of her heart, anticipation for God knows what, exciting every fiber of her being.

"You're a distraction," Carson muttered, brown eyes flickering between her hazel, which were taking in the fresh cut on his cheek and the one on his lower lip. Was it bad that it just made Noelle desperate to kiss him? Her mouth dried at their closeness, the music still playing nothing but a hum she couldn't recognize mixed with the pelting rain. How did they always end up in each other's personal space? How come nothing ever came from it? Carson's gaze dropped to Noelle's lips, and she swore her breath was gone. "You weren't even there tonight, and I couldn't get you out of my damn head. Cost me the fucking match."

Oh. Oh. What the hell was she supposed to say to that?

Hell, it would be a miracle if she could even form a coherent thought after Carson's clear yet devastating words. He lost the match because he couldn't get her out of his head? The very statement had Noelle tensing in astonishment, lungs burning for air she failed to inhale because of the shock stilling her in every way.

Pressing her lips together as her heart hammered in her chest, Noelle took in every detail of Carson's face at that moment, giving her thoughts a second to realign. His long lashes, the tip of his nose slightly flushed from the rain, not to mention the water slickening his skin, the two small slashes on his face were red with dried blood. She wanted to kiss the cut on his lips better.

She didn't realize Carson had taken that moment to memorize every feature of her face too.

"Should've been thinking about where to throw my next punch, next kick," Carson was saying, his low rasp pulling Noelle out of her thoughts as she blinked back up at his eyes—dark eyes that she felt were staring right through her. "Instead, all I could think about was you walking the fuck away from me. Destroyed every ounce of my focus."

Noelle found it difficult to swallow the lump forming in the middle of her throat; she found it difficult to breathe because every time she inhaled, all she could smell was the scent of rain and pine clinging to Carson. She found it difficult to believe that he lost a match because she was the reason for his inability to focus, to think of anything but her.

She had been on his mind, just like he had been on hers.

Still, she wasn't going to let herself believe this so easily. She wished her voice was stronger, steadier, more confident when she spoke instead of it coming out as a whisper. "Hard to imagine a fighter like you letting some girl get in your head like that."

It was a small yet pleasant surprise when Carson's lips curled in slight amusement, a scoff escaping him. "Think I'm realizing you're not just some girl," he responded, his own voice a quiet murmur as his gaze unwavered from hers.

Noelle's breath stilled in her throat, unsure if she heard him right. She was unsure if his words held the obvious meaning she picked up on. She didn't want to just assume and end up embarrassing herself, but the way Carson was staring at her with intense dark eyes seemingly staring into her goddamn soul, Noelle was sure there was no other meaning behind his words.

Everything stilled in the next moment, the world coming to a seeming halt despite the steady pour of rain outside. The music was still playing with some soft melody Noelle didn't recognize because all she could focus on was Carson, towering over her as his gaze flickered around her face. The air between them practically crackled with the same anticipation that was exciting their hearts.

Despite her chest threatening to burst open and her throat drying at their closeness at being crowded by Carson and despite having room to move back, Noelle couldn't help the sudden urge to push his buttons to see if she could get some kind of reaction out of him. "Sounds like a bunch of bullshit," she taunted practically, lifting her chin slightly with her eyes on his.

His eyes darkened even more, narrowing at her words as a hint of challenging anger flashed across his face. His shoulders squared slightly as his lips pursed at Noelle's goading. The mildly irritated look on Carson's face, funnily enough, had Noelle's stomach twisting in excitement.

But then, Carson seemed to recognize the mirth Noelle couldn't keep from dancing in her light eyes as she looked at him. The corners of her lips twitched into a smile she tried to keep at bay. Noelle couldn't help herself; this entire situation was nerve-wracking and unexpected with Carson's presence, but the excitement was bubbling relentlessly.

His shoulders relaxed, all forms of irritation and anger seemingly leaving him with a sharp exhale, and Carson pursed his lips. Noelle could tell just by the slight twitch of his mouth that he was preventing his own smile. She realized at that moment that him being disgruntled and maybe offended with her for running out on him a few days ago seemed to be the last thing on his mind. There they were, the two of them standing toe to toe with the blood in their veins simmering with anticipation, looks of nothing but want and need etched across their features. The second Noelle's gaze flickered to Carson's lips, body tensing ever so slightly in anticipation, she knew he caught the movement. It was at that moment that Carson seemed to finally let his guard down for her and threw caution to the wind.

"It's not," Carson gruffed, his movements swift as his hands grasped Noelle's face and pulled her towards him. He ducked his head to press his lips to hers in a near-bruising kiss.

Noelle's response was instant—never once hesitating, never pausing to comprehend what was happening. Moving her lips with Carson's was instinctive. Her eyes closed at the toe-curling force he kissed her with, her heart going into overdrive. *Finally*, she couldn't help but think.

There was nothing gentle or slow about this kiss. Noelle absolutely had no complaints, feeling herself melt into Carson's lips and into his large hands grasping her cheeks as his fingers lightly tangled into her hair. She stumbled closer on the tips of her toes, pushing herself closer to Carson's height as their chests pressed together to get rid of any unwanted space between them. The front of her clothes dampened against his rain-soaked body, but the warmth he engulfed her in had her paying it no mind.

Both of their senses were invaded by each other as Noelle gave into the desire she probably had the moment she met Carson and sucked on his plump bottom lip. Her knees threatened to give out as a rough moan resonated from the back of his throat and into her mouth. Noelle took advantage of his parted lips, her tongue meeting his in a greedy dance Carson easily took the lead on. She used his grasp on her face to pull her closer in appreciation. She couldn't possibly be any closer to him, but it still wasn't enough.

It was like weeks of figuring out confused feelings—their own and each other's—and pure desire of being able to just hold each other was finally being paid its due. At this moment that seemed to be inevitable, all they could do was be overwhelmed by each other.

Noelle felt Carson's wet yet surprisingly warm hands on her face; the metal of his rings a cool, stark contrast that had her gasping. He reveled in the way her hands fisted the front of his wet shirt, right below the neckline before sliding up and briefly pausing at his shoulders until finding home on the sides of his neck. Her warm touch was a welcomed stranger on his wet skin. She could taste the cigarettes and mint in his mouth, like he chewed some gum after taking a smoke, and he was willing and able to suck off the cherry ChapStick she wore.

Carson was drenched from the rain. Noelle could feel some droplets of cold water on her skin, but she couldn't bring herself to care if her clothes got wet the closer she pressed herself against Carson, feeling the delicious pressure of his hips against hers. When Noelle's lips moved against Carson's a certain way, his hands slid into her hair and he tightened his grip, not enough to hurt her, as he groaned into her mouth.

She quickly realized through her muddled mind overtaken by everything regarding Carson that she had touched the cut near

172

the corner of his lips. "Sorry," she breathed into his mouth with her eyes still closed and her brows furrowed.

His teeth lightly clasped around her lower lip, pulling it back and taking in the hooded gaze she was staring at him with. Her eyes clouded with the same desire Carson's already clingingly wet pants were tightened with. Shit, he was ready to take her right in the middle of the damn store with the way her hands felt on him and the addicting taste he couldn't get enough of.

He let go of her lip. Noelle's insides melting like ice over fire. "Don't be," Carson rasped. He didn't mind it. In fact, Carson enjoyed the pressure of Noelle's lips against his own cut. Her light eyes peered up at him through her lashes, and Carson was surprised to find himself needing a moment to let this moment sink in, to properly appreciate what he just did.

Closing his eyes, Carson kept his hands in Noelle's hair. It was just as soft as it had felt that night in her bed. He pressed his forehead to hers, their noses brushing together as Carson inhaled a deep breath, the kind of deep breath he needed after a fight to allow his body to relax from the adrenaline of the fight. Only this time, Carson needed to calm down from the high of finally, finally, finally getting to feel the softness and taste the sweetness of Noelle's lips. So he held her in place with his hands holding her head, letting their warm breaths puff against each other's kiss-swollen mouths. Carson vaguely recognized "I Found" by Amber Run softly playing through the store, his heart thundering as he wondered if Noelle felt like the world was floating away from her too.

He had been cold from the rain, but now, he was on fire.

I kissed Carson. I just kissed Carson. Those were the only thoughts Noelle's brain was processing at the moment—nothing less, nothing deeper. She was incapable of thinking of anything further than the notion of her lips meeting Carson's. She didn't want to take this long-craved moment to think about what the hell this meant and what Carson meant about it. Those were questions she could drive herself crazy by overanalyzing and overthinking later tonight. For now, all she could do was keep her warm hands on his neck with his forehead against hers. Her parted lips that let out soft pants, mixing with his own, curling into a small, giddily content smile.

But then, a deafeningly loud clap of thunder roared across the sky, cruelly breaking the blissfully content silence Noelle and Carson had enveloped themselves in as they appreciated the afterglow of a kiss neither of them planned. Noelle's eyes flew open at the startling noise, her breath catching in her throat as her hands dropped from Carson's. She unexpectedly stumbled back, the thunder catching her off guard since she was too busy being satisfied with the way her lips were tingling from being pressed against Carson, for still being able to taste his minty tongue.

Opening his eyes, Carson straightened as he saw Noelle turn her gaze towards the door. She watched the rain pelt harder outside, her lips parted to catch her breath. He couldn't help the smirk threatening to tug his own, noticing the way her mouth was slightly pink and swollen from entangling with his. His boyish smugness flooded through him, his own lips still tingling with the desire to claim hers once more.

Much like Noelle, he didn't want to think about anything other than the fact that he was here and that he had done the one thing he had been battling with himself on doing for the past few days. Carson didn't want to ponder the inevitable thoughts of what to do next or where to go from here; he just wanted to pat himself on the back approvingly for coming to terms with the fact that, yeah, he really did have undeniable feelings for Noelle.

So without giving it too much thought, without letting any of the nagging voices at the back of his head get the better of him, Carson reached forward and gently grasped Noelle's hand in his. Her gaze instantly snapped down to the way his fingers curled around hers, her own slowly returning the gesture as she lifted her gaze to meet his. Carson smirked softly—a small little smile that didn't hold any of the smugness he was feeling moments before.

"Come on." He tugged at her hand slightly, nodding towards the door. "I'll take you home." No way was he letting her go out alone in this rain at this time of night.

She blinked up at him. The offer took her by surprise, but really, at this point with Carson, what didn't? The tall drenched boy wanted to kick himself for even giving her the impression of him not wanting to do something for her in the first place. Carson didn't regret many things, but for the first time, Carson regretted ever being even the smallest bit of a jerk to the pretty girl in front of him.

"Okay." She smiled, showing off the dimples Carson fought the ridiculous urge to poke. Instead, he felt his lungs swell up at the sight of her smile; she had such a gorgeous smile.

He couldn't keep his eyes off of her; not when she put away the rag she had been cleaning with, not when she moved around the counter to grab her things, not when she approached him by the doorway and clicked off the lights. He didn't leave her side; not as he stood over her with his jacket off and holding it above her head to shield her from the rain as she locked up the store, or when the rain drenched him once more yet he kept the jacket over her, trying to keep her head as dry as possible.

Despite the low jazz music playing through his stereo and the rain echoing as it hit the glass and roof of the car, there was silence during the drive as all either of them were privy to were the sounds of their pounding hearts that would give the thunder a run for its money. He was drenched and the rain had gotten her only a little. The heater of the car was already working on drying them, yet the last thing on their minds was the pouring rain.

The silence in the car was anything but tense. It wasn't like the first time they were in Carson's car alone together on their way to Max's house. This time, it was the kind of quiet that allowed Noelle to focus on biting back the goofy smile threatening to split

175

across her face; it allowed Carson to keep his attention on the road, keep his grip tight on the steering wheel even if his right hand was itching to let go to rest on Noelle's thigh just for the sake of being able to touch her.

But was he allowed to touch her? He kissed her impulsively, and he had gotten lucky that she didn't push him off or slap him. He was lucky she had accepted the desires that he so desperately needed to quell by just pressing his lips to her. After kissing Noelle the way he had, Carson realized his want and need for her only intensified, but . . . baby steps. If any, at all.

However, he understood that figuring everything out wasn't for tonight as he pulled up in front of her house. Tonight was for them to replay the head spinning, dizzying kiss their lips craved more of in their minds, to silently ask themselves what the other person meant by it as they laid in bed at night, hoping they both wanted the same things. But were Noelle and Carson completely sure of what they wanted? Had either of them established what they wanted the other to mean for them?

Carson was pulled out of his thoughts as he heard the seatbelt zing back into place, glancing over to see Noelle picking up her bag with one hand on the door handle as she looked at him. He wondered if feeling his breath catch in his throat was something he needed to get used to around Noelle.

"Thanks for the ride, Carson." Her voice was soft and low, as if not to disturb the personable silence they mutually created around them.

Oh, how fucking desperately Carson wanted to kiss her again, but he wasn't sure if that was pushing it, if it was something she wanted. She might have kissed him in the store, but Carson didn't want to just assume she would be willing to do it again.

"Come to my match tomorrow?" Carson asked instead. He didn't often do back-to-back matches a few days in a row, but it was his last match of the week and, shit, he wanted Noelle there despite constantly telling himself she didn't belong in Astros. Her

176

absence during the last few matches hung over him like a dark cloud, an unexpected storm, and he knew her presence was the only way for it to dissipate.

She gazed at him. Her hazel eyes were lit up by the street lamps outside, looking at him almost scrutinizingly. Carson wondered what she could be thinking before feeling the words die in his throat when she shifted slightly to face him. "Might need a little convincing," she mused.

Carson didn't miss the way she leaned closer, and once again, he was surprised to see the mirth in her eyes, challenging him to make the next move. Carson couldn't help but wonder how he could have missed the minx-like personality Noelle seemed to carry, but fuck it if Carson didn't find it the hottest thing ever.

An airy scoff of a laugh escaped his smirking lips, and he didn't need to be told twice as his right hand pressed against the area under her chin, cupping it with his thumb on one side of her jaw and his fingers on the other and then pulling her cupped face towards him as he met her lips halfway with his own.

He felt Noelle smile against his lips. He felt his own mirroring the action as he worked to pull a slow, sucking kiss from Noelle's mouth as he held the bottom of her face in one hand. Carson had kissed off most of her ChapStick, though the cherry-flavored lip balm lingered slightly as he sucked the rest of it into his own mouth. His pants were strained when he heard Noelle let out a quiet yet satisfied moan that he swallowed.

Shit. It was only the second kiss and he never wanted to fucking stop. Never wanted to stop her lips on his or their noses pressing against their cheeks.

"Okay," Noelle breathed, pulling away in need of air. Her eyes fluttering open to dazedly look at Carson. He brushed his thumb over to join his fingers on the other side of her jaw, and Carson never understood what it felt like to melt in someone's touch until Noelle turned her head ever so slightly to press a kiss to

177

his palm. She smiled at him, lazy and sweet. "I'll come to your match."

Without another word, another kiss, Noelle smiled that pretty smile before opening the door. The roar of the rain made Carson blink back into reality as he watched her shut the door behind her and run up to her front door in the rain. He watched from where he sat in the driver's seat, looking through the rain-pelted window to watch Noelle open the door to the house. Her silhouette turned around to offer a quick wave before shutting the door, and Carson fell back in his seat as reality replaced Noelle's presence.

He let out a deep breath. He was in trouble, but he was completely okay with it.

CHAPTER SIXTEEN

"I really miss him, Ellie."

Noelle felt her stomach churn, the queasiness having nothing to do with the mild cold she had developed overnight. She was in the rain for maybe five seconds but apparently, walking into her air-conditioner-blasting house was enough for her to wake up with a stuffy nose and phlegmy throat. During times like these, she wondered if she had a sensitive immune system.

That had nothing to do with the way her chest tightened as she gazed at Andrea's sad face; her younger sister stared longingly at their father's picture on the mantle under the TV. His smiling face, while comforting almost every day, felt a bit haunting at this moment. Those blue eyes only Andrea inherited were frozen to reflect the smile on his face forever. All the girls were super close with their father, but Andrea and he were joined at the hip. She was the one who most often had days of missing him terribly; today was one of those.

"I do too," Noelle sniffled, mildly irritated for having both a congested and runny nose. She rolled her lips into her mouth as she followed Andrea's gaze to their dad's picture, wondering what he would do to comfort her younger sister. Then Noelle sat up, smiling. "Come on, let's go to that Froyo place he took us to, the one in Columbus Circle."

179

Andrea dragged her eyes to Noelle before giving her a once over, a dull excitement present amongst the sadness in her eyes. "You're sick though. Shouldn't you rest or something?"

Noelle scoffed, waving her off as she stood up from the couch. "It's just a little cold. I'll be fine," she assured even if the mild soreness in her throat was irritating. Sitting around at home was too boring, and even if she was capable of joining Beverly at work, Noelle would rather be with Andrea today. "Get dressed and we'll leave in a few."

They split as they went to their own rooms to change out of the pajamas they had been lying around in. Though, it was still a few minutes until noon. Noelle changed into some shorts and pulled out the first crop top from her closet after a shower, pausing in front of her mirror as she debated to do anything to her face. She settled for a coat of mascara and her cherry ChapStick before grabbing her things and heading downstairs.

"You didn't have to do this, you know," Andrea's quiet voice sounded over the radio once they were in the car since Beverly opted for the subway.

"Shut up. Yes, I did," Noelle responded instantly as she made a right turn, the wheelchair folded in the back rattling slightly. She used to hate driving in New York; she always thought that was a skill she wasn't capable of possessing, but her parents sat with her in the passenger seat until she could drive, and now, it was as easy as breathing. Plus, Noelle was always willing to help her sisters feel better if she could. "We're gonna eat some frozen yogurt and chill in Central Park and get our mind off of everything."

Andrea was silent for a moment before she raised an eyebrow. "Are you trying to get your mind off Dad, or is there something else bothering you too?"

It was creepy how well Noelle and her sisters could read each other.

Still, for all their insights on their sibling, Noelle was sure Andrea couldn't see the thoughts and images flashing through her mind—ones that made Noelle's grip on the steering wheel tighten and her stomach to twist in unfiltered excitement. For a moment, and most of the previous night, all Noelle could think of was Carson showing up at the store out of the blue, of him kissing her and touching her in a way she had been craving probably since the moment she met him.

She always thought his lips were begging to be kissed, and now that she finally had, she was desperate to do it again.

It was true that Noelle was still trying to process how last night came to be. How did Carson feel about her? What did that kiss mean to him, if it meant anything at all? Her excited twist transformed into a breathless, gut-wrenching churn at the thought of Carson kissing her just for the fuck of it. But the look in his eye . . . a kind of softness she hadn't expected especially when he asked her to come to his match tonight despite looking bothered when she did show up on her own whim. It was enough to hold Noelle over into believing that Carson wasn't randomly showing up into her store and kissing her senseless for no reason.

There had to be a reason. Noelle was sure Carson wasn't someone who did anything without one.

"The only thing that's bothering me is this cold," Noelle responded, trying to ignore the way her lips were tingling once again. It was as if Carson was kissing them. The genuine cough that followed her words only solidified her statement; she wanted this little Froyo trip to be about them and their dad. Boy troubles weren't on the agenda even if the boy was Australian and gorgeous and basically a god.

Noelle inhaled as sharply as she could through a semi-congested, semi-runny nose as she pulled into a handicapped parking spot in the area closest to the frozen yogurt joint. She really needed to better herself on pushing Carson out of her thoughts. Thinking about him at first was hard enough, but now that she had felt his lips on hers and his taste on her tongue, it was nearly impossible.

181

After helping Andrea into her wheelchair, the two girls made their way inside the parlor, which was somewhat busy akin to the foot traffic outside. *It could be worse*, Noelle mused since it was the middle of summer and tourist season. She knew Central Park would be crawling with people like ants on a picnic.

"I can't believe you like that." Noelle scrunched her face up in distaste, glancing down at Andrea's cup. "It's gross."

"You just have no taste," the seventeen-year-old shot back, her attention not deviating from her cup of dark chocolate frozen yogurt with coconut shavings. Meanwhile, Noelle just shook her head and Andrea laughed. "It was Dad's favorite! It's good."

The smile remained on Noelle's face as she scooped up her own Froyo. "Dad had a weird taste," she commented. Okay, so maybe dark chocolate and coconut shavings weren't the weirdest of tastes, and while Noelle liked the smell of coconuts, she didn't enjoy the taste and dark chocolate. Noelle wanted to cringe at the mere thought of the taste.

When she noticed her sister shudder in disgust, Andrea snorted. "You're a dramatic bitch."

Noelle let out a faux affronted gasp before shoving a spoonful of strawberry banana frozen yogurt in her mouth while crossing her ankles. She sat on a stoned wall that only came up to her hips when standing, and Andrea sat right in front of her. Noelle shrugged with a grin. "I'm not gonna apologize for liking what I like."

The cold treat in her mouth seemed suddenly hard to swallow as, somehow, her brain decided to take her words and morph them into a thought revolving around Carson. Had she truly expected to keep him off her mind for too long? Noelle would be lucky if she didn't crave for his lips once again since the moment she woke up.

Kissing Carson was earth-shattering. Him showing up at the store after hours in the rain and kissing her after appearing to be mad at her for avoiding him over the course of a few days was a kind of act she needed more than just a day to process. Noelle wasn't going to lie, she may have pinched herself a bunch of times in bed, wondering if this was some kind of dream.

One—or two—kiss from Carson and Noelle was even more into him than she thought possible. Funny how it only took that for Noelle to realize that she had been around him long enough to decide whether or not she liked him. It was almost funny because Noelle had only ever seen Carson at his toughest, when he was constantly carrying that confident, don't-look-at-me vibe so effortlessly. God knows what would happen if there was another side to Carson she had been missing out on.

"I miss him a lot, you know."

Andrea's soft voice over the sound of busy New York City yanked Noelle right out of her thoughts, pushing Carson all the way to the back of her mind as her gaze flickered to Andrea. Suddenly, she was reminded why they were here in the first place and felt a rush of guilt. She shouldn't be sitting around thinking about kissing Carson when she came out here to be there for her sister.

"I do too," Noelle offered, looking down at her cup to swirl her melting frozen yogurt around. Honestly, Noelle might not talk about her father too much, but, God, she missed him every day. His absence was heavily noticed in the house, void of his deep laughter that always brought a smile to Noelle's face and the scent of his special chocolate chip pancakes that Noelle just couldn't seem to get right. "Sometimes . . ." she trailed off, eyebrows furrowing at nothing in the distance. "Sometimes, I wake up and think he's still around, you know? It used to be every day when it first happened and now it's not as often but," Noelle let out a sigh, feeling the familiar burn in her eyes that almost always occurred at the thought of her father, "it still sucks."

That was a pathetic way to end her sentiment, but it was nonetheless true. It sucked not having their dad around; nothing filled the void his lively presence used to fill. Even three years later with the smell of chocolate chip pancakes that weren't made by him lingering in the air and the sound of his laughter only echoing through the walls either by distant memory or an old video on one of their phones, the reality of him being gone was akin to feeling her insides shrivel up slowly and painfully. At least, that was what it felt like for Noelle.

"He would've been proud of you and Bev, you know," Andrea spoke up while resting her sunglasses atop her head to squint up at Noelle, uncaring for the sun shining down on them. "The bookstore was his life and business has never been better. I think—" she paused, a smile slowly lighting up her face as Noelle held her breath. "I think by keeping the store and all the stories in it alive, you're kind of keeping him alive too, you know?"

Shit. If Noelle was trying to hold back her tears before, now there was no stopping the waterworks.

She did manage to hold them back, feeling the weight of Andrea's words sit heavily and longingly on her heart. Her seventeen-year-old sister really knew how to bring Noelle's emotions out.

"He'd be proud of you too, you know," Noelle assured with a grin, eyes glassy with unshed tears. Their surroundings were nothing but background noise to them, the only indicator of them being the sun on their backs and the light breeze. She put her nearly empty cup aside, hands on the stone ledge she was sitting on. "Especially for pulling yourself together. I remember you being so angry after . . . after the accident. For not having Dad or your legs, but you got through it. And you're here. You fought and Dad would've been so proud."

Noelle didn't even want to think about the days, weeks, or months following the accident that killed their dad and paralyzed Andrea. They were all hurting so badly, and fourteen-year-old Andrea had to deal with not just one loss but two. Noelle would never tell Andrea of the countless nights she cried in her room, in the bathroom, wherever she could when she thought of the pain her sister was in, in the first little while that Andrea was in the

184

wheelchair. The loss of her father and watching her little sister go through something so awful felt like a hand had her heart constantly enclosed in it, painfully squeezing the organ every time Andrea even so much as winced at the nerve pain she used to feel before she ultimately lost feeling in her legs.

"Oh my god! Elle!" Andrea's surprised gasp pulled Noelle out of her thoughts once more, staring at her sister in alarm. When she saw Andrea's mouth dropped open in shocked amusement, she followed Andrea's wide-eyed gaze next to her before Noelle's own eyes widened at the sight she was greeted with. How the hell had she not noticed an adorable little dog licking away at the inside of her leftover frozen yogurt cup?

"Umm . . ." Noelle stretched the word, an incredulous laugh escaping her as her gaze flickered between the black-and-white dog and her sister, who looked just as amused. The dog had a collar, so she assumed it wasn't a stray as she glanced around for a potential someone looking for their pet. "Hi, buddy." She finally giggled, reaching over to carefully pet the pup's head.

The small fluffy dog lifted its head away from the cup long enough to let out a chipper yip before it began eating away the contents of Noelle's cup, which, at this point, she considered was the dog's.

"He's so cute!" Andrea gushed, rolling her wheelchair forward a bit to get closer to the stone ledge Noelle sat on. "Oh my god, Elle! Look at his little face!"

Noelle couldn't help but grin as she looked at the dog, not even bothered that the little guy decided to finish off the rest of her frozen yogurt. Thankfully, it wasn't a chocolate-flavored one, and it seemed like the dog was enjoying it. "I wonder who he belongs to," she mused, her fingers still gently rubbing the top of his head as she glanced around with squinting eyes. "His owner's probably looking for him."

Andrea rubbed his back. "Can we keep him if we don't find his owner?"

185

Noelle shot her sister an amused yet flat look, unsurprised at Andrea's desire to steal away the dog. Though, she couldn't blame Andrea for her words. This was the cutest little—

"Oreo!"

Her hand froze atop the dog's head. Noelle wondered if she somehow imagined the familiar voice amongst the busy hum of Central Park and if her mind was playing tricks on her because New York was so fucking big and what were the odds that when Noelle successfully followed the voice over her right shoulder, she caught sight of Carson jogging down the light hill behind her.

At this point, the way her heart started to quicken should've become a familiar sensation whenever Carson came around, but Noelle still found her breath hitching in her throat as she saw him near them. He had a red and white trucker hat on— Noelle didn't possibly understand how he managed to make that look good—that allowed his dark hair to curl out from under it. He wore sunglasses that hid his eyes behind the darkened lens, but she didn't miss the way his jog slowed down into a walk as he neared them. His lips parted ever so slightly, almost unnoticeably, when he realized who he was approaching.

Of course Noelle noticed his lips. She couldn't stop thinking about those goddamn lips.

"Carson?" Andrea grinned as she instantly recognized him, drawing the older boy's gaze towards her. "Wait. Oh my god, is this your dog?"

Noelle's fingers may still be scratching the dog's head, but her eyes were on Carson as he stood on the grassier side of the ledge as opposed to where Andrea was on the pavement. She greedily wondered if he was looking at her from behind the sunglasses, her curiosity intensifying when Carson's head ticked her way ever so slightly before he subtly shifted. His broad body shielded her from the sunlight shining behind him.

He was totally looking at her.

"Yeah, he's mine," he answered, his attention back to Andrea as a small hint of a smirk graced his lips while glancing at the small animal among them. "This is Oreo."

Oh god, he has a dog; he has a dog named Oreo as if he couldn't possibly get more attractive, Noelle internally groaned. Her smile absentmindedly widened when Oreo lifted his head from the now empty cup, bumping it against her palm when she stopped scratching him. Her heart soared as she continued her fingers' movements.

Moments later, Oreo shuffled towards the brim of the ledge that he and Noelle were on before ultimately jumping onto Andrea's lap. "Oh, man." She giggled, giving Noelle her empty cup to put to the side as Oreo stood up on his hind legs with the front two against Andrea's chest as he licked at her chin, which emitted more giggles from the seventeen-year-old. Clearly, her focus on Oreo had her totally ignoring the mild bruise and cut that could be seen on Carson's face from his fight. "I'm stealing your dog," she said to him.

He chuckled lowly, and Noelle tried not to be obvious in the way her back straightened when Carson moved forward before bending down to sit on the ledge next to Noelle. Unlike her, his feet touched the ground as he laced his hands in the space between his thighs. "If he ever goes missing, I'll know where to look," Carson mused, lifting an eyebrow at Andrea who just grinned innocently before giving all of her attention to Oreo.

Carson's arm barely brushed against Noelle's, but the heat of his body was enough to stall Noelle's breath in her throat. Unfortunately, the mild cold she was fighting off irritated her a bit too much as she began coughing with a groan amongst the coughs. She turned away from Carson and covered her mouth with her left elbow. "God," she wheezed slightly. Her nose wrinkled in annoyance as she tried to clear her throat, the mild burning sensation ever present.

"Here." Noelle glanced at Carson, blinking at the water bottle he was offering, and it was almost embarrassing how that simple action spurred the butterflies in her stomach. She took the bottle, smiling gratefully. Carson's own lips curled slightly as she drank from the bottle without touching her lips, not wanting to get him sick too. "You good?"

"Yeah," she breathed once capping the bottle and handing it back to him with a soft thanks. "Was in the rain for, like, ten seconds and I ended up with a cold."

Carson's eyebrows furrowed slightly at that, and Noelle's heart stumbled when she saw the flash of regret across his features. Did he feel guilty for not providing her with an umbrella or something, for her getting caught in the rain? She pressed her lips together, preventing the smile from growing, both endeared and amused at his reaction. There was no reason for him to feel any bit of guilt, yet it warmed her nonetheless.

When Carson didn't say anything, Noelle felt the need to fill the silence that settled between them. Andrea had rolled away with Oreo, playing with him with the small stress ball she carried with her everywhere since the accident. "Are you training today?"

"Yeah," he responded, shoulders squaring as he sat up. Even while sitting, he unsurprisingly dominated her in height. Then something shifted in his features—Noelle noticed—as he faced her slightly. She wished she could see his eyes. "If you're sick, you don't have to come tonight."

Noelle rolled her lips into her mouth while glancing at him. She suddenly felt nervous for a moment as if she hadn't received the biggest show of emotion from Carson last night when he had his lips against hers, a bit unsure of herself. "Do you . . . not want me to come?"

The uncertainty she heard in her own voice prickled Noelle's skin; she was a confident girl, and while Carson caught her off guard, she no longer wanted to feel or act as though she was afraid of saying the wrong thing in front of him. Feeling any of that

188

doubtfulness seemed a bit redundant to her after last night, and even though Noelle didn't want to get too ahead of herself, she couldn't keep the excitement from bubbling or her heart from feeling like it was soaring in her chest at the sight of Carson.

"I do." His words were sure, and as if that wasn't enough, Noelle truly felt her stomach plummet in anticipation when Carson took off his glasses with his cap shielding him from the sun as he leaned closer. The sight of his deep dark eyes demanded Noelle's attention as she couldn't find herself looking away, her heart familiarly picking up its rhythm as Carson stopped a handful of inches away from her face. He was close enough for her to smell his deliciously piney scent but still too damn far.

When one corner of his lips tugged up slightly and his gaze dangerously dropped to her lips, Noelle held her breath. "I told you last night I wanted you there, and I still do," he mused in a low, accented voice.

Wow, Noelle felt like she was gonna throw up from the thrill Carson's words sent her, but that wouldn't be cute, so she invited the air into her lungs before quickly searching for the confidence she knew she had. Almost reluctantly, she leaned back slightly as she raised an eyebrow at him. "Can't blame me for double checking. You have a habit of looking pretty annoyed when I show up at Astros," she pointed out.

The heat that Carson felt rise in his cheeks was unexpected, rolling his lower lip into his mouth as a small yet sheepish smile tilted on his face. Normally, Carson wasn't really one to regret his words or actions, but now, he felt like a dick for making it seem like Noelle's presence at Astros bothered him. While it wasn't her attendance that unsettled him, it was the other people that were there. He knew the kind of people—kind of men—that frequented Astros, and Carson was quickly realizing he didn't want any of them to give Noelle a second glance even if he knew her presence demanded it. It was hard to look away once it landed on Noelle, and that was another thing Carson was admittedly happily coming to terms with.

Honestly, why would I ever want to look away? Carson thought. With his eyes meeting Noelle's, Carson pressed his tongue to the back of his teeth at the sight of her light eyes as it shined brightly, and Carson just knew it had nothing to do with the sun over their heads. He could make out the deep green flecks in the light hazel as it was no longer hidden and there for him to admire in all their glory. Quickly regaining track of his thoughts, Carson lifted his chin slightly. "Show up tonight and you'll see I'll be anything but annoyed, babe," he told her lightly.

Babe. Babe, babe, babe. How could one word stop Noelle's world from spinning?

Her heart threatened to jump out of her chest, mouth drying slightly as she picked up on the mischievous glint in his eyes. If his words didn't hold the subtle thrill they did, Noelle would definitely be able to tell by the slight challenging quirk of his brow that Carson was flirting with her, and both of them were consciously aware of it.

Her lips pouted into a small smirk, the action successfully catching Carson's attention. "That's romantic," Noelle drawled sarcastically.

"What gave you the idea that I was romantic?"

Noelle's grin widened at the teasing lilt behind his words, a strange kind of giddy bubbling up at the fact that Carson was joking about romance with her. "I don't know," she hummed knowingly, feeling the fire in her cheeks at the next words to spill out of her mouth. "Coming into my store in the middle of a storm and kissing me was quite the gesture. Even Shakespeare can't write romance like that," she added teasingly.

Carson pressed his lips together at Noelle's words, scoffing lightly through his nose as he tried to fight off the smile threatening to grow. The light teasing and the way Noelle started to clap back at him were something akin to refreshing, and Carson couldn't help but revel in the fact that she was acting around him the way she acted with the people she was comfortable with. The knowledge of her being comfortable around him made him happier than he would admit.

"Guess I'm just full of surprises." *Like you*, he wanted to add but didn't just yet want to let Noelle know her power of catching him off guard.

Noelle's smile widened slightly at his words, showing off her dimples as her eyes remained on his. God, was she ever aware that Carson was full of surprises? "If you want me to come to your match tonight, then I will." Noelle decided with a tight grip on the familiar confidence she knew she possessed yet somehow lost when it came to Carson.

Her heart practically bolted out of her chest at the small yet satisfied grin curling at Carson's kissable lips. "I'll look for you."

*   *   *

Noelle felt terrible—both literally and figuratively; the former because throughout the course of the day her mild cold had just gone downhill, and the latter because she felt bad about being unable to attend Carson's match. Her sore throat intensified, her voice hoarse every time she spoke. It was irritated further whenever she coughed with phlegm stuck in the back of her throat. Her eyes were itchy too, but while she didn't have a fever, she did have some chills. She wondered if it was the end of the world with her miserable mood.

Her love for the rain was easily replaced by irritation due to this cold.

"Take some NyQuil before you go to bed, okay?" her mother said as she grabbed her keys from the small table by the front door.

191

"I already did," Noelle lazily drawled from where she lay on the couch, a throw pillow covering half of her body as she watched an episode of *Suits*.

She heard her mom let out a huff. "Then why are you up? Go to sleep. Don't fight the medicine."

Noelle waved her mom off, telling her she would sleep in a little while. Dr. Simon let out another sigh, bid goodbye, and left the house. It was nearing ten o'clock that night, but her mom had a surgery scheduled and was headed to the hospital. Andrea was busy in her room, and Beverly hadn't returned yet from Carson's match, which only made Noelle let out a disappointed breath. She wished she was there.

Her eyes felt heavy, the drowsy effect of the medicine already kicking in though she kept her eyes open, absentmindedly watching the show playing on the TV. Noelle couldn't help but wonder if Carson was as disappointed in not seeing her tonight as she was about not attending. She texted to let him know she couldn't make it, and he said it was okay but that was it. Noelle still felt down. Sure, the violence and blood during matches weren't something Noelle was a complete fan of, which was funny because that was why people attended them in the first place, but honestly, she was a fan of one of the best fighters there.

She hadn't been to any of Carson's matches for nearly a week, and tonight, she would have finally gone back to Astros. The place itself always made her feel uneasy, but she allowed herself to forget that discomfort whenever Carson took the ring. She had been looking forward to going tonight, especially when Carson literally, personally told her he wanted her to be there; her health kicking her in the ass and preventing that from happening was a low blow.

It was about ten minutes after her mother left that Noelle's phone let out a beep, and she picked up her phone to see that Beverly had informed her that the match was over. Carson had won, and she was staying over Aiden's. Noelle put her phone back on the coffee table, burying her face in her throw blanket as she coughed into it.

Ugh, I want to die.

Around ten-thirty, she decided to call it a night since she could barely keep her eyes open. Her head felt heavy from the NyQuil, her nose congested and throat itchy as she shut off the TV and stumbled to her feet as she draped the blanket around her shoulders. She made her way towards the stairs, wanting to just collapse on the bed and not think of missing Carson's match or her health, only to freeze after switching off the living room lights when a knock sounded at the door. The light above the door was on, illuminating the small space. Noelle frowned at the door as she wondered who the hell was knocking.

Her phone let out a *ding,* and when she checked the message, she nearly dropped the device as she read Carson's name and then his message.

Open the door.

Noelle's heart dropped to her stomach, her eyes widening as her gaze snapped back to the door just a few steps away. *Carson is here?* Suddenly, she felt as though her dry throat had nothing to do with her cold as she took slow steps towards the door; her drowsy mind was wondering if this was some kind of joke. Maybe the NyQuil was making her delusional or something. What the hell was Carson doing here?

As if ripping off a Band-Aid, Noelle gripped the doorknob after unlocking it. She swung the door open and froze in the entryway at the sight of the tall figure standing right there. He stood in jeans and a grey tank with a beige button down on top, undone with the sleeves rolled to show off the tattoos on his wrist and hands. The sight of him had her staring at him in disbelief with her lips parted, and Noelle wondered if the NyQuil had her somehow hallucinating the image in front of her. She was pretty drowsy, but she hoped to any god listening that this wasn't a trick of the medication. Her gaze dropped to his hand. She noticed the brown

Panera bag he held, bewilderment mixed in with confusion etched on her face as she forced her gaze back up at him.

"Carson . . . hi," she breathed out with left hand still gripping the doorknob as she stared up at him. He still had the two cuts on his face and the bruise was fading. Noelle was relieved to see that there weren't any new ones added. "What're you doing here?"

"You're sick," Carson stated matter-of-factly as if that explained his unexpected arrival. Then he lifted the bag, his dark eyes meeting her hazel ones. Noelle was surprised to see what she thought was uncertainty flash in his brown irises.

"Got you chicken noodle soup because, y'know, everyone likes chicken noodle soup. And it always helps me when I'm sick so, uh, yeah . . ." he trailed off, his words sounding unsure. Air rushing out of her lungs, Noelle suppressed the urge to coo 'aww' because this was too fucking sweet. If she was doubtful about her feelings for Carson before, then that was no longer the case because Noelle was positive she could feel her heart swell in her chest at Carson's gesture. She knew he won the fight thanks to Beverly, and normally, he would be out celebrating with everyone else, but he was here at her house with soup because she was sick. Noelle just knew that she had fallen a little bit more for him already.

"That's—" Noelle's lips split into a grin, suddenly not so tired anymore despite the NyQuil running through her system. She fought the urge to lean against the door like some lovesick girl as she peered up at him. "You didn't have to, Carson. This is so sweet of you."

Carson smirked as he lowered the bag, raising an eyebrow at her. "Don't go spreading that around. I've got a reputation to maintain," he jibed lightly.

She snorted, rolling her eyes as she stepped aside to let him in. "Come on in, tough guy." Noelle chuckled, watching as Carson's smirk transformed into a genuine smile—one that made her insides flutter because she didn't get to see it often enough, and when she did, it was a memorable moment.

Sniffling, Noelle led Carson towards the kitchen and felt his gaze on her back. It wasn't until they passed the stairs where there was a small mirror on the wall that Noelle cringed slightly. She caught a glance of herself with the haphazard bun that has messy strands sticking out and her nose pink from sniffling and blowing. Safe to say she didn't look her best, and while she knew it wasn't a big deal because surely Carson didn't expect her to look like she had her life together when she was sick, it still made her feel slightly insecure to look like this when Carson looked like the opposite.

"It's still hot," Carson's deep voice pulled her out of her mildly self-deprecating thoughts. She looked at him with confused brows as he stood on the end of the counter. She slowly made her way over. "Have it before it cools down, yeah?"

Noelle hummed in tired appreciation, unable to keep the small smile from tugging her lips as she grabbed a spoon from the drawer and a bottle of hot sauce from the cabinet. As she poured some into the soup, the steam immediately floated once Carson popped the lid off. "How'd your match go?" Noelle asked.

Carson folded his arms on top of the counter, leaning forward as Noelle stood to his left. He glanced at her. The way the blanket fell over her shoulders and the tendrils of hair fell out of her bun made her look so damn adorable, and Carson didn't find anything or anyone adorable other than Oreo. The smile that played on his lips was difficult to keep away. "I won, so about how you'd expect."

She couldn't help but roll her eyes as she took a spoonful of the soup, wincing ever so slightly as it burned her tongue but reveling in the warmth it gave her throat.

"A little bit of modesty is good for the soul, you know," Noelle quipped with a quirk of a brow. She wasn't sure if she would ever admit that Carson's cockiness was something she found so damn attractive.

"Just bein' honest." Carson chuckled deeply, feeling his shoulders relax at Noelle's grin. He had been nervous, honestly, when he was driving over to Noelle's house, wondering if it was a good idea for him to show up in the first place but then he decided fuck it and bought her some soup because he wasn't going to show up to her house empty-handed knowing that she was sick. "Is it good?" he asked, nodding towards the cup.

"Mm-hmm," she hummed sleepily while swallowing a spoonful of soup, chicken, and noodles. Somehow, the familiar soup tasted even better because it was from Carson. Propping her left elbow on the table, Noelle rested her cheek against her palm and twirled the spoon in the cup as she brought her gaze back to Carson. She failed to ignore the excited twist in her stomach as she realized he was already looking at her. It was a nice change from her stomach feeling mildly queasy throughout the day. "I think you bringing me soup totally counts as you being a romantic."

She was referring to their conversation from earlier at the park today, of course. Carson huffed out a laugh as he bowed his head, shaking it a bit. If anyone else told him he was romantic, Carson would tell them to fuck off, but Noelle teasing him about it lightened his chest and made him want to prove to her just how romantic he could get.

"Just don't tell anyone," Carson jested, his eyes watching Noelle's eyes fall shut as she scoffed out a smile at his words. Her right hand picked up a spoonful of soup as she put it in her mouth. She was practically falling asleep standing up. "You tired?"

"Drank some NyQuil earlier," Noelle drawled, her eyes still closed after swallowing the soup.

Carson furrowed his eyebrows, staring intently at Noelle who had her eyes closed and cheek on her palm. He realized just how sleepy she looked. He knew the medicine's drowsiness could take a quite toll, and that seemed to be the case for Noelle. "Wanna go to bed?" he asked, his voice automatically softening as he straightened.

"No." Noelle shook her head, finally opening her eyes as she forced herself to fruitlessly blink away any sleep as she, too, straightened and shot Carson a half-sleepy, half-determined look. "I wanna finish the soup."

But, shit, did she also want to go to sleep.

Carson's presence made her want to stay up all night if she had to. For shit's sake, he was at her house with soup he bought for her because he knew she was sick, and Noelle didn't want to let any of this go to waste.

"You can barely hold the spoon, Noelle."

Yeah . . . it would be great if she didn't feel like she was about to pass the fuck out.

She pouted at the spoon as if it was its fault she couldn't get a firm grip on it anymore. At this point, there wasn't much of a difference if she was drunk or drowsy off NyQuil.

Nonetheless, she was surprised when the spoon was no longer in her grasp. She blinked in confusion, and as an attempt to get rid of her sleepy state, she watched Carson move to stand next to her. Noelle watched in surprise as she hugged the blanket closer around her shoulders while Carson dipped the spoon into the cup and scooped up chicken, noodles, and some broth. When he raised it above the cup, his expectant stare met her stunned one. He tried to fight off his amused smirk.

"Come on now, you've only got some left," he said.

Instead of doing as he said, Noelle's lips parted as she stared up at him. He's so tall . . . and pretty. "You're gonna feed me?" she dumbly asked. She didn't even cringe at her question; she was too tired to care.

Carson's smirk softened while taking in her wide-eyed look, and even he couldn't deny that he melted on the spot at the sight of her. "Wouldn't be the first time," he pointed out.

Noelle sniffled before opening her mouth, and Carson fed her the spoonful. His lips parted slightly as if he was feeding a baby and gestured for her to do the same. At this point, he didn't bother hiding his smile as Noelle chewed with closed eyes, her lips forming a smile of her own. Noelle definitely thought the soup tasted better when she was being fed by Carson.

It was a quiet moment between the two of them for the next few minutes as Carson fed her the soup, making sure to get every bit of chicken and noodles. Noelle dutifully ate every bit of it. She was growing sleepier by the second, the medicine demanding for her to go to bed, but being with Carson felt much more inviting than her bed. He looked so gorgeous next to her under the glow of the overhead kitchen light that Noelle didn't want to tell him to leave; she didn't want to be by herself when he was already here.

She didn't even notice that Carson had thrown out the bag and the now-empty cup, putting the spoon in the sink until he was turning to face her once more. Noelle still had the blanket around her, and as she stared up at Carson with his brown eyes and dark curls and stupidly handsome face, she wasn't able to keep in the next few words from spilling out of her mouth.

"Can you stay the night?"

Carson swore his heart fell to the very bottom of his stomach. He couldn't even keep his cool when his eyes widened at Noelle's question. He sucked in a sharp breath because, once the fuck again, Noelle had taken him by surprise. The plan—not that there was much of one—was to come by with the soup. Okay, so it might have also been to start making up for him being an ass to her when they first met and to just keep Noelle company if she wanted him to. He wasn't going to lie; he missed seeing her at Astros, feeling disappointed that she couldn't make it tonight but not wanting her there anyway if she was too sick. Bringing soup over was just an impulsive thing, something Carson felt compelled to do, but him saying no to Noelle after asking him to come up to bed with him even if it was just to lay down together would be a crazy thing to do.

When he didn't respond soon enough, Noelle offered the smallest of smiles. "You don't have to . . . if you don't want," she muttered, taking a breath through her stuffy nose. "I mean, I'm sick so I won't blame you if you don't—"

Carson instantly cut off her backtracking. "I want to." Noelle shut her mouth, taking a soft breath because she may or may not have risked embarrassing herself when she asked that question, but Carson's agreement was enough to warm up her cheeks, enough to remind herself that feeling hesitant and maybe even a little bit insecure around Carson should become something of the past.

He noticed. Carson saw the hesitation in Noelle's eyes once she had asked him; he noticed the way she took in a breath as if preparing herself, through her drowsiness, for the rejection Carson would send her way. At that moment, he realized he didn't want Noelle to feel like that towards him. He knew, from their recent interactions, that they were growing to be comfortable around each other—fuck, Carson wasn't even going to think about that kiss from last night—and Carson was determined to get rid of any apprehension Noelle may still have.

"Let's go."

Noelle smiled a small, sleepy smile as they left the kitchen, then turned the lights off as they went up the stairs. "Wait. I actually think Bev might have some of Aiden's pajamas, if you want them for the night," she said as they walked the familiar way to Noelle's bedroom.

Carson paused in front of Noelle's bedroom, glancing down the hall to where Noelle was still lingering by the stairs. He didn't want to send her off back downstairs to Beverly's room, but Carson would be lying if he said he was comfortable sleeping in the skinny jeans he had on now. While he wouldn't give a flying fuck if he slept in his underwear next to some girl, Noelle wasn't some girl and he was sure as hell not going to treat her like one.

So he pulled away from Noelle's door. "I can go get them."

"It's fine," Noelle assured, her throat no longer aching as much when she took off the blanket. "Can you put this on my bed?"

Carson nodded as Noelle tossed the blanket from where she stood. He caught it in one hand as Noelle disappeared back down the stairs. He entered the room, flicking the switch on the wall that illuminated her room. After putting her blanket on the bed, Carson quickly went to the bathroom across the hall and used the toilet before heading back to Noelle's bedroom, running his ring-clad fingers through his hair just as Noelle returned.

"Here you go." She smiled, and Carson took the black-and-blue plaid pajama pants he recognized as Aiden's. Carson noticed her smile, which only showed hints of her dimples, was as sleepy as it could get as Noelle moved around the room to go towards the dresser to pull out some clothes. "I'll be back," she hummed before disappearing out of the room.

Without much thought, Carson took this moment to take off his shoes and remove his jeans and boxers after emptying his pockets, pulling on the far more comfortable pajamas. When he dropped down to the same side of Noelle's bed as he had the last time, Carson let out a content breath. Really, he couldn't believe he was back here again, in the same bed he probably had one of his best sleeps in, waiting for the pretty girl to return to her bedroom. It was the kind of déjà vu he most definitely welcomed.

He had never done this before, never voluntarily and wholeheartedly got into another girl's bed just for the sake of company or for the sake of comfort. Carson didn't like to include that one relationship he had back in high school. He thought of himself as a different person back then because he never did now what he did back then. But this? Wanting to just lay with a girl? That was something he did back then, and he found himself

200

missing that kind of closeness with someone without sticking something in somewhere.

As he settled on the bed with Noelle's fruity scent mixed with something of her own, Carson felt his shoulders relax because he couldn't help but feel so damn comfortable in here. He had only ever felt comfortable, utterly at ease, in only a handful of places and who would've thought Noelle's room would be added onto that list? There was such a homey essence in here with the pictures and the books and little tokens that made Noelle's room hers. Carson was kind of proud of himself for not feeling too freaked out over the comfort he felt.

He sank against the pillows behind him, his feet free of socks as he slid under the covers while he remained sitting up. He was waiting for Noelle to return. He had been staring at the ceiling, blinking in surprise because of how he hadn't noticed the few glow-in-the-dark stars that were stuck up there, when her voice suddenly sounded out of nowhere.

"It's kind of unfair you're in my bed like that, and I can't kiss you."

Carson straightened his head, his eyes finding Noelle as she entered her room and shut the door behind her with her gaze on Carson as her lips formed a pout. His own lips parted as a breathy scoff of a laugh escaped him, eyebrows shooting up in surprise because, fucking hell, Noelle couldn't say shit like that without expecting him to want to act on it.

She wandered towards the bed, the overhead light off and just the bedside lamp on. She was dressed in her own pajama pants and tee with her hair loose around her shoulders. Leaning forward, Carson raised his eyebrows in amusement despite the fact that he so desperately wanted to kiss her too. He couldn't fucking stop wanting to kiss her once again.

As Noelle came to sit on her side of the bed, Carson knew what she meant by her words. "Who says you can't?" he teased, unable to help it.

Noelle's shoulders dropped, her pout intensifying into a whining one. "Carson," she complained. His grin widened at that, and Noelle was instantly smiling back because how could she not when Carson was showing off his perfectly white teeth, and the crinkles by his eyes made her heart thump even more than normal. He has the prettiest smile. *Fuck.* He was doing a silent laugh, one that shook his broad shoulders, and Noelle didn't ever want him to stop because it was just so adorable. "The universe is against me," Noelle declared dramatically, huffing jokingly as she slid herself down to lie down.

With that, she laid down on her side and pulled the blanket up with her back to Carson, and she swore she would've fallen asleep right in that moment when her head hit the pillow but then the lights were off. She felt Carson shift behind her, and Noelle felt his arm slide over her waist and effortlessly slide her closer until her back and his chest were pressed together. Noelle swallowed inaudibly at the immediate warmth she felt of him against her, of smelling his familiar scent, and if she didn't feel herself die a little in that moment, she sure as hell did in the next.

That was when she felt Carson use his free hand to pull the blanket down a bit and brush her hair away from her shoulder, then, all of a sudden, the unmistakable pressure of his lips on the side of her neck was the reason her skin felt like it was on fire. It had nothing to do with the cold she had.

Noelle's heart beated rapidly. She could hear the pounding in her ears as she felt Carson's nose and lips on her neck along with the ends of his curls tickling her cheek and jaw as she stared wide-eyed at the wall in the darkness of her room. Carson's soft lips worked at her skin, and Noelle inhaled a choked gasp when his teeth dug in slightly, her eyes fluttering when he continued his unexpected ministrations of sucking and licking at her skin.

Oh god. Is this happening? Noelle rolled her own lips into her mouth, inhaling sharply and trying to hold in any sound threatening to escape her because, holy fuck, this felt so good. She knew what
202

kissing Carson felt like; it was something she never wanted to stop doing, but Carson's lips on her skin felt otherworldly. The softness of his lips paired with the bite of his teeth and warm soothing of his tongue had Noelle's stomach twisting tightly, and the sleepiness in her head was replaced by pleasured dizziness.

"Just because you can't kiss me . . ." Carson's low, gruff voice broke through the silence once he most definitely finished leaving a mark. His lips moved a little bit higher, and Noelle felt her damn abdomen quiver in pleasure as his lips brushed against her. "Doesn't mean I can't kiss you," he spoke.

He was doing it again, and this time, Noelle shut her eyes and her hand went to grip Carson's, which was resting against her stomach, as he repeated his actions.

"Carson," Noelle gasped quietly, reveling in the way she felt his lips curl slightly. "Don't start something you can't finish."

He chuckled against her, the sound coming from deep in his chest that Noelle felt on her back and her sleepy yet hyperaware mind couldn't help but think that this guy was absolutely going to be the death of her. Noelle could also feel his half-hard length against the thin material of his pajamas, and she knew this couldn't go on because as much as she wanted this to keep going, she was most definitely not having sex with Carson while she was sick, but he didn't stop as Noelle felt his teeth once more, the mild pressure so goddamn pleasurable. She didn't even dare try to focus any of her attention on wondering what the fuck was happening; she was only focused on enjoying the softness of Carson's lips and the fire he was igniting in her veins.

"I have every intention of finishing this, darling," Carson hummed after his tongue finished soothing Noelle's warm skin, pulling back ever so slightly to admire the second darkening mark that stood out against her skin even through the darkness of the room. His smirk, though Noelle couldn't see it, was back on his face as he settled his head back down with hers resting comfortably in the space beneath his chin. "Just you wait," he promised lowly, squeezing her hand.

Noelle let out a sharp breath through her nose, briefly wondering how the fuck things had escalated that fast but not at all complaining. In fact, she so desperately wanted to feel Carson's lips against her once more, but the moment he pulled back, the drowsiness decided to make its way back into Noelle's system, not even giving her a chance to revel in the small afterglow of the knowledge of having hickeys on her neck left by Carson as her already closed eyes remained so in an attempt to go to sleep. It was annoying how the NyQuil demanded for her to go to sleep right this moment, to not even give her the luxury of bathing in the thrilling high Carson's lips on her skin provoked.

It didn't take long for her to fall asleep after she came down from the excitement of Carson's actions. Her breathing slowed down, and her hand still grasped Carson's. As comfortable as Carson was in this position, of having Noelle so close as his own quickened heart calmed down from what he just did out of no-fucking-where, he couldn't stay in bed much longer and slowly pulled away from Noelle. Making sure he only got up from the bed when Noelle was completely out, Carson clenched his jaw before making his way out of the dark room and into the hallway. He headed towards the bathroom to relieve himself of the tension he brought upon himself from getting a taste of Noelle's skin.

If only she joined him in the bathroom to help him out of his little—big—problem. Carson squeezed his eyes shut against the locked door, letting out a sharp breath. Man, they hadn't done much, and Carson could tell he was already in deep. The only way he was able to ease the hardened tension he was experiencing was to think of the ways he was going to fulfill on the promise he just made to Noelle.

CHAPTER SEVENTEEN

Noelle truly didn't want to be one of those girls who thought being with a guy made everything better, but she was having a really difficult time preventing herself from turning into one when she woke up the next morning feeling far better than she had the day before. Her cold had been mild, sure, but she hadn't expected to wake up to a comfortable throat and a mostly clear nose. She most certainly expected to wake up next to the one guy who had been on her mind for the past few weeks, who had fallen asleep right next to her with his arms around her waist and face in the crook of her neck.

But she didn't.

When Noelle turned over, ready to feel Carson's body next to hers, she was met with nothing but disappointment and the imprint of where he slept. Her sleepy eyes narrowed in tired confusion, brows furrowing as she slowly propped herself up. She noticed Carson's things from the bedside table were gone and Aiden's pajamas were folded at the end of the bed; nothing was left but crumpled sheets where he was and his lingering pine scent clinging to them.

He was gone, and Noelle felt a dull thud of disappointment land on her heart as she pressed her lips together. She wondered why he left; she wondered if he regretted showing up last night as she let out a sigh and reached for her phone. It wasn't until she

205

looked at the message on her screen that her disappointment, hurt, and hint of anger completely dissipated.

I'm sorry I left before you woke up. Had to get to work but I'll see you later, yeah? Hope you're feeling better, babe.

It was ridiculous how Noelle had to contain the squeal threatening to escape her, like she was some kind of lovesick teenager, even if she couldn't help but feel like that at this moment. Carson had sent her the message about an hour ago, and her previous disheartened emotions were replaced by a cheek-aching grin and an erratic heartbeat. Fucking crazy how Carson could induce these reactions out of her by just a damn text.

"Wow, bitch," she whispered to herself through her smile, getting off her bed to get ready for the day. It wasn't until she started washing her face in the bathroom when she noticed the discoloration on her neck. All the air rushed out of her lungs when her mind was slammed with last night's memories. How in the world did she forget Carson's lips and teeth kissing, sucking and biting her skin? She desperately hoped that the first time she felt that kind of sensation wouldn't also be her last.

And then, she vaguely remembered Carson making her a promise before she had drifted off to sleep—a promise that turned her legs to jelly and her stomach to lurch in anticipated pleasure. He promised he would finish whatever the hell he was starting last night; he basically promised to take the mere act of leaving hickeys a few steps further, and they both knew what that meant.

Noelle splashed her face with cold water once more, letting out a deep breath. Carson basically confirmed the two of them would eventually act on whatever this was between them—this pull they both so obviously felt towards each other, like magnets slowly but surely coming together—and Noelle decided the promise of sex was so much worse than wondering if it would ever happen in the first place.

*　　　*　　　*

206

"Hayes!" Carson stopped as he heard Darryl's voice call for him over the music playing through his headphones, stilling the punching bag as he caught sight of the older man a few feet away. "Come to my office."

Carson frowned as Darryl walked off, unstrapping the gloves he decided to train with today and shoving his headphones in the pocket of his athletic shorts. Darryl rarely ever called anyone to his office, which wasn't really even an office. It was just an old storage room with a desk and chairs that Darryl occupied whenever he was at Astros. Carson's curiosity got the better of him as he stepped inside and shut the door behind him.

"You're cutting in my training time, Darryl," he pointed out with a quirk of a brow.

"Sorry about that." Carson noticed Darryl didn't seem the least bit sorry as he sat behind his desk, staring up at him with pursed lips and determined eyes. "Milner is back."

Carson's entire body tensed at his words as he took in a calming breath, though that could never be enough to relax him at the bombshell that was just dropped. The very name boiled Carson's blood, burning his veins with a level of anger that was reserved for Doug Milner. The biggest asshole Carson had ever met, a guy who used to fight at Astros and was one of the best— behind Carson—who talked as much trash as he threw punches and kicks. He and Carson used to be at each other's throats; Carson had never despised someone as intensely as he did Milner. Milner wasn't also one to shy away from throwing punches at not only Carson but his friends too. Arguments between he and Carson often transitioned into Milner throwing punches at Carson and the boys, and there had been times when he had landed a fist on Levi and Max. While they weren't as proficient in fighting as Carson or even Aiden, they definitely threw some punches of their own back.

Safe to say that no one got along with Milner, and Carson had been smug and satisfied when the fucker moved out of New

207

York and went to who-the-fuck-cares after their last match that had ended in Carson breaking his jaw with a well-timed, well-forced right hook. Now that he was back, especially at Astros, Carson knew things were going to get shitty.

"He's coming back to Astros?" Carson questioned through a steady voice even though he knew the answer already.

"Yes," Darryl answered. Carson's jaw clenched as his lips curled into an annoyed sneer. Darryl sighed. "I'm telling you this as a heads-up, Hayes. Any issues you have with Milner, either keep it in the ring or on the streets. I don't want any petty bullshit when you're not in an actual match. Save the punches for then, alright?"

Carson let out a scoff, hands clenched as he crossed his arms. He was fucking pissed because he figured he would never have to see Milner again when he left nearly a year ago, but now that the fucker was back, Carson knew he wasn't going to suddenly become a changed person or some shit. He would bet the money he made in here that Milner was the same asshole as before, and he knew his return would eventually mean the two of them would face off in the ring.

As much as Carson didn't want to see Milner again, he couldn't wait to get any anger, irritation, and fury he felt towards him out on the ring against him.

"He might show up tonight." Darryl pulled Carson out of his thoughts, the warning tone in his voice not going unnoticed by the Australian who narrowed his eyes. "So keep your focus on your match and don't worry about him, okay? Not until you have to."

Even Darryl knew that problems between the two fighters were sure to arise at Milner's arrival, and Carson wondered if he had enough self-control to not deck the guy the second his eyes inevitably landed on him.

"Did you give him the same warning?" Carson questioned, lifting his chin.

A wry smile tugged at Darryl's mouth. "I'd be an idiot not to." He leaned back in his chair. "And he'd be an idiot not to listen, but we know how he is."

Carson snorted. "An idiot."

"Just keep it together, alright?" Darryl said with a pointed raise of his eyebrow. "You wanna punch him, then do it in the ring or away from Astros. Don't make me suspend you."

His words made Carson scoff with a roll of his eyes. "Fuck off, you don't suspend anyone," he said, deadpanned.

"I might start." Then Darryl chuckled at Carson's unimpressed expression because he clearly wasn't bothered or worried. "Alright, get out."

*   *   *

"Did you miss me?"

Noelle's back straightened at the breathy Australian voice against her ear as she took a breath through her nose to accompany the way her heart skipped a beat. She felt Carson right next to her as he came to stand on her right. She tugged her lips upwards and shot him a glance. They were in the middle of Astros, minutes away from Carson's match to start. She and all their friends were standing in the very back of the excited crowd since there was another match going on at the moment between two fighters Noelle didn't give a damn about. While the others were watching with half interest as they conversed, none of them noticed the proximity between Carson and Noelle as they stood at the end of the line.

"Wouldn't have to if you didn't sneak out on me this morning," Noelle shot back in a low voice, standing with her arms crossed over her chest as she looked up at Carson.

He, in turn, let out an airy chuckle with a shake of his head, straightening as his dark eyes scanned the room. Noelle couldn't help but think that he was looking for something, wondering what

209

it was but forgetting all about it when he spoke up again. "I left you a text," Carson playfully defended, the familiar smirk on his lips. It was a sight Noelle adored. "A man's gotta work."

Noelle rolled her eyes, though the smile on her face said loud and clear she wasn't bothered by it at all. "Excuses, excuses," she hummed, face scrunching up when she saw one of the fighters deliver a nasty roundhouse kick to the face.

She felt Carson's gaze on her. The weight of it was one Noelle was willing to carry and then she heard him click his tongue in mock disappointment. "You covered them up."

She tensed at his words, breath stilling for a moment as her fingers itched to brush against the spot on her neck that Carson was obviously referring to. The marks he left were light and, fortunately, didn't take too long for Noelle to cover them up, but when she was doing so, it felt as though she was covering up some kind of secret. While she was more than willing to let the two sizable marks be noticed by anyone who happened to glance her way, going to work with hickeys on her neck wasn't professional even if it was her store.

"Sorry to disappoint," Noelle replied with a teasing smile, trying not to focus on her fluttering insides as she watched Carson's gaze flicker from her neck to her eyes. The way he just looked at her, no matter the circumstance, always had Noelle holding her breath because of the mere intensity of Carson's stare. It was as if he wasn't just looking at her but seeing through her every time he did.

The smirk was back in full-blown arrogance. "Doesn't matter," he hummed, looking back at the ongoing match that was about to come to an end. "Next time, they won't be so easy to hide."

Noelle's jaw dropped slightly as his words registered, wide eyes staring up at Carson incredulously as the smirk widened on his face. He was not even looking at her when the crowd began cheering as the match ended. She both could and couldn't believe

210

those words had come out of Carson's mouth yet another promise made by him that she excitedly realized he had every intention of delivering on. It was torturous, really, knowing Carson wanted the same things as she did but neither of them acting upon it just yet. Noelle didn't think either of them had a clue what they were waiting for, but maybe that wasn't such a bad thing. The waiting was thrilling, the anticipation of knowing something was going to happen but not when it kept Noelle on the tips of her toes.

Carson making these kinds of vows left and right only served to intensify her feelings and desire for him.

Before she could even hope to respond to Carson's words—not that her blank mind could even think of anything—Aiden was ushering Carson off because it was his time to fight.

"Stay close," Carson told her quietly, nodding to the others before he left with Aiden. While his words were unnecessary because no way in hell would Noelle deviate from her group, she still felt an endearing warmth bubble in her chest.

Along with Levi, Max, and Beverly, Noelle moved through the crowd until they were standing in the front. Soon enough, Aiden had joined them once Carson was up in the ring with his muscle tee discarded. Noelle couldn't help but let her eyes trail over the tattoos on his chest and arms.

Noelle hadn't expected to feel something akin to relief at seeing Carson in the ring after about a week of not attending any of his matches. Sure, every time but the last was because she was avoiding Carson out of—what she thinks of as now—utter stupidity, and she had been looking forward to seeing his match last night. Admittedly, she had gotten something better when Carson showed up at her house—the side of her neck under the foundation was proof of that—but something about seeing Carson in the ring was a different kind of experience.

At first, she had obviously been all kinds of apprehensive when she first showed up at Astros, intimidated by Carson's overwhelming presence, and it was crazy to think that was only weeks ago. Here she was now, at the same shady place with the same shifty people, and somehow, Noelle could pay attention to no one but just one of the men in the ring. She was aware of the kinds of people she was surrounded with—how could she not with the continuous deep cheers and boos and shouting going on—but her eyes were trained on Carson's golden-inked skin and the mess of black curls she wanted to run her fingers through.

She followed every movement—the thrust of his punches, his back muscles shifting under his unfairly smooth skin, even the way the two necklaces he wore swayed and swung when he ducked and lurched.

Unsurprisingly, the match ended quickly with Carson winning each round without letting a single hit land on him. The crowd was mostly filled with manly cheers. Noelle couldn't help but think how fucking hot that was—how he dodged and blocked every hit that came his way effortlessly. He was definitely on his A game; he didn't even look like he broke a sweat by the end of the third round, and Noelle couldn't keep the admiration off her face as she watched the smug smirk tilt his lips when he was announced the winner.

"I think that's the quickest you've won," Max commented when Carson walked over, drinking from a water bottle.

Levi smirked, quirking an eyebrow. "Definitely been making a comeback from that loss the other day. Back on your game, aren't you?"

Carson scowled, though no real irritation was present, as his throat worked when he swallowed a mouthful of water before turning his head away slightly. "Fuck off," he grunted. His dark eyes then met Noelle's, features softening a bit. "Just needed a little luck," he added.

Noelle's pressed lips curved into a smile at his words, feeling her heart swell because it was obvious he was talking about her and really he shouldn't say stuff like that because he was only feeding into Noelle's ego. Her cheeks heated up as Carson's smirk widened, clearly catching sight of her trying to fight off the smile.

"Drinks?" Aiden suggested, arm finding home around Beverly's shoulders.

Everyone hummed their agreements as it was heard over the dying buzz of Astros since there were still some people around. "You guys go ahead," Carson said as he nodded towards the back. "I'll meet you outside in a few."

As they moved towards the doors, Noelle fell to the back of the group while walking. As she walked past Carson when everyone was already up ahead, she hooked her pinky along Carson's and grinned. "I'll buy you your first congratulatory drink."

His lips curled up into a smile, and Noelle felt her own smile widen when he curled his pinky around hers in return. Carson then used the small grip to raise their hands, and Noelle swore her heart burst through her chest when Carson brushed his lips to the back of her hand, his eyes glinting.

"Wouldn't have it any other way, love," he chuckled lowly.

Kill me, why don't you? Noelle almost melted at the spot, mouth drying at the little gesture as Carson released her hand before nodding his head to where the others went off. With one last smile, she followed everyone out of Astros and a few ways away where the cars were parked in a small parking lot next to the building. Noelle couldn't help but think of how the back of her hand was tingling from where Carson's lips touched her skin, shaking her head at her own absurdity but also figuring that her skin lighting itself on fire because of Carson's touch wasn't the most out-there thing.

Carson and Max's cars were parked right next to each other. Noelle leaned against the hood of Carson's car with her arms crossed over her chest, absentmindedly listening to her friends' chatter as her eyes stared, unfocused, at the pavement beneath her. It was a cool summer night as the wind filtered through her hair, the faint smell of cigarettes and New York lingering in the air as the low buzz of people nearby talking sounded muted in Noelle's ears.

She was lost in her own world for minutes she couldn't count with a small smile playing on her lips as she thought of the guy they were waiting for, her stomach swirling with a familiar excitement that was always present with Carson.

"You good?" She heard Aiden's voice call, her head snapping up to see Carson walking through the building's double doors with his duffel hanging off his shoulder. Noelle assumed they had been waiting for a few minutes because Carson's hair was damp, indicating the quick shower he probably took, as he walked over to them.

"Ready to drink," Carson responded with a wry grin, digging something out of his front pocket as the jingling of keys sounded in the air.

He neared his car where Noelle stood, his eyes finding hers. The smile that twitched at her lips was instinctive when he subtly nodded towards his vehicle, a silent request for her to ride with him.

The others went to Max's car and promptly drove off, but just as Levi went to grab the handle for the backseat of Carson's car once it was unlocked, a male voice cut through the air before anyone could get inside.

"You gonna leave without saying hi, Hayes?"

Noelle paused with her hand on the door handle as she looked to her right, catching sight of a man exiting Astros with his gaze firmly set on Carson. He was tall with broad shoulders and sizable biceps and short dirty blonde hair. Noelle raised her eyebrows as he made his way over confidently, glancing over at Carson and blinking in realization when she saw his previous soft smirk was replaced by a scowl that sent a shiver down her spine. She hoped to never be on the receiving end of a scowl that held such ferocity.

"Got better things to do, Milner," Carson responded. Noelle flinched slightly when he tossed his duffel in the backseat and slammed the door shut, the action shaking the car. She noticed the change in his entire demeanor, the smugness of his victory replaced by palpable irritation directed solely at the stranger. "How about you walk back into Astros or, better yet, go back to whatever hole you crawled out of." It wasn't a suggestion; it was more of a warning.

"And miss catching up with you and your buddies?" Milner responded with a raise of a brow. His dark eyes then slowly and purposefully trailed over Noelle, her skin prickling uncomfortably under his unwanted perusal. What the fuck was it with men who hung around Astros staring at women as if they had never seen a female before? When a sneer of a smirk curled at his lips, Noelle knew whoever this guy was, she didn't want to be around him. "Looks like you got some hotter ones to hang around you, huh?"

Oh god, gross. Noelle's face scrunched in distaste as she felt a hand on her shoulder before Levi's incredibly tall and broad body stood in front of her, shielding her from Milner's sight. On the other side of the car, Noelle saw Carson's glare intensify as he took a step to where Milner stood.

"Look at her again and I'll rip your eyes out," he threatened angrily, almost sounding like a growl with his voice dangerously carrying out the words.

Noelle might have felt uncomfortable the moment Milner's eyes landed on her, but with Levi in front of her and Carson once again defending her, she felt herself relax a bit. The feminist in her wished she didn't have to depend on a guy or two to protect her from another creep, but Noelle knew when to be grateful for having a friend in Levi and a . . . whatever Carson was to her.

"Oh, that's right." She heard Milner speak up once more in a knowing tone where she could just hear the smirk in his tone. "Davey told me some bitch has got you wrapped around her finger. Pathetic, if you ask me."

215

Noelle knew from the match she attended that the Davey Milner was talking about was Boman. If her distaste hadn't been apparent before, it was now with the way her nose wrinkled and eyes narrowed into a glare. She couldn't see Milner thanks to Levi using his body as a shield, but she already wanted to smack the sneer off his face that she just knew was there by the sound of his voice. Milner's words weren't important; all she heard was him calling her a bitch without basis.

"'Ey!" Noelle's eyes widened at Carson's loud voice. It was the most vocal she had ever heard him, watching as he stormed away from the car and to where Milner was. She heard Levi curse under his breath before taking a few steps forward, allowing her to catch sight of Carson face-to-face with Milner around Levi's body. "Don't fucking talk about her like that. You don't want your first night back at Astros to end with a broken nose, Milner, so fuck off and get the hell out of here."

The tension in the area was almost suffocating. Noelle wondered why she was still surprised with shit hitting the fan when it came to her and her friends lingering outside on sidewalks and getting threatened by random men that show up out of nowhere, but this Milner guy wasn't a random dude, which she could clearly see by Carson and even Levi's reactions. Some kind of history was obviously present. There were less than a handful of other people lingering about, but they were minding their own business, save for a few curious glances thrown their way.

Before Milner said anything, Levi walked away from Noelle as she stayed by the car. She watched as he grabbed Carson's shoulder and tried to pull him back. "Come on, Car. You know he isn't worth it."

Milner's attention shifted to Levi, tilting his head ever so slightly as he regarded the blond. "How you doin', Levi?" His lips twitched into a smirk. "Last time we met, you're the one who left with a broken nose, right? Good to see you got that shit fixed."

216

His words unexpectedly made Noelle's jaw drop with her eyes on Levi as she watched the normally smiling man clench his jaw in contained anger. Meanwhile, Noelle's stomach twisted at the knowledge of this Milner guy most likely breaking Levi's nose. Levi was tall and broad, but he wasn't a fighter. She didn't want to know the circumstance that transpired that event, but she did feel the heated prickle of anger at Milner doing that to Levi. Uncharacteristically, Noelle hoped Levi or Carson or any of the other boys hit Milner right back—only ten times harder.

Levi might be a giant, but Noelle couldn't see him throwing punches at all. The fact that someone took a swing at him really pissed her off.

"Yeah?" Levi responded, his own broad shoulders squaring. "Maybe now that you're back, I can finally press charges against you like I planned before you ran out of town like the damn pussy you are."

Noelle's lips parted in a choked gasp. She covered her mouth with one hand because this was totally an inappropriate time to let out the laugh that was threatening to escape. Levi pressing charges against an asshole who broke his nose was definitely not a laughing matter.

Obviously, Milner agreed because he took a warning step closer to Levi while maintaining eye contact with the man who was much taller than him. "The fuck did you just say to me?" Milner spat out.

Noelle inhaled sharply. Men really needed to control their goddamn anger.

"You heard what he said," Carson spoke up, not even acknowledging Levi's hand on his shoulder. Noelle could only see his back as she noticed the rigidness of his shoulders. "You wanna throw a punch? Schedule a fucking match with me, and we'll have it all out. Until then, stay the fuck away from me, my friends, and my girl."

Noelle forgot how to breathe.

217

Time seemed to freeze as she wondered if she had heard him right, if Carson had actually called her his girl, as if he referred to her that way all the damn time. She was aware of her jaw slackening, her mouth and throat drying at his words. The thundering of her heart echoed in her ears, deafening Noelle to her immediate surroundings. Was it just a slip of the tongue? Did Carson actually mean to call her his, or did he not even notice it happen? Noelle couldn't deny the thrilled flutter of her stomach as her mind registered what he said. She hoped to any and every entity out there that Carson meant those two mundane words that held so much more weight than imaginable. This circumstance was clearly not ideal for her to start dissecting and overthinking this; why these guys were getting in each other's faces, but what could she do? Noelle's heart had a lot more power over her mind.

She barely registered Milner's scoff. "Don't worry, you'll get your fucking match." She heard him say. She didn't even acknowledge his departure until Levi and Carson were turning to walk back over after talking amongst themselves for a moment.

My girl. My girl, my girl, my girl.

It wasn't until Carson was standing in front of her that Noelle realized what or who she was looking at. She blinked up at him in an almost confused daze because, wow, this was some information to process. She wanted to know who this Milner guy was, what was his history with Carson and Levi and any of the other boys if there was any, and she so desperately wanted to know if Carson meant what he said or if she was just overthinking it like a freak.

"'M sorry about him," he murmured once he was close enough, an apologetic frown furrowing his brows as he looked down at Noelle as if it was his fault some asshole started mouthing off on them.

Finally breaking out of her reverie, Noelle offered him a reassuring smile, lightly tugging at the hem of his black tee with her fingers as she tilted her head slightly at Carson.

218

"You got nothing to be sorry for, Car," Noelle said, forcing herself to focus more on what was happening than the two words her obsessive mind sunk its fingers in and wouldn't let go of. When he took a breath with the frown still in place, Noelle widened her grin to get him to relax. She flashed her dimples Carson melted at the sight of. "Come on, I owe you that drink."

She felt proud when she saw the light crinkles appear by Carson's eyes as he smiled in response, his stance relaxing from being so tense before. He took one step further and pressed a kiss to the crown of Noelle's head. Her entire body flushed at the sweet gesture as she watched him walk around the car, slightly stunned.

"Wait," Levi's voice suddenly broke through. Noelle would've felt bad for forgetting about his presence if it weren't for the fact that her entire body was tingling from Carson's small kiss. Glancing at Levi, Noelle saw his drawn eyebrows and slightly widened eyes, a finger waving back and forth between her and Carson as he stammered incredulously. "Are you two . . .?"

Noelle rolled her lips into her mouth. This time, her cheeks felt like they were on fire at Levi's probing stare because, really, she didn't even know how to answer his unasked question. She and Carson, in her opinion, were definitely not just friends, and even though they hadn't discussed any of it, she wanted to both go with the flow and also know what the fuck was going on; she was aware of Carson's feelings, to an extent. Noelle knew Carson liked her. He basically admitted it. She wondered if he said anything to anyone else.

Carson merely sighed at his friend as he opened the door. "Get in the car, Levi," he said before ducking inside the vehicle.

When Levi's demanding stare shifted to Noelle, she fumbled for a nervously awkward smile before opening the door and getting in as well, wondering if putting herself in an enclosed space with Levi and Carson was a good idea at all.

*   *   *

219

"So who's Milner?" Noelle questioned, a form of greeting as she reached the bar and stood next to Carson who was waiting for his second beer after Noelle had bought him his first when they arrived. She faced him with her left side leaning against the bar as he leaned his front against it, arms folded on top.

Carson looked at her, taking in the raise of her eyebrows as she looked at him. Noelle knew he expected her to ask the question sooner rather than later, unable to help herself especially after Levi told Max and Aiden about their encounter with Milner. She saw the way their expressions darkened in hostility. Nothing was said after that as the subject was quickly changed, but Noelle was too curious for her own good to let it go so easily.

"A son of a bitch," he responded factually.

A small wry smile tugged at her lips, left elbow propped on the counter. "I gathered that much," Noelle mused. She glanced to her right where everyone else sat at the booth, their laughter and chatter mingling with the rest of the bar along with the music playing. The colors of the neon signs planted on the walls of the bar reflected against the patrons gathered, washing them in reds and purples and blues. Her eyebrows lowered slightly and her gaze was on the blue-eyed boy at the table. "Did he seriously break Levi's nose?" she asked Carson.

A long sigh escaped through Carson's nose as he straightened, nodding his thanks to the bartender as his pint of beer was placed in front of him. "Yeah," he answered with a clench of his jaw. Noelle could see him starting to get riled up about it once more. "Gave Max a black eye once too."

"Jeez," Noelle breathed out with wide eyes, unsure if she should be surprised or not. Just five minutes with Milner, and she could tell the guy had some serious issues, especially with Carson and the boys. "Is it bad that I hope you guys hit him back?"

Noelle knew her dislike of violence was changing ever since she met Carson because the sight of him in the ring got a kind of reaction out of her that she had never felt before. The way his body curved and moved when he was fighting was mesmerizing, and she wondered if she should be worried that the sight of people fighting was now something she enjoyed. She felt as though she could watch Carson fight all day, but if a hit were to land on him, Noelle knew to expect a wave of fright and worry to wash over her.

Carson's lips tilted into a small smirk behind the rim of his glass, his throat bobbing up and down as he drank the beer. "You know I did," he hummed as he set his glass down. Carson turned to face Noelle, peering down at her with dark eyes glinting under the bright, neon lights of the bar as he tilted his head slightly. "But I don't think Milner's all you wanna talk about right now."

My girl.

Noelle's heart thumped in her chest, but she somehow managed to maintain a cool façade though she felt her neck tighten in anticipation. She had most definitely been wondering about Carson's words since he uttered them about twenty five minutes ago; it was amusing how crazy she could drive herself over the course of less than half an hour in regards to something the man she was so fucking into said. While Noelle thought Carson had experienced a slip of the tongue, him knowingly bringing it up told her loud and clear that he knew exactly what he said.

Oh god. Noelle could feel her stomach being tickled as if butterflies were let loose, and it so didn't help that Carson was looking at her as if he could see right through her. She knew she had joked a while back that she was easy to figure out, to read, but when Carson was so blatantly doing it, Noelle felt the urge to turn away from him because she was hesitant of letting him find out just how much she liked him. Mostly out of anxiety that he didn't like her back as much, but when Carson locked his gaze with her, it was hopeless for Noelle to try and look away.

Still, she couldn't help but give in to the embarrassed heat of her cheeks as she—god knows how—maintained eye contact. "I don't know what you're talking about," Noelle bullshitted. She

221

realized briefly at that moment that she had a habit of talking in circles with Carson.

Of course, he saw right through her. Carson let out a breathy scoff of a laugh, his left arm moving to slide around Noelle's waist to pull her closer. He caught her slightly off guard as the action pressed their chests up together. Her breath caught in her throat, tilting her head back to look up at him despite the excited knots her stomach was tying itself into.

"It wasn't something I just let slip, Ellie."

She felt like melting. That was the first time Carson referred to her by her nickname, and she prayed it wouldn't be the last. It was so fucking soft. Staying silent, Noelle swallowed inaudibly when she watched Carson's eyes flicker around her face and the corners of his lips curling upwards as he leaned his head down a bit. All she could smell was him.

Noelle's nimble fingers once again played with the hem of Carson's shirt, twisting and twirling the soft material as the world around them seemed to slip away. How could he read her mind so damn easily?

"I don't remember asking for that kind of title," Noelle teased in a meek attempt to not give away her delighted nervousness.

Carson grinned, a full-on smile that crinkled the corners of his eyes and showed off his perfect teeth before he bit down on his lower lip while still smiling as Noelle didn't even try to calm her suddenly erratic heart at the sight. She wished he smiled more, the kind of smile that lit up his dark eyes and softened his features, because it was already becoming one of her favorite things to look at. He smiled and suddenly every weight that fell upon Noelle's shoulders lifted just for those few moments, and she savored it.

She felt Carson's left hand slide to her lower back as he pushed her closer and upwards to minimize the distance between them while watching Carson's hooded gaze drop to her lips. His tongue swiped his lower one, and Noelle had to refrain herself from just kissing him right there. When his eyes met hers once more, Carson's voice dropped to a murmur as he squeezed his hand against her back.

"It's yours to take."

Noelle's heart dropped to her stomach at his words, quiet and honest and only for her to hear. *How did all of this happen so quickly?* Noelle asked herself. In, what, a matter of a month or so, they went from being complete strangers to whatever the hell they were doing now, and Noelle absolutely had no complaints. She was dizzy with her feelings for Carson and how they were standing pressed up against each other with no care in the world.

Which was why, when those words left Carson's mouth, Noelle took in a quiet, almost shuddering breath before propping herself on her toes and pressing her lips to his. Her eyes fluttered shut at the first anticipated touch. His response was immediate, tilting his head to not even waste a moment as he deepened the kiss. His tongue brushed the seam of Noelle's lips as she parted them without hesitation and dove into the taste of him as well as the beer he drank. Her hands slid up before she pressed them against Carson's cheeks, absolutely loving how they felt in her palms as the mild stubble he was sporting scratched against her chin. Noelle was surprised she could even stay upright as her head spun.

Carson's hand went from her back and lowered it until it was pressed against the swell of her ass, his touch igniting a fire even through the shorts she was wearing. Noelle let out a startled laugh against his mouth when she felt him cheekily give her a squeeze. He grinned against her lips, and Noelle couldn't help but let out a content sigh through her nose as she realized that according to Carson's words, she could do this all day.

"I knew it!"

Unfortunately, it seemed that Levi wasn't going to grant her that luxury as his loud voice rang throughout the bar and over the music. Carson grunted before reluctantly pulling his lips away

223

from Noelle's inviting ones. He wanted to smirk at how Noelle chased his lips with her own before her eyes dazedly opened, and she pouted up at him. Carson held in a groan at the inviting sight.

His heart was pounding in his chest, something that rarely happened to him when it came to a girl but he knew to expect something with Noelle as his lips begged to kiss hers again. He stopped himself, turning to look at the table where his friends were and catching sight of all of them staring at them incredulously, except Beverly who had a satisfied smile on her face. The boys' expressions, however, ranged from disbelief to downright astonishment.

Looking at Levi, Carson raised an unimpressed brow. "I totally knew there was something going on!" Levi shouted while pointing at them accusingly.

Pulling herself out of her reverie, Noelle raised her eyebrows at the seemingly proud Levi, her cheeks warm from the afterglow of kissing Carson. He sighed as he picked up the glass with his free hand before he nudged her to walk over, his hand sliding up to her back as he followed behind her. They reached the table in time for Max to guffaw at Levi.

"Since when?"

Slowly lowering his finger as Noelle and Carson stood at the end of the table, Levi smiled sheepishly. "Half an hour ago," he admitted.

Noelle pressed her lips together to keep in her laugh, though the smile couldn't be kept off her face as Carson draped an arm around her shoulders after she retrieved her beer from the table and took a sip. The weight of his arm was so comforting, but the sight of his tattooed hand and wrist was knee weakening. And those rings on his fingers? Noelle had to bite the inside of her cheek because she shouldn't be this attracted to a man's hand.

The boys all stared at Levi in bewilderment while Beverly snorted, leaning back in the booth. "I knew for, like, weeks so fuck outta here, Levi," she stated smugly and triumphantly.

"What?" Aiden laughed, staring at his girlfriend with wide eyes. "And you didn't say anything?" Before she could answer, his hazel eyes flickered up to Carson as he leaned forward. "How come you never said anything?"

Max scoffed, pressed against the wooden wall at the end of the booth as he lazily gestured to Carson. "Since when have you known Car to be vocal about his feelings? Other than when he's in the ring?"

Noelle rolled her lips into her mouth, though she was still smiling. *He's been pretty vocal about his other feelings to me*, Noelle thought.

"Fuck off," Carson retorted, though there was a light laugh in his voice. "Just because I don't have heart-to-hearts with you, doesn't mean I'm incapable of them."

Noelle couldn't keep the snort from escaping as she tilted her head up at him, raising an amused eyebrow. "Are you saying we've had heart-to-hearts? Because that's a lie."

"Really?" Carson hummed, tilting his own head away as he squinted up at the ceiling, like he was seriously considering something. Then he looked down at Noelle before smirking. "I think that night at the bookstore and last night were all pretty emotional."

A disbelieving yet airy laugh escaped Noelle as she widened her eyes at Carson, amused at the teasing raise of his eyebrows and the way he so casually referenced the two intimate moments between them. She didn't mind though because it was a beautiful reminder that this was reality and those events had actually transpired; that he wasn't just that tough fighter she met and was someone who had a soft, kind side she was lucky enough to experience; and that she didn't just imagine or dream up the dizzying kisses she had shared with Carson—or, in last night's case, been given by Carson.

"Wait, last night?" Beverly sat up, interrupting the small grins Carson and Noelle were sharing as they looked at the blonde

225

who was leaning forward and staring up at the two with narrowed, accusatory eyes. "What happened last night?"

"Oh god," Noelle muttered, unable to stop herself from hiding her smile in Carson's side, pressing her face against his shirt as she felt his body shake with slight chuckles. She had completely neglected telling Beverly what happened last night when Carson showed up at their house since Beverly stayed at Aiden's, and Noelle hadn't talked to her until they got to Astros. It wasn't something she wanted to tell her sister through texts or at a fight. Hell, even Andrea didn't know that Carson had been over that night. So far, Noelle kept it to herself like it was her own little secret to hold.

Levi, on the other hand, was smirking at Beverly's increasing curiosity. "Guess you don't know everything, huh, Bev?" he remarked, shooting her a look.

When she heard her sister let out a low growl of complaint, Noelle took in a deep breath—inhaling Carson's pleasantly familiar scent—as he squeezed her shoulders in amusement. Beverly was totally not going to let her off the hook.

CHAPTER EIGHTEEN

A groan sounded from behind Noelle. "Alright, now, you're just teasing me on purpose."

Grinning, a blush spread across Noelle's cheeks as she straightened to stand properly. She turned around to catch sight of Carson standing right behind her. She saw the appreciative look in his eyes before his lips tilted into a smirk, and she clicked her tongue at him while crossing her arms.

"You're not allowed behind the counter if you don't work here," Noelle retorted, eyeing where he stood.

She stayed in her spot as Carson raised an unimpressed eyebrow, taking two steps towards her in the limited space until he was towering over her smaller frame. His tattooed hands gripped her hips to pull her towards him. Noelle let him without argument, looking up at the Australian.

"What if I've got an in with one of the owners?" Carson mused in a low voice.

Noelle knew it was unprofessional of her to cozy up to Carson behind the counter during business hours, but his touch over her clothes was burning into her skin and, really, she could never think straight with him so close to her. After weeks of only seeing him as someone standoffish and only getting physical when it came to violence, Noelle reveled happily in Carson being flirtatious and getting his hands on her in any way he could. It was such a fucking good change.

Before Noelle could say anything, like tease Carson that just because he more or less lay his claim on her three nights ago didn't mean he could hope over the counter, he continued to answer his own question.

"She's dating my best friend, so I don't think she'll mind," he teased, smirk widening into a shit-eating grin.

It took a second for his words to register in Noelle's mind as she blinked up at him in mild bewilderment. When she noticed the mirth in his eyes and the words referring to Beverly instead of her clicked in her mind, Noelle let out an affronted scoff as she stepped back with a dismissing swat to his chest. Carson let out a laugh as she tried to move away, his grip on her hips keeping her in place as she playfully glared at him.

"Get out of here," she declared with a shake of her head, though she made no other move to push him back or get away herself.

"You know I'm kidding, darling." Carson laughed, and Noelle pondered if her heart would ever stop doing a flip at Carson referring to her by cute pet names that melted her from the inside. "'M here to see you before I go to work. Brought you coffee—cream and sugar, right?"

It was then when Noelle noticed the plastic coffee cups from Dunkin Donuts resting on the counter—she mentioned it a few nights ago how she preferred their coffee over Starbucks—and the smile was back on her face in full force as she looked back at Carson.

"I thought you had a reputation to maintain of not being a romantic?" she hummed, arms wrapping around his waist as she tilted her head back to look up at him. "You're just destroying it yourself, you know."

Carson smirked, lowering his head as he bumped his nose with hers. "Ask me if I give a shit, doll," he rasped before slanting his lips over hers.

Noelle couldn't help the giggle as she kissed him back, muffled by Carson's lips. Pushing herself up on her toes, Noelle wrapped her arms around his neck to keep him close. She tasted a mix of his minty toothpaste and the bitter coffee he had been drinking, not too surprised she liked the combination. It was a taste of Carson; of course she liked it.

When Carson tried to deepen the kiss, Noelle reluctantly pulled away. She put herself back on her feet as Carson groaned at the loss. She let out a laugh as he opened his eyes.

"Sorry, bub." She smiled, her heart skipping a beat as she used the term. Her right hand slid around, so her thumb could brush along his soft lips, lightly wiping away the lipstick that made his lips seem pinker. "Not here."

Carson let out a long sigh, his arms going around her shoulders and hands linking before he quirked an eyebrow with a mischievous glint in his eyes. "Then how about tonight?"

Noelle fought her grin from widening, her heart thumping as she was momentarily reminded of Carson's promise of having every intention of finishing what he started a few nights ago. "I would, but I've got plans with Camille," she told him, looking up at him as her fingers lightly trailed up and down his back. "You free tomorrow?"

"Yeah. I finish training around seven," Carson answered, catching sight of someone approaching from his peripheral before pulling away from Noelle. "You have a customer."

Carson noticed the smile on her face was ever present, genuine as she and the customer engaged in small talk about the books she was scanning. He wasn't surprised that Noelle seemed to know what each of the books were about, an excited gleam in her eyes as she talked about them to the equally interested customer.

It was alarming how much he liked her. It happened in a matter of days, didn't it? How his initial indifference—maybe annoyance, but that just rightfully made him feel like an ass—had so easily transformed into not being able to keep his eyes and hands

229

off her or keep from adoring the sound of her laugh. Carson was aware that, at first, his growing feelings for Noelle were a lot too quickly, but just as fast as his feelings developed, he accepted them. Why try to win a fight he knew he would lose? While Carson hated losing, he didn't mind it this time.

"So who're you up against in your next match?" Noelle's voice pulled Carson out of his musings, prompting him to look at her facing him once more. She was leaning against the counter as she picked up the coffee he bought for her.

"Arnie Lance," Carson answered, knowing the name meant nothing to Noelle. "Decent fighter. Should be fun."

Noelle chuckled before having to turn around to tend to another customer. Carson pulled out his phone to check the time, realizing he would be late to work if he didn't leave now. So he stood up and came up behind Noelle just as she bid the customer goodbye, reaching for his own coffee as he pressed his lips to her temple.

"I'll talk to you later, yeah? Have fun tonight," he murmured, squeezing her hip with his free hand.

She hummed, his soft gestures leaving her breathless as her eyes followed Carson walking around the counter and towards the door with an all- straight back and broad shoulders as she enjoyed his lingering scent for a moment. Noelle watched as Carson opened the door, her smile reappearing when he looked at her over his shoulder and threw her a quick grin. The giddy feeling bubbling in her stomach stayed long after Carson was gone.

*   *   *

Noelle hadn't expected her night to go slightly downhill after having dinner with Camille and a few of their other friends. She had been having fun. At home, she got ready before bidding goodbye to Andrea who was off to a summer camp in New Jersey for the next month before stuffing herself silly with some hibachi

230

and enjoying the company of Camille, Sera, and Tanya especially since she hadn't seen the latter two for a while. They had gotten dressed up, gotten dinner and then dessert at a nearby Cheesecake Factory before going to DUMBO in Brooklyn to take pictures in front of the water and Brooklyn Bridge. It had been fun; Noelle was having a blast, laughing and snapping picture after picture until it was nearing eleven o'clock and they decided to head home because it was a weekday after all.

It wasn't until after Sera and Tanya bid goodbye to walk to where they found parking for Sera's car and the other two were headed to where Noelle parked hers that things took a turn. Her car was on a back road behind a building full of restaurants. Just as she and Camille approached it, one of the back doors of the building opened and out stepped a guy Noelle had only seen once but had made enough of an impression to allow her to forget him so easily.

"Ah, Hayes's girl, aren't ya?" Milner mused knowingly once his eyes landed on her, slowing his walk down just as Noelle did. Her hand lightly grasped Camille's wrist to keep her from walking. Noelle took in a breath, wondering why this shit kept happening to her. "Can't say I mind running into you. Or your friend."

When his eyes trailed appreciatively over both girls, Noelle and Camille's faces scrunched in distaste. They exchanged glances of exasperation. There weren't many people around at the narrow street they were on, and the only lights were the ones filtering out of the ground floor windows of the buildings they were in between. Noelle hoped someone would walk by or out if things got . . . difficult.

"Good for you," Noelle responded before using her grip on Camille to usher her towards the street so she could walk around to the passenger's side of her parked car. Camille shot her a silent questioning look as she went, wondering who the hell this guy was. "Unfortunately, we gotta go."

231

Her heart thumped when she tried to reach the door with keys in her hand but stopping short when Milner smoothly got in her way.

"What's the rush?" He tilted his head, his voice cool as his left hand was pressed against the window of her door. Noelle could see Camille's eyes widening. The sixth sense women seemed to have alerted them of a threat that was seemingly going off for both of them. "I just wanna chat."

Noelle's jaw clenched, her body rigid in alert. "About Carson?" she shot back.

A grin stretched across Milner's thin lips, though the sight of it did nothing to rid of the unease Noelle was feeling around him. In all of Brooklyn—in all of New York—why did she have to be in the same place as this guy? Milner lifted his chin slightly as he regarded her.

"Smart girl."

"Smart enough to know to stay away from you," Noelle sharply responded as she grabbed the car door handle and tried to open it despite his hand still on the window. "Get your hands off my car."

When she tried to open her door, a startled gasp escaped Noelle as Milner's free hand shot out to grab her wrist. His grip was not even in the same neighborhood as gentle. Her jaw loosened in pain at Milner's tight grasp, his large hand wrapping around her wrist and squeezing it. She genuinely feared that he would snap her bones. Camille, from the other side of the car, let out a protesting exclamation of her own as she noticed Noelle's grimace.

"Hey, get your hands off of her!" Camille demanded, though Noelle detected the panic wavering in her voice. "I'll call the cops."

"You got somewhere to be?" Milner questioned in a steady voice, utterly ignorant of the fact that Camille had spoken. Noelle picked up the controlled anger behind Milner's tone. This was crazy. What the hell was he angry for? Just because he had seen her

232

with Carson didn't mean he could get in her face and nearly break her damn wrist. She watched with wide eyes as a mocking knowing look dawned on Milner's face as he nodded slowly. "Oh, right. Probably off to see Hayes, aren't ya?"

Noelle clenched her jaw as he gave a squeeze to her wrist, trying with all her might not to show the pain or fear he was successfully instilling while her heart pounded in a way she hadn't felt in years. It was thundering against her ribcage, provoked by the same kind of fear she had felt once more when she was in the hospital, waiting to find out the fate of her father and sister. This time, Noelle's dry mouth and hammering heart were in honest-to-God terror of her wrist snapping because this man in front of her was angry and he was an actual fighter. Noelle would be flat-out lying if she didn't feel even the slightest bit fearful of her life right now.

She didn't get to respond to Milner, too frozen in shock and pain, but he continued along in a dark tone that had her nerves standing on edge.

"When you see him, tell him I'll be waiting for our match." Noelle's eyes were glued to his, knowing that he could probably see the alarm in them, but she somehow maintained their gaze. She looked into his dark eyes that weren't nearly as comforting and lovely as Carson's were. She knew he was aware that he was freaking her out because his lips curled into a near sadistic smirk as if he was getting off on instilling such panic in her. When he leaned closer, Noelle instinctively moved back while wincing at his grip. "And this time, he's gonna be the one crawling out of the ring with broken bones."

Noelle felt her body freeze at his words. The pain in her wrist was pushed to the side as she saw the dangerously serious look in Milner's eyes. He wasn't joking, not in the least. His threat against Carson was successfully planting and growing a seed of justified terror. It wasn't just a threat; it was a promise of revenge.

When Milner shoved her hand away with a force that caused Noelle to stumble as her hip hit the car, she felt her heart in her throat as he literally smirked in satisfaction. The entire encounter probably lasted just a minute or so, but the way Noelle's heart began to race and the terror that sank in her bones made it seem like it dragged on. What kind of low-life man enjoyed hurting a woman? She glared after Milner, which didn't faze him in the slightest as his warning eyes went from her to Camille before he turned around and walked off, tall and proud for intimidating two women.

It wasn't until he disappeared down the block and moved out of sight around the corner that Noelle released a long shuddering breath as she pressed herself against her car. Her left hand came up to lightly brush along her right wrist where the dull ache of Milner's hand still remained.

Noelle's heart was hammering so loudly in her ears that she didn't even hear Camille's hurried footsteps until her best friend was right in front of her, blue eyes widened in fright.

"Holy fuck, Noelle! Are you okay?" she hastily asked, casting her gaze down to Noelle's hand. "Shit, how hard did he grab you?" she gasped, cursing softly. Camille's phone was in her hand as if she truly had been ready to call the police.

A bewildered, disbelieving daze had fallen upon Noelle as her mind tried to process what had just happened. She blinked down at her wrist in mild confusion as she also tried to make sense of Camille's words. Her unplanned confrontation with Milner had Noelle's thought process become blanketed in a layer of numb discombobulation, a shocked ringing in her ears as if she had been hit in the head a bunch of times. Only it was her wrist that was in pain.

She followed Camille's slightly horrified gaze, her reaction slow until her eyes landed on her wrist. The glow of the streetlamp above them showed the barely-there marks that were reddening on her skin. Noelle bruised like a peach, so the near-instant appearance of the bruises-in-the-making wasn't a surprise, though it did take a moment for her mind to catch up with the fact that these were signs of someone practically manhandling her—signs of Milner searing her skin without her consent.

"Noelle, hey." Camille snapped her out of her thoughts, causing Noelle to finally look at her worried best friend. "Who the hell was that? Does he know Carson? Are you okay?"

Her last question was stressed, ducking her head slightly so her eyes met Noelle's determinedly. "I'm fine," Noelle responded slowly, almost unsurely because if she was being honest, she wasn't fine. She was shaken from Milner's words and actions, her eyes dropping to her wrist as she noticed the imprint of his hand angrily standing out against her skin. "W-we should go home," Noelle stammered as she let out a deep breath, her heart still pounding in her chest.

Camille kept her gaze on Noelle, the concern swimming in her bright blue eyes because she was still reeling from what had just happened too and had so many questions that she didn't think Noelle could answer right now.

"Okay," Camille said instead. "Do you want me to drive?"

"No." Noelle shook her head, throat working as she swallowed inaudibly. She clutched her keys in her palm as the metal bit into her skin while telling her heart to calm the fuck down. Milner was gone by now, so why did her insides feel like they were shriveling up and her heart wasn't slowing down? "I-I'll drive. Let's go."

The car ride was silent other than the radio playing the top hits, the music only serving the purpose to fill the gap Camille might have used to ask questions. As Noelle drove, each ray of light from the buildings or streetlamps they drove by washed over her wrist. Her attention was constantly being drawn to the reddening marks where the muscle still ached with a dull throb.

235

When Noelle pulled up in front of Camille's house, the blue-eyed girl didn't move. "Are you gonna tell me what that was about? I'm kinda freaking out over here, Elle," she asked.

Noelle squeezed her eyes shut and clenched the steering wheel, releasing a deep breath as she found her voice. "Not tonight, Cami." She met her friend's disapproving stare. "I'll tell you later. I just . . . I wanna go home."

There was only one person Noelle wanted to talk about this with, and she wasn't sure how she should go about telling him.

When Camille finally and reluctantly got out of the car and bid goodnight, Noelle drove off to her house. She tried her best to obey the speed laws, but she wanted to get home quickly. Noelle's ears were ringing as she stepped inside, absentmindedly greeting her mother who was sitting on the couch watching TV and drinking a cup of coffee as she was dressed to go to work at this time of the night.

Noelle didn't care where Beverly was; she was probably at Aiden's or something as she headed straight for her room. Her lungs burned for a breath she didn't inhale until the door was shut behind her.

The last thing she wanted to do was call Carson. She didn't want to bother him by informing him of what happened, but she knew she had to. There was obviously some serious bad blood between him and Milner, and she knew Carson would be pissed if she kept this from him. So she pulled out her phone and held it in her right hand, which wouldn't stop shaking. The sight of the marks on her wrist were even redder because all of the blood that was gathering under the skin, which frustrated her so she switched her phone to her left hand instead.

Sitting on the edge of the bed as the line trilled, Noelle's knee bounced uncontrollably. Her breath got caught in her throat when the line picked up, and Carson's voice sounded through the speaker.

"Hey, you done already?"

236

Noelle pressed her lips together as the sound of his accented voice was somewhat succeeding in calming her erratic heart, which she couldn't at least do.

"Yeah," she breathed out, clearing her throat when it got caught. "We . . . I, uh, just got home."

She could hear how unsteady her voice was, so she shouldn't have been shocked with Carson's immediate response. "Noelle, what's wrong?"

Glancing down at her wrist, Noelle tried to turn her hand over and, shit, she hated herself when she felt her eyes burning with tears she wasn't aware she had been holding back. The bruises on her skin hurt, yeah, but not enough to draw tears. She knew she wasn't crying because of the pain; she was scared and intimidated by Milner's presence and words and grip, and even if she was in the comfort of her own bedroom, the fear that had balled up in her throat was finally taking over and she let out a choked breath.

"I saw Milner."

*   *   *

Carson was seeing red.

Fire had sparked in his blood the second Noelle told him she ran into Milner, intensifying with rage when she told him what he said and what he did. By the time Carson picked up on the shallow breathing and sniffles from Noelle's end, which was an obvious indicator that she was crying, all bets were off and Carson had snatched up his keys and slammed his apartment door shut. He headed to the one place he knew Milner would be. He was also aware that he was definitely playing into Milner's taunts, but Carson didn't care—not when Noelle was involved, not when Milner thought he could get away with confronting her for no goddamn reason other than to get under Carson's skin. Well, mission fucking accomplished.

The short drive to Astros only served to let Carson's bubbling anger grow, his palms stinging from his death grip on the steering wheel and jaw beginning to ache from how tightly he was clenching it. It was all he could do to control his rage, to not let his utterly pissed off mood make him run over a pedestrian or crash into another car. He couldn't help it. He was furious that Milner had the audacity to talk to Noelle, to fucking touch her without her consent and threaten her as a way to get to Carson. He was not going to let that fucking go.

When he arrived at Astros and allowed a sliver of patience to park his car in the only available tight spot, Carson threw open the doors to Astros, not even acknowledging how the heavy doors slammed against the wall or the looks he was receiving from the handful of people there. His entrance was overpowering their training session and the music playing, but as soon as their eyes landed on him and landed on the unfiltered dangerous aura he was radiating and the wrathful scowl twisting his features, they all knew not to get in a very pissed off Carson Hayes' way.

"Where's Milner?" he demanded as he took a few steps inside the building, not catching sight of his victim amongst the men there. When no one responded and only continued to throw wary glances his way, Carson's already thinning patience snapped. "Where is he?!" he roared, clenching his fists.

His voice bounced off the walls and deafened the music, his shoulders shaking as his blunt nails dug into his palm as he waited for an answer.

"He's taking a smoking break out back," one of the men Carson didn't recognize, nor cared for, answered.

Carson didn't need to be told twice. His movements were sharp as he stormed across the building, his narrowed eyes only having tunnel vision as his gaze locked on the door leading towards the back alley where he often took his own smoking break. The door rattled on its hinges as Carson pushed it open and stepped out

238

into the alley, his gaze immediately landing on the dickhead he was on the hunt for.

The banging of the door caught Milner's attention as he leaned against the wall and a half-finished cigarette between his fingers while he raised an eyebrow at Carson. The smell of trash and nicotine was overpowered by the blood boiling in Carson's veins, by the echoing sounds of Noelle's hesitant tears in his ears as Carson made his way to Milner without a moment's pause, not letting him register what was happening as Carson drew his fist back as he neared him and let it fly forward so his knuckles and rings came in contact with the bone of Milner's jaw.

The anger and adrenaline were taking over every part of Carson's being, not allowing him to register the sting in his fingers because fighting with rings was not a good idea, but he couldn't give a single fuck. Milner stumbled with a grunt, his cigarette dropping to the ground as his back slammed against the wall. Carson didn't give him any time to prepare as his hands fisted the front of his shirt to hold him up before letting his left hand deliver a second punch to Milner's jaw, this time letting him fall right to the ground.

"The fuck did I tell you about staying away from her?" Carson snarled, his accented voice thick with vengeance as Milner struggled to his feet as a glare of his own on his features. "I'm gonna break your fucking hands for putting them on her," Carson added as he stalked near Milner in the wide alley.

He watched as Milner spat the crimson liquid on the ground as he stood up, wiping his mouth with the back of his hand as his gaze met Carson's.

"Just wanted to send you a little message, Hayes." He shrugged, his lips curling into a smirk that showed off his blood-stained teeth. "No harm in that."

Carson's body was on fire from the rage fueling him. He wasn't one who took threats and throws against his family and friends lightly. When one of the people who he couldn't stand

239

blatantly got in the face and bruised his girl? Carson was blind to everything except the unadulterated fury he was keen on letting out on Milner.

"You wanna send me a message? Face me like a man," Carson said angrily, almost sounding like a growl. "Don't even think about going near her."

Milner's smirk turned mocking. "Unfair that you get to keep that little tight piece for yourself."

Carson's jaw locked. He wouldn't be surprised if he left with his fingers broken from ring-impacted punches.

∗   ∗   ∗

The dishwasher clicked shut after Noelle put in her dirty plate, having just eaten a slice of the chocolate cake Beverly had gotten for kicks the last time she went grocery shopping. It was nearing midnight and Noelle was alone at the house. Her mom just left to go to work, Beverly was spending the night once more at Aiden's, and Andrea was at a sleepover a couple houses down. Noelle didn't mind being alone. Sure, she was still a bit shaken from what happened earlier with Milner with the forming bruises on her skin as a reminder, but she would rather not explain anything to her family when she could just sit by herself.

She had told Carson what happened, down to the last word Milner said and the grip he had on her. Noelle could still recall the shivers that ran down her spine at Carson's darkened tone after hearing what she had to say, promising that he would see her later before hanging up. She knew Carson probably went to see Milner. She knew, from what she knew of Carson and what she had seen of Milner, that things had the high potential of turning ugly, but all she could do was sit in her house and let her knee bounce with worry and teeth nibble on her nails as she wondered what was going on right then.

Distracting herself by eating cake and trying to watch her show weren't working out too well, and Noelle had to stop herself multiple times from reaching for her phone and texting Carson to check in. They had only officially gotten together just a few days ago. She didn't want to seem annoying, but she couldn't help but stew in her anxiousness.

It was fifteen minutes past midnight when the doorbell ringing had her jumping from where she sat on the couch. Her heart was hammering for some reason as she paused the TV and got up, hurriedly making her way over to the front door. Noelle didn't even pause to ask who was on the other side, which would've been smart since it was past midnight. Instead, she unlocked the door and swung it open. Her heart was suddenly in her throat when she registered the sight in front of her.

"Told you I'd see you later." Carson grinned lazily.

It wasn't his presence or smile that had Noelle's stomach lurching. It was the fact that he had to lean against the doorframe to keep himself up, the cut across his right cheekbone where blood was gathered, staining his skin, and the way his hands—the knuckles angrily red and blotchy—were clutching his left side. The breath stilled in Noelle's lungs as her eyes trailed over every wrinkle in his shirt, the tousle of his mild curls, and most importantly, the blood sticking to his beautiful golden skin.

"Carson," Noelle breathed out, her grip on the doorknob tightening as she felt her heart beginning to pick up its pace. "Oh my god! W-what happened?"

She knew what happened; of course she did, but that didn't stop her from asking as she quickly muttered a quiet 'come here' before gently taking his right arm and placing it around her shoulders to help him inside. Noelle was used to carrying Andrea's weight, so even though Carson was significantly heavier than her, she didn't find it too difficult to hold him up. She didn't care if his weight was crushing her; he was hurt and the only thing on Noelle's mind was trying to find a way to make him feel better.

241

"I'm fine, love," Carson reassured, though the slight strain in his voice told her a different story once the door was shut and she was helping Carson further into the house. "Nothin' that's never happened before. Just need t' sit down."

Noelle's own breathing was growing shallow from the worry twisting her stomach, the tips of her left fingers grazing Carson's hand that was still holding his side.

"You're bleeding and practically limping, Car. You're not fine."

She had so many questions about what went down and how he managed to get here from wherever he was in the state he was in. Seeing Carson in fights at Astros was one thing, but this was completely different. This wasn't a scheduled match. He hadn't won money off of it. While she had seen him battered and bruised, she had never seen him unable to completely support his own weight. He wasn't dragging his feet nor was he falling over, but it was obvious his side was hurt, hindering him from walking properly.

He didn't say anything in regards to her words. "Can we go to your room?" he responded instead.

Noelle bit her lip as she casted a glance towards the stairs before looking up at Carson. The muscle in his jaw was jumping and the tension in his neck was obvious as his Adam's apple bobbed.

"Can you make it up the stairs?"

Carson nodded, his curls falling across his forehead as he straightened. She saw him squeeze his eyes shut for a brief moment as he put more pressure from his hand to his side, then inhaling sharply through his teeth before he took the first step towards the stairs. Noelle instantly walked along with him.

Getting up the stairs wasn't as much of a struggle as she had worried, Carson's boots thudding heavily on the steps as he let go of his side to use the railing for additional support just in case. Noelle could hear him breathing through his nose, her heart twisting at the thought of this being even the slightest bit of struggle for him. Carson was always so quick, so effortless in his movements. She would be lying if she said having to help him up the stairs wasn't causing a dull ache in her chest.

He got hurt because of her. She knew it may be irrational for her to take all the blame because it was Milner that did this, and while Noelle hoped Carson sent him worse off, she still hated seeing him in this state.

"We should clean you up," Noelle murmured once they reached the top of the stairs and made their way down the hall. "Let's go to the bathroom, okay?"

"Yeah, okay," Carson breathed raspily, allowing Noelle to take them to the bathroom across the hall from her bedroom.

Once inside, Noelle had Carson sit on the closed toilet seat, hearing him grunt as he leaned back and tilted his face upwards. He closed his eyes with a slight furrow in his brows. Under the bright lights, she saw the blood already drying on the long cut, and despite the presence of the crimson liquid, she could see that the wound wasn't that deep; thankfully, just long in length.

Since her mother was a doctor, there were first aid kits in every room of the house, so Noelle pulled it out of the cabinet under the sink and made sure there were bandages and antiseptic cream to be used before pulling out a clean rag from the cabinet by the shower.

"I'm gonna clean the cut, Car," she informed him softly as she crouched in front of the dark-eyed man. She looked up at him from her position as she rested her hands on his knees. "That okay?"

He nodded, opening his eyes as he gave her a small half smile. He looked as tired as Noelle expected. He was just silent as his dark eyes watched her, breathing calmly as Noelle stood up to bring the first aid kit over. She didn't want him to stand even if she needed him to be near the sink to clean the wound. Instead, Noelle found a small plastic container and filled it with cool water and soap before also bringing those over with a soft, soaked washcloth in hand and putting it on the thick rim of the bathtub next to them.

Noelle knew she would have to crouch over him because of his seated position, but as if Carson had been reading her mind, he looked up at her.

"It'll be easier if you sit on my lap, sweetheart," he said.

Her eyes flickered to meet his, widening slightly with worry as she glanced at his left side that he had been holding. "But your si—"

"'S okay, Ellie." The softness in his voice had her breath faltering accompanied by that same small smile tilting at the corners of his lips. She couldn't believe how handsome, so effortlessly gorgeous he looked at this moment even though he was hurt. "Trust me, I've been worse."

As if that makes me feel any better.

When she hesitated, Carson pushed himself up against the toilet a bit more, not even wincing as he did so even though a sharp pain spread from his side, courtesy of the kick Milner had delivered. Carson knew he had no broken bones, but it still hurt like a bitch. He patted his jean-covered thighs.

"Sit."

She pressed her lips together, wondering if it was the appropriate time to feel her heart hammer in her chest as she moved forward and spread her legs just enough before carefully settling down on Carson's lap. Noelle straddled him, the material of his jeans rough against her own bare thighs thanks to the night shorts she wore, her lack of underwear and the material of the shorts too thin for her to not feel the jeans against her pathetically clothed center.

Fucking hell. Not right now, she scolded herself, but her thoughts were hard to control when she felt Carson loosely grip her hips. Noelle's gaze flickered down to his hands. Shit, she loved the bracelets and rings he wore on his tattooed wrists and fingers, but she also made a mental note to get him ice for the bruises on his knuckles.

With a dry mouth, Noelle finally looked back at Carson. She felt her breath catch as his dark eyes instantly met her hazel ones. Once again, it was like he was staring into her soul as Noelle brought up the damp rag in her right hand, and though it still twinged a bit in pain after having iced it, it was surprisingly steady. She used her left to allow her fingers to cup his stubbly chin.

"What happened?" she asked again, her voice soft and quiet as if to not disturb the silence of the house and the one that comfortably existed between them.

The white rag was pinkening with Carson's blood as he let out a sharp breath through his nose. "Fucker pulled out a blade on me," he responded, the exasperation and underlying anger clear in his tone. "I knocked it out before he could swing it again."

Noelle swallowed inaudibly as her brows twitched into a frown. While she was glad Carson had gotten rid of the blade before any more damage could be done, she also wished he had never gotten this cut in the first place. She wished none of this ever happened. When she efficiently got rid of the blood on his skin, Noelle let out a shaky breath while turning Carson's head to face her again.

"I'm sorry this happened," she mumbled.

Carson pulled together, not liking the guilt he could hear in her voice. He knew that she knew this wasn't her fault, that his confrontation with Milner would have happened for one reason or another, but he did hate that it occurred because Noelle was thrown in the middle of it. He would have happily kicked Milner's ass whenever he felt like it, but Noelle getting involved stirred a painful discomfort in Carson's stomach he needed to ease.

When her right hand reached into the tub to drop the rag into the soapy water container to let it soak, his eyes followed the movement before his left hand gently grabbed her fingers. Carson brought her hand over, the familiar angry fire lighting in his chest as

245

his eyes landed on the hint of the bluish-purple bruises around her wrist. They weren't that prominent, but against her pale skin, they were obvious and Carson felt the urge to kick Milner in the gut with a new intensity.

If anyone should be feeling any guilt, it was Carson. It was his past with Milner and his present with Noelle that made her a target. While he couldn't have known Milner and Noelle would run into each other tonight, Carson still felt a sense of failure on his part for being unable to keep her away from him.

"I'd do it again," Carson told her truthfully, pushing aside the anger for Milner and replacing it with honest reassurance for Noelle. The fingers of his other hand brushed along her wrist as his jaw clenched momentarily. "And I'd have no regrets," Carson promised, meeting her eyes once again.

The firm honesty in his voice had Noelle taking in a deep breath, thinking that so much was happening so fast but then realizing that if Carson liked her for even half as long as she had liked him, it didn't matter. It had been over a month since they left, and developing feelings for him came just as fast. Noelle still felt her heart leaping at the fact that Carson liked her just as much as she liked him, which was a crazy, head-spinning, and beautifully overwhelming amount.

She smiled that soft smile Carson adored, hinting at her dimples but not showing them. "That's pretty romantic," she jested slightly as she picked up the washcloth and squeezed out the excess water.

A breathy, silent laugh escaped Carson, feeling the tension lift from his shoulders as Noelle brought the wet washcloth up to his face.

"Hold still," she instructed before dabbing the cut with a featherlight touch.

Carson didn't even flinch at the sting of anything touching the fresh cut as his brown eyes remained on Noelle. Her gaze was focused on what she was doing, but her cheeks were heating up

246

under the weight of Carson's eyes on her. Her heart never paused in the leaps it was doing as she cleaned up the cut. His hands were back on her hips, but his fingers had snuck under the hem of the loose tee she wore. His warm fingers against her skin sent sparks of heat throughout Noelle's body as she swallowed inaudibly; that mixed with the cool metal of his rings had Noelle's dry throat working.

Of course, because nothing ever went unnoticed by Carson, he noticed the tension in her neck. He smirked because he knew he was the cause of it. His thumbs began rubbing small circles against her skin. The gesture made Noelle pause, which he felt because she had briefly stopped cleaning his cut and bit the inside of her cheek.

Yeah, that's not distracting at all, her thoughts drawled, continuing her ministrations while trying—and failing—to appear unaffected.

"Alright," she breathed, eye on the newly cleaned cut that was now just a long pink, not deep, gash across his cheekbone. Noelle put the washcloth back in the container and picked up the antiseptic cream from the kit.

"Wait, gross, no." Carson shook his head, trying to lean away from Noelle when she squeezed some out on the tips of her two fingers. He hated the smell of it, and he sure as hell didn't want his face to smell like it.

She shot him a mildly incredulous look, not expecting to see Carson with his face scrunched up in distaste as a laugh threatened to bubble past her lips.

"Are you serious?" Noelle raised her eyebrows. "I know you know that you need this, so it doesn't get infected."

"Yeah, but . . ." Carson hesitated, eyebrows lowering into a complaining frown. "It just smells," he whined.

She had never seen him look so pouty; she never thought his raspy voice was capable of sounding high-pitched when he whined like that. She broke out into an amused grin.

247

"Car, it's odorless."

He blinked. "Oh." His cheeks warmed up in slight sheepishness, but the giggle Noelle released had his lips tugging up. He was no longer embarrassed for appearing even the least bit bratty. Carson watched as Noelle brought her fingers up and took in a sharp breath at the cold cream against the cut, slightly stinging as Noelle offered a soft apology.

They were so close as Noelle's fingers gently soothed the cut, only being able to hear their soft breathing and feel the steady thrums of their hearts. Carson reveled in Noelle's fruity scent and her doing the same of his outdoorsy, piney one. Their entire focus was on each other.

"Done," Noelle's sotto voce sounded, leaning back slightly and reaching over to rip off some toilet paper to wipe her two fingers clean from any residual cream. As she dropped it in the trash, her hazel eyes met his brown ones. "I'll get you some ice for your knuckles and side," she said.

She made a move to get off, but Carson's grip on her hips tightened, keeping her seated on his lap.

"No," he said. He didn't want her to go; he was enjoying her on him too much. "Don't need any ice. Just need you," he cut her off in a low tone when Noelle parted her lips to protest.

Noelle's heart jumped in her throat, her lips parting at the utter honesty in Carson's tone. Though she knew he needed ice more than he needed her, the fire still ignited across her skin at his words. Her body melted when Carson leaned towards her, closing the distance as her eyes fell shut just as his lips pressed against hers. Noelle inhaled deeply through her nose, her hands cupping Carson's jaw as she moved her lips against his in the slow, soft kiss that turned her insides into jelly. She could already feel her head spinning at the gentle pace of the kiss. It was different than the ones they had shared; it was unrushed as their lips moved in synchronicity.

248

She was not sure how long they had been kissing, but it was enough for her to pull away and trail kisses down Carson's strong jaw. Her head ducked to let her lips and tongue and teeth work down his neck and return the favor he had done days ago and left her own marks against his pretty skin. Noelle heard Carson let out an appreciative groan as she nipped, working on her fourth mark. It gave a small boost to her ego because she was the one who got him to make a sound as sexy as that.

She brought her lips back to his in a slow, sucking kiss that erupted wild butterflies in her stomach. When Noelle felt Carson's blunt nails digging into her skin with the metal of his rings biting, she let out a soft moan into his mouth.

"I need you too," she whispered.

Her words, just as sincere as Carson's, had him groaning before nipping at her lower lip. Carson pulled back ever so slightly, brushing his nose against hers and keeping his eyes closed.

"Then let me take you to your room, darling," he practically begged.

Noelle felt her heart drop to her stomach from anticipated excitement, feeling his warm breath against her lips and forehead against her own.

"Please," she consented instantly.

Carson didn't hesitate as his hands went from Noelle's hips to slide under her thighs, his feet firmly planted on the ground as he stood up and lifted her up with him. Noelle's arms instantly wrapped around his neck and her legs around his hips at the unexpected gesture.

"Wait, your side. I can ju—" she said worriedly, her eyes widening slightly in concern.

"I got you." He let out a breath to prelude his rushed words before capturing her lips in another slow kiss.

Yeah, his side was protesting as he carried Noelle out of the bathroom, but the tightness in his pants was a lot more demanding as Carson blindly walked towards Noelle's bedroom, seemingly having her house mapped out. He kept kissing her, relishing her chest pressed against his as he walked them through the open doorway of her room and kicked it shut behind him.

Noelle's fingers, which had been entangled in the curls at the back of Carson's head, tugged at his hair slightly, which elicited a guttural groan from him that allowed Noelle to meet his tongue with her own. It was slow and sensual in the way the kiss deepened, and Carson made his way towards the bed and stopped at the right place from memory to crawl onto the mattress on his knees before bending to lower Noelle. Their kiss never broke, a lazy tangle of lips and tongues and teeth as Carson's hands slid from her thighs and went up her sides, then going under her shirt and all the way up. His knees rested on either side of her hips as Carson's thumbs brushed right under her bare breasts. His cock hardened even more at her lack of bra.

"As cute as this is," Carson mumbled against her lips, his eyes opening only slightly to let his hooded gaze drop to the picture of Bambi on her shirt. He looked back at Noelle, her light eyes glinting in the darkness of the room, save for the lights filtering in from her parted curtains. "It needs to come off."

Noelle giggled breathily as Carson's fingers pulled off her shirt as Noelle lifted slightly to get it off. Once Carson discarded the piece of clothing on the floor behind him, he pulled back to admire the view in front of him. He let out a groan, sitting back on his legs as to not put his weight on her.

"You're so perfect," he praised.

Her cheeks flushed a happy pink at his words, which were followed by him coming down to kiss her once again and his hands cupping the soft flesh. Noelle moaned into his mouth as Carson's calloused fingers had their way with her breasts, cupping and squeezing and tugging at her already hardened nipples due to the cool air of the room. It may be cold in here, but Noelle felt like she was on fire.

Much to her chagrin, Carson pulled away from the kiss. She was desperate to follow his lips with hers, but her head dropped and tilted back when she felt him wrap them around her right nipple, giving it the kind of attention she craved. His warm tongue circled her nipple before tugging at it lightly with his teeth. Noelle closed her eyes and let out a breathless whimper through parted lips, her fingers still tangled in his hair as his other hand squeezed her left breast and rolled the nipple between the pads of his finger and thumb.

Holy shit. She thought kissing him was dizzying, but this was leaving her without any air to breathe.

When he treated the other breast similarly, Noelle couldn't help but open her eyes and watch as Carson licked and sucked. His eyes were closed and his lashes brushed against his cheekbones. Noelle felt her stomach stirring and bit her lower lip at the waves of pleasure his mouth was bringing her.

One of her hands slid down from the back of Carson's head. When she felt the collar of his shirt, she tugged at the back of it.

"Take it off, please," she breathlessly pleaded, and Carson realized if she ever asked him to do anything in that voice, he would do it in a heartbeat.

So he sat up, taking a moment to admire the way Noelle's chest moved from her breathing. His throat was drying at the sight of her breasts slick with his saliva. Carson could hear his heart pounding in his ears as he reached one hand to the back of his shirt, pulling it off in one swift motion and tossing it to the floor, ignoring the cool chains and pendants he wore against his heated skin because he couldn't believe the sight in front of him. He couldn't believe the girl with the glazed hazel eyes and swollen lips was his. She was dizzying and addictive. He adored every inch of her, and he couldn't wait to show her just how much.

While he admired her, Noelle was doing the same as she took in his toned torso and tattoos—the ones he got for his family

251

and for himself. She took in the hickeys she had left on his neck, a show of her actions, but the black ink and purpling marks weren't all that were sticking out against his golden skin because Noelle's eyes drifted to the yellowing bruise on his left side. It was a bit too large for her liking as she saw it through the limited light of the room and slowly sat up.

She took in a breath, steadying her wild heart as her fingers barely brushed against the tender skin, the guilt from before coming back at the sight of the bruise. When she pulled her lower lip into her mouth, Carson's hand came up to cup her cheek, his thumb gently releasing her imprisoned lip.

"Look at me," he told her gently as he ducked his head. So she did as she swallowed at the intensity of his kind stare that contradicted the harsh cut on his cheek. It was a look he kept for only those close to him. "I'm okay. I've seen worse."

Noelle let out a sharp breath, hearing the mild summer wind outside over her heart and realizing that having Carson so close was the only thing keeping her warm.

"That doesn't make me feel any better, Carson."

His lips tugged upwards into a smile. He used his light grip on her cheek to bring her forward and softly bite down and tug at her lower lip before releasing it.

"Then let me try to help out with that."

And then he was kissing her again, enjoying the faint taste of chocolate she had eaten before pushing her back until she was lying down again and then dragging his lips away from hers towards her jaw and down her neck. Noelle savored the feel of his full lips against her skin as an appreciative moan falling past her while Carson sucked and nipped on a particularly pleasurable spot. His actions were slow, taking his time on leaving his mark on one spot of her neck before moving on. He dragged his mouth lower and lower all the while making sure to leave purplish marks on her collarbones and the swell of her breasts as well.

252

The left side of his torso was still experiencing a dull throb of pain as he moved himself further down on the bed, but Carson paid it no mind because his entire attention and energy was focused on the stunner of a girl beneath him, whose moans and soft whimpers were more empowering than any crowd during a match.

When he trailed kisses all the way down her torso, the cool pendants of his necklaces did what the air couldn't and raised goosebumps on Noelle's skin. Carson moved to rest on his knees on the floor, his hands on the back of Noelle's knees to pull her down closer to him as she let out a startled gasp. Smirking and reaching the waistband of her cute little night shorts, Carson paused and glanced up at Noelle.

"Baby, can I take these off?" he questioned.

Fuck it if Noelle didn't melt at the husk of his voice. She looked down at him, wondering how they hadn't truly even done anything yet but she still felt like she was seconds away from coming undone. Her lips parted, licking her bottom lip. Carson knew he would have to take his pants off soon because the sight was so fucking hot.

"Yeah," Noelle answered with an absent nod. "Yes, Car."

He didn't wait a moment longer as his fingers hooked into the band before dragging the shorts down her leg. Carson felt his entire body clench because she was dripping. The sight of her slick folds was enough to send Carson over the edge, and he couldn't wait to get to know every single inch of this gorgeous girl's body.

"Shit, Ellie," he breathed as he discarded her shorts, his hands on her inner thighs to push them apart and open her up to him. "Been dying to have a taste."

Noelle pressed one hand against her forehead when she felt Carson draw circles on her inner thighs, the subtle action sending an unexpected wave of pleasure.

"God, yes, Car. Please," she said, breathlessly begging. Her head still against the mattress, Noelle looked down at him as her

253

face scrunched slightly. "I need you. Need your mouth and your fingers. Need all of you," she pleaded.

She wasn't even embarrassed that she was already begging for him, not when she saw Carson smirk before his lips trailed kisses up the inside of her right thigh—all teeth and tongue and leaving marks. He got close to where she needed him most. He was right there, but he suddenly switched to her other thigh. Noelle's chest fell with a heavy breath at his purposefully slow movements. Each nip and suck had Noelle begging for more.

"Can't wait to taste you," he breathed, his breath teasing Noelle's heated core before her mouth dropped open at the little kitten licks he taunted her pussy with. Noelle had to stop her entire body from spasming when Carson's tongue slowly entered her.

Her strangled moan and his satisfied groan were music to each other's ears—Noelle motivating him and the sound he made vibrating through her entire being as both of her hands found home in his hair once more, keeping him close as his tongue worked her over.

Carson watched while savoring her taste. With her back arched and head tilted back in pleasure, he was completely entranced at how fucking beautiful she looked like this, how her pretty lips parted open in a breathless gasp when he shifted lower to push one finger into her folds.

"So pretty like this," he remarked breathily, reveling in the way her fingers tightened around his curls and watching as Noelle's glazed-over eyes watched him lick his lips that were wet with the taste of her. Carson pressed a kiss to her clit, adding a second finger and increasing the stomach coiling pleasure she felt. "So pretty for me."

His lips wrapped around her clit as his fingers continued their ministrations. Carson forced himself to keep his eyes open, so he could keep them on Noelle as her moans were accompanied by her trying to close her thighs as she tilted her head back, giving Carson the stunning view of her pretty neck and the darkening marks littering her skin. She was utterly his. He couldn't help but muse as the rim of his ring added on to the pleasure he was generously giving her.

Carson used his free hand to keep her left thigh spread, quickening his pace until he felt Noelle clenching around his fingers. The room was filled with the sounds she made. She whined when Carson suddenly pulled his fingers out because she was so close.

"Oh god," she panted when his fingers were replaced by his lips and tongue. "Shit, Carson, I'm clo—"

Her words were cut off with a choked cry as Carson shifted, wrapping his arms around thighs and pulling her even closer. He lifted her hips off the bed. The new angle his tongue was hitting was enough to have Noelle seeing stars and squeezing her eyes shut at the toe-curling end she finally reached, the moan her star-seeing orgasm accompanied causing Carson to groan against her as she came right on his tongue. He didn't think he would ever get enough of her taste.

Carson pulled back with one last kiss to her clit, and Noelle used the grip she had on his hair to tug him up. His body easily followed her lead as she pulled him down and pressed her lips to his, their tongues instantly meeting. Noelle moaned into his mouth as she tasted herself and not for the first time did Carson think this girl would be the end of him as his left hand dragged up her body, feeling her smooth skin under his touch before his hand found her throat.

Before he could do what he wanted, Carson paused briefly before deciding against it. With lips still on hers, he began to move his hand away from her neck. He wasn't sure if Noelle would want that. He didn't want to make her feel uncomfortable in any way. However, as if realizing what he was about to or what he was hesitating to do, Noelle's right hand grasped his tattooed, bracelet-covered wrist and kept his hand in place.

"Please," she mumbled against his lips, dragging hers against his. "Do it. Do whatever you want."

Shit, I didn't need to be told twice.

His hand splayed at the base of her throat, putting just the right amount of pressure in the front as he used his fingers to do the same on the sides of her neck. Noelle's lips parted against Carson's as the unadulterated pleasure she felt from Carson's grip unforeseen yet so fucking dizzying. No one's ever choked her before—hell, she never trusted anyone enough to—and the pressure Carson was putting along with his cool rings biting into her skin had Noelle's stomach recoiling wonderfully.

He was obsessed with her, with the way she tasted and felt and sounded, and Carson knew he would never be able to have enough of her, especially when her fingers worked on the buckle of his belt.

"Off. Need you now," she instructed hoarsely through a fucked voice.

Carson kissed her lips before pushing himself off the bed, his swollen lips already missing Noelle's as he got to his feet on the floor. His eyes never left Noelle's as the air between them was alive with thrilled, euphoric electricity while she pushed herself further up on the bed. Carson let out a shameless groan when she pulled her lower lip into her mouth, watching as he worked at his belt.

He took it off as it clattered to the ground, removing his shoes and socks before hastily unzipping his jeans. The urgency to be on her, inside her, with her was getting the better of him as he shoved his pants and boxers down his legs, wincing only slightly when he bent and his side protested at the action. Carson barely registered it though, along with the thud of his pants because of his phone and wallet in the pockets. The only thing he could focus on was the woman in front of him, her breathing as shallow as his because of the intense anticipation of what was about to happen— what they had both been waiting for to happen.

Noelle didn't feel the least bit embarrassed when she felt her mouth practically water at the sight of Carson, completely bare and all for her. She took a brief moment to admire every part of him—from his tattooed arms and biceps and collarbones to his toned chest and strong thighs. It was all an indicator of how well he treated his body, of how stupidly gorgeous he was.

When Carson crawled back on to the bed on his knees, he made his way back to her by trailing kisses from below her belly button all the way up her stomach, torso, the valley of her breasts, and neck before finally reaching her lips. Noelle felt like her body was on fire. Carson's lips were leaving scorches in their wake as she sighed into his mouth, feeling his hardened length against her thigh and her heart threatening to burst through her chest.

"So beautiful," Carson rasped against her mouth. He realized the way his heart pumped during a fight was nothing compared to the breathlessness he felt at this moment with his front flush against hers and his cock twitching in impatient anticipation. "Need you so bad, Ellie. Can I have you?"

"God, yes, yeah," Noelle whined, her senses overwhelming as she couldn't possibly wait a second longer. Her hands cupped his cheeks as she felt the hard lines of his jaw in her palms, his chest against her own as his necklaces sensually dragged against her fiery skin. Her eyes met his as he hovered over her with only inches between them as she took in his dilated pupils and pink lips. She was obsessed with every feature of his as her thumb tenderly brushed the skin right below his cut. "All of me, yeah. Just need to feel you, Car."

Their noses brushed together, heavy breaths mingling in the silence of the room as their blood rushed in their veins and hearts pounded in their ears. Their senses were just full of the other, unable to be close enough.

"I'm on the pill," Noelle volunteered breathlessly.

Carson's heart jumped up to his throat as her words registered in his mind, and he dropped his forehead to her collarbones as an aroused groan escaped him at the mere thought of being able to feel Noelle without any filter.

"You're gonna kill me," he quipped against her skin, voicing the thought that always seemed to flutter around his mind where Noelle was concerned. Reaching his hand down, he gripped the base of his cock and brushed the tip against Noelle's sensitive folds that pulled a soft whine from her, which caused him to smirk as he slanted his lips over hers in a kiss not as gentle as the ones before, the adrenaline in his veins energizing his movements.

"What're you waiting for?" Noelle muttered against his lips when she didn't feel him in his entirety, pulling back slightly as a smirk of her own tilted at her pink mouth. "Get on with it."

Narrowing his eyes, Carson's smirk widened at Noelle's bold impatience while staring down at her as he couldn't help but think how perfect this beautiful, sexy girl was and that she was his.

"Whatever you say, love," Carson marveled before, without another moment's pause, he moved his hips and sank himself into Noelle's heat. The sensation of her walls snugly around him made Carson release her lips. Their foreheads were pressed together as both of them let out loud, impassioned groans at this new feeling.

He bottomed out with Noelle inhaling sharply as she tilted her head back at the maddening way he filled her so completely, so full, and she could already feel herself drawing to the edge at how tantalizing Carson felt. He, in turn, dragged his lower lip along hers as he released shallow breaths, his heart in his throat as he held himself up with his arms. Both of them were taking a second to process this moment, to revel in the new level of intimacy they had been craving. It wasn't until Noelle clenched around him that spurred Carson on, breaking every strand of patience and control he had as he pulled out almost completely before snapping his hips forward.

The gratifying mewl that escaped Noelle at the rough movement prompted Carson to pick up his pace. He couldn't help but kiss her for what felt like the hundredth time but still ignited a fire just like the first. It was a messy kiss with tongue and clashing teeth, rushed with the heat coursing through their veins and the waves of bliss stealing their breaths and writhing their bodies, the pleasure even more enjoyable for Noelle as his stubble scratched her chin.

"So good, Car," Noelle babbled softly, moving her legs to wrap around his hips and lock her ankles at his back. The new angle as she pushed himself more into her had Noelle quickly approaching the edge. Carson buried his face in the crook of her marked neck because he didn't think he had ever felt euphoria this intensely before. One hand returned to her throat, his fingers finding home around it. Noelle's heart felt as though it was going into overdrive. Her nails scraped lightly against his scalp as he groaned against her skin. "God, I feel so full."

Shit, she really was going to be the end of him. He kissed her collarbone and sat up slightly while his other hand held her thigh, and his rings bit into her skin as his hips never once ceased bucking forward, overwhelmed with how well he fit inside her.

"Take me so well, baby," Carson rasped, unable to stop the praise from falling past his own lips as he licked at her. "Like you were made for me."

Noelle believed that wholeheartedly.

It wasn't long until both of them were reaching their end, their stomachs coiling as Noelle felt her muscles quivering at her fast approaching orgasm.

"Let me how pretty you look when you cum, Ellie," Carson urged as he let go of her thigh to prop himself up, allowing his other hand to come up and rub loose circles over her clit with his thumb.

It took all of Noelle's willpower to open her eyes, to look up at the stunner of a man who was bringing her the kind of ecstasy she had never felt before, who lit up her body in every way with a fierce fire, every nerve within her body igniting with life. When her eyes met his, she was done.

Carson let her ride it out, the warmth of her releasing around him quickening his own approaching orgasm as the sound of skin slapping against skin and their mingling moans electrified the air. Noelle's lips parted with a heavy gasp as Carson kept going, loving the feeling of him within her sensitive heat and wanting to always remember this moment of how her name fell past his lips in a euphoric groan when his own orgasm finally washed over him and she felt him deliciously spilling inside of her.

Their breaths were heavy, disrupting the silence of the room as Carson, after a moment of pausing to catch a breath, pulled out of her tenderly. Unhindered groans sounded from both of them at the loss of closeness. Carson laid down beside Noelle, their chests heaving and hearts only just starting to slow down. His head was against the pillow as he wrapped his right arm around her shoulders and pulled her over. The desire to be close to her was never going to disappear.

Noelle rested her cheek against his shoulder, her hand resting against his chest as they basked in the afterglow of the rapture they had just experienced without anything keeping them apart, with their skin warm and flushed and heads swimming in pure delirium. They knew they should clean up, but they were too comfortable on the bed next to each other, too overwhelmed and sensitive to do anything except bask in each other's presence.

With his arm wrapped around Noelle's shoulder, Carson's fingers lightly ran through her hair as he felt her legs move until a blanket was sliding up his bare legs. Noelle reached for it to bring it up and cover them up.

"Sleepy?" he mumbled because, really, falling asleep with her in his arms—beautiful and fucked and his—sounded like the best thing.

She hummed in response, her cheek against his shoulder as she reveled in the warmth the blanket and Carson's body provided. She was exhausted and sore and felt so taken care of.

"You gonna stay the night?" she rasped.

260

Carson twirled a strand of her soft hair around his finger, pressing a kiss to her temple as his own eyelids felt heavy.

"Don't wanna be anywhere else."

CHAPTER NINETEEN

As her finger trailed over the hickeys on her neck, Noelle couldn't help the warm blush that spread across her cheeks as last night's events replayed in her mind like her favorite movie—not only were there marks left by Carson's lips on her neck but there were also the faint imprints his rings left when his hand wrapped around her throat, pink and welcoming. There were matching ones on her inner thighs, which she had only noticed when she slid her shorts up, and more purple marks on her collarbones and the tops of her breasts. She couldn't help but think how pretty they looked against her skin.

Last night was, to put it bluntly, earth-shattering. Noelle just knew she wasn't going to be the same after it. Sex with Carson had been a near religious experience; she had never called out God's name so much.

Returning to her bedroom, Noelle felt her heart flip at the sight of Carson on his feet with jeans and shoes back on as he straightened after grabbing his shirt off the floor. His eyes instantly went to her as she entered the room, taking in her makeup-free face and messy hair in all its adorability as Noelle came to stop in front of him.

"I'm sorry, I have to go to work," Carson apologized, his shirt still in hand. Once Noelle was close enough, he wrapped his fingers around the drawstrings of her shorts to tug her close until she was flush against him.

"Don't apologize." Noelle chuckled, both of their voices laced with sleep as she dragged her hands up his arms and rested them on his biceps. "I gotta get going soon too."

Carson smiled, his eyes a bit sunken with sleep and his hair a curly mess. Noelle couldn't help but think he couldn't look more adorable if he tried. The purple marks on his neck, courtesy of her, just added on to his already incomprehensible attraction. He glanced at her bedside clock that read 11:23 AM.

"I think you're already running a bit late," Carson teased with a smirk.

"What can I say?" Noelle grinned lazily. "I went to sleep pretty exhausted."

Her words widened Carson's smirk, arrogant and proud as his hand came up to brush a lock of her hair behind her ear. Just as he did so, Noelle's eyes caught sight of his fingers, and her expression dropped as she pulled back, gently grabbing Carson's wrist and turning his hand so she could observe his fingers.

She had gotten so caught up in the overwhelming bliss last night that she hadn't taken a moment to properly notice Carson's hands. His knuckles were a fading reddish-purple color that weren't all too new because of the punches he was always throwing, but what was new were the additional bruises that discolored his skin right under the rings he wore—something she never saw before.

"Shit, Carson," Noelle gasped, her eyes widening as her fingers were still wrapped around his wrist and her other hand came to gently touch the tips of his fingers while taking in the small cut under the rings as she carefully slid them forward. Carson took in a breath and Noelle's worried gaze lifted to meet his eyes, but his gaze was on their hands. "These look worse than your regular bruises. What happened?"

Each finger that was decorated with rings on both of Carson's hands looked the same—cut and bruised more than usual.

"Didn't take my rings off with Milner. Not the smartest idea on my part."

Noelle huffed incredulously, both of her hands holding his as she looked at the bruises on his fingers, not nearly as pretty as the ones on his neck. The bruise on his side was turning a bluish black, and Noelle's heart tugged in her chest because she hated seeing him hurt. Before they got together, she would wince and have to look away when she went to a match and saw Carson get hit. Now, Noelle knew if she had to see that again, she would definitely feel her heart stop functioning.

"Are your fingers okay though?" Noelle asked worriedly, raising her eyebrows in concern.

"They're fine," Carson assured with a light chuckle, maneuvering his fingers so he could pull her hand towards his lips and press a kiss to the back of it before putting his shirt on. Noelle didn't miss the sharp intake of breath he took when his torso stretched at the action, pulling his shirt down and covering the bruise on his side. When he saw the unconvinced look Noelle was giving him, Carson grinned as he intertwined their fingers and nodded towards the door. "Come on, babe. Walk me out."

She shot him an unamused expression before letting him drag her out of her bedroom, a giggle falling past her lips as Carson raised their joined hands to twirl her forward. As Noelle practically skipped past him towards the stairs, she let out a startled yet giddy shriek when Carson's hand cheekily slapped her ass.

"Hands to yourself, Hayes!"

Carson laughed loudly behind her, his footsteps thudding on the stairs as he followed after. "I can't help myself!"

Her giddiness prompted by Carson was abruptly cut short when they reached the bottom of the steps because the last thing either of them had expected was for Noelle's mom to be standing in the living room. Noelle stopped short with Carson right behind her as her mother raised her eyebrows, looking stunned and confused at the sight of her hickey-covered daughter with a man she didn't recognize who had a cut on his face and similar marks on his neck.

264

"Mom." Noelle's heart dropped to her stomach because this was just not how she wanted her mom to find out about her relationship.

"Noelle," her mother's calm, almost indifferent voice sounded as she dropped her purse to the couch. Her eyes flickered to behind her daughter's shoulder. "Who's this?"

"Um, this is Carson," Noelle introduced, feeling pretty damn nervous all of a sudden because she had a feeling this wasn't going to end too well. She glanced at the man behind her, shooting him a helpless look as Carson raised his eyebrows, looking a bit shocked and even slightly uncomfortable under Dr. Simon's scrutinizing gaze. "Carson, uh, this is my mom, Malorie."

Carson cleared his throat as he moved forward, his right hand stretching out as he neared the couch.

"It's good to meet you, Dr. Simon."

Noelle bit the inside of her cheek as she watched her mom glance down at Carson's hand and raised a plucked eyebrow. She knew that her mother's medical eye had immediately taken notice of Carson's bruised fingers as she took his hand and shook it, her eyes also taking in the pink cut on his face as well.

"You too, Carson," she replied smoothly. Noelle knew, with a sinking heart, that her words weren't all-too true.

When they dropped hands, Noelle bit the inside of her lower lip as Carson turned to face her. He took a breath of his own as he rubbed his hands down his jeans.

"Well, I'm gonna get to work," Carson said as he walked backwards towards the door, his dark eyes meeting Noelle's alarmed ones.

Noelle knew Carson could tell she was worried, almost descending into a state of panic over her mother's reaction of finding them like this—a mix of bed and sex hair and hickeys peeking out from under their shirts, not to mention Carson's own bruises. She noted the hesitation in his eyes, reluctant to leave Noelle to deal with this on her own, but she knew he couldn't stay.

265

It might be less ugly with him gone, plus the last thing Noelle wanted to do was further subject Carson to the look of contempt her mom was doing nothing to hide as she looked at Carson. It pricked something sharp in Noelle's blood, wanting to tell her to knock it off.

Noelle was a grown woman, and Carson a grown man, but she wasn't excited to face her mother's wrath nor did she think Carson was prepared to face the disapproval either. He deserved better than that.

Hastily, Noelle followed Carson towards the door as he opened it and stepped out. She ignored the way she felt her mother's gaze burned a hole through her back. She offered Carson a reassuring smile that she knew she wouldn't be convinced of herself.

"I'll talk to her," she whispered as Carson stepped outside, the determination in her voice replacing the panic she had been showing moments before.

She wanted to reassure him. She wanted him to relax the tension she could see tensing his muscles and noted with relief when some of it seemed to melt away. He offered a small smile, his appreciation obvious.

"Call me later, yeah?" Carson murmured, and because he was obstructed from Dr. Simon's view, he took the chance to kiss Noelle's forehead before jogging down the steps and down the sidewalk. Noelle let out a breath because this was not how she wanted the morning after she and Carson finally slept together to go.

"Last time I checked, you were with Isaac," Dr. Simon's hard voice sounded when Noelle shut the door. It took all the twenty-two-year-old's might to not slam her head against the door. How could she have forgotten that she and Isaac were playing around with their parents' poor set up? She hadn't even seen Isaac in a while, and frankly, it really did completely slip her mind that they were loosely trying to fool their parents. It wasn't like her

266

mom was home often enough to ask or know about what was going on in Noelle's life, so it hadn't been important to Noelle. She was too preoccupied with the man that she *actually* was trying to build a relationship with. "What the hell is going on, Noelle?"

Before she could help herself, Noelle shut her eyes and let out a groan, turning to face her mother.

"Mom, Isaac's gay. Carson has a better chance of getting with him than I do," she exclaimed.

Dr. Simon blinked. "Levi's son is gay?"

Noelle bit her lower lip, a wave of guilt washing over her for revealing Isaac's secret when she had no right to. Shit, what if her mom divulged this to Dr. Grant? He should be told that Isaac is gay by no one but Isaac himself.

"Then why have you been telling us you're going out?"

"Because he hasn't come out to his dad yet, and we actually do hang out because we're friends." Noelle sighed. "Isaac's actually dating Benny. They're pretty cute."

Her mom tilted her head ever so slightly, the information sinking before she seemed to accept it rather quickly.

"Huh. Well, good for them." For a moment, Noelle thought all was well in the world until her mother frowned at her. "But who's this Carson and how long have you been seeing him? Do you have any idea how strange it is for me to see my daughter in the state that you are with the man who did this to you?"

Noelle's face flushed, knowing full well her appearance blatantly showed what her and Carson had been up to last night. While she didn't regret it, it was embarrassing to be inquisitioned by her mom like this.

"Mom, you're making it sound like he did something wrong," Noelle huffed, feeling like a twelve-year-old caught making out on the couch than the age she was. She should really consider moving out, so she didn't get caught in this uncomfortable situation. "He's . . . Carson's my boyfriend."

267

She shifted on her feet, not out of discomfort but what she recognized as giddiness at referring to Carson as that. Still, the term 'boyfriend' in regards to Carson felt so mundane; he was anything but. It just seemed so normal, and that was definitely not an attribute Noelle contributed to Carson. Nothing about them seemed normal, honestly, but Noelle wouldn't have it any other way.

"Where did you meet him?"

"He's a friend of Aiden," Noelle answered. She definitely wasn't going to divulge in the circumstances of her and Carson's meeting, but she knew her mom liked Aiden. Maybe knowing Carson was a friend of his would lean her mother off a bit.

Her mom's eyes were still narrowed and Noelle was already tired of this interrogation. She knew she couldn't blame her mom for wanting to know who her daughter was involved with, but Noelle didn't appreciate the distaste her mom was displaying, especially towards Carson. The poor guy practically ran out of here, and though Noelle was surprised at his unexpected change in demeanor, she couldn't exactly blame him for it. Still, it was completely out of character.

"Why did he have bruises on his hands? And a cut on his face?" her mother demanded as if she was listing off reasons why she didn't like Carson rather than what she noticed on him. Dr. Simon let out an impatient huff as she crossed her arms over her chest and Noelle took in a sharp breath.

Oh god, not the 'Mom Pose'.

"Honestly, Noelle, what kind of man have you gotten yourself tied up with?"

"A good one," Noelle responded instantly, her voice as firm as her trust behind those words. "I think you should have some faith in who I'm seeing. I'm a big girl."

Her mother's jaw clenched at Noelle's ignorance of the questions she asked, staring at her daughter in momentary frustration. If there was one common trait all three of her daughters

268

shared, it was their set determination and stubbornness. It was useless arguing with any of them most of the time, so Malorie Simon ignored the matter all together.

Picking up her purse, she merely sighed. "I hope you know what you're doing," she said vaguely before disappearing up the stairs.

While Noelle was grateful the matter was dropped, she knew that eventually she would need to get her mother to come around, to not remain in silent scrutiny or ignore the fact that her daughter was in a relationship. Noelle knew that before her dad's passing, before her mom threw herself into her work and didn't spend nearly as much time with Noelle and her sisters as she used to, her mother would've been and stayed all over this situation. She would want to know everything.

Now, it seemed like she couldn't get far enough.

*   *   *

"You look like shit, but you also look like you had a wild night," Aiden observed with a raise of an eyebrow as Carson entered his office, sitting down on the chair on the other side of his desk with a soft groan. "The hell did you do?"

"A lot," Carson grunted, leaning back in the cushioned chair as he loosely crossed his arms. He had returned home after leaving Noelle's house, feeding Oreo and calling for the dog sitter before taking a shower and heading to work. He felt fresh and new yet still a bit sore for more reasons than one.

Aiden raised an eyebrow, hazel eyes flickering over his friend, at the cut on his face before ultimately landing on Carson's hands. Eyes widening, Aiden sat up and leaned forward with hands on the table.

"What the fuck happened to your fingers, Carson?" he demanded.

Pursing his lips, Carson let out a deep exhale through his nose as he debated on whether or not to tell Aiden the truth, but his friend had seen his hands. Aiden wasn't going to let go of his prodding.

"Got into it last night. You should see the other guy. Didn't end too well for him," he admitted, taking on a lighter tone as an attempt to ease the tension radiating off of Aiden.

"And what the fuck about you?" When Aiden's eyes skimmed over Carson's fingers once more, he clenched his jaw in knowing frustration. "You punched with rings, didn't you?" he said as he looked Carson in the eyes.

When Carson didn't respond, he merely sat with a cool expression on his face because, really, he wasn't afraid of Aiden. He knew his friend would be disappointed. Carson never fought with rings; it was a bad idea. Instead of only hurting his opponent, he was risking his bones breaking even more than he already did with the added pressure of the metallic jewelry. He had only ever done it once in an actual match and his fingers almost broke, unable to take part in the next few matches. Carson had been pissed on losing out on the money. Carson knew that Aiden was only looking out for him, but he wasn't going to apologize for his actions.

"It was Milner," Carson told him, watching as Aiden's expression dropped and darkened while leaning back. Carson's own anger from last night was resurfacing at the mere mention of the asshole as he let out a frustrated sigh. "Noelle ran into him last night when she was with Camille. He put his hands on her, Aiden. Threatened both of us. I wasn't about to let him get away with that."

An angered yet incredulous expression furrowed at Aiden's brows, lips tilting into a frown. "He put his hands on her?" he repeated. The fire that lit up his eyes was similar to the simmering flames Carson was trying to keep at bay. "He recognized her?"

"Of course he fucking did," Carson scoffed, face twisted in profound irritation towards the subject of their conversation.

"So what'd you do?"

Carson shot him a look. "What do you think? This isn't just paint on my hands, Aiden."

"For fuck's sake, Carson," Aiden huffed, rubbing his hands down his face in exasperation. "You didn't kill him, did you?" he asked, shaking his head.

"No, unfortunately," he responded dryly.

Aiden pursed his lips. He didn't need his best friend having a run-in with the law. "What'd you do after?"

Last night's events—the good ones—played through his mind as the thought of the pretty girl softened his aggravated thoughts.

"Went to Noelle's."

He watched as Aiden slowly raised his eyebrows and parted his lips.

"You slept with her," he deduced in an even tone.

There was a look on Aiden's face Carson didn't entirely like—a look that he recognized could be seen as hesitated disapproval. Suddenly, Carson was frowning because why was his best friend looking at him as if he just did something wrong?

"Why're you making it sound like I made some kind of mistake?" he asked in a steady voice as he stayed calm and cool.

"Because I'm thinking you did."

The flare of irritation Carson felt before was now directed at Aiden along with a hammering sense of panic because this was his best friend. Why was he saying this? Aiden knew Carson better than anyone, and even though he might give him shit, Aiden's opinion meant the world to him, but if his best friend was going to tell him something he didn't want to hear regarding Noelle, Carson genuinely didn't think he had the stomach to hear it.

Still, he masked that with his default cold anger. "What the fuck, Aiden?"

"Dude, you're my brother, okay? But Noelle's like a sister to me and I don't want to see her getting hurt." Carson's jaw

271

clenched as he was about to retort that obviously he didn't either. "Hanging around you—around us, really—attracts enough attention to her when she comes around Astros, but what do you think is gonna happen if people find out she's your girl?"

Carson could feel his heart quickening its pace from Aiden's words, a seed of furious panic planting itself in his stomach.

"They know better than to try anything."

"Most of them do, yeah." Aiden agreed with a nod, lacing his hands together on the table. "But people like Milner and Boman, they don't give a fuck. Both of them have already targeted her in some way just by being seen with you. You know the kind of men they are. They've got no respect for anyone."

"You think I don't know that?" Carson huffed through narrowed eyes, sitting up and ignoring the dull pang in his side as he leaned towards the table. "You don't think I feel like shit knowing that she's got a bruise around her wrist because someone from my life decided to fuck with her? Milner and Boman are lucky I didn't break their necks on the damn spot."

"I know you feel guilty," Aiden responded, his voice still as calm as ever, utterly opposite of the agitation noticeably rising in Carson's. "But once guys like them see just how close you are, you know they'll use her to bait you whether it's in the ring or out. So my question to you, Car, is . . ." he trailed off, almost hesitant to ask, effectively thinning Carson's patience. "You really wanna do this with Noelle? Or is she just another one of your hook ups? Because I swear, you may be my best friend but if you screw over Bev's little sister, I'm gonna—" he finally uttered.

"Are you fucking with me right now?" Carson demanded, glaring eyes widening in incredulity and never did Carson think he would ever feel his blood boil towards his best friend. He was genuinely disgruntled and offended that Aiden would even suggest that he was merely fucking around with Noelle. Did his friend think Carson was incapable of having feelings for someone? "You honestly think I'm just messin' about with her?" He clenched his

272

jaw once. "I like her," Carson added firmly. Those were words he hadn't properly uttered to anyone but himself, not even explicitly to Noelle, and they still didn't feel like enough. When it came to her, he *couldn't* get enough. Even now, his fingers tingled with the desire to run over her smooth skin again, his lips craving her taste.

Aiden pursed his lips, once again looking like he was going to regret whatever he was about to say. Carson wanted to tell him to spit it the fuck out already.

"Are you sure? You sure you like her enough to keep her close and have to look out for her around those fuckers? Because they aren't people Elle can handle herself, and I know you know that. She isn't some girl you can have your fun with and then just ditch. She's one of us, Car."

Carson was trying really hard not to feel as though Aiden was coming at his throat, but that was proving to be difficult when his words hit him harder than any fist. He wondered if it was his lack of past relationships or the fact that he mostly only ever hooked up with women that drove Aiden to the conclusion of him not treating Noelle right. Maybe it was both, but Aiden knew why Carson didn't get into relationships. He knew he didn't truly get with anyone unless he truly liked them, so why did it suddenly feel like he was being attacked for the decisions he made his friends respect him for?

The fact that Aiden assumed Carson would ditch Noelle both warranted waves of heated indignation and an uncomfortable twist in his gut. Carson didn't get in relationships just for the fun of it; he wanted to be in them when his feelings for a girl were too much to ignore. With Noelle, Carson knew what he felt for her was something to go after. He liked her in a startling way he had never liked anyone before. While that kind of scared the shit out of him, he still wanted it with her.

"So what?" Carson felt like his jaw was about to break from how hard he was clenching, his teeth grinding together because he already hated this conversation. He hated the thought of his best friend thinking so low of him. "You think I'm not good enough for her?"

Just merely uttering those words left a bitter taste in Carson's mouth, his entire body tensing as he prepared himself for potentially hearing Aiden's answer—words he might not like. Carson didn't give a shit about what people thought of him. The only opinions that mattered to him were of his family and his close friends, and if Aiden told him he thought he was making a mistake with Noelle, Carson knew he was in deep shit. He dreaded Aiden's answer, but he also couldn't help but feel angry at his friend for planting this seed of doubt in the first place. He was suddenly reminded of this morning, of the look Noelle's mother wore on her face as she took in the sight of Carson in jeans, a wrinkled shirt, and messy hair with bruises and hickeys alike.

He knew she was judging him, and Carson felt microscopic under her scrutinizing stare. It didn't take a genius to figure out that Dr. Simon wasn't thrilled to meet him—never mind the circumstances of their meeting. Carson would be lying if he said he wasn't worried about the opinion of the mother of the girl he was seeing. Selfishly, he hoped Noelle's mother wouldn't somehow convince her to stop seeing him but then Carson figured he knew Noelle, and he knew she didn't do anything unless she completely wanted to. She wouldn't end something right when it began starting. Still, Carson couldn't help but compare Dr. Simon's judgemental glare to the words his best friend was uttering, to the thoughts he was implying.

Isn't Aiden supposed to have my back?

"You know that's not it," Aiden said with a sigh, a pointed expression on his face. I know you don't get into relationships without being one hundred percent about them because you know that anyone who's got an axe to grind with you may find a way to use her against you. Boman and Milner already have. I just don't want you to get blinded by how much you like her when it comes to dealing with those assholes. They don't have morals like we do.

274

If they're crazy enough, they'll do anything for the glory and the money that comes with fighting at Astros. Or they may just be out for blood. I don't want Noelle to get caught in the middle of that."

"I don't either."

The anger left Carson, replacing it with frustration over the truth Aiden was spewing. Carson knew how some of the men at Astros were, how they gave zero fucks because most of them had nothing left to lose. There were times when men who used to frequent the matches, whether they were fighters or guys who lost too much money, would confront one another and, more often than not, people would end up in the hospital or in jail. Carson would know; he had put some of them in the former and the latter. Well . . .

"Last time, you got off lucky. I've got a feeling if Noelle was involved, you're ready to put someone in the hospital again. And I'm scared that you're gonna end up behind bars again."

It was like Aiden had read Carson's thoughts when he said those words, the dark-eyed boy shifting in his seat as he pursed his lips. "I wasn't charged, Aiden."

"Yeah, I know. You got lucky because then both of you would be in deep shit, but you still spent a few nights in jail, and frankly, I'm not interested in seeing you end up in prison." Aiden shook his head, the serious expression on his face not once wavering. "There's nothing wrong with defending or protecting the people you care about, but you can't lose yourself in the anger where you lose all of your control, Car." Gesturing to Carson's fingers, Aiden added, "You damn near broke your fingers because Milner put his on Noelle, and while I don't disagree with your actions because of your history with him and the fact that he had it coming, you can't fly off the handle. Keep yourself in check."

Carson took a breath, not entirely appreciating this lecture or the fact that Aiden brought up Vince Reichs. He was also a fighter at Astros, back when Carson was starting out, but had long since quit after a particularly ugly brawl the two of them had outside of the ring. It had happened on the streets, attracting the attention of police officers who happened to be on the scene to catch the perfect moment of Carson beating Vince into unconsciousness. Never mind the fact that Carson was suffering from broken bones of his own, Vince was taken to the hospital and Carson was arrested for assault and battery.

Vince didn't want to press charges. With a shady past of his own, he didn't want any of that being brought to light, and just like Carson, he didn't want Astros to be involved because for many of the men there, that place was almost like a safe haven—violent but a haven. So after he fully recovered in the hospital, not sustaining too serious injuries, he told the police he didn't want to press charges. Since the cops had better things to do and didn't want to spend their resources on a stupid street brawl, they released Carson after four days in the county jail. Carson had avoided any run-ins with the law ever since.

"I'm not gonna let anything happen to her," he said, looking Aiden dead in the eye as he sat up.

"I know that. Question is, are you gonna let anything happen to you?"

CHAPTER TWENTY

"What are you doing here?"

Noelle would be lying if she said the smile on her face hadn't strained slightly at Carson's flat greeting, gulping inaudibly as he continued his punches at the sandbag that hung in front of him. Her grip on the bag she held tightened.

"I brought you lunch," she informed him, lifting the bag of food from the deli he said he had been craving lately. Honestly, Noelle felt as though she found her soulmate—someone who loved Fairdown Deli almost as much as she did. "Got you the chicken parm panini."

A gloved punch was delivered to the bag, Carson not even glancing her way. "You didn't have to do that," he muttered.

"It's no biggie," Noelle assured with an airy laugh, which sounded slightly nervous to her own ears. Right away she could tell something was off about Carson, which she noticed, especially because he had been acting just how he did when they first met. In fact, he had been acting this way since the day following them falling into bed together. And that had been just two days ago. "I wanted to come see you anyway."

Amidst his movements, Noelle picked up the way Carson's jaw clenched. Her skin prickled when he didn't stop. "I'm a bit busy, so you can just leave the bag on the bench," he grunted.

Noelle blinked before her brows furrowed, annoyance tightening her jaw at Carson's rude dismissal. She knew he had been acting off, but him blatantly telling her to leave was new and, frankly, hurtful. She glanced around, relieved that Astros wasn't busy at this moment before looking back at Carson with an affronted glare.

"What's going on with you?" she questioned, not beating around the bush. It was funny; the moment she and Carson hooked up, letting their bodies speak to their attraction to one another rather than using words, all of Noelle's initial thumb-twiddling nervousness around Carson dissipated. Seriously, if she was intimidated by her own . . . whatever Carson was to her . . . then that would be a problem. "Why're you in a mood?"

Once again, he didn't dignify her with so much as a glance as he swung a right hook at the bag. "I'm not in a mood," Carson denied, his hard tone completely contradicting his words.

Noelle scoffed, hiking up the strap of her purse on her shoulder. "You're kidding, right?"

When Carson didn't say anything and only continued to assault the sandbag as his muscles rippled with every move he made, Noelle's irritation was beginning to be accompanied by worry because he hadn't even looked at her since the moment she announced her presence.

"Carson, can you just stop for a second?" she begged, stepping around so she was next to the punching bag, though she smartly put some distance to avoid getting hit by it.

When she was fully in his view, Carson reluctantly stopped, relaxing his stance as he straightened and his dark eyes finally slid over to her. Noelle took in the thin layer of sweat on his skin and appreciated how cute he looked in the grey beanie that was covering his head and hiding his curls, but she didn't let that distract her from what was going on, especially when she noticed the way Carson was looking at her—indifferent and distant. Just like he used to when they first met.

Her chest twisted uncomfortably. She had gotten so used to the fond, soft looks and knowing smirks he sent her way that

Noelle forgot the unease this particular look brought on. What had happened that warranted this reaction from him?

"What's going on?" Noelle repeated, keeping the anger she felt at bay but unsuccessful in hiding the hint of desperation her voice carried.

Carson shrugged as if he had no idea what Noelle could be talking about as his gloved hands hung at his sides. "I told you, I'm busy. You're getting worked up for no reason."

Her jaw hung slightly in disbelief. "Really?" Noelle rhetorically asked before scoffing. "I'd believe that if it weren't for the fact that you've been acting weird for the past few days. Are you mad at me? Did I do something?" she questioned, genuinely wanting to get to the bottom of this. Because if Carson was upset with her, she didn't want them to hide from the issue. In Noelle's opinion, they had been dancing around their feelings by themselves for too long to not handle any issue head-on. The best way to figure things out was together.

"No, Noelle. You didn't," Carson huffed, his expression not easing up. "And I haven't been acting weird."

"Yes, you have," she stressed, eyebrows raising in mild disbelief that he hadn't noticed it himself. "You have been ever since that morning." And then a horrific thought crossed her mind, one that hadn't before and suddenly, Noelle wished the ground would swallow her whole because all the self-doubting and insecure thoughts were making their way to the forefront of her mind. Her mouth dried, inhaling sharply yet quietly as she voiced her newborn fear with a tight throat. "Are you . . . do you regret it?"

She hated that her voice sounded so small. She loathed that she seemed as insecure as she possibly could get, but Noelle couldn't help it. She knew if that was what this was, if Carson was acting this way because he wished he never had sex with her and he was suddenly regretting everything, she knew she would be done. Noelle didn't think Carson was capable of being an asshole like that, of being so inconsiderate, but jumping to the worst possible

279

conclusion was her first reaction. She hoped to God it was an unwarranted one. She wanted to give him the benefit of the doubt, but fear stemming from insecurity was a heinous thing.

She watched as Carson's eyes softened despite his hardened expression, and maybe that was a baby step in the right direction.

"No, Ellie, I don't regret it." Noelle took in a breath, his words calming her down somewhat and the use of the nickname helped. Carson rubbed at the tip of his nose with the back of his wrist since his hand was covered by the glove. "But I can't do this right now, alright? So you . . . just go home, yeah? Or back to work. Whichever," he continued, his Adam's apple bobbing up and down.

The frown was back in place on Noelle's eyebrows, eyes widening questioningly. Carson had taken the brief easiness he brought with his first few words and twisted them in bewilderment at his finishing ones. Noelle's heart thrummed as she tried to make sense of what he was saying; she tried to understand what in the hell was going on.

"Can't do what right now, Carson? What the hell are you talking about?" The frustration was clear in her tone and the way her frown intensified. Noelle wished Carson would stop being so cryptic and just spit out what he meant to say.

"I just need to figure some shit out for myself, Noelle. 'S got nothing to do with you, so stop trying to interfere," Carson snapped, scowling in the same kind of frustration Noelle felt.

Now, she was staring at him in surprise, not expecting him to sound so harsh when all she was trying to do was figure out what was wrong. Yeah, she might have been pushing, but there was something clearly bothering him and Noelle didn't like seeing Carson pull into himself when she was there to help out. He was hiding from her when she was prodding him to come out into the open. She was just trying to help.

Although, now, it just seemed like she pissed him off.

Noelle swallowed the small lump that had formed in her throat at his hard words and glare; she pushed down the hurt and surprise and anger that he wouldn't tell her what was going on. Instead, she just pursed her lips and gave a single nod, diverting her gaze because she had never wanted to be on the receiving end of one of Carson's scowls, and right now, she was.

"Okay. That's fine. I'll leave this here and go," she said evenly, feeling the clench in her heart.

Her movements were almost robotic, feeling like she wasn't in her own skin when she could feel the tension radiating off of Carson's body, throwing her mentally off-balance as she placed the bag on the bench behind him. Noelle could feel Carson's gaze burning her back as she began walking away with her shoulders squared and not bothering with a goodbye because even though she was hurt at his behavior, she was also pissed. Yet, she hoped that he would stop her, that he would tell her to come back so he could explain why he was so angry.

But Noelle was already out the door. And Carson hadn't stopped her.

*   *   *

When Carson opened the front door of his apartment after some incessant knocking, the last person he expected to see was his older sister. Kira Hayes stood in the hall with a purse in one hand while the other gripped the handle of a carry-on suitcase and a smile on her face. His eyes widened at the sight of her, his lips automatically stretching into a grin despite the shock of her presence as he laughed out.

"Kira! What're you doing here?" he asked, pulling her into a hug.

"Came to visit my favorite brother, of course." She giggled, Australian accent lost amidst living in Canada since she graduated college six years ago. Carson rolled his eyes good-naturedly at her words, being her only brother, as he grasped her carry-on and pulled it inside as she walked in. "I had some vacation days from work, so I thought I'd drop by for a few days."

Carson's smile strained briefly as he shut the door, her words settling in his mind. He loved his sister, always was down to spend time with her, but her being in New York and obviously staying with him wasn't ideal, to say the least. Not when he was dealing with his insufferable issues about his relationship. Not when he had a few matches at Astros lined up. Not when she had no idea that *that* part of his life even existed. He was lucky his few cuts and bruises from before were pretty much gone or else the curious questioning would have started already. Kira knew everything about him, but she needed to remain oblivious to this.

"That's great." Carson cleared his throat, hoping his hesitance didn't show. "Do Mum and Dad know you're in the States?"

"Yeah, I'm visiting them once I leave here," Kira responded as she dropped her purse on the couch before letting out an excited exclamation when Oreo ran into the room, and she scooped the pup up. "Oh, I missed you the most!" she commented as Oreo licked at her chin.

"I don't see Oreo giving up his bed for you to sleep in," Carson grumbled as he dragged the suitcase to his room before returning to the living room and joining his sister on the couch.

Kira grinned as Oreo settled on her lap once she folded her legs under her to face her brother. "So tell me, what's new with you? You're practically dead on social media. How am I supposed to keep up with you?"

"So sorry about that," Carson said dryly.

Kira nudged his knee. "So?" she stressed with a raised brow. "What's new? How's work? How're the boys? Anyone new in your life?"

Carson's heart thudded for a brief moment. "Work's fine." He wasn't totally lying—both the gym and Astros were fine. "The boys are good. And, uh . . ." He paused at the last question. Carson

282

was never one to keep much from his family, with the exception of Astros. "I've, uh, started seeing someone," he slowly admitted.

He saw the instant excitement in Kira's dark eyes as they widened in slight disbelief. His sister was well aware of his tendency to only dive into relationships when he was truly hooked on a girl, when he knew it could mean something, when the girl was too special to not even try with. So no doubt Kira would jump on the hope of trying to get as much information out of him as she could regarding a potential relationship. She grinned, the genuine happiness in features that resembled his own bright ones. They only differed in the sense that she had recently dyed her dark hair blonde.

"Really? Who is she?"

Carson took a breath, arm draping over the back of the couch. "Her name's Noelle. She's . . . she's amazin', really." With a frown tilting his lips, he remembered what happened early today. "Way too good for me," he added.

"I'm sorry, what?" Kira blinked, head tilting forward as if she misheard him. "Too good for you? Why the hell would you say that?"

Aiden's words and Dr. Simon's reaction from days ago were suddenly brought to the forefront of Carson's mind. His jaw clenched because Carson prided himself in not letting what others thought get to him. While, at the end of it, Aiden had voiced his support for Carson's relationship with Noelle, Carson still couldn't shake his words out of his mind. He couldn't erase Dr. Simon's displeased expression from his eyelids. He couldn't stop thinking about the fact that Noelle being with him was a risk that didn't come with any other relationship. Was he really that selfish that he would rather her be with him than to keep her away for her own safety?

When the mere thought of her brought a smile to Carson's face, he knew the answer was yes.

"I didn't see it coming, Kira. I fell for her so fucking fast," Carson finally confessed with a sigh, leaning his head so it was resting against the palm of his hand with his elbow propped on the top of the couch. "She's so good, so caring, fuckin' obsessed with books and isn't afraid to speak her mind." Carson looked away at nothing in particular as the words just effortlessly flowed past his lips. "Noelle's beautiful and smart, and I'm just—"

"Kind, brilliant, and the best person to exist," Kira finished firmly, her determined features and pointed raise of brows solidifying her statement. "Why would you even think otherwise?" she asked with a scoff.

"I met her mum a few days ago and it just . . . didn't go too well," Carson confessed, shrugging one shoulder and deciding to keep Aiden out of it.

Kira frowned. "How come?"

When it came to talking to his sister, nothing was off limits. Still, when it came to talking about his sex life with his sister, Carson still felt a warmth spread across his cheeks. "She, uh, caught us the morning after Noelle and I, you know, hooked up." He chose his words carefully, awkwardly, not one to choose the wrong thing to say and piss his sister off.

Realization dawned on Kira's face as she pressed her lips together, the corners twitching in a lame attempt to hinder her smile from widening, but she couldn't stop the amused laugh from escaping, her hand covering her mouth and eyes crinkling much like Carson's did as she muffled her laughter, all the while Carson shot her an exasperated look.

"Oh god, that would happen to you."

Carson wasn't as amused. "It's not funny."

"It's hilarious," Kira countered with a giggle. When she took note of Carson's flat expression, she sobered up moments later, fighting off the smile. "Come on, Car. If Noelle's mum saw you guys in your, um, state . . ." Her childish giggle had Carson rolling his eyes. "Then you can't really be surprised if she didn't

284

welcome you with open arms. At the end of the day, Noelle's still her daughter and knowing she was doing what you guys were doing without even knowing who you are wouldn't warrant the most pleasant reaction from her. You can't take it to heart, pal."

And that had never happened. Carson had always been confident in himself, sure of every move he made and everything he did and said, taking pride in who he was and sure as hell taking pride in his fighting. Noelle's mother, in just a few short minutes, seemed to dismantle everything in him effortlessly. Not to mention, when it came to Noelle, it seemed like Carson's self-doubt was as strong as ever, though it had nothing to do with her. Noelle did nothing wrong; Carson was just swimming in a pool of apprehension others seemed to want to drown him in.

"Hey, I've never known you to let anyone get in your head," Kira hummed, poking Carson's knee as she ducked her head to connect their gazes. "She must be really special if you're working yourself up over this."

Carson smiled wryly, unapologetic. "You've no idea," he answered.

But then, Carson remembered Noelle showing up at Astros earlier today, trying to get him to talk after noticing the way he was closing into himself. He was aware he was doing it, and Carson wished he could handle things like this better; he wished he could talk about what was bothering his heart as easily as he could confess to Noelle how he felt once he had come to terms with it a hundred percent. When it came to troubling matters of the heart, Carson was notorious for keeping his issues to himself rather than talking them out, and he knew that was what Noelle was looking for today—for them to figure this out together.

And Carson had basically kicked her out.

With a groan, Carson dropped his head as his forehead rested on his arm, squeezing his eyes shut. "I'm such a dick," he muttered.

Kira raised her eyebrows, sifting her fingers through her blonde hair. "Did you push her away when she called you out on your shit?" she asked knowingly.

It was terrifying how well his sister knew him. "Yes."

She clicked her tongue. "That's a good quality for her to have, especially if she's dating you." There was a teasing tone in her voice as Carson felt her hand rub at his back. "It'll be okay, little brother. You obviously want this to work. Instead of keeping it to yourself, talk to Noelle. Tell her your fears and doubts. I know you hate letting others know your weakness, but you gotta make an exception with her."

It was funny. Kira knew that fact about Carson without knowing just how far it extended into his life—to a part of his life that she didn't even know existed, but that statement was the truest it could be in the ring. He made sure his opponents only ever saw his punches and kick, never what could be used to their advantage.

While two assholes already used Noelle against him, Carson knew that more than anything else, she was his good luck charm—one he needed to get back and apologize to for being an ass.

"You haven't screwed up yet, Car," Kira said, her hand still rubbing his back comfortingly. "Stop fighting yourself and start fighting for her."

*   *   *

Carson watched as Kira happily chatted with Beverly after he introduced the two, all the while he remained next to the fantasy section of the bookstore. He was absentmindedly holding a book he had no interest in reading, his dark eyes wandering around the store in search of the Simon sister he really wanted to see.

He and Kira ended up at Simon's Stories the next morning because his sister wanted to visit the store Carson was always sending her books from, and when she found out that Noelle worked there, she was practically dragging her brother out the door.

286

So here they were, and while Kira and Beverly had hit it off almost right away, Carson was left standing in the middle of an aisle, trying to catch sight of Noelle.

When he caught sight of her over the shorter shelves, walking out of the backroom with a bunch of hardcovers in her arms, Carson made sure to shove the book in his hand back in its appropriate spot on the shelf before quickly making his way over. He dodged customers and shouldered around shelves, his eyes never leaving the top of her head. Her hair was styled into those braid crown things Carson saw his sister wear often.

He slowed down when he neared her, watching from the end of the aisle as Noelle held five thick books in one arm and placed one in her other hand on the shelf. Carson felt his heart give a tug at the sight of her, at the memory of how rudely he had dismissed her yesterday and he felt like an asshole all over again. He remembered the look on her face—hard and disappointed and hurt because he wasn't letting her in when he was supposed to . . . because he was supposed to; she was his girl. Carson shouldn't have let his insecurities get the better of him.

"Hi, Ellie," he greeted as his fingers lightly trailed along the shelf, biting the inside of his cheek when he noticed the nervous tilt his voice took.

Noelle looked over and Carson watched as her eyes widened ever so slightly, lips parting at the sight of him. She clearly hadn't expected to see him, and Carson couldn't help but feel guilty because he knew her surprise was due to their encounter yesterday.

"Hi," she slowly returned, her eyes on him as she put in the book. "What're you doing here?"

Carson's lips twitched into an almost sheepish small smile as he took a few steps closer. His steps were hesitant because he could tell that Noelle's guard was up, wary of his presence and what it might entail. Carson wanted to punch himself. They seemed to be going backwards in their relationship, and Carson wanted to fix that as soon as he could.

"Came to see you, of course," he truthfully answered, shoving his hands into the pocket of his green hoodie. He wore a leather jacket on top as well despite it being the start of July, but Carson grew up in Australia and Carifornia, so a New York summer was child's play.

"Really?" Noelle drawled sarcastically, rolling her eyes as she returned her attention to the shelf while she continued her work. "So it's okay if you come to my work when I'm busy, but if I do that to you, you're allowed to kick me out." She said it like it was a fact, her tone indifferent, much like Carson's had been.

He hurt and angered her, and Carson wanted to kick himself for it.

"I was out of line for that, and I'm sorry," Carson immediately apologized, taking a few steps closer to her. He noticed the way her jaw clenched, her gaze dropping slightly as she shoved a third book into the shelf. "I was dealing with some of my own shit. I pushed you away, and I shouldn't have."

Noelle's gaze flickered over to him, her eyebrows drawn together slightly as their gazes locked. He saw the worry and curiosity that swam in her light eyes as it shone through behind the guard she had half-heartedly set up at the sight of him. With a slight shake of her head, Noelle hugged the two remaining books she held to her chest.

"What, Carson? What're you dealing with that you're not telling me?" she asked, her tone taking a gentle turn.

She took a step closer with her features soft and eyes earnest as her free hand came to grasp at his wrist, most of it still hidden in the shared pocket of his hoodie. Her hand came in contact with the bracelet he wore, the metal cool against her skin, and suddenly Carson's chest was tightening in the most pleasant way just by Noelle's presence. He had been hiding in himself after meeting her mother and that conversation with Aiden, and despite that being something Carson was used to doing, he knew he had to change it. Shoving his feelings down instead of talking about them

288

with Noelle was only going to hurt their relationship, and this was one Carson wanted to last.

"I want to tell you," Carson said, watching as those five words had Noelle's face falling before he pulled his hand out so he could turn his hand over and grip hers. "But not now and not here, okay? Right now, there's someone here that wants to meet you and all I gotta ask is you don't bring up Astros because she doesn't know I do what I do," he added quickly.

Confusion scrunched Noelle's features—Carson wanted to fucking melt at how adorable she looked—as she blinked up at him. "Who?"

As if on cue, Carson saw Kira coming down the aisle over Noelle's head before looking back at her and answering with a helpless smile.

"My sister."

Noelle's eyes widened at his words, her lips parting in surprise as she saw Carson nod to something, or someone, behind her before she turned around and caught sight of a beautiful woman making her way over. She was tall and blonde and most definitely Carson's sister. Kira, Noelle knew, especially from the tattoo of her name on Carson's arm, but before Noelle could even comprehend anything further, the woman grinned.

"You must be Noelle! I've been hearing a lot about you, and it's so great to finally meet you."

Suddenly, Noelle was being pulled into a hug, her hand dropping from Carson's wrist to return the hug since her other arm was caught behind her front and Kira's. Her heart did an excited leap because Kira's perfume was fresh and sweet and homely, and because Noelle was meeting someone from Carson's family and he had *talked* about her. That little mundane fact widened Noelle's smile as they pulled away from the hug.

"I'm Kira," she introduced, her accent Australian and adorable. "And, like I said, so excited to meet you."

"You too," Noelle sincerely responded as she looked up at her. Kira was tall, like her brother, and Noelle felt so short between them. "Did you just arrive in the city?"

"Last night, yeah," Kira nodded before her dark eyes flickered around the store, her smile widening. "I have to say, I adore your store. Hope you don't mind, but I'm looking to spend hours here as long as I'm in New York."

Noelle smiled, elated that Kira seemed to love the store almost as much as she did. "I don't mind at all." She laughed. "You can spend as much time here as you want." She glanced up at Carson next to her, her smile teasing as she added, "Anything for a Hayes."

His heart sped up at the sight of her smile directed towards him, almost threatening to burst out of his damn chest. He loosely strung an arm around her waist, ducking his head to press a kiss to her temple. He felt at ease for the first time in days, knowing that Noelle wasn't as pissed at him as before because they were going to talk about what had been bothering him. Carson had no intention of hiding from her anymore, and he was going to fucking try and get his shit together.

"Tomorrow night, yeah? I'm so excited."

Carson was pulled out of his thoughts randomly at his sister's voice, tuning into the conversation as he blinked in mild confusion. "Tomorrow night?" he repeated with a slight frown.

Both women looked at him. "Levi and Aiden's party," Noelle told him with a quirk of her brow as if he should know. When she said that, he did know. His friends' birthdays were a little over a week apart, and they had been planning on throwing them a party at Barcade with a shit ton of their friends. It was in a nicer part of Brooklyn. It was a bar and arcade mixed into one for overgrown children like Carson and their friends. Since both Levi and Aiden had been dying to go, they had managed to rent it out for tomorrow night. It was gonna be a surprise.

290

"Right, right." Carson nodded, glancing down at Noelle. "Want me to pick you up?" he asked.

Noelle's gaze returned to his, her eyes narrowing as she tilted her head challengingly. "Just to give me a ride or so we can talk?"

Carson pursed his lips at her words, the controlled look in her eyes telling him she wasn't budging on this. She wanted to talk to him about what had been going on and she wanted to do it soon, which Carson didn't blame her for. When he saw the knowing look cross over Kira's face, he knew his sister picked up on what Noelle meant and shot him a pointed look of her own, silently telling him to say yes or else he would regret it. He had no doubt he would.

He knew he owed it to her. He was an ass, and he owed her an explanation and he was going to give it to her.

When Kira subtly slipped away, Carson turned to face Noelle, noticing the determined pout and tilt of her lips, her eyes never leaving his as she waited for him to answer. Carson wasn't going to lie despite knowing it was his rude behavior that had Noelle showing him such a firm stance, he wholeheartedly admired and appreciated that she wasn't shying away from any of this. It was a reminder that in a relatively short amount of time, they had come a long way from him brushing her off and her averting her gaze out of nerves.

Carson reached his hands to cup Noelle's face, feeling her relax slightly but never wavering her gaze as he brushed his thumbs against her cheekbones. He ducked down a bit, unapologetically letting her see the sincerity and honesty he was feeling that he didn't let her see for the past few days. When he saw just a little bit of the hardness in her eyes melt away, heard her take in a soft breath, Carson knew he never should've fucking let what anyone else thought of him get into his head. All that mattered was Noelle, and he was an idiot to think so otherwise.

"We'll talk," he promised, his voice low and truthful as the buzz of the store slipped away. It was just him and Noelle; it was always just him and Noelle. "I'll tell you all about why I was being an asshole, and I'm gonna hope you'll forgive me and kiss me and everything will be okay."

"You should've told me without being an asshole in the first place," Noelle pointed out, her skin warm at Carson's touch yet feeling shivers run down her spine at the feel of his rings. She surprised herself by finding the willpower to reach up with her single free hand and grasp Carson's wrist, pulling his one hand away from her face and doing the same with the other. She saw his expression fall slightly, the mild panic crossing his features because she knew he was wondering if she was rejecting him at this moment. "But when you do tell me and your reasons are valid, then I'll for sure forgive you and kiss you and everything will be okay. For now, though, I gotta get back to work. I'll see you tomorrow, alright?" Noelle assured him with a gentle smile before Carson's unease took over.

Carson felt his tensed shoulders relax, wanting to give Noelle a look for scaring him like that. He genuinely feared for a brief second that Noelle was going to pull away from him when she forced him to let go of her, but then he nodded, letting out a soft breath as he shoved his hands back into the pocket of his hoodie and squared his shoulders. When his initial panic dissipated, his lips twitched into a smile at the sight of Noelle's as she backed away.

"I can't get a kiss before you go back to work?" he asked, his tone only half joking as he lifted his chin a little. It was kind of pathetic that he felt like he might be overstepping when he asked that, and Carson knew he had no one to blame but himself.

But then, Carson felt his chest lighten when he saw Noelle's smile widen slightly and she stopped before making her way towards him again. His heart sped up like a teenage boy's when she neared him, though he didn't mind at all. Stopping in front of him, Noelle got up to her tippy toes before pressing her lips to his cheek. Carson didn't at all feel disappointed when he knew the stain of her faded pink lipstick was on his skin.

292

She pulled back, her soft smile a beautiful sight to Carson's eyes. Noelle winked as she approached the other end of the aisle.

"It's all you get . . . for now," she promised before she disappeared around the corner.

CHAPTER TWENTY-ONE

Once making sure her silver hoops were secure in her ears, Noelle gave herself a satisfied once-over as she smiled approvingly at herself in the mirror. She had just finished getting ready for Levi and Aiden's surprise party, smoothing down the simple thigh-length sleeveless dark blue dress and making sure her makeup was okay before grabbing her things to head downstairs. She heard the whistle of the light breeze outside through the opened bedroom window. Carson would be here soon to pick her up so they could go to Barcade, but before they did that, Noelle knew that the two of them were due for a talk.

It was not like things were technically bad between them; it was just that there was definitely an issue Carson was dealing with that he wasn't letting Noelle in on, and if that was affecting their relationship then she wanted to know what it was, especially if she could somehow help him out. Noelle knew that Carson had the habit of keeping troubling feelings to himself since she was prone to do the same, though not as much as he did. And things weren't going to work out between them if they didn't communicate. If the mere thought of that made Noelle's stomach queasy, she didn't even want to entertain the thought of things truly ending before they even started because they couldn't talk to each other.

She had fallen for Carson so fast. Her feelings were deeper than she initially thought, and she desperately wanted things between them to work out.

Lost in her thoughts, Noelle left her room and began making her way down the hall to the stairs, only to stop when her mom came into view with a cup of green tea in her hand and already in her pajamas. Dr. Simon blinked at the sight of her daughter.

"I thought you left with Beverly," she said.

Noelle tried not to roll her eyes. For her mom being a renowned surgeon, her observation skills never seemed to apply too heavily on Noelle.

"She's keeping Aiden busy until the surprise party. Carson's picking me up in a few minutes."

Noelle saw the flutter of distaste flash across her mother's face, sparking annoyance in Noelle's blood.

"Hopefully, he doesn't look the mess he did when I met him," Dr. Simon breezily commented as she began walking towards her room, consequently passing Noelle as she did so.

"You can't judge him based off of that one brief interaction, Mom," Noelle stated as she turned around to stare at her mom's back.

"It was our first meeting, Noelle, and it was obviously after you slept with him." Noelle's face flushed heatedly at that. "You kept him a secret and told me you were dating Isaac when you've been running around with some boy whose hands looked like they'd punched a wall over and over again. What am I supposed to think?"

"That he's more than what he appears to be," Noelle responded with an exasperated sigh, hands flailing about. "Just give him a chance, Mom." Quietly and almost reservedly, she added, "I really like him."

Dr. Simon stopped right in front of her bedroom door at Noelle's last few words, head turning ever so slightly as she considered her daughter's words. Just when the sliver of hope was widening, Noelle's shoulders dropped when her mom sighed.

295

"Not tonight, Noelle," she said before disappearing into her room and shutting the door behind her.

Noelle clenched her jaw, disappointedly nodding to herself as she looked away at nothing in particular. The lack of interest her mom showed in her life was painful, something Noelle hadn't grown used to since her dad's death even if she kept telling herself it was fine. It wasn't fine, but the ringing of the doorbell had pulled her out of her thoughts instantly.

When Noelle opened the front door to reveal her boyfriend, she had to stop her side from falling to the door at the sight of Carson. She had seen him in athletic clothes, in jeans and casual button-downs; hell, she had seen him naked, but she had never seen him dress up too much, and right now, he looked absolutely delicious.

From his black shoes and slacks to the black button-down with white stripes tucked in, the three buttons undone, along with his dark hair curling atop his head and tattoos peeking on his collarbones, Noelle's knees weakened at the mere sight of the unfairly attractive man. The dull glow from the light above the front door shone down on him, his bronze skin glimmering under it.

If she wasn't totally speechless, she would definitely have mused, *hubba hubba.*

"Wow," Carson's low voice sounded appreciatively, snapping Noelle out of her daze.

A smile spread across Noelle's face, her cheeks flushing at the sight of Carson's dark-eyed gaze unabashedly roaming over her figure. She raised her eyebrows once their gazes locked. Her heart fluttered like it always did as her smile widened.

"I could say the same for you." When Carson smirked and let out a scoff, she nodded her head into the house. "You wanna come in?"

Carson sucked in his lower lip, glancing over his shoulder at the sight of the silver car parked right along the curb that he knew belonged to Noelle's mother.

"How about we talk out here?" he asked, looking back at Noelle with a hopeful glimmer. "It's nice out."

Furrowing her brows in confusion, Noelle offered a single nod as she stepped out and locked the door behind her before facing Carson. The front step of her house was relatively wide with black metal railings around it, save for where the three stairs to the pathway were, as they both leaned against the railing. Noelle looked at Carson as he faced straight ahead, leaning forward on the railing with his arms on top and hands interlocked. She waited for him to speak.

"I know I've been acting like a dick for a few days," he started, fingers absentmindedly twisting one of the rings he wore as he stared ahead. Noelle gazed at him as she leaned on her right side, so she could look up at his pretty profile, the way the muscle of his jaw was jumping and the subtle breeze was teasing his curls. "But it had nothing to do with you. It was just . . . things were said and I didn't handle hearing them the best way."

"What things, Car?" Noelle gently asked, not wanting to push too much but knowing this conversation needed to happen.

He was silent for a moment, the distant car horns being the only sounds disrupting the moment as Noelle watched Carson thoughtfully contemplate to utter his next words. And she waited patiently and carefully, only wanting him to speak when he was ready. Carson had never struck Noelle as someone who would openly talk about his feelings or his troubles so easily, and that was okay. The fact that he wanted to share this with her, something that had been obviously bothering him, was already a step in the right direction after the few steps backwards he had been taking when he closed off the past couple of days.

Carson bowed his head, his curls sweeping his forehead before he turned his head to look at her.

"Your mum's not too fond of me, is she?" he asked with a self-deprecating small smile, tilting his lips.

Noelle blinked at him, her lips parting because she hadn't entirely expected that. She hadn't expected Carson to outright ask that particular question. Her breath stalled in her throat, mentally cursing her mother for not even being capable of pretending to be pleasant when she first met the Australian. Noelle straightened slightly, hand gripping the cool narrow top of the railing.

"Carson—"

"It's okay, Ellie," he cut her off, sandwiching her hand on the railing by putting his own on top. Carson shrugged subtly. "It was obvious when I met her that morning, and I don't blame her for not liking what she saw. But—" Carson let out a breath, squinting up at the dusk sky. "Just the way she looked at me and then that conversation with Aiden just really set me off," he continued.

The clench of her heart couldn't be ignored, and Noelle's disappointment in her mother's brief interaction with Carson only intensified.

"I—" She didn't even know what to say or what she wanted to say. "What did you and Aiden talk about?" Noelle managed to ask despite not getting her thoughts together.

"You," Carson answered easily, a soft smirk on his lips as she raised her eyebrows. His smirk turned into a small smile. "And us. He was asking if being with you was something I was sure of," he added.

Noelle's heart came to a stop, her lips pressing together as she swallowed the hesitance down. She wanted to know what had been bothering Carson and had been adamant on hearing from him, but she wasn't going to lie if the direction of his conversation with Aiden wasn't worrying. What even prompted this kind of talk?

She stayed quiet; she didn't want to say anything because she wanted to hear Carson without prompting anything out of him.

Safe to say, she could feel the relief relax her muscles when Carson turned his body slightly to face her.

"Obviously I said I was," he assured her. He looked down at her, their gazes locked as he squeezed her hand. "Not to get all mushy on you, love, but after the past few days of me acting like a complete idiot, I realized you're one of the few things I'm sure of."

Oh shit. Was Carson ever not gonna surprise her? Render her speechless by his quiet yet breathlessly genuine words?

Noelle took in a soft breath, pressing her lips together as her eyes remained locked with Carson's dark ones, completely taken with the sincerity in his eyes and voice. She felt the smile tugging at her lips, her senses overwhelmed by the look on Carson's face and the wonderfully pleasant piney scent mixed with cologne he was engulfing her with.

"If I'm being honest with you, Ellie," Carson's quiet voice brought her back to reality, watching as he picked up her hand that he was holding to let it dangle between them, his ring-clad fingers interlacing with her own. "After meeting your mum and talking with Aiden, I just . . . I got to thinking and not all of it was good, and I started worrying if—"

"If what?" Noelle prodded, drawing her eyebrows together as she squeezed his hand slightly, tilting her head a little as she kept their gazes locked. What thoughts had been running through his mind that had him so worked up?

Carson pursed his lips as he inhaled sharply as if he was trying to muster up the courage to get the words out. Noelle waited patiently because if he needed a moment to push himself, then she knew he really was trying. Despite this being a new thing for him, he was willing to air out his vulnerabilities. She knew that he was well aware he had to be open with her for any of this to work between them, and despite being in the dark for the last few days, Noelle's patience remained as he gathered his thoughts. She kept her eyes on his and saw the way his gaze softened, his broad shoulders relaxing just a bit.

"If I wasn't good enough," Carson finally admitted, the sheepishness heavy in his tone, "for you."

His words had her reeling slightly, leaning back as she frowned up at him incredulously. For a second, she pondered if she heard Carson right, but the close-lipped, ingenuine smile on his lips and the way his gaze dropped to their interlocked hands had Noelle instantly realizing that this was what it was. This was what had been weighing down on Carson, had him acting distant and unavailable, and for Noelle to finally find out it was because of that had her heart breaking.

He didn't think he was good enough for her? Why did he regard her with that kind of pedestal as if she was higher than him in any kind of way? If he really did thought that much of her, could he not tell that Noelle felt the same way about him? Could he not tell that he was larger than life, someone who didn't have to fight for attention because he had it, someone who Noelle couldn't believe she was lucky enough to be with?

It was funny; the two of them thought the world of each other but forgot the feeling was completely mutual.

Noelle was feeling so many things at the same time, her heart thudding in her chest to keep up with the emotions running wild. She was irritated with her mom for sparking that impression in Carson's mind, mildly annoyed with Aiden for questioning Carson like that, and nothing but overwhelming adoration for the man in front of her who looked the shyest she had ever seen him. Carson looked like a mixture of embarrassed for revealing the truth but relieved that it was out there, and Noelle was proud of him for finally talking to her. Sure, it took him a few days but baby steps. They were kind of new at this, but they would get the hang of it.

She was a believer that actions speak louder than words in some scenarios, and Noelle believed that this called for it. With a small scoff of a laugh, she took advantage of the slight boost of height her wedges gave her and reached her free hand to the back of Carson's neck.

Effectively pulling him down, Noelle only caught a brief look at Carson's surprised face before she connected their lips, her eyes falling shut at the familiar feel and taste of his lips. Each kiss always picked up her heart, her insides melting into a puddle caused by the warmth Carson spread through her. She felt his free hand on her side, exposed through the side cutouts of her dress and smiled at the feel of his skin on hers, his ring biting familiarly.

It was a sweet kiss, slow and sucking as they breathed each other in to retain in memory, as if they hadn't already, but it ended too soon—much to Carson's disappointment. He blinked his eyes open slowly because, shit, she made him dizzy in the best way possible. His tongue peeked out to swipe at his lower lip as Noelle's eyes followed the movement and felt her lips curl at the sight of her faded pink lipstick on his mouth, knowing her own was probably smudged.

They were still close, chests pressed together and noses brushing. The tips of Noelle's fingers slid into Carson's hair at the back of his head as her eyes locked on his.

"Next time you get the silly thought of not being good enough for me," she began, her voice low but holding nothing but honesty, "remember that you're a better man than anyone else I could've ended up with. Don't compare yourself to anything or anyone, especially to me. You're who I want to be with."

Carson knew that some people he knew would call him a complete pussy for feeling as though his heart was fucking soaring in his chest at Noelle, for feeling like absolute mush at the clear candor in her words, but he couldn't give a damn. He knew, at that moment, that he had been an utter idiot for ever keeping his feelings from her, for hiding from her because he was too stubborn to openly talk about what had been bothering him. How could he ever keep her out when she had accepted his feelings so easily and so readily?

And her admittance of wanting to be with him? Carson was putty in her hands if he hadn't already been before.

He smiled, breathless because she made him feel so much. His arm slid around her waist to keep her close. Carson nudged his nose with hers, eliciting a soft giggle from her.

"Think it's obvious you make me a better man," he murmured earnestly as his hooded gaze remained on Noelle.

Noelle felt her cheeks flush, giddy and so head over heels for him as she hooked her arm around his neck and pressed a quick kiss to his lips.

"Weren't you listening?" She grinned at the subtle raise of his eyebrows. "You already are."

*   *   *

"Surprise!"

The looks on Aiden and Levi's faces, bewildered and shocked and totally elated, widened the grin on Noelle's face as she laughed and clapped along with everyone else. The birthday boys had just arrived with Beverly and Levi's brothers, who were both in town for this occasion, and the look of astonishment on their faces gave away the happiness they felt at the fact that they just hadn't expected this.

Barcade was packed with the boys' friends as the joint was rented out for this party with silver letter balloons spelling out Levi and Aiden's names. Noelle hugged Aiden and Levi, wishing them a happy birthday before the party started. Drinks were served, music was playing, and almost every arcade game was being used while others either gathered around to watch or mingled with one another.

At one point, Noelle had joined Beverly, Kira, and a couple of other people she had only met that night while taking shots at the bar. She only took a few, enough to give her a pleasant buzz but not enough to get her tipsy. Once she was done drinking for now, as well as taking countless pictures with the girls, Noelle caught sight of Carson playing one of the games and walked over, weaving through the partygoers to reach him.

She came up next to him, her left arm winding around his waist and leaning her cheek against his bicep. She felt his arm move as he played with the knobs and buttons, his gaze glued to the screen. Noelle watched as he played, her eyebrows furrowing at the alien fighting game he was playing.

"I can't tell if you're winning or not," she hummed in confusion.

"To be honest," Carson chuckled, still playing the game, "I can't either. Think I'm losing actually."

Noelle smirked, turning her head to press her chin on his arm so she could look at Carson. His teeth were sinking into his lower lip, his brows furrowed slightly in concentration. It was the same kind of look he had in the ring, though less intense and angry, and it was the kind of look that weakened Noelle's knees.

"I'd expect you to put up more of a fight," she teased, her right arm going around his torso so both of her arms were around him. "Are you telling me I've been dating a loser this whole time?"

Carson barked out an incredulous laugh, turning his head to look at her with dark eyes dancing with mirth. The robotic music was still playing from the game, but neither one of them was paying any attention to it.

"What'd you just say to me?" Carson demanded playfully.

She giggled lightly. "I called you a loser and judging by the results, you definitely are one," Noelle clarified when she heard the arcade game let out a tune that indicated the game was over. Dropping her arms from around Carson and taking a step back, Noelle clicked her tongue teasingly with a shake of her head. "Pretty disappointing." She smirked before promptly turning and walking away, though not before her grin widened at the sight of Carson's eyes narrowing tauntingly at her.

Unfortunately, Noelle didn't get too far because right when she was walking past the bathrooms towards the bar, a hand wrapped around her arm and pulled her towards the bathrooms. Noelle's startled yelp was drowned by the music and games and people chattering before it transitioned into a laugh when she recognized Carson pulling her along, stumbling only slightly to keep up when he yanked her into the single unisex bathroom and shut the door before pressing her up against it.

"First, you call me a better man," Carson spoke up, pressing his front to hers as she looked up at him with wide, excited eyes. The heat of his body radiated on to her as she felt his hands deliciously slide down her sides before coming around back, his large hands cupping her ass perfectly to keep her close. Their faces were inches away as they breathed each other in and basked in the proximity. "Then you call me a loser," Carson continued, tilting his head slightly to regard her teasingly. His hands squeezed her ass while Noelle's lips parted as she sucked in a soft yet sharp breath. Carson smirked knowingly. "I'm having trouble keeping up, darling."

Despite feeling her breath catch and stomach flutter excitedly, Noelle couldn't cease her teasing streak as she quirked an eyebrow.

"Maybe I should add slow to that list too."

Something flashed in Carson's eyes—dark and mischievous and challenging—effectively causing Noelle's heart to leap because that look he wore effortlessly pooled wetness to her very core. She felt his hands slide to her thighs before going under her dress. Noelle's breath hitched at the feel of his warm hands against her already heated skin, the coolness of his rings biting. Noelle's breath once against stalled when Carson's thumbs hooked into the waistband of her underwear.

And then he smirked—dangerous and arrogant and unforgiving.

"You're gonna regret that one, sweetheart," he vowed.

Before Noelle could comprehend it, her panties were ripped right off. The cool air rushed to her heated core as she

304

gasped in shock, gaping at Carson as her hands gripped his biceps while glancing at the ripped piece of cloth he held between ring-clad fingers.

"You owe me a new pair," she stated, her mind mildly hazy from excitement and shock because no guy had literally ripped her underwear right off of her, and Carson doing so sent a rush of heat through her body, igniting a fire only he was capable of setting off.

The smirk never wavered from his plush lips, his gaze locked on hers as he stuffed the flimsy fabric in the back pocket of his pants without hesitation. With his hands on her hips and her dress bunched at them, he dropped down to his knees right in front of her and groaned appreciatively at the sight of her bare and ready for him. Noelle's chest sank with a sharp exhale, her head against the door and the sounds of the party muffled as all she could think about was Carson.

So that was all she did—think about Carson as her fingers tangled in his curls while his mouth worked wonders and his hands held her in place. She thought about Carson when he made crude sounds while eagerly taking in every bit of her release and watching her fall apart above him within moments. She thought about his own pretty parted lips and satisfied groans when she decided to return the favor and release him from the confines of his pants and boxers to give him the kind of head-spinning pleasure from her own mouth the way he did with hers. And, shit, did she only ever think of Carson when he propped her on the edge of the sink and sank into her to the hilt. Their kisses were a mess of teeth and tongue and senses overwhelmed with the presence of each other.

When they walked out once they were done, two dizzying orgasms providing them the kind of bliss they craved, Noelle was thankful she had worn a dark dress to cover the wrinkles it adorned. Carson felt like a smug son of a bitch at the feel of her panties still in the back pocket of his pants.

They weren't too subtle walking out of the bathroom, their lips swollen and hair kind of messy with their hands interlocked as

305

they emerged. Fortunately, no one was really paying attention, but when Carson kissed the back of her hand and gave a wink before walking to where Max and a couple of other guys stood, Noelle couldn't keep the lazy, blissed-out smile from her face as Aiden approached her with a quirk of a knowing brow and a bottle of beer in hand.

"You know, since it's my birthday, I think I'm supposed to be the one to be rewarded with birthday sex," he mused jokingly, coming up to lean against the bar with Noelle.

She glanced at him, tearing her gaze away from the bustling party as she raised her own eyebrows at the older man despite the blush on her face at his insinuation.

"I think you've got the wrong sister for that situation, Aiden." Noelle chuckled, nodding to where Beverly was playing against some guy at one of the games across the room. "Bev's right there."

Aiden laughed, left arm propped on the bartop as he glanced at Noelle. "I'm glad things between you and Car are okay."

The smile on Noelle's face diminished slightly as if she was suddenly remembering that she and Carson had a gravelly couple of days. She knew part of it was her mom's doing, but she also remembered what Carson said about his conversation with his best friend.

"Things wouldn't have gotten even slightly messy if you hadn't made him doubt his relationship with me in the first place," Noelle mused as she glanced down at her feet.

Aiden's smile wavered slightly as he straightened, his dimples disappearing. Noelle could see the guilt flash in his light eyes.

"Listen, Noelle. I was only looking out for you and—"

"And I appreciate that, Aiden. I do," Noelle cut him off, her tone calm and neutral as she faced him properly. "But that's not for you to do, okay? I also get that you were looking out for him too, but your conversation didn't just make Carson doubt our relationship, he started doubting himself, and I know I don't have to tell you that that's not a good look on him."

Aiden's lips parted at her words, the regret clear as day and Noelle honestly felt bad about making him feel this way at his own birthday party. She couldn't help but feel slightly annoyed with him. She knew he and Carson were best friends and she admired the brotherhood they had, but instead of encouraging Carson to not listen to his insecurities, Aiden incidentally fed into it.

Noelle sighed, not wanting Aiden to feel like shit, especially now that whatever happened was in the past because her and Carson were okay and happy. They had talked and worked it out, and there was no reason for them to dwell on this.

"I really like him, Aiden," Noelle told him, repeating the same words she told her mom earlier tonight with just as much honesty. "And I don't care if being with him means having to deal with assholes like Boman and Milner."

Carson told her about that little bit too, about him worrying about the kind of men he was involved with who had already looked at Noelle wrongly. She had been endeared and touched by his concern for her, but she also reminded him that her feelings for Carson were a hundred times stronger than any fear she might have of facing those men again.

"I appreciate you looking out for me—for us—but trust me, being with Carson is the best thing for me and I wholeheartedly believe that."

The curly-haired man regarded her for a moment, his eyes and ears catching every bit of genuinity Noelle spoke with before a smile spread across his face. Noelle couldn't help but mirror it with a raise of her own eyebrows in expectant confusion, his grin ridiculously contagious as she waited for him to say something.

"I'm assuming you know Car only ever dates someone when he's completely sure that the relationship is worth pursuing, right?"

"Yeah . . .?" Noelle sounded slowly and unsurely, frowning slightly as she wasn't expecting that from him.

Aiden's grin widened as he held up his beer in a form of cheers.

"I'm glad he's found someone completely worth it."

CHAPTER TWENTY-TWO

"I kinda find it funny that the first time I come to your apartment is not even to see you," Noelle said as soon as Carson opened the door, blinking in surprise at the sight of his girlfriend. She giggled at the dumbfounded expression on his face, reaching on her tippy toes to press a kiss to his lips. "Hi," she hummed before walking further into his home.

"Uh, hi." Carson laughed lightly, confused at her arrival but not at all complaining as he shut the door and turned in time to see Oreo run into the living room and right towards Noelle. He watched with a fond smile on his lips as the little pup pawed at Noelle's legs before she giggled and picked him up, letting him lick at her chin. "Not that I'm complaining, love, but what're you doing here?"

"Kira didn't tell you?" Noelle questioned, cradling an all-too-compliant Oreo as Carson shook his head. "She wanted to do last minute shopping, and I offered to go with her." With a quirk of an eyebrow and a smirk tilted at her lips, hinting at a single dimple as she added, "Need to replace that underwear you destroyed."

An arrogant smirk curled at Carson's lips just as Oreo jumped out of Noelle's arms and onto the couch, slowly making his way over to her.

"Yeah, you're not gettin' those back. They're mine now," he informed her as his arm hooked around the back of her neck to pull her closer. The very piece of underwear they were talking about—navy blue and lacy—was currently in Carson's drawer, his new favorite possession as of last week. He ducked his head, pressing a kiss to her smiling lips. "Welcome to my crib," he added as an afterthought.

Noelle laughed against him before pulling back, her hazel eyes wandering around to take in Carson's home. His arm slowly withdrew from her, watching as she began walking around to observe every aspect of his apartment. It was obviously nowhere near as big as her home, but it was Carson's. It was more than enough for him, but he would be lying if he said he wasn't wondering what Noelle thought of it.

He watched as she approached the wooden mantle under the television, her fingers dancing over the few picture frames he put up. They were all either pictures of him with the boys or with his family. Each picture brought a smile to Noelle's face because, while Carson put up a tough exterior, one that she was so glad didn't exist around her anymore, it was beyond obvious that he loved the boys and was such a family man. It made liking him all the more effortless and breathless.

She also really liked the framed posters he had on his wall, a knowing smirk tilting her lips at the *Rocky* poster in addition to posters of bands and artists she vaguely knew of but didn't listen to too often. He had a small bookshelf in the corner filled with movie DVDs and books alike, and each piece of decoration and furniture gave her such a Carson vibe that she couldn't help but adore them.

Still, she couldn't help but tease him as she turned to raise an eyebrow at the dark-haired man. "You could use some plants."

Carson chuckled, sitting down on the couch. "I'll put that on my shopping list," he mused.

Noelle grinned, walking over as Carson expectantly put one arm on the armrest of the couch and reached his other hand out for her. He grabbed her hand and pulled her onto his lap and legs to rest on the couch.

"What're your plans for today?" she asked, her right elbow resting on his shoulder and fingers playing with the curls atop his head.

He tilted his head towards her hand, unabashedly enjoying the feeling of her fingers entangled with his hair as he moved his head just to brush his lips against her jaw. "Taking Oreo for his annual checkup and then a training sesh with Aiden."

"Hmm, speaking of that . . ." Noelle paused momentarily to giggle at the tickle of Carson's growing stubble scratching her skin, the sensation welcome and enticing as her free hand cupped his chin to press a brief kiss to his lips. Shit, she always wanted to be kissing him. "Does Kira really not know about what you do at Astros?"

"No, she doesn't," Carson answered, his right hand coming to rest on her thigh, which was exposed by the shorts she wore. Everywhere he touched, it was like he was leaving a searing imprint on her skin, and Noelle didn't mind. "If she, or my parents, found out they'd . . ." Carson shook his head. "Don't wanna worry them, y'know? It's best if they're left in the dark about this."

Noelle understood that; she did, but still, she couldn't help but frown as her hand released his chin to drop to her lap. "I get that, but, like . . . what if something serious happens, Car? They shouldn't find out about this part of your life if you're seriously injured or something."

Carson shot her a look, raising his eyebrows, almost unimpressed. "Been doing this for years now, Ellie, and that hasn't been a problem so far. It's not gonna happen any time soon," he drawled.

Her head cocked exasperatedly, hand dropping from his hair. "You can't know that, Car. What if—" she pointed out.

"Hey, stop with the 'what ifs' alright?" Carson cut her off, a frown drawing his eyebrows together in mild irritation. Noelle pursed her lips as he vaguely gestured with his hand. "The only way

311

that's gonna happen is if someone beats me. And if that happens—which, I shouldn't have to remind you, rarely does—then it's not before the other guy has a couple of broken bones." He looked away. "I don't need you doubting me now," he grumbled.

"Hey." Noelle frowned, her fingers lightly flicking his nose as Carson automatically scrunched his face up in response. "I'm not doubting you. I'm worried about you. There's a difference."

Carson relaxed under her, realizing he had been getting annoyed for no reason because she was allowed to be worried about him, just like he was about her when it came to certain things. Plus, in Noelle's defense, she had more of a reason to fret over Carson because of the violence he voluntarily took part in. Hiding it from his family wasn't as difficult as one would imagine. Sure, Carson hated lying to them, hated having an important part of his life hidden from them, but it was what was best for everyone. He didn't want to worry them. As long as they saw him healthy and happy, then everything was okay.

"I know. I'm sorry, baby," Carson rasped, tilting his head to brush his lips along hers. He could faintly smell and taste her cherry ChapStick. "I'll be fine, okay?" He tilted his head to lock their gazes. "And if I'm not, you can totally kick my ass."

That prompted a small smile to tug at Noelle's lips, her fingers lazily hooking around the two necklaces he wore. "Getting your ass beaten by a girl won't be good for your reputation, you know."

Carson grinned widely, the kind where the crinkles by his eyes appeared and his cheeks pushed up adorably, making Noelle's heart soar because it was such a fucking gorgeous sight. He squeezed her. "I'd be honored to have my ass kicked by you."

"That might just be the most romantic thing I've ever heard." Kira's voice had Carson's gaze flickering past Noelle as she looked over her shoulder, his cheeks flushing slightly at the sight of the older woman's amused smirk as she stood in the entryway of the short hallway—dressed and ready to go.

312

"You know me," Carson snickered, smiling cheekily at his sister as he rested his chin on Noelle's shoulder. "'M the most romantic guy in the world."

Noelle couldn't help the laugh that escaped her despite the flush on her cheeks, remembering the few conversations she and Carson have had about that very topic. Honestly, she thought he was pretty damn romantic.

"Alright." She giggled slightly, patting Carson's thigh as she looked at Kira. "You ready to go?"

Kira grinned as she tied her blonde hair back into a ponytail. "Yeah."

Carson reluctantly unwound his arms from Noelle so she could stand up, getting to her feet as she picked up her purse and followed Kira out the door. The blonde called a goodbye to her brother before leaving the apartment. Before Noelle left, she pulled Carson by the front of his shirt to press a kiss to his lips.

He returned the kiss without hesitation, a soft groan rumbling at the back of his throat as Noelle teasingly bit his full lower lip. "Have a good day, Car," she mumbled before pulling away completely.

He watched as she walked away, shooting him a grin over her shoulder that just screamed of her slyness because Carson knew she knew what kind of effect she had on him. Carson narrowed his eyes, leaning around the doorframe as Noelle caught up with Kira down the hall.

"Oi, sweetheart, make sure your new panties are the lace kind!" he called out to his girlfriend with a smirk.

Noelle gasped as she shot him an incredulous look, surprised he had so openly shouted that down the hallway while Carson smirked cheekily and shamelessly.

"Don't be a freak!" Kira shouted right back, protectively draping her arm around Noelle's shoulders.

*   *   *

313

Jab. Jab. Duck. Cross. Hook. Duck. Kick. Jab. Kick.

His moves were precise, dodging the swings of Aiden's arms perfectly while delivering a kick in return before his fists came in contact with the punching pads his friend wore. Soft thuds of other people at Astros punching sandbags and their partner's pads could be heard throughout the area over the music guitar heavy playing, but Carson's focus was on his own training session.

He had been at it for hours now, bench presses and weight lifting and push-ups out of the way before the ring became available, and he and Aiden claimed it. Carson paid no mind to the sweat he could feel running down his face, neck, arms, and back. He was too focused on perfecting every hit and making sure he was light on his feet. The adrenaline in his veins wasn't as intense as it was during an actual fight, but it was enough to keep Carson excited while training. Being fatal was never his goal—just making sure he could induce maximum damage without actually killing someone. Lots of the other fighters in Astros didn't seem to have the same mindset as him though.

Eventually, he and Aiden called it quits and finally stepped out of the ring to let someone else have a go. "You've any plans?" Carson asked as they headed towards the locker room.

"Yeah, Bev and I have dinner reservations to celebrate our anniversary."

Carson shot him a quizzical look as he quickly did the math in his head. "Anniversary?" They had already celebrated their one-year anniversary just a little while back. "Which one?"

Aiden chuckled slightly as he unstrapped the punch pads and dropped them on a bench they walked past. "Fourteen months." At the disbelieving raise of Carson's eyebrows, Aiden shrugged. "It's her lucky number, which apparently calls for celebration. Who am I to say no?"

A smirk came across Carson's lips. "Whipped."

"And you're not?" Aiden shot back quickly.

314

Carson pursed his lips, not being able to argue with that. "The fact that you'd throw my weakness in my face wounds me, Aiden."

"You know what wounds me?" Carson's movements froze right when he opened his locker, his jaw instantly clenching as he noticed Aiden tense next to him at the sound of the aggravatingly familiar and sarcastic voice. "The fact that you and I still haven't seen the inside of a ring."

With a jaw tight enough to shatter his teeth, Carson turned around to direct his glare at Milner, who stood just a few feet away with an unjustified arrogant tilt of his head as he gazed at Carson challengingly. The Australian, if he weren't so pissed at Milner's mere presence, would've laughed because the last time he saw Milner, Carson left him with bruised skin, battered ribs, and blood all over his face—not to mention fingers that Carson hadn't broken, unfortunately, but left in a state that would definitely cause Milner pain to so much as twitch them.

Seems like now that he was healed, the fucker was back to running his mouth as if he hadn't gotten his ass beaten the last time he pissed Carson off.

"What, you haven't gotten your ass kicked enough?" Carson responded with a bemused quirk of his eyebrow, though the fiery hatred in his eyes could be seen from miles away. He squared his shoulders and lifted his chin as Carson mockingly shook his head once. "What difference does it make if it's in the back alley or in the ring? You'll end up knocked out anyway."

Milner twitched his jaw, his own short fuse threatening to go off before he scoffed out a smirk. "We'll see about that when the match is over and I'm the one walking away with the money." His smirk widened, a taunting jeer in his voice. "And maybe with your little girlfriend too. She looks like a good time," he added.

Fucking hell, Milner was lucky Carson was at least trying to keep his word to Darryl of not colliding Milner's head with the wall since they weren't in the ring. Carson couldn't believe the son of a bitch. Milner's arrogance in just mentioning Noelle was enough to warrant a fist to his face, and Carson's blood seemed to set on fire at the sound of Milner uttering his girl's name, fighting the urge to rip the bastard's tongue right out.

"From what I can tell you've already lost to Car twice since coming back," Aiden piped up, his tone turned mocking. "I doubt third time's the charm for you, man." He took a step forward, and Carson noticed the way his best friend's eyes narrowed threateningly. "And don't fucking bring his girlfriend into this."

Milner's sharp gaze snapped to Aiden, irritation twisting his features. "Fuck off, McGrady. This is between me and Hayes," he snapped.

"Then keep her out of it," Carson demanded. Seriously, he just wanted to take a shower before heading home, and he couldn't even do that without Milner showing his damn face. Still, Carson wasn't going to let him get away with using Noelle in his pathetic threats. Taking a step forward, Carson narrowed his eyes. "You want a fight? I'll give you one. But bring her into this again and I don't give a fuck about the money. I'll put you in the ground without a thought."

The asshole smirked, unfazed by Carson's words as a satisfied glint flashed across his eyes. "Good." Milner nodded. "Two days."

Carson paused for a moment, remembering that Kira's flight was that night around the time the matches usually started. He hadn't been scheduled for one, so he had offered to take her to the airport. No way was he backing out of that, but he nodded at Milner.

"Fine. But it's gonna have to be pushed 'til ten," he said.

Milner shrugged indifferently. "So long as you get your ass in the ring, Hayes. I could give a shit what time it is." He began walking towards the door, throwing Carson a smug smirk. "See you there," he said.

When he left, Carson let out a sharp breath through his nose as an attempt to calm the simmering anger that always threatened to blow around Milner and guys like him before he turned to his locker once more.

"So Thursday night then?" Aiden raised a brow, opening his own locker up.

Carson began pulling out whatever he needed. "Looks like it," he grunted, shutting the locker before facing his friend. His expression was serious, his features set in a hard line as Aiden glanced at him expectantly. "You can't tell Noelle and Beverly about it."

"What?" Aiden laughed confusedly, frowning when he saw the determined look in the dark-haired boy's eyes. Aiden shut his own locker, the smile fading and frown deepening. "You don't want them there? It's an important match, Car. They'd wanna be there."

"I know, but I'm telling you, Aiden, Noelle can't be there," Carson stated, not budging from this. "You and I both know it's not gonna be an easy fight. It's gonna be the ugliest one yet, and I can't have Noelle standing there."

Aiden was still bewildered, unsure of what was making Carson come to this decision. Beverly came to every one of his fights, and Aiden knew Noelle liked being there too to show her support. They all did.

"What? You're gonna get distracted by her or something?"

Carson's patience was practically gone. "Goddamn it, Aiden! I don't want her seeing that fight!" he snapped, his hand slamming into the locker next to him as his loud voice bounced off the walls. He glared at his best friend, who to his credit wasn't fazed by Carson's outburst as he glared at him. "I don't want her around with that much blood, and to be fucking honest with you, I'd rather not have my girl be in the same room as the fucker who had the balls to put his hands on her."

Aiden pressed his lips into a thin line, taking note of the aggravation in Carson's tone and tense muscles. He was already getting worked up over this.

"You know she's gonna be upset you kept this fight from her," he calmly informed him, knowing he was only stating a fact Carson was already aware of.

"You think I don't know that?" Carson shook his head, a sharp breath escaping him as he glanced around the empty locker room absentmindedly, his body heated from not just the training session but after that short conversation with Milner. The bastard would be lucky if Carson let him walk out of that ring with his feet intact. If he thought Carson was going to let him get away with even mentioning Noelle, he had another thing coming. Carson should've truly put him out while he had the chance. "I love her too much to let her watch this fight."

They had slipped. The words had slipped effortlessly out of Carson's mouth, and he wouldn't have even thought twice about it if it weren't for Aiden's eyes widening in shock, staring at Carson in disbelief.

"You what?" Aiden practically choked out.

Carson looked at Aiden with a slightly confused furrow, unsure of what Aiden meant or was referring to. And then his own words replayed in his mind, a loud echo ringing in his head, and suddenly, realization crashed into Carson like an eighteen wheeler and his heart stopped beating in his chest.

It was comical, the way Carson's features had gone from annoyed because of Milner to completely taken aback by his own confession, his mouth clamped shut and his Adam's apple bobbed because he *loved* her.

There wasn't enough oxygen in the world to allow Carson to breathe as he tried to come to terms with what he just blurted out without a thought. Aiden stared at him silently in his own state of shock, waiting for Carson to accept what he just said. His ears were deaf to all sounds, save for the thundering of his heart, its quickened pace showcasing the excitement of Carson's words. With each second that passed by, the more Carson thought about it, the more he realized that it was fucking true.

He and Noelle haven't been together long, only over a month or so. He had known her for only a little longer than that, but the relative shortness of their relationship didn't seem to matter. Carson knew his feelings for her were stronger than what he had ever felt for anyone before. He knew that he hated himself if he upset her, felt his heart leap out of his chest at the sight of her smile, knew his favorite flavor was her cherry ChapStick, and was ready to do some serious damage to anyone who tried to fuck with her. She had easily, effortlessly become one of the most important people in his life—his favorite person.

For someone who had taken a minute to accept that he had feelings for Noelle in the first place, Carson, at that moment, readily and wholeheartedly accepted the fact that he was in love with her once the initial astonishment settled.

Because he did.

He didn't care that they hadn't been together long. He couldn't help how he felt about that beautiful girl with the prettiest dimpled smile and the kindest eyes and a bright personality that outshined anyone else he had ever met, which contradicted the fact that her favorite writer was Edgar Allan Poe. The more he thought about it, the more breathless he felt in the best possible way because he loved Noelle.

And the best part was, he wasn't scared at all.

CHAPTER TWENTY-THREE

"You told me you loved her day before yesterday. Why the hell haven't you told her yet?" Aiden scoffed as he and Carson quickly crossed the street, five seconds left before the pedestrian signal flashed red again.

Carson shot Aiden an exasperated look as they turned right on the sidewalk to continue walking. "Because I'm not gonna just blurt it out, Aiden," he huffed, reaching up to push his hair back. "It has to be, like, said at the right moment."

"Aww, Car!" Aiden giggled, his voice turning high-pitched with its teasing as he reached out to nudge the dark-eyed man's arm who promptly tried to shuffle away. "You're so romantic!"

Carson's smile turned wry as he thought of his many conversations with Noelle and how Kira had said the same thing the other day. "That's what they tell me."

They approached the store amidst their bantering, walking into the familiar space filled with books and somewhat busy with customers wandering around. Right away, they spotted the older Simon sister at the counter.

"I'm here to whisk you off for lunch," Aiden announced as they approached the register.

Beverly looked up from the notebook she was writing in, a smile spreading on her face as she shut it. "About time. I'm starving," she teased, walking around the counter as her eyes shifted to Carson. "Hey, Car! Elle's in the back."

Carson nodded with a smile, already making his way towards the back room as he heard Beverly call for one of her employees to man the register while she stepped out. He glanced around as he made his way to the back, appreciating the effortless coziness this store consisted—not only were there shelves in the middle but there were some built into the walls, creating corners of worlds ready to be read and explored. Carson hoped to do that someday.

He entered the back area that served as a sort of a break room, his eyes immediately landing on Noelle. She was already on her break, laying down on the dark green couch with her head on the armrest. She was oblivious to Carson's entrance behind her as she busied herself on her phone. She wasn't doing anything out of the ordinary, but she was easily the prettiest girl Carson had ever met.

"Delivery for Ellie Simon," Carson announced his presence with a one-knuckle knock on the door frame. Noelle's neck craned, looking behind her as a grin spread across her face when she realized just who she was looking at.

She sat up, pulling her hair over one shoulder as she grinned up at Carson after catching sight of the Burger Heaven bag he held. "Don't know what I'm happier seeing," she teased as he entered the room. "The food or the guy bringing it."

Carson rolled his eyes good naturedly, walking to the round plastic table as Noelle followed after him. "We both know it's the food," he responded, sarcasm dripping from his voice as he shot her a pointed look.

He had settled the food down just as he spoke, giving Noelle the opportunity to grasp Carson's cheeks and pull him towards her. She gave him a proper greeting of a kiss that familiarly set fire to Carson's skin. When she pulled away, Carson automatically tried to chase her lips, which earned a grin from Noelle as her thumbs briefly circled his cheeks.

"We both know it's you," she mumbled, pressing another kiss to his lower lip before pulling away to sit down on one of the chairs.

His heart thudded. Shit. He was so in love with her.

"So," Noelle spoke up once more as Carson took the seat next to her, bringing it upon herself to pull out their food. She smiled at the mac and cheese container for herself, handing Carson his sandwich before she popped the lid. "Shouldn't you be spending the day with Kira? Isn't she leaving tonight?"

Suddenly, Carson's turkey sandwich seemed hard to swallow. "Yeah," he managed to speak out after taking in the bite. "I'm gonna stay with her at the airport until she boards so, you know, I wanted to see you before because I'll be there for a while."

Lie. Lie, lie, lie.

He hoped Noelle wouldn't pick up on him being unable to look her in the eye when he said that, his attention falsely fixated on his food. His fight with Milner was tonight, a secret kept from Noelle and her sister because Carson knew if Beverly found out, then Noelle would too. He hated asking Aiden to lie to his girlfriend, but he had no choice. Carson refused to have Noelle there and was willing to deal with the consequences of her potentially being angry at him for it, but it was for her protection.

Though no matter how many times he repeated that in his mind, it didn't make lying to her any easier.

"Aw, you're so cute!" Noelle grinned. Carson wasn't surprised that he didn't feel the ball in his chest loosen in relief at her obliviousness. He was an asshole. As she swallowed a spoonful of mac and cheese, she tilted her head. "Your parents live in California, right? Do you visit them?"

"During the holidays, mostly." Carson nodded, grateful to get his mind off of the lie he told Noelle, but it was hard to get rid of. "I went to see them for Christmas and stayed until after New Year's."

Noelle raised a brow. "Seeing them this year?"

322

Carson snorted, thinking of the conversation he had with his parents a few days ago on FaceTime with Kira. "No, they've already booked a holiday couples' cruise."

His words prompted Noelle's grin to widen. "I think your parents might be the cutest couple on earth."

He smiled, wholeheartedly agreeing as he took a sip of his water, then he leaned towards Noelle and pouted slightly. "What about us though?" he asked.

Noelle looked at him, her light eyes twinkling as she cupped his chin. Her fingers squished his cheeks together and puckered his lips in the process. She wanted to take a picture of Carson's face, the sight in front of her levels of adorable she couldn't comprehend.

"Take me on a couples' cruise and we just might be."

Carson laughed loudly, his eyes crinkling as Noelle joined in. Her dimples made an adorable appearance and made Carson's heart pound. She was so beautiful. He was so in love. And he was an asshole for lying to her.

*   *   *

It would be a lie if Carson said he was satisfied that Milner's jaw didn't crack under his fist, though watching him tumble to the ground would be enough for now, but just as fast he went down, he got back up, not sparing a second as he launched himself at Carson. He felt Milner's arms wrap around his torso, pushing Carson back. Before he could take him too far, Carson jabbed his right elbow into Milner's back, causing him to stumble slightly. Carson took the opportunity to jerk himself to the right, effectively getting out of Milner's grip while kicking out his foot so it could come in contact with Milner's side and put some distance between them.

They were only in the first round, and while Carson had gotten a few hits on Milner, he was repaid by a sharp kick to his side and a hit to the face. He knew that was bruising, but the adrenaline pumping his veins made him numb to any pain as usual. He never focused on an injury until the match was over.

Carson could taste the blood in his mouth, the copper tang not too heavy because he knew it came from a cut on his lip. His eyes never left Milner's as he spat the crimson liquid onto the canvas floor before wiping his mouth with the back of his hand.

Milner was back on his feet across the ring, his breathing heavy. "Not doing so hot, Hayes?" he called, fists already up and back bent slightly in a defensive position. "That has anything to do with the fact I don't see your chick in the crowd?"

What was it with guys bringing up or trash talking their opponent's girls in the ring? Carson had never done it as he didn't find it necessary to degrade a woman like that, and it never happened to him until Noelle. Now that it was coming from assholes like Milner, Carson was even more keen on knocking the air out of the son of a bitch.

So Carson didn't dignify him with a verbal response. Instead, he swiftly made his way to Milner, quick like lightning, and attacked.

*   *   *

"Take them off."

Carson panted heavily, trying to catch his breath as he glared up at Aiden, irritated by the demanding tone in his voice. Aiden didn't waver, a scowl of his own twisting his features as he stared down at Carson expectantly. The fighter, in turn, didn't look any less irritated as he slid off the rings decorating his fingers, holding back winces when the jewelry twisted against his bruised digits.

When Carson shoved them into Aiden's arms, the hazel-eyed man cursed before dropping them into Levi's hand. "Are you trying to shatter your fucking fingers?" Aiden demanded, staring at

324

Carson in angered incredulity as he picked up the roll of protective wrap. "The hell were you thinking?"

"That I wanted to make him fucking bleed," Carson snapped back, the muscle in his jaw stinging as he spoke. As Aiden crouched in front of him to redo Carson's wrapping, the fighter's gaze went to the other corner of the ring where Milner was being taken care of by his own buddies. A smirk tugged at Carson's lips at the sight of the blood smearing under Milner's nose and the corners of his mouth. "'S working pretty well."

Levi scoffed from above him, arms crossed over his chest after pocketing Carson's rings. "Making him bleed shouldn't have to mean breaking your fingers in the process."

"Yeah. You're tryna make it through this fight, remember?" Max added in with a raise of his brows.

Carson rolled his eyes, already heated from the fight as his bruised fingers clenched around the water bottle he was quickly draining. The second round had just ended with Carson winning, and while he was satisfied with that victory, he was determined to win the match as a whole. There were more people here than usual. This fight was one that people had been anticipating since Milner returned because his rivalry with Carson was no secret. While Carson knew winning this match would bring him a pretty penny, he was more sick and tired of hearing Noelle's name or her mere mention from Milner's damn mouth. He was sick of Milner walking around like he owned the damn place when Carson had beat him more than once. Carson was determined to put him in his place.

He couldn't lose his head though; he knew that. If he got too pissed off, if he let Milner get under his skin, then his hits would get sloppy and Milner would get the better of him. While that was the last thing Carson wanted, he hated to admit that it was already happening in the past two rounds.

His bruised torso, jaw, and fingers along with cuts on his lips and bleeding nose were all proof of that.

The more he sat in the corner, letting his friends take care of him for the two-minute break, the more his attention kept wandering to the injuries he sustained. He had purposefully yet foolishly left the rings on his fingers, and every time he punched, he could practically feel his bones wavering under his skin. Carson was aware it was a stupid decision on his part, but all he could think of was bringing maximum damage. While Carson was sporting injuries of his own, Milner was worse off than him.

"Your teeth are still intact, right?" Aiden's voice brought Carson back, making the darker-haired man scoff in affronted annoyance.

"I'm gonna pretend you didn't just ask me that," Carson grunted as he stood up, inhaling sharply through his teeth at the throbbing sting that traveled up his side, originating from where Milner had landed a kick. He could feel himself limping too because of another kick that had hit him in the back of the knee. Carson clenched his jaw, ignoring the stinging pain the action brought. He planned on ending Milner if that was the last thing he was going to do.

Carson didn't pull back his hits. He didn't, for a second, think about any damage his body might have sustained when Milner struck back. Despite the hindering pain in his leg, he didn't stop from being light on his feet. He was determined on winning this fight, determined to instill maximum damage on Milner, to the point where he focused more on his offense than defense.

While Carson could hear his friends shouting at him from the sidelines, telling him to block the punches Milner launched and the kicks he threw, Carson didn't entirely listen. His focus was his own attacks and Milner's stupidly smug expression every time he landed a hit . . . and Noelle.

Because, of course, Carson was thinking about Noelle. At this point, everyone who frequented Astros knew of her relationship with Carson and knew that Milner was openly using her to antagonize Carson. With every contact of Carson's fists and feet against Milner's body, it was an obvious message to him and anyone else who tried to start something with Carson that they couldn't possibly win. In fact, there were two messages Carson knew would reach anyone watching.

Don't voluntarily pick a fight with Carson Hayes, and never bring his girl into it.

*   *   *

"I'm not kidding!" Beverly laughed, only intensifying Noelle's laughter as the younger woman pushed herself into the back of the couch, her hands on her cheeks in incredulity. "Like, it was so awkward! Aiden started choking and I just couldn't speak."

"Holy shit," Noelle wheezed, her cheeks hurting from how much she was grinning. "Louisa really gives no fucks, huh?"

Beverly shook her head as she exhaled sharply, laughing in lingering disbelief. "Apparently not." When her light brown eyes met Noelle's, they widened slightly as she confessed. "She told me that Aiden once said he wants, like, eight kids. Eight!" Noelle's jaw dropped. "I love him, but I'm sure as hell not popping out eight goddamn kids. There's only so much pain I can put myself through."

Noelle genuinely couldn't stop laughing at her sister's expense, clapping her hands. She knew she probably looked like an overzealous seal, but this was just too funny. Beverly was informing Noelle about something that had occurred when Aiden's mother and siblings had come to the city the other day. They came the day before yesterday for dinner with Aiden and Beverly and then decided to stay over at Aiden's place for an extra day before having lunch with him and Beverly and heading back home.

And, apparently, lunch included Aiden's mom questioning him and Beverly when the hell they were going to tie the knot and pop out some grandbabies. It didn't matter to Louisa McGrady that Beverly and Aiden have only been together for a year, which was

327

too soon for either of them to think about marriage or children. She had put them on the spot and just imagining their comical reactions had Noelle launching into a fit of giggles. The fact that Aiden supposedly wanted eight kids was even more ridiculous.

"It's not funny!" Beverly exclaimed, though she laughed as she grabbed onto a couch cushion and hit Noelle who merely took the hit on her arm as she continued giggling. "What if it was you and Carson, huh?"

Noelle's laughter died, her eyes widening as she shot her sister an incredulous look. "Whoa, hey, okay! Carson and I have only been together for, like, over a month or something. I think you're jumping the gun there, Bev."

"It doesn't matter. You'd be just as embarrassed if someone started asking you about babies," Beverly retorted with a smug grin as Noelle's face flushed hotly. Having kids was just not something Noelle thought about even before meeting Carson. She hadn't been with him long enough to even entertain the idea jokingly, but Noelle couldn't lie. The implication of being with Carson long enough for that to happen kind of excited Noelle.

For a second, she selfishly wished she was with him but then squashed that thought away. He was with his sister, and she was spending time with her just as they should be. She would see him tomorrow or something.

"We're not talking about this." Noelle laughed, albeit a bit nervously as she tried to change the topic. As if the universe was on her side, the doorbell rang and she got up. "Saved by the bell," she sang, causing Beverly to roll her eyes and click her tongue.

Noelle laughed as she reached the door, opening it and raising her eyebrows at the sight of Max and Aiden standing there. Noelle would've been happy to see them if it weren't for the grim looks on both of their faces.

Her smile wavered, her eyebrows twitching into a frown. "What're you guys doing here?" she asked. Her gaze flickered between the two, her stomach knotting as she gestured for them to come inside. "What's the matter?" she added hesitantly.

The two men exchanged looks with one another as they entered, Max pursing his lips and Aiden's Adam's apple bobbing before they looked back at Noelle. Behind them, Beverly stood up with a curious, confused frown and raised her eyebrows at Noelle, but Noelle could only focus on the two men. Their eyebrows were drawn together in dreaded worry, and Noelle felt her heart pick up its pace. Whatever they had to say, with both hesitant on saying it, only made Noelle more nervous. Weren't they supposed to be having a boys' night out with Levi?

"It's Carson," Max finally said, effectively causing Noelle's heart to jump in her throat because why were they here about Carson? Wasn't he at the airport waiting for Kira's flight to take off? The way Max was playing with the bracelets on his wrist made Noelle nervous. "I . . . he's hurt, Noelle."

Her mouth dried as Beverly's eyes widened, but Noelle's gaze was on Aiden and Max as her eyes widened in confusion. Had she heard him right? Carson was hurt? Why the hell was he hurt? Noelle knew the possible answer to that because what else could explain it, but she didn't want to believe it because that would mean he lied to her, and she couldn't possibly understand why.

She parted her lips. "Wha—"

"His match with Milner was tonight," Aiden spoke up, her gaze instantly snapping to him as he uttered those words. Noelle inhaled sharply, heart pounding.

What the fuck? Why the hell hadn't he told her? Why did he lie about being with Kira? What the fuck was going on?

Aiden took a step towards her. "He won. He beat Milner, but he's hurt pretty bad."

Noelle couldn't breathe. Beverly rushed over, holding her sister's hand because she knew she needed it; she knew Noelle needed something to anchor her. It felt like her insides were twisting and tightening in painful discomfort, constricting her lungs

329

and cutting off air as she processed Aiden's words. By the looks on their faces, she knew it was serious. She knew that Carson must be really hurt for them to be here to relay this to her, and all Noelle could do was feel a tight ball of worry in her throat. She squeezed Beverly's hand.

He needs to be okay. Carson has to be okay.

She was trying to maintain her breathing even if air seemed difficult to come by. "Where—" she choked out as she willed herself not to cry.

The words died on her tongue, but thankfully, Max understood. "He's at his apartment. Levi's with him," he supplied.

Noelle let out a sharp breath. "If he's hurt, why the fuck isn't he at the hospital?" Beverly exclaimed.

"You know why, doll," Aiden calmly responded and Noelle understood too. She knew of Carson's distaste of hospitals.

Although she understood why he didn't want to go to the hospital—she wasn't much of a fan of them herself—Noelle couldn't help but curse Carson's stubbornness. Her panic was building, her mind conjuring up gruesome images of him beaten and bloody and unable to stand on his own two feet if Aiden and Max showed up with grim faces to deliver her the news in person. She was pissed and in disbelief that Carson didn't so much as hint at the match, but her worry was far greater.

Aiden's throat worked, worrying his lower lip before sighing reluctantly. "I, uh, think you should go see him."

Even though her heart was threatening to burst out of her chest, her head dizzy with the knowledge of her boyfriend injured and incapable of staying on his feet and dreaded fear closing up her throat, Noelle didn't have to be told twice. She grabbed what she needed, slipped on her shoes, and was gone quicker than anyone could blink.

CHAPTER TWENTY-FOUR

Three years ago

The smell of disinfectant had never seemed so strong before. Noelle's nose began to go numb because of the pungent stench, but that wasn't a focus of hers. Her knee bounced erratically, timed with the nervous beating of her heart, throat tight with worry and lips chewed out, all the while wondering if they were okay.

Noelle refused to cry, not until she knew what exactly was going on. Beverly had practically bitten all of her nails off next to her and her mother's pacing was only growing her anxiety. She didn't think her mom had ever been on this side of the hospital scene; her mom had always been the one in the ER or in the operating room, saving lives instead of waiting to find out if her colleagues could save the lives of her husband and youngest daughter.

A few of the other doctors and nurses were lingering around the waiting room as well, those who weren't treating Mr. Simon and Andrea, in show of support. Noelle wondered if they didn't have patients of their own to go see, but that thought went as quickly as it came. She didn't care. She just needed to know if her dad and Andrea were okay. She couldn't handle the ball heavy with lead and dread sinking in the pit of her stomach, the nausea it induced threatening to make her throw up even though she didn't know what was going on.

Someone needed to tell them what the fuck was going on.

"Malorie." The sound of one of the surgeons, Dr. Tanaka, Noelle briefly remembered, had everyone's heads whipping to where his voice came from. Noelle and Beverly automatically stumbled to their feet as they saw him approach with Dr. Wendell by his side. Noelle's red-rimmed eyes scanned their faces in hopes of being able to read their expressions, but even though these two had just treated family members of one of their colleagues, one of their friends, they still managed to expertly school their expressions.

"How are they?" Noelle's mom said, which were the first words that flew out of her mouth. Her widened eyes stared at them expectantly, dread swimming in her eyes. Noelle's hand grabbed Beverly's. "How're Henry and Andrea?"

Dr. Wendell spoke up first, her voice gentle yet firm and professional as she explained Andrea's injuries. Broken ribs and right arm, a concussion and shards of glass that have left several cuts on her skin. Noelle swore with each injury listed, her heart sank lower and lower into her stomach, her lips quivering and nose stinging and eyes burning at the thought of her little sister being in so much pain. God, all Noelle wanted to do was get to Andrea, hold her hand, and lay down next to her.

"There's something else," Dr. Wendell hesitantly spoke up once more, and this time, Noelle could detect the emotion in the older woman's voice. She could detect the benevolent, concerned tilt Dr. Wendell's voice took, and she assumed Beverly did too with how her hand squeezed Noelle's. Dr. Wendell's gaze flickered between Dr. Simon and her daughters before she let out a breath and looked back at her friend. "Malorie . . ."

Dr. Simon straightened, knowing that look and that tone of voice all too well as her jaw clenched. Noelle had never seen her mother look so calmly terrified.

"What?" she demanded. "What is it?"

332

Noelle guessed Dr. Wendell threw caution to the wind with how her face transformed into regretful sorrow, only serving to skyrocket Noelle's anxiety. The hospital was busy, but it had never been quieter. It was like everyone was holding a breath, waiting for Dr. Wendell's next words.

The surgeon swallowed. "Andrea suffered from severe spinal cord damage . . ." Dr. Wendell shook her head slightly, and it was obvious she couldn't keep her own emotions at bay. "I . . . there was nothing we could do, Malorie. She's paralyzed."

Noelle felt like she was going to throw up.

She didn't know how many minutes had passed as they processed this information. She didn't know what to do with the knowledge of her younger sister, only fourteen years old, never being able to walk again. Noelle's eyes were wide and unblinking and burning, her knees threatening to give out from under her because she just couldn't seem to process this. She didn't want to accept this. Andrea had her whole life ahead of her. Now, she was confined to live it on a wheelchair.

"What about Henry?" Dr. Simon's hoarse voice asked after minutes of incomprehensible silence. She was wringing her fingers together, her wedding band the only piece of jewelry on her. Noelle felt her breath still in her throat as her gaze flickered to Dr. Tanaka. Noelle couldn't take anymore bad news. "Is Henry okay?"

Dr. Tanaka's expression broke, the older man's features turning into one similar to Dr. Wendell's. Noelle began shaking her head because she knew she wasn't going to like whatever he was about to say. She knew the fresh wave of tears burning her eyes were justified.

"I . . . I'm sorry, Malorie." *Oh god, no.* "There was nothing we could do, but . . . Henry was DOA."

Dead on arrival.

This time, Noelle did throw up.

*　　*　　*

The circumstances were different drastically. Noelle knew that, but that didn't mean she didn't feel the same nauseating worry eat up inside her as she tried to make her way to Carson's house as quickly as she could. She jumped into the car and drove, having no patience for an Uber or a subway as she made her way to Brooklyn. There was no music playing in the car, only the sound of her heart beating erratically and her thoughts screaming at her.

Carson has to be okay. He is fine. Noelle kept repeating that in her head like a mantra as if the more she said it, the truer it would get; as if he would be perfectly okay when she would walk through his apartment door.

Her grip on the steering wheel tightened, too many emotions overwhelming her. Her concern and worry for Carson's well-being was accompanied by confused anger. She was pissed that Carson hadn't told her about his fight with Milner. It was something she knew was coming eventually; she knew the two fighters needed to act on their animosity for each other sooner or later, but she just hadn't expected Carson to hide it from her. She was worried and angry and, frankly, hurt.

Beverly obviously didn't know about the match either, which told Noelle that Carson had specifically asked Aiden and the others to keep it from both of them. He had gone out of his way to leave Noelle in the dark, and even though Noelle wanted answers, her desire to make sure that he was okay won out.

She found a parking spot fairly quickly and was quick on her feet, her fingers nervously wringing together and her eyes glued to the numbers on the elevator as it too slowly took her to Carson's floor. As soon as she reached the door with her heart pounding, Noelle knocked a bit too hard though she didn't care, ignoring the light sting in her knuckles as she didn't stop until she heard the lock click and the door swung open.

As much as she adored Levi, Noelle was disappointed that he answered the door. "Where is he?" she questioned hastily, not even waiting for the blond to step aside as she pushed her way into the apartment. Her hazel eyes darted around the empty living room, swiveling around to look at Levi once more. "Levi, where is he?" Noelle repeated desperately.

She registered the worried look on Levi's face, clear and on full display with his curls being tied back into a bun as he nodded forward. "In his room."

Despite the fact that Noelle had never been anywhere in Carson's apartment except for his living room, it was like her feet were moving on their own accord as she walked down the short hallway, easily finding the doorway to Carson's bedroom. When she stepped in without a moment's thoughts, Noelle's heart dropped like dread was anchoring it down.

He wasn't even sitting on the bed. Instead, Carson was on the floor, propped up with his back against the bed and head tilted all the way back to rest on the mattress. Noelle's hand fell away from the door, the strap of her purse falling from her shoulder to the crook of her elbow before she ultimately let it fall on the floor with a thud, an unsteady inhale shaking through her.

She wanted to cry at the sight in front of her.

The blood under his nose was unsuccessfully cleaned off because a light pink-reddish tint was still smeared on the area, a cut right in the middle of his bottom lip making it seem pinker and fuller than usual because of the slight swelling. There was already a bruise yellowing and darkening around his right eye, dark curls matted against his forehead. His right arm was thrown around his torso, his bruised and raw fingers gripping his side. By the looks of his digits, Noelle knew he must've fought either the entire or some of the fight with rings on.

Even with her lips pressed together, Noelle could feel them quivering as her breath remained uneven. Her feet slowly but surely moved her to where her boyfriend sat. She wasn't sure if Carson even noticed her presence, though she knew that Oreo did as the pup, laying on his paws next to Carson with his chin rested on

Carson's thigh, lifted his head to regard her. Noelle felt her heartstrings tug. Oreo clearly knew Carson wasn't okay, unable to do much but to sit next to him in hopes for comfort. Noelle knew it was appreciated.

"Carson," she breathed out, her voice breaking the pained silence hanging in the air as she walked further into the room, eventually kneeling to the Australian's left side. Her fingers itched to touch him but Noelle hesitated, unsure of where he was really hurt and if he would want anyone to touch him after going through a brutal fight the way he did. She felt her throat tighten when Carson drearily blinked open, his head still leaned back on the mattress yet turning slightly towards the sound of her voice. "Hey. Hi, baby."

She was angry and scared and hurt and upset, but above all, she was concerned over his well-being. She needed to make sure he wasn't fucking dying.

Carson's brows furrowed as his dark eyes landed on her, causing Noelle to let out a soft breath. She was terrified but relieved to see his pretty brown eyes.

"Ellie," he breathed out, his Adam's apple bobbing as if just uttering her name pained him. Noelle winced alarmingly as Carson tried to sit up, his face scrunching in pain as he hissed through his teeth. She could only hold her breath at the look on his face as Carson forced his eyes open, brows still drawn together. "What're you doing here?" he croaked.

Noelle attempted to swallow down the emotion lumping in her throat, trying to force a gentle smile to grace her lips despite the heaviness sitting in her chest at the sight of Carson. He may have won the fight, but he was bruised and bloody. Noelle couldn't stand to see him like this. Tears were already burning her eyes, threatening to escape, but she forced them back as her fingers carefully sifted through his hair to push them back.

"Came to make sure you were okay, bub." Her voice was thick and shaky. "Heard you won."

336

Carson let out a breath, his chest sinking. Noelle noticed the thin sheen of sweat coating his skin. He was in a grey tank top, dark in some spots due to his sweat and tattoos on display. Now that she was right next to him, Noelle noticed the few bruises darkening his golden skin on his arms. Was there a part of him left uninjured or untouched?

"How did you—"

"Aiden and Max told me," she cut him off, already knowing what he was going to say. "Told me about your fight. Told me you were hurt."

Despite her worry over Carson, Noelle couldn't keep the hurt from seeping into her unsteadily calm tone, her fingers still carefully tangled into his messy curls. His gaze was on hers and she reluctantly met his eyes, knowing that she had nothing to hide from and it was Carson who was in the wrong. But he was hurt and so obviously in pain. Noelle didn't want to do this right now.

"Baby, I'm—"

"You need to go to the hospital, Carson," Noelle cut him off, not needing to hear his apology right now. She definitely wanted to hear what he had to say, but the main priority was to make sure he was taken care of. A fresh trickle of blood was seeping down from his left temple through a cut she hadn't noticed before, his black eye was swelling slightly. Noelle wanted to make sure he didn't have any broken ribs.

His reaction wasn't surprising. Carson immediately shook his head, leaning away from Noelle as he shut his eyes and scrunched up his face, the movement disturbing his body.

"No. No hospitals. You know that, Noelle," he grunted out. Oreo shifted at Carson's movement, moving back as he peered up at the two of them curiously.

Noelle clenched her jaw. She wasn't going to take no for an answer, not when he lied and kept this from her and not when he was this injured.

"Carson, you need to get checked out," she persuaded, hoping to keep the annoyed edge out of her tone. They wouldn't get anywhere with her simmering anger stemming from hurt and his own short fuse. "Your fingers could be broken, and we need to make sure your ribs aren't either. Or that you have a concussion. You could—"

"I've been doing this for years," Carson reminded her with a sigh, and Noelle would be lying if she said she wasn't surprised that he sounded more tired than annoyed. Normally, when the topic of him going to the hospital came about, he bit the head off of whoever brought it up. Though Noelle figured she couldn't entirely blame him for being more exhausted than anything. "I'll just ice everything, and it'll be okay."

She gaped at him, leaning back a bit as her jaw dropped slightly. Was he kidding? Noelle knew Carson was a grown man who was capable of taking care of himself, but his refusal to go to the hospital when he was bleeding and bruised and couldn't even sit up properly was just fucking stupid. She wasn't going to let him sit with possible broken bones and a concussion. She was scared for him—not to mention pissed off, which was why she didn't feel too ashamed when she ducked her head slightly to connect their gazes.

"Carson," she started with her hand on one shoulder, hoping it wasn't injured as his gaze lazily dragged to hers. "You can't just keep a fight like this from me and sit in this state and not expect me to want you to get checked out." She swallowed at the way he took in a deep breath as if trying to keep himself together. "I know you hate going to the hospital but—" She was definitely about to guilt trip him, but it also most definitely came from a place of wholehearted concern for this beautiful man she was so head-over-heels for. "Do you trust me?"

A sharp breath escaped Carson, sounding almost disbelieving as he tiredly frowned up at her. He was going to pass out eventually, his body unable to keep him up or awake after such a brutal, lasting fight. His movements were slow and lazy, showcasing his exhaustion clearly, but his eyes were locked on hers. Noelle felt that same rush of overwhelming, pleasantly blissful emotion she always did when his dark irises met her light ones, and she knew no one else would ever make her feel the way Carson did. No one would compare, which was why she needed him to let her take him to the hospital.

When she was driving over to Carson's apartment, her mind overrun with all kinds of worry-filled, horrific thoughts. Noelle also kept praying over and over again that he was okay. Just like she had been praying over and over again the day she lost her dad and her sister lost her legs. It didn't matter what it was. Just knowing someone she cared about so deeply was hurt in any way had Noelle's insides shriveling up as if they were about to wither away. The devastating thought of something seriously bad happening to Carson had bile rising to the back of Noelle's throat.

He looked at her; he looked at the determination etched onto her face and the worry and concern drawing her eyebrows together and tilting her lips downwards. His bruised, slightly swollen fingers itched to reach forward and tuck away the light brown strands of her hair that fell forward and framed her face. The fact that a small twitch in his fingers hurt told Carson that he really should get them checked out.

His throat worked, not even having to think about Noelle's question. "Yes," he responded raspingly.

Noelle's lips twitched slightly, her hand gently cupping his right cheek. Her touch was light as a feather, barely making contact with his bruised jaw as she briefly rolled her lips into her mouth. Her emotions prodded Noelle to practically beg.

"Then please let me take you to the hospital. I promise, nothing . . . no one is going to question you on your injuries. I'll make sure of it."

It was in the way the desperation was effortlessly sounding in Noelle's voice, the unadulterated anxiety scrunching at her features, the fact that he lied to her and was the reason for how she was feeling, and the fact that he loved her so damn much that had Carson finally conceding.

"Okay."

Containing the breath of relief that immediately escaped her was hopeless as Noelle blinked away the tears she managed to keep at bay, offering Carson an appreciative smile. Despite her anger, Noelle leaned forward and pressed a kiss to his forehead. Carson's eyes shut at the touch, taking in a soft breath as Noelle pulled away and sat on her haunches and turned to face the door.

"Levi, come here!" she called out.

The blond appeared a second later, his concerned eyes flickering between Noelle and Carson as he entered the room.

"What's going on?" he asked.

"Help me get him to my car," Noelle instructed. "I'm taking him to the hospital."

Levi's bright blue eyes widened at that. "Whoa, wait! Really?" If Carson's refusal of going to the hospital wasn't apparent with him, it definitely was in Levi's reaction.

"Yeah. Now, come on!" Noelle impatiently gestured. Her heart was pounding because of Carson's state and because of him agreeing, and she wanted to get him in her car before he had the chance to change his mind.

It was a team effort between Noelle and Levi to help Carson up with putting on the least amount of work for him. They had to move him carefully to his feet before they could start walking with either one of Carson's arms thrown around Levi and Noelle's shoulders. Levi's arm was wrapped around Carson's upper back due to his height while Noelle's was around his waist as they slowly moved out of the apartment, to the elevator and then towards Noelle's car.

Every grunt and pant of breath that escaped Carson had Noelle's heart clenching because the mere sound of him in any kind of pain made her chest ache. Noelle's teeth began hurting from how hard she was clenching her jaw as an attempt of keeping back her tears, blinking them away every time they blurred her vision and taking sharp breaths through her nose to try and steady her racing heart.

"Do you want me to come with?" Levi asked once they had successfully and carefully placed Carson in the passenger seat, letting out a breath as he ran his fingers through his blond curls.

"No. I think it'd be better if I just took him in," Noelle told him with a grateful smile. She was kind of irritated with him, Aiden, and Max for not telling her about tonight, but she knew they only did it because Carson asked. This was just something she needed to talk to him about, and as pissed as she was, Noelle needed to make sure he was alright before letting him know of her simmering anger. "The others might still be at my house, so—"

"I'll just go to them," Levi finished with a nod. He clenched his jaw under the facial hair he was sporting, his eyes flickering to the car behind Noelle. Carson could be seen sitting back, his head leaning against the headrest with eyes squeezed shut. "Take care of him, yeah? Let us know if you need anything and keep us updated."

"Of course." Noelle nodded, smiling as Levi kissed the top of her head before opening the car door for her. She didn't see him get into his own car until she was halfway down the street. Noelle let out a drawn-out breath, the soft hiss of air filling the silence of the car.

She glanced at Carson from her peripheral, an uncomfortable furrow in his brows and his eyes still closed while his hand once again gripped his side and cut lips pursed. The overhead street lamps illuminated him every five seconds, highlighting the chisel of his jaw but making his bruises and cuts and streaks of blood stand out. Noelle returned her gaze to the road, her grip on the steering wheel tightening and her heart pounding. He wasn't saying anything, and while Noelle hoped it was because he was just saving his energy, the worry was relentlessly eating away at her.

341

*   *   *

"What do you mean I can't see her?" Noelle demanded, clenching her hands into fists to keep herself from slamming them onto the receptionist's desk. "She's my freaking mother! Page her! She'll come!"

"She's closing up a patient right now, miss. I can't just call her away from a surgery if it isn't an emergency."

Noelle wondered if Carson's choice of career was rubbing off on her because she found herself fighting the urge to throw a punch at the woman's face. Though, to be fair, she had heard her mother complain about Donna Filch, the receptionist, a number of times.

"Were you listening? It is an emergency! My boyfriend is hurt and—"

"Then have one of the ER doctors here take a look at them," Donna snapped, gesturing towards the bustling ER behind them. She was clearly getting as fed up with Noelle as she was with her. "I'm not calling out one of our surgeons just because—"

"What's going on?"

Noelle instantly turned around at the sound of the familiar voice, her eyes landing on Dr. Grant—Isaac's dad. She felt a little bit of relief in her otherwise tensed body, not once relaxing since Max and Aiden had showed up at her house. Noelle pushed away from the desk to face him.

"Dr. Grant," she breathed out, and for a moment, she remembered that Isaac had yet to come out to his dad. She wasn't sure if the façade of them being interested in each other was still up, and she only had half a mind to keep at it. "Is there any way you can get my mom? I . . . my friend. He's hurt and I just . . . I need my mom for this. Please," she explained hastily.

Dr. Grant regarded Noelle for a moment and saw the distressed look in the young girl's eye before his own eyes went to

342

the only person sitting on one of the side waiting chairs. Clearly injured and in pain, his head leaning back against the wall and eyes shut, oblivious to the bustling emergency room around him.

"Alright." Dr. Grant nodded before gesturing to a male resident standing next to him. "Hill, get that young man to bed three. Dr. Simon's going to be with him shortly."

Noelle watched as Hill moved to where Carson was, a breathless, absent smile on her face.

"Thank you," she said to Dr. Grant before turning to be with Carson. A mental note was made in the back of her mind to properly thank Dr. Grant later, but her focus was Carson at the moment.

Noelle stood by Carson's side, antsy on her feet once he was on the hospital bed. The ER curtain was drawn to hide them from the rest of the busy area as Hill took all of Carson's vitals. She was at least a little bit glad to see that Carson's eyes were open—as much as his right eye could be due to the bruise—tired and lazy and staring up at the ceiling as Hill took his blood pressure and what not. All Noelle could do was stand next to the bed and bite at her nails, the worried expression permanent on her face.

"You're makin' me nervous, love," Carson rasped, his head against the pillow as he tilted it slightly to gaze up at her. "Sit down, yeah?"

He was hurt and in pain, but Noelle still wanted to smack him upside the head because *she* was making *him* nervous? She would be lucky if she had nails left to bite once the night was over. She merely clenched her jaw in response, biting her tongue from saying anything she may regret, something Carson shouldn't have to hear now while he was finally being checked out by professionals instead of just icing everything.

Still, the soft smile he gave her, not entirely taking up his face because of the black eye and the cut lip and bruised jaw, had just the tiniest bit of her resolve melting. Just as she was about to sit down, the rings on the curtain rod sharply hissed as it was pulled open, and the curtain turned to catch sight of her mother standing there in her dark red scrubs.

Noelle saw her mother's eyebrows shoot up as she took in their presence. She saw the way Carson's Adam's apple bobbed at the sight of his girlfriend's mother, and Noelle instantly stepped out of the area and drew the curtains behind her once more to face her mother.

"Can you please take care of him?" Noelle quietly said to her mother while they were out of Carson's sight.

Dr. Simon frowned slightly, her hair tied back into a ponytail as she crossed her arms over her chest. "What happened to him?"

Noelle didn't want to lie to her mother, but at this particular moment, it didn't matter what Noelle did or didn't want. Was it awful that she didn't care about lying to her mom? Carson's secret wasn't something of hers to share. She had already done so with Camille and didn't plan on doing it with her mother of all people, not with how her mom had so obviously judged Carson. If Noelle disclosed he was in the state he was in because of illegal fighting, then the reason Carson hated coming to hospitals would become reality and Noelle wasn't going to make Carson regret trusting her with this.

"There were some guys." Her mouth was running with the lie before she could stop herself, but the guilt behind it was nonexistent. "He was walking back to his apartment after picking up dinner for us and they were just . . . they jumped him." It was pure bullshit to her own ears, and Noelle hoped it only sounded like that because she knew it was a lie and that her mother would believe it. She hoped her utter desperation for Carson to be better wouldn't make her mother question anything. "Mom, please. He hates hospitals. He's not . . . he doesn't want to press charges or anything. Can you just help him?"

Her heart was in her throat, tight and dry and hoping that her lie and the genuine distress she was displaying would be enough for her mom to help without any questions. Noelle was well aware that her mom didn't like Carson when she first met him. She knew that her own relationship with her wasn't the best, but her mom was truly the only person she trusted with this. She seriously hoped her mother would help.

When her mom finally let out a breath and nodded, her features relaxing into agreement, Noelle felt her stomach churn in anticipation.

"Alright. He'll be under my care specifically," her mom said, relief washing over her.

Noelle blinked a couple of times, quickly and in relief as she let out a slow breath. She nodded as her mother opened the curtain once again. Hill was still doing whatever the hell he was supposed to do as Noelle followed behind her mom, moving around her to get to Carson's side. She noticed the way he was sitting up now, his dark eyes on her mother, apprehensive and hesitant as Dr. Simon talked to Hill before flickering to her mom.

She noticed the way his Adam's apple was bobbing nervously, and despite everything she was feeling, Noelle still offered him a reassuring smile as she got to his side.

"I'm sorry you had to lie to her," Carson whispered to Noelle when he saw that her mom was busy talking to the younger resident.

Just like you're sorry you lied to me? God, how she wanted to say that. She hoped her neck didn't tense as she swallowed inaudibly, her hand gently resting on his wrist because she didn't want to touch his injured fingers. Noelle wasn't entirely sure if she was justified in her anger. She wasn't sure if she had the right to feel upset and pissed that he kept this from her because, really, what was the point of lying to her? She knew the fight would happen, but the fact that he didn't want her there hurt her feelings. Carson knew she liked being there to support him, and if this was a big one, why didn't he want her there?

Her heart tugged, her light eyes meeting his dark ones, soft and kind like they always seemed to be for her. His full lips were formed into a soft pout, the cut visible. Noelle, like always, wanted to kiss him—like that would make his pain go away. Just the way he looked at her made it so hard for Noelle to be mad at him, tempting her to only focus on the fact that the feelings of want, adoration, worry, desire, and love she had for this man were so much more stronger than the anger and hurt she currently felt.

Noelle bit the inside of her lower lip as her mom turned to face them after speaking to Hill, trying to suppress the breathless shudder that threatened to pass through her at the realization as her eyes remained on Carson even though his attention was on her mother.

Oh god. Holy shit.

She loved him. So much. That was why being angry at him felt even more painful than it already was.

CHAPTER TWENTY-FIVE

"My daughter seems to care a lot about you."

Carson felt his heart thud against his chest, much like it always came to do whenever Dr. Simon's was present. It was his second day at the hospital. He was instructed to stay in bed, so he could recover. Carson was a lucky son of a bitch. His body had been screaming in pain, but there were no broken bones. There were bruises and cuts and a bit of swelling and a whole lot of ache but nothing was broken or fractured. He hoped the same couldn't be said for Milner.

He swallowed at Dr. Simon's words. It was crazy yet kind of believable that her being in the same room as him made him tense. True, it mostly had to do with their first meeting; something he didn't think either of them would forget, but ever since he was admitted into the hospital last night, he had been in the same room as Dr. Simon multiple times and his muscles went stiff every time she came into view. However, she didn't have that same cold demeanor she had when they first met; she was professional, making sure she was taking care of Carson to the best of her abilities.

"I care about her a lot too," his low voice responded with his eyes on the splints on his fingers. He had no broken digits, but he had contusions that warranted some of his fingers splinted or taped together to heal. But Carson's focus was on the girl he was waiting to arrive after Noelle's mom had kicked her out, so Carson

347

could get some rest and she could go home and get sleep too. He knew he scared and worried her beyond belief last night, and Carson hated himself for freaking her out like that. The absolute least he could do was listen to her and let her bring him to the hospital—where, again, he felt guilty for having her lie to her mom. She did it for him, but Carson still felt badly about it.

"She looked frightened for you," Dr. Simon mused, standing at the end of Carson's hospital bed as she glanced up at him from where she was looking down at his chart. "I hope you're feeling better so she feels better."

There was a light, teasing tone in her voice that had Carson inhaling softly as he looked at the older woman. Was she warming up to him? Or did she just feel bad about him lying beaten and bruised? His body was sore, which wasn't new for him, and the swelling of his right eye was only just starting to go down. It wasn't too bad since Carson could still see out of it, but he most definitely was sporting a black eye.

"I am." Carson nodded. Sure, he wasn't feeling a hundred percent better, but the drugs he was given and the way parts of his arms and legs and torso were wrapped definitely helped a little bit. Carson let out a breath, lips pursing momentarily. "I didn't mean to scare her like that," he said.

Dr. Simon regarded him for a moment before an almost sad small smile tilted at her lips. "I think it just brought up some unwanted memories for Noelle. Waiting for us to finish our exams on you, I think, reminded her of . . ." Carson noticed the way Dr. Simon's brows drew together, her throat working as she looked down at the chart once again and breaking their gaze. "Of when Andrea and their father were brought in," she finished in a somewhat quivering tone.

Carson felt his throat tighten as guilt rushed through him at Dr. Simon's words. He knew last night was a mess, he knew it from Noelle's expressions, and he knew it from when the boys and Beverly visited him earlier. They lightheartedly brought get-well-
348

soon balloons and flowers to liven up his room all the while not refraining from informing Carson how distraught Noelle was when she found out about him.

The last thing he wanted to do was never have Noelle relive such a horrible day because of him—or relive it, period. She didn't really talk about her father much, but Carson knew it was because it pained her to speak of him, instead just mentioning him every few conversations if something in particular reminded her of him. The thought of her remembering the day she lost her father and Andrea was paralyzed because she was so worried about Carson made acidic, guilt-ridden bile rise in the back of his throat.

How the fuck could I have put her through that?

Dr. Simon left soon after that, telling him that she would be back in a little bit with his discharge papers. He didn't have to stay at the hospital since he didn't need anymore tests to run; his head was fine and so were his bones. All he needed to do was keep the splint on his fingers for a few days so they could heal, and Carson was already used to living with bruises. Besides, Carson was eager to get out of the hospital. They made him uncomfortable, and the sooner he got out, the better. Noelle was, in fact, on her way over to pick him up and take him back to his apartment, getting out of work early for it. The boys wanted to come too, but Carson knew they all had work and frankly wanted to spend some time with Noelle, especially to apologize.

He knew he fucked up, and he was determined to make up for it.

While he waited for Noelle, Carson managed to get himself out of the bed and walk over to the bathroom after picking up a change of clothes Aiden had brought for him when he and everyone else came to visit earlier. Carson's body ached with his movements, his muscles protesting as he walked into the bathroom. He had to bend and stretch to pull off the hospital gown and slide on the sweatpants and shirt, which took him a second to do because of some of his fingers being taped or splinted.

349

He took a look at himself in the mirror after changing, pursing his lips and not even flinching when the cut on his lower one stung slightly at the action. The swelling of his right eye had gone down overnight. Now, there was just a bluish-black ring around it along with another bruise on his left jaw and a cut along his temple. His nose still felt a bit sore, but nothing just a little bit more icing wouldn't fix.

Carson sighed. While feeling triumphant over his victory, he still let a lot of damage get done to him, but remembering the crack of Milner's nose under his knuckles made him feel a little bit better.

When he stepped back into the room, Carson took in a soft breath at the sight of his girlfriend now standing there. "Hi, Ellie."

"Hey," Noelle returned, her tone not unkind but cautious. She didn't make a move to come closer to him, standing towards the end of the bed while Carson was near the side. A small smile twitched at her lips and Carson could instantly tell she was forcing it. "How're you feeling?" she asked.

He would be an idiot not to notice the slight tension in the air, in the way she hadn't greeted him with a kiss like she usually did or how her smile—small in size—didn't reach her light eyes.

"Just a little sore," he answered, trying not to give away that he so clearly noticed her tense demeanor. Carson held the railing of the bed for support because he couldn't be up on his left leg for too long. "Nothin' I'm not used to."

Noelle's throat worked with her already forced smile plastered on her face. Carson hated that she looked so uncomfortable, so stiff around him. It was like a weight was being pressed down on his chest. Watching the woman he loved act so rigid around him as if he was a stranger rather than someone who knew every inch of her in any every way possible made Carson's inside twist painfully—a kind of ache worse than the current soreness of his muscles.

Instead of responding to his words, Noelle gave a single nod. "My mom said you can leave now so, uh, you ready to go?" she asked.

"Uh, yeah." Carson nodded, trying not to let the frown furrow his eyebrows at Noelle's distant demeanor. "Yeah, I'm ready."

Noelle nodded once again before taking it upon herself to grab the duffel bag Aiden had brought that Carson put his clothes back in, hiking it over her shoulder before offering another small smile. "Let's go then."

She turned and walked out of the room. Carson remained standing by the bed for a moment longer, staring after where she had disappeared. He clenched his jaw and ignored the stinging pain. It didn't take a genius to see that Noelle wasn't her usual self, her short statements and fake smiles adding onto the tense demeanor she adorned. Carson felt himself grow anxious. She was mad at him, wasn't she?

Carson was barely scared of anything, but the fact that Noelle hadn't yet acknowledged her anger towards him was absolutely terrifying.

$*$ $*$ $*$

Carson had been punched, kicked, and thrown but he had never felt as though he was suffocating. He never let anyone get their hands on him long enough to give them the advantage of cutting off his air. Who would've thought the first person to forcefully, without his consent, deprive Carson of oxygen in the worst way would be the same person he was so hopelessly in love with? Who would've thought she had that kind of power over him without even touching him, without even looking at him?

He had never been comfortable with feeling powerless. It made him feel vulnerable and naked and went against who he was as a person, but when he had come to terms with his feelings for

Noelle in the first place, he always had an inkling that this girl would ruin him in the best way. Right as they entered his apartment after a fifteen-minute car ride of suffocating silence that Carson could physically feel wrapped around his throat and cut off his air, he genuinely felt like a lamb waiting to be slaughtered.

Carson's fearlessly knocked down opponents significantly larger than him, but at this moment, he was actually scared of his five-foot-five, near pixie-like girlfriend.

It was only a momentary comfort when Oreo ran up to him once they entered the apartment, bringing a relieved smile to Carson's face as he forced himself to bend down to pick Oreo up. Carson ignored the way his muscles ached at the action, not quite completely healed, but he didn't care as he stood straight and let his little pup lick at his face.

"Hi, buddy," he whispered, cradling Oreo in the crook of his arm to be careful of his fingers. He kissed the top of Oreo's head. "Missed you."

After a few more licks and some nuzzling, Oreo jumped out of Carson's grip, and he let out a breath as he heard the thud of his bag drop on the floor. He turned around to see Noelle looking down at the bag after letting it fall from her grip. He watched as she glanced around the apartment at anywhere but him.

"Do you, uh, need anything?" she asked.

Carson lifted his chin slightly as he regarded her. He could practically see the guard she had up, and there was a tight ache in his chest at the fact that the girl he loved was acting as if she didn't know who he was. When Carson was in pain, he also managed to get angry—short fuse and all.

"Are you asking to be nice or because you actually care?" he retorted with a slight cock of his head, and the second the words left his mouth, Carson knew it was the wrong thing to say.

Noelle's gaze instantly snapped towards him, her brows drawing together and eyes narrowing. "Are you actually questioning if I care about you?" She scoffed, the sound disbelieving and incredulous as Carson took a small breath.

Oh shit, Carson thought as he noticed the purse of her lips. *I've gone and pissed her off even more.*

Noelle vaguely pointed at him, the gesture absentminded as she tried to collect her thoughts. "You've got no right to say that when you know damn well I wanted to be at that fight, and you just refused to let me know about it."

Carson clicked his tongue with a slight shake of his head, backtracking as a feeble attempt of damage control. "Ellie, that's not what I meant. I—"

"What the fuck were you thinking?" Carson's eyes slightly widened at Noelle's raised voice while staring at her in shock because the amount of anger that dominated her words was unexpected. The fire in her eyes almost burned him as he took in her fierce glare. "How could you not tell me about the match, huh? What? Did you think I would be against it or something? I knew your fight with Milner was inevitable, but I really would've fucking liked to have been there."

"I know," Carson responded, his tone conciliatory as he tried to appease the situation. Seeing and hearing Noelle so pissed at him uneased him; it made him want to make things right as soon as possible. "But it was a tough one, baby, and I didn't want you to see something like that. It was so much more intense than any other one you've been to and—"

"And what?" Noelle cut off with a sarcastic tilt of her head, her arms crossed over her chest. "You didn't think I could handle seeing something like that? Please, Carson. I'm a grown ass woman who doesn't need you to decide what I can or can't handle."

Carson clenched his jaw, holding back the wince the action enticed as he took in a sharp, steadying breath. His leg was hurting from standing up for too long, but that was the last thing on his mind. The first being his very angry girlfriend. He knew she was right; he knew that he shouldn't be making decisions for her, but

353

his own experience with Astros and the people there gave him an insight that Noelle didn't have.

"It wasn't about you not being able to handle it," he began, taking a step closer to her. Noelle kept her ground, still a few feet away. "It was about making sure if shit went sideways, you weren't caught in the same room as—"

"Boman and Milner?" Carson pursed his lips. He might love the shit out of Noelle, but he was getting irritated with her for not letting him finish what he was saying. Noelle paid him no mind; she didn't even care as she let out a scoff and ran her fingers through her loose hair before staring at him with disgruntled incredulity. "For fuck's sake, Car! We've been over this already! I don't care what they do or—"

"But I do!" Carson exclaimed, his raspy voice loud in the tense quiet of the apartment as Noelle pressed her lips together. At the back of his mind, Carson couldn't help but notice in overwhelming relief that he hadn't scared her with the raise of his volume. If she had so much as flinched, Carson would hate himself for it. Instead, she stood her ground with her jaw clenching, then he remembered his own irritation. "And I'm not about to let you walk into Astros with those fuckers thinking of ways to get to you, so they could get at me."

Noelle rolled her eyes, clearly not as affected at the thought of some random, sleazy guys approaching her as Carson was.

"What? You think they're gonna jump out of the ring and come for me?" She shook her head, waving her hands as if getting rid of the conversation. "That's not even the damn issue, Carson. The problem is that you fucking lied to me about the match, and not only that, you made the boys keep it from me and Bev. Why couldn't you have just told me you didn't want me to come?"

Why hadn't he just done that?

Carson knew that if he asked, Noelle would've been cooperative and didn't attend the match if he really didn't want her to. Carson knew if he had just explained himself, she would've appreciated it and listened to him.

He knew all of that, so why the fuck didn't he do it?

"I just . . ." he paused, taking in a somewhat unsteady breath as his gaze remained locked on hers, his dark brown clashing with her hazel ones. Carson's chest tightened at the confused hurt in her eyes. He hated that he was the cause of it. "It was an ugly match, Noelle. I didn't . . . didn't want you to worry."

Noelle's chest fell as she let out a sharp breath, her eyebrows that were scrunched together rising at his words as she stared at him in disappointed disbelief.

"Didn't want me to worry?" She licked her lips, subtly shaking her head as her shoulders sank and arms uncrossed, falling to her sides. "What the hell do you think I felt when Aiden and Max showed up at my doorstep to tell me that you were hurt? You don't think I was worrying then?" she asked with an almost defeated yet exasperated tone.

The anger was seeping back into her voice. Carson swallowed his own because he knew he wasn't justified in it.

Even though she was furious, Noelle still sounded breathless with concern and fright. The hurt expression on her face dried Carson's throat.

"You don't think I was fucking terrified when I saw all those bruises and blood on you?" Noelle shook her head, her lower lip quivering. All Carson wanted to do was wrap his arms around her and apologize profusely for scaring her like that. He felt like an asshole even if his intentions for his actions had been pure. "You have no idea what I felt, thinking the entire night that you were with your sister, only to find out you were bleeding on your apartment floor."

Carson blinked a couple of times because he honestly hadn't expected for his eyes to burn with unshed tears at the thought of scaring Noelle like that. His chest felt heavy, the soreness of his muscles not even coming close to the clench of his heart as he tried to swallow the lump in his throat. His injuries from the fight felt like nothing compared to the agony Noelle's words brought.

How could he not be in pain, knowing he made the woman he loved feel the way she was feeling?

How could he not feel the tears burn his eyes when Noelle's were already wetting her cheeks?

"It may not be that serious, and I'm not gonna apologize if you think I'm being overdramatic, but last night, I felt like that same nineteen-year-old girl who raced to the hospital to find out her dad died out of nowhere." Carson's lips parted and he wanted to throw up because Dr. Simon had been right. Noelle had unequivocally relived that tragic day because of him. "There's always a chance you might get hurt during a match, and I know that, and so far, I'm still sane." Noelle's gaze met Carson's as she shook her head, exhausted and disappointed and tormented. "But not telling me about it and leaving me to wonder if you're okay is a surefire way of driving me crazy."

"I'm sorry," he said, not knowing what else to say, his accented voice thick and croaky. The few feet of distance between them seemed like miles, but Carson couldn't bring his feet to move towards Noelle, like he didn't deserve to be near her for putting her through that kind of pain. Carson knew he couldn't have known that last night would've brought up some unwanted, terrible memories for Noelle but he still blamed himself. "You didn't deserve . . . I'm sorry, Ellie. I'm so, so sorry."

I love you.

He wanted to say it. He so desperately wanted to say it, but Carson didn't want the first time he said those three monumental words to her to be a way of getting her to forgive him right then and there. It might explain why he did what he did, why he lied to her and kept the match a secret, but he wasn't going to use it as an excuse. He loved her, and he should've been honest with her, but instead he kept something from Noelle that elicited a kind of fear in her he never wanted her to have, especially because of him.

She looked at him with hazel eyes that Carson found himself often getting lost in yet right now, they were glassy. Carson watched apprehensively, desperately as Noelle looked away and blinked back tears and reached her hands to wipe at her cheeks.

"I'm, uh . . ." Noelle took a breath, nodding to herself as she wiped her hands down the sides of her shirt and swallowed. She looked at him, her expression still sad and hurt and a little bit angry. "You're okay by yourself, right?" She didn't wait for him to respond. "I think Aiden is gonna come by in a bit. So I'm just, um, I'm gonna go."

Carson took a step forward, his heart jumping in his throat as she took a step back towards the door. "Noelle, please—"

"I know you're sorry," she said, the smallest of smiles on her face, barely tilting her lips as she looked at him. Carson froze where he stood. "But I just . . . I need to get my head on straight. Need a little bit to figure out—"

Carson couldn't help the words that spilled past his lips out of pure distress, a kind of desperation he had never felt before. "Figure out if you'll forgive me or if you want to still be with me?"

Noelle's eyes widened slightly, her breath hitching. "My feelings for you haven't changed," she told him, the firmness in her voice actually bringing Carson a mild peace of mind. She still felt the same. "But you still kept something important from me and I know you were just . . . trying to protect me, but I still need a minute to process this. You can't expect me to be okay with this so quickly. I'm sorry, I just . . . I need to get it together."

"Don't be sorry," Carson instantly responded, taking the last few steps towards her as his Adam's apple bobbed in his throat. He didn't blame Noelle for needing some time for herself; he knew that she deserved it after being scared to death over last night's event and consequently remembering the day her dad died as a result of it. Carson stood in front of her, his height easily dominating Noelle's as he peered down at the hazel-eyed girl. Even with some of his fingers splinted or taped together, Carson didn't let that stop him from—albeit, awkwardly—grasping Noelle's hand. "You've got nothing to apologize for. I'm the one who screwed up and if you . . . if you need a few days away . . ." God, Carson selfishly didn't want that to be the case. "Then you do that."

Her eyes searched his, her expression softening. This time, the smile on her face, even though small, seemed genuine.

"I don't need a few days away, Car," Noelle muttered with a small shake of her head. "We're still us. We're still a team. You just . . ." she trailed off, an almost sheepish chuckle escaping her as she shrugged. "You gotta let me get my head back in the game."

He nodded. Right. Carson could do that. Definitely.

Carson licked his lips, just barely feeling the cut on his lower one. "Whatever you want, sweetheart," he mumbled, his gaze dropping to their awkwardly held hands. He meant it, whatever Noelle needed to make sure that she was okay. He wanted to help her, to be there for her as she tried to deal with the memory of her dad and what seeing Carson like that did to her, but if she wanted to work through it by herself, he couldn't force her to let him help.

Maybe they would be okay.

But then Noelle dropped his hand and took a step back. Carson watched as the girl who might as fucking well be the love of his life tensed up slightly as if she was suddenly unsure how to act. Carson's heart thumped in his chest as she backtracked to the door with an awkward, nervous smile on her lips as she blindly reached for the doorknob behind her and successfully pulled the door open.

Carson wished the smile on her face was the real one he was in love with instead of the fake, forced one she currently adorned.

"I'm glad you're okay, Car," she murmured quietly before she left the apartment within a blink of an eye, the door clicking shut behind her.

Or maybe Carson was screwed. Maybe he should've told her he loved her in case the 'us' Noelle had been talking about was in more trouble than Carson thought.

While that notion felt like an iron punch to the gut, Carson still swallowed down the fear and pained apprehension it brought because he was a fighter, and fighting for his relationship with Noelle was much more important than some match at Astros.

Her fruity, wonderful scent lingered in his apartment—just a whiff of the girl who Carson wished hadn't left.

CHAPTER TWENTY-SIX

The plan wasn't to avoid Carson, and even if it was, it would be a shitty plan because there had been brief text conversations between the two the next day. The day after that, Noelle was being dragged to have lunch with him, Beverly, and the rest of the boys.

It was not like Noelle could cut off all contact with Carson. She was still angry at him for lying. She was still trying to calm herself down after establishing that Carson was safe and okay, but she wasn't about to just push him away because that was not what she wanted. She wanted him badly and desperately, but she still needed some space—just a little bit.

It was tricky. Noelle was still reeling from everything, but she also wanted to just be with Carson—hold his hand, kiss him, and hug him. Noelle felt like she was being pulled in two different directions. She was mad but, shit, she just wanted to be with him.

Being mad at someone you love was a pain in the ass.

"I don't know how you do it," Beverly mused, her fingers dancing over the row of lipsticks on Noelle's dresser. They were getting ready for the lunch, which would be happening at Max's place. Beverly was looking to use some of Noelle's makeup. The twenty-five-year-old looked at Noelle through the reflection as she applied mascara. "If Aiden pulled that shit with me the way Carson did with you, I'd probably be on my way to prison for murder."

Noelle sighed, twisting the mascara container shut as her shoulders sank. "You love him too much to do that," she pointed out with a knowing raise of her eyebrows before averting her gaze as she put away the mascara. A definite crime of passion. "Same goes for me," she added, mumbling.

Beverly froze, staring at Noelle with widened eyes trained on her instead of her reflection.

"You love him?" The surprise was evident in her voice, her gaze burning Noelle's skin. "Have you told him?" Beverly asked, her voice suddenly softening.

"No." Noelle shook her head with another sigh, rolling her lipstick-free lips into her mouth. "I mean, I want to tell him but it's just . . . with what just happened, the timing didn't seem right."

Beverly ticked her head, drawing her eyebrows together in mild confusion. "I don't think there's a wrong time for telling your partner you love them," she stated.

Noelle chewed the inside of her cheek for a moment. "I just want us to get past this first and . . ." she admitted, trailing off and looking down at her yellow-painted nails with a conflicted frown marring her eyebrows. She suddenly looked hesitant.

"And what?" Beverly gently prodded, frowning in concern over her sister's clear uncertainty.

"What if he's not ready for that yet?" Noelle desperately asked, the scared tone evident in her voice. She didn't doubt Carson's feelings for her, but Noelle was in love with him. What if that was too fast for Carson? She wasn't one to throw around the notion of loving someone lightly, and she knew Carson wasn't either, so this was a pretty big fucking deal. Her apprehension was warranted in Noelle's opinion. She didn't want to sound like she didn't have faith in Carson because she did, but there was still a small part of her that was afraid she would scare him off.

"That man looks at you like you hung the damn moon, Ellie. I'll honestly be surprised if he isn't ready yet, even if this is Carson we're talking about," Beverly assured soothingly while rubbing Noelle's back. Noelle looked at her sister, a hopeful light lifting her face slightly, as Beverly grinned. "You're a catch. He'd be an idiot not to love you."

At that, Noelle let out a laugh, grateful to have Beverly to pull her out of her doubts. It was a scary thing, realizing you were in love whether it was with someone you were in a relationship with or not. Noelle wanted to tell Carson how she felt because the words were on the tip of her tongue, but she was holding them back. It wasn't the best time to tell him yet; things between them were kind of tense and Noelle was still trying to get over the fact that he lied to her.

Noelle suppressed a groan. Why couldn't she have fallen in love when their relationship wasn't hitting a rough patch?

When Beverly went to her room to change clothes, Noelle also changed out of sweats and into a simple dark purple T-shirt dress and sneakers before grabbing her purse and heading downstairs. Pouting her lips thoughtfully, Noelle decided to quell her growling stomach by having a little snack before the lunch. She entered the kitchen and opened the fridge, smiling in satisfaction at the sight of the bowl of cut cantaloupe sitting inside.

She was probably going to spoil her lunch, but keeping Noelle away from her favorite fruit was nearly impossible.

"You look nice." Noelle glanced up from where she was leaning forward on the counter with a piece of cantaloupe in her mouth as she caught sight of her mother entering the kitchen. When Dr. Simon saw what Noelle was doing, she chuckled knowingly. "Couldn't wait for lunch?"

"It's just a light snack," Noelle defended lightly, stabbing another piece with her fork.

Dr. Simon hummed as she filled up the kettle with water before putting it on the stove. "Are you going to see Carson today?"

Noelle paused her chewing momentarily at her mother's question, trying to detect her tone of voice. She didn't sound like Carson's name was a bad taste in her mouth.

"Uh, yeah," she answered cautiously.

"How's he feeling?" Dr. Simon questioned, turning around to look at her daughter. Her genuinely curious look had Noelle swallowing her piece of fruit, mildly surprised at her mother's interest in her boyfriend.

"Um, he's fine," Noelle straightened, nodding slightly. Even though she hadn't seen Carson since the day before yesterday and even though she was still harboring some annoyed feelings for him, Noelle still checked in on him to make sure he was alright. She pleaded with him to take his pain medication if his body hurt too much instead of being a stubborn boy and riding out the ache.

Dr. Simon nodded slowly in acknowledgment, and Noelle couldn't help but eye her mother curiously, dubiously. She was kind of surprised her mom would even bring Carson up in the first place. After Noelle brought Carson to the hospital, she didn't see much of her mom except when she visited the hospital because of her mother's hefty schedule. This was the first time in the past few days they were in the same room that wasn't in Carson's hospital room.

And then her mother really took her by surprise.

"He's a nice boy." Noelle's eyes widened ever so slightly because Dr. Simon's words were a complete opposition of her first impression of Carson. The small smile playing on her mother's face had Noelle's heart pounding. "He sustained all those injuries, but all he seemed to worry about was if you were okay after seeing him like that. He was undoubtedly in pain and yet his main concern was you. He put your state of mind above his own physical well-being and that's . . . admirable."

Noelle's breath hitched in her throat, taking note of the fond tone in her mom's voice. She didn't want to get her hopes up, but if Noelle didn't know any better, it seemed like her mom was warming up to Carson. It was wild to Noelle because him being at the hospital was the second time they interacted and, really, it wasn't any better than the first time they met. Honestly, the only two times Dr. Simon saw Carson were the morning after obviously sleeping with Noelle and the night he was brought bloody and bruised to the hospital. Both impressions weren't the best, yet her mom seemed far less judgmental this time around.

The turnaround she was getting from her mother really was dizzying, but Noelle didn't really want to question it.

"You should bring him for dinner one day. I'd like to get to know him," her mom mused. Noelle supposed her shock and curious interest was written across her face.

Okay, did Noelle step into a different universe, or was she being delusional? Because, frankly, those were the only two options that seemed probable at this moment.

"You would?" Noelle choked out, astonished.

There goes not wanting to question it.

However, in Noelle's defense, she really hadn't seen this coming.

"Yes," Dr. Simon hummed with a soft smile gracing her lips, a kind of smile that Noelle hadn't seen in a while. That realization was saddening, no doubt, but the fact that she was able to receive it then was too gratifying to ignore. "I think giving the man my daughter loves a chance is the least I could do," she added, offering a light shrug.

Noelle felt the air rush out of her lungs and, at that moment, she felt strangely emotional. She didn't even question how her mother knew that she loved Carson; she didn't even deny it because it wasn't something she ever planned on arguing. At that moment, all that mattered was that it seemed like Noelle's relationship with her mom was starting to work its way through, and she wasn't at all surprised that part of it had to do with the man she loved.

Before Noelle could respond, her mom continued conversationally, "I'm not sure how much I believe that he got jumped when you brought him to the hospital." Noelle froze, her eyes darting to meet her mom's who wore a wry smile. "Given that the first time I met him, he had bruises then too, but that's his business," she added when Noelle was about to interrupt. What she would say, she had no clue. She was too frozen in shock that her mom seemed to pick up on the lie easily and seemed . . . at peace with it but then Dr. Simon's gaze softened, a maternal worry crossing her features that made Noelle's heart stop. It had been a while since that look had been directed towards her. "I just need to know, are you safe? You won't get hurt? Is there—"

"Mom, it's all good," Noelle reassured quickly, pushing past the lump forming in her throat because, God, the wall that had been built between the two of them was finally starting to crumble. Instead of feeling any resentment towards her mother for icing her out for so long, Noelle was ready to work towards what their relationship used to be. She didn't want to spend another moment living a life where her mom was a ghost—barely there. She was already one parent down. So Noelle smiled, true and sincere. "Despite what you've seen of him, Carson's a good guy. He wouldn't . . ." Noelle's throat worked, replaying her and Carson's last conversation in her head. "He wouldn't let anything happen to me."

Her mom looked at her for a moment, critical as she tried to detect a lie, but Noelle knew she wouldn't find one. Dr. Simon smiled warmly, the sight of it bringing a smile to Noelle's face too, then her mom nodded in acceptance.

"Then that's all that matters."

*   *   *

Lunch had been an uneventful affair. Max, who Noelle was surprised to learn was actually a really good cook, had put out a nice

365

spread with Levi butting in that he helped. Max clarified that Levi had set the table and bought the drinks. They all chatted while they talked, and as they sat across the table from one another, it seemed as though Noelle and Carson couldn't stray their gazes from the other for too long, somehow always finding each other's eyes.

When everyone had finished eating, they all retreated to the living room to wind down. The TV was playing to serve as background noise while they talked amongst themselves along with music Levi insisted on playing softly. It wasn't until Noelle was returning from the bathroom that she noticed Carson wasn't sitting with everyone. She frowned in confusion when she glanced around.

Her eyes landed on Aiden, who she guessed knew what she was looking for because he nodded right at her.

"Fire escape," he mouthed.

It happened to be at the end of the hallway she had just come from. With a grateful nod to Aiden, Noelle turned right back around and headed back down the hall. She turned at the corner towards another hallway, where at the end of it was the fire escape. As she got closer, Noelle caught sight of Carson sitting on the iron steps. She ducked her head under the open window.

"Hey," she greeted softly.

Carson, who was looking out at the neighborhood below, turned his head to look at her with a cigarette between his fingers that were no longer splinted. He had grown irritated and had insisted his fingers were fine. His expression softened at the sight of her, sitting up slightly.

"Hi."

Noelle's lips twitched upwards. "Can I join you?"

He nodded and Noelle sat on the windowsill before swinging her legs over, not particularly caring if she flashed her boyfriend as she stepped outside. It was kind of cold for a late July night, the level of Max's apartment provided some wind as Noelle stepped in front of Carson. She peered at him, the soft glow of the buildings around them shadowing the fading bruises on his face.

366

When she saw him arrive at Max's apartment, Noelle had been relieved to see Carson's bruises were already healing even if the discoloration added a violent type of beauty to his features.

They were quiet for a moment, distant car horns sounding and fading while the music playing inside was soft. Noelle peered down below. It was dark and quiet.

"Have I told you that you look gorgeous tonight?"

Noelle's head turned back to Carson, her gaze softening at the sight of him looking up at her innocently from where he sat. She smiled slightly, unsurprised at the warmth on her cheeks. She leaned back against the metal railing.

"Thank you," she murmured, shuffling towards him slightly. "You're feeling better, right?"

Carson nodded as he took a drag, turning his head away from her to blow the smoke out moments later before looking back at her.

"Yeah."

When Noelle quirked a dubious brow, Carson let out an airy laugh, his shoulders straightening. "I promise, Ellie. The pain meds your mom prescribed work wonders."

Noelle smiled in relief before shooting him a look. "You better not be trying to train already."

A wry smile tugged at his lips. "I'm not," he assured, the tendril of smoke curling up from his cigarette. "The matches at Astros are shut down for a bit."

Her eyebrows shot up at the news. None of the boys had mentioned that. "How come?"

Carson rolled his eyes at whatever the reasoning might be. "Apparently, the cops got an anonymous tip about the fighting, so Darryl put a pause on things until the heat dies down," he told her.

Nerves twisted in Noelle's stomach. If the cops were sniffing around Astros, then Noelle was more than glad Carson was staying away. She didn't want to think about what would happen if they caught him taking part in illegal fights. She didn't want an image of him in handcuffs to ever come true.

"An anonymous tip?"

"I'm positive it was Milner," Carson said, unable to keep the sneer from creeping into his voice at the mention of the loathsome man. Even Noelle's lips curved downwards. "He's pissed he lost to me again. I don't think he's coming back to Astros, so he probably thought to shut down the whole thing as his goodbye present."

Noelle scoffed, not at all surprised. It sounded like exactly the petty thing Milner would do, uncaring of those he potentially got in trouble with the law. Even though everyone at Astros, whether they were the ones fighting or the ones betting, knew what they risked by being there, but that didn't give Milner the authority to throw them under the bus.

"If it dies down this time around, how do you know he's not gonna keep talking to the cops?" Noelle questioned, crossing her arms over her chest.

Carson took a drag of his cigarette, the end burning a bright ember, before releasing the smoke. "Darryl said he'd take care of him, which I don't doubt. He's gonna keep Milner from squealing and send him packing at the same time."

Noelle didn't want to think what that would entail; she wouldn't concern herself with it. She very well knew there was a side of Carson's world revolving around the ring she wouldn't understand nor that she would want to. While she accepted that her boyfriend was one of the best fighters, she would leave it at that. She was well aware it was a risk to even be at Astros as often as she was, though she didn't care, not when it came to Carson. Maybe it was foolish, but love tended to make fools out of everyone, didn't it? Noelle accepted it for Carson.

She rolled her lips into her mouth, distractedly nodding as she recalled the conversation she had with her mother before she left the house. Noelle glanced away, absentmindedly looking at the

368

building next to them while feeling Carson's gaze on her. She could always feel him looking at her, and while she had grown accustomed to it and she had grown to revel in it and enjoy it, she felt nervous just like she used to when she first met Carson.

"My mom wants you to come over for dinner sometime," Noelle blurted out.

The sound of Carson coughing had Noelle snapping her gaze back to her boyfriend, her eyes widening in worry as he coughed into his free fist. His eyebrows were drawn together and his face was slightly scrunched in discomfort as he tried to regain his breath. Noelle stared at him in concern, unsure of what she should do as Carson finally wheezed out a final cough before staring up at her with his dark eyes widened.

"I . . . she wants me to what?"

Noelle didn't blame Carson for sounding so shocked; he was completely taken aback with her words because that was exactly how Noelle had felt when her mom said it to her.

"Yeah," she breathed out with a laugh. Suddenly, all Noelle could feel was her heart pounding, a prickle of fear, and the one emotion she had penned just for Carson. Her chest was right, her body tensing slightly and wondering if she really was gonna do this. If she really was going to say this.

"She wants to get to know the man I love."

Shit. She said it. In a way, she said it.

She bit the inside of her lower lip as she carefully watched Carson, silent and kind of shy and a little bit worried because what if she said it too soon? What if they weren't ready for that?

But then she noticed the way Carson's lips parted, his eyes slightly wide under the few stray curls falling across his forehead and disbelieving, and the cigarette that was nothing but a butt falling from between his fingers and through the metal flooring of the fire escape and all the way down to the ground. Noelle noticed Carson's chest sink heavily as a breath escaped him and her heartbeat could be heard in her ears and felt in her throat.

Suddenly, he was on his feet, his tall figure towering over her. Noelle tracked his movements, taking in the way his eyebrows were drawn together in stunned relief. Noelle parted her lips in surprise until Carson's hands were cupping her cheeks and his lips were on hers.

Noelle stumbled at the sudden force behind the gesture, only getting her footing when one of Carson's arms slid around her waist to keep her in place. Her hands pressed against his chest, fisting it as her lips moved against his instantly and tasting the nicotine as his tongue slipped past her lips and caressed hers. Noelle was sure her heart was ready to burst out of her chest. She hadn't kissed Carson in only a few days, and she was an idiot to think she could've gone a second longer.

It had only been three days but, fuck, she missed him. It felt like a lifetime.

Noelle had almost forgotten what preceded this kiss until Carson's hand went from her cheek to the back of her neck, keeping her in place as he ended the kiss yet kept his forehead against hers. Noelle breathed heavily, her breath stolen from that kiss and her eyes still closed as she felt Carson's nose brush against hers.

And then he gasped airily, his breath fanning her mouth.

"I love you too. Fuck. I love you too. So much," he murmured.

Oh god. Was it inappropriate to cry at this moment?

Her grip on his shirt tightened, her breath hitching in her throat as Carson's quiet words echoed in her head. It wasn't the first time that Carson made Noelle feel like she was floating on cloud nine. It was because he loved her. He loved her too. He loved her.

Every ounce of hesitance and fear was immediately wiped away, and Noelle felt dumb for ever feeling like that in the first place.

Opening her eyes, Noelle looked up at Carson as she swallowed before parting her lips, a breathless laugh escaping her as she noticed Carson already staring at her. He grinned, wide and beautiful and unconditionally happy. Noelle was sure, if it was possible, she fell a little more in love with him. She felt like she was free falling, though not at all terrified because she knew Carson was there to catch her before she hit the ground.

Her cheeks hurt from smiling so much, her hands coming up to cup Carson's jaw and her touch gentle in case he was still in pain, though from the force of that head-spinning kiss, she doubted it. Noelle pressed her lips against his once more, melting into Carson's touch.

"I love you," she murmured for the first time.

*   *   *

They were a mess of tangled limbs and never-ending kisses, skin against skin and never not touching one another. All they could sense, feel, and think about was each other, searing kisses igniting their blood like fuel to a fire. The absolute last thing Carson and Noelle wanted to do was let go of each other, her fingers tangled in his curls as he buried his face in the crook of her neck. He groaned against her skin as her teeth lightly bit into his shoulder.

Carson rocked into her, slow and soft and steady, as Noelle's breathless sounds were music to his ears. Everything about this moment was so intimately perfect, not a single thing to be changed. His lips had been everywhere, kissing every inch of her skin as he memorized every piece of her. Noelle hadn't hesitated on doing the exact same thing to him, her own lips dragging along and soft kisses trailing up his body and over his tattoos until her mouth finally slanted over his.

He had so much goddamn love for her.

"Car," Noelle breathed against his skin, her fingers tightening around his curls in the most dizzying of ways. "I'm . . . keep going, please."

Her wish was his command.

When they finished, they were wrapped up around one another and utterly out of breath but full of love. Neither of them wanted to be anywhere else. Noelle gasped slightly as Carson pulled out slowly, falling on to the mattress next to her with a satisfied groan rumbling deep from his chest.

They were quiet for a moment, catching their breaths because even though they had taken it slow and taken their time with one another, it still rendered them breathless and dizzy with pleasure and bliss and everything else relating to it. That was okay because this was exactly where they wanted to be, how they wanted to be, and who they wanted to be with.

Carson's fingers lightly trailed up and down Noelle's arm, his own wrapped around her shoulder as she laid with her cheek pressed against his chest, her eyes closed against the steady thrum of his heartbeat. Her finger was grazing against his skin, drawing nonsensical patterns before twisting around the chain of his necklace and playing with the pendant.

He stared up at the ceiling, utterly content with having her so close. Nothing else seemed to matter at this moment, and Carson couldn't believe he had gone the past few days without her. It was less than a handful of days, sure, and it could be argued that he was becoming dependent on Noelle's presence, but fuck it if he cared.

He loved being with her, loved having her around, loved her. But knowing that she felt that way about him too brought on a kind of high Carson had never experienced before. Honestly, forget weed or alcohol or cigarettes, Noelle was the most addicting of them all.

Fuck, he was so lucky to have her.

"Y' know I really am sorry, right?" Carson found himself murmuring into the quiet of the night, his voice a low rasp. Noelle's mindless playing with his necklace paused. "Lying to you, worrying you like that . . . I really am sorry about it."

Noelle kept her gaze on her finger wrapping around his chain, Carson's heartbeat calming as she rolled her lips into her mouth briefly.

"I know you are," she answered just as quietly. With a sigh, Noelle lifted herself up slightly, still pressed into his side and folded her arm on his chest to be able to look at him in the eye, prompting Carson to turn his head slightly to meet her gaze.

"I get why you did it, Car, I do, but . . ." She offered an unapologetic small smile. "I'm always gonna worry whenever you have a match, and there's nothing you or I can do about it. I obviously don't want you to stop fighting just because I'm worried, but I'd rather be at Astros than be oblivious to the fact that you're in the ring."

Carson pressed his lips together guiltily, knowing full well that Noelle had a point and that she was right. He knew it was the not knowing that really bothered her. Hell, it was what happened when her father and sister were taken to the hospital. At that moment, Carson promised himself that he would never put Noelle through that again. He could take any punch or kick thrown his way—that kind of pain was doable—but the ache that struck every fiber of his being when he made Noelle angry or hurt her in any way, he knew that was something he could not handle.

He pushed himself up a little, resting his weight on the elbow behind her as he faced her with their bare chests pressed together. For a moment, Carson couldn't help but admire the beauty in front of him; Noelle's long eyelashes framing her gorgeous hazel eyes and messy hair and swollen lips and just glowing. How the fuck had he gotten so lucky?

"I won't ever do something like that again," Carson promised, tangling his legs with hers under the sheets, earning a small smile from Noelle. "And I love it when you come to my matches." He bumped his nose with hers, feeling himself smile effortlessly even though his cheeks warmed slightly. "You're my good luck charm," he admitted.

The smile that instantly spread on Noelle's face made Carson's heart soar, the sight utterly breathtaking as she ducked her head slightly with a light chuckle. She looked back at him, her eyes taking a mischievous glint as she quirked an eyebrow.

"Am I really? Because you beat Milner without me being there," she countered, though there was nothing but playful teasing in her tone.

Carson scoffed out a laugh, feeling any remaining tension he might have felt leave his body because they were okay. "Only because I was thinkin' of you the entire time. See? Good luck charm."

Noelle rolled her eyes, letting out a scoff of her own as she poked his chest to push him back. "Sounds like a bunch of bullshit."

A memory instantly sparked in Carson's mind, immediately remembering that night in their bookstore where he was drenched in rain and annoyed beyond belief that the girl he liked had been avoiding him for days on end. The night when he finally kissed her right after she said the exact same thing she just said, after weeks of deliberating and coming to terms with his feelings.

Here they were now—in love and so fucking happy.

"Really?" Carson hummed coyly, smirking as Noelle raised her eyebrows, unable to keep the sly smile off of her own face because she too remembered that night. How the hell could she not?

Carson leaned closer, not that there was much distance between them in the first place, looking as if he was going in for a kiss and bypassing her lips at the last second to connect his to her jaw. Noelle's lips parted as Carson's traveled down.

374

"I'd be happy to prove that it's not," he mumbled against her skin.

He felt her hand slide up his chest to the back of his neck, keeping him close.

"Might take some convincing," she breathed out.

In a blink of an eye, Carson had Noelle on her back as she let out a startled yet giggling yelp. She stared up at him with eyes widened giddily and excitedly as he grinned down at her, the pendant of his necklace grazing her bare chest. Carson leaned down to connect their lips in a soft, sucking kiss. "We've got all night, love," he murmured.

They were okay. They were happy. They were in love.

EPILOGUE

Holding back the tears was nearly impossible for Noelle. She was unable to keep them at bay as she watched her sister and new brother-in-law do their first dance as husband and wife. It was a beautiful sight, watching Beverly look gorgeous in her perfect wedding gown and Aiden handsome as ever in his fitted black suit slow dancing to their mutual choice of Elvis Presley's *Can't Help Falling In Love*. They both looked so happy, so in love. Noelle had no choice but to cry.

It didn't help that her hormones have been so crazy lately.

An arm wrapped around her waist, pulling Noelle into a familiar comforting embrace before Carson's voice lowly chuckled into her ear.

"D'you need another tissue, love?"

Noelle scoffed at the teasing tone in her boyfriend's voice, turning her head to narrow her eyes up at him. "Don't make fun of me," she whined, the tissue clenched in her hand practically soaked with her tears. Honestly, Noelle was surprised her makeup was still intact. "It's your fault I'm more emotional."

Carson hummed doubtfully. "No, I think it's just because your sister got married," he mused, his left arm around her waist tightening as his hand rubbed her noticeably swollen belly. "Don't blame the little one for this."

Noelle's free hand covered Carson's, a soft smile tilting at her lips. She was four months along, not too big that she couldn't fit into the bridesmaid's dress without a few alterations. Her hormones were already crazy. Her emotions were definitely heightened lately and, honestly, bless Carson for dealing with her day and night.

"I don't blame Dahlia. I blame Dahlia's father. There's a difference," Noelle quipped with a smile, making Carson roll his eyes in amusement, though the smile on his face was nothing but fond.

Why wouldn't it be? In four months' time, baby girl Dahlia Hayes would come into the world. Carson couldn't be more excited if he tried. He and Noelle had been together for nearly three years now, their happiness never ceasing all this time. About a year and a half after they first got together, Noelle moved into Carson's apartment. Another year after that, Carson and Aiden decided to open up their own gym in Brooklyn with the leftover money they had. A few short months after that, Carson decided to quit fighting at Astros.

Noelle asked him time and time again if that was truly something he wanted to do. She knew he loved fighting; she knew he had been doing it for years and it was something he was good at. She didn't want him to regret quitting something he enjoyed, but Carson was adamant on it. The gym had no problem becoming successful to the point that Carson didn't need the extra income from Astros as the co-owner of the gym plus working as a personal trainer for several of their clients. So he told Darryl goodbye and that this chapter of his life was over. While Darryl was sad to see him go, he was more than happy and proud that one of his best fighters found the life he was looking for. With the gym and Noelle's bookstore bringing in money, the two of them lived a more than comfortable life together.

Now, she was pregnant, and their little family of three—the two of them plus Oreo—was growing into a family of four.

"If I remember correctly," Carson hummed as his gaze turned at the bride and groom with a smirk growing on his lips, "I was just doing exactly what you asked me to. You're the one who ended up pregnant because you forgot to take your pill."

Noelle's eyes instantly narrowed once again, taking a step away from him to prop her hands on her hips. Everyone was focused on the newlywed couple, not paying any attention to Carson and Noelle.

"Are you saying you regret getting me pregnant?" she huffed.

Carson's smirk dropped, his eyes blinking wide at the accusatory glare Noelle was shooting him. He needed to tread carefully, realizing he was on dangerous territory with his hormonal girlfriend. He had to say the right thing to defuse the little bomb. Yet another way Noelle kept him on his toes. "What! No, of course not!" he placated and wondered since when Noelle's glare made him so jittery. Definitely when she first started becoming increasingly hormonal. "You know no one's as excited as me to have this baby!"

Apparently, it was the wrong thing to say.

Noelle raised her eyebrows, an offended look washing over her pretty face. "So you think I'm not just as excited as you are?" She leaned towards him and Carson's eyes widened slightly. He wished that someone was around to pull him out of his girlfriend's wrath, but everyone was too busy watching Aiden and Beverly. "You don't think I can't wait to hold our daughter?"

Jesus Christ. Carson could feel himself losing his cool under her severe stare. "I . . . uh, I mean—"

Suddenly, Noelle's scowl crumbled as she began giggling, amusement dancing in her hazel eyes as she leaned away from Carson. She covered her mouth to muffle the sound, not wanting to draw attention, but the mirth in her eyes was clear and Carson was staring at her with his own eyes slightly widened in disbelief and shock.

What the fuck?

378

"Oh god, Car!" Noelle giggled, shaking her head as she looked up at him with a wide grin. Her free hand gripped his bicep, squeezing it comfortingly as she laughed. "You should have seen the look on your face! You looked like I was about to eat you or something!"

Carson's chest deflated, his shoulders sinking as he rolled his eyes and shook his head away from Noelle, who was still giggling as if it was the funniest thing in the world. He pursed his lips as he bemusedly stared at her. Noelle's mood swings were no joke, and her clearly having her fun with them just to get a rise out of Carson wasn't as amusing to him as it was to her.

"I would make a joke about your pregnancy eating habits, but I don't want a plate to my head," Carson shot back.

Noelle's laughter silenced. "Don't you dare."

Carson snorted, the smirk back on his face as he wrapped an arm around her shoulders and pulled her in, pressing a kiss to her temple.

"Can't believe I'm stuck with you," he teased. "You definitely got pregnant on purpose."

Noelle scoffed, rolling her eyes at him. "Please. You couldn't live without me."

Carson smiled against her hair. She wasn't wrong.

*　　*　　*

Somehow, they all ended up at Simon's Stories after the reception.

Even Beverly and Aiden, who were supposed to go back to their place to pick up their bags and leave for their honeymoon, but their flight wasn't for another few hours. When they walked into the bookstore, cheers sounded from everyone already there—Noelle, Carson, Andrea, Camille, Benny, Isaac, Levi, Max, and their respective girlfriends.

"I'm surprised you didn't walk in in your wedding dress," Andrea joked when her eldest sister strolled in arm-in-arm with her new husband, dressed in comfortable pants and a blouse.

Beverly rolled her eyes, makeup still done, as she locked the door behind her before she and Aiden walked over to them.

"How much of a dramatic bitch do you think I am?" she snorted.

Noelle laughed, leaning her head back against Carson's chest. His arms were around her as she sat in the space between his legs. The store had expanded over the past two years. The corner store next to theirs went out of business, so they bought the space for themselves. The blackboard wall had been knocked down and there was a small cafe built in, akin to how there were Starbucks in Barnes and Noble, but that same wall had been rebuilt further along because it was popular amongst the customers. Noelle and Beverly really wanted it around.

Everyone was spread out on the couch or the stools they brought over from the cafe with Noelle and Carson sitting on a floor cushion with his back against the couch occupied by Max, his girlfriend Olivia, and Camille.

"You had a ten-tier cake," Noelle teased. "That's the epitome of dramatic."

Beverly stuck her tongue out, and Noelle smiled innocently, feeling Carson's hands on her belly. She was still in her maid of honor dress, a pretty baby blue gown with spaghetti straps. It was simple and comfortable, which was particularly fortunate for Noelle and her bump.

They fell into a lull of conversation, and the contentment Noelle felt only intensified when she felt the soft yet noticeable kicks her little one was freely giving out.

"She's active tonight, huh?" Carson's quiet voice murmured, his lips brushing along Noelle's ear.

Where his hands were was where little Dahlia was kicking as if she knew where her father was. It was beautiful and brought a smile to Noelle's face.

"Yeah," Noelle hummed, their voices lost amongst the chatter of their friends and family. "At least she's not kicking me like I'm a damn soccer ball." She paused before adding, "Or a punching bag."

Carson smirked, letting out a breathy chuckle. "Definitely Daddy's girl," he mused, fingers tapping Noelle's belly lightly. "Either a soccer star or a fighter in the making."

Noelle grinned slightly. She had found out just a few months into being with Carson how he had grown up playing soccer. He was good at it, which wasn't surprising at all, until his love for fighting won out. Then, his love for family was unbeatable.

"You just had to have hobbies involving loads of kicking and punching, huh?" Noelle asked wryly, shooting him a dry smile. "I'm being bullied by my own kid." With a huff, she added, "Why couldn't you have been into, like, cricket? She doesn't have a bat in there to abuse me with." She knew she sounded ridiculous, but it was fine. Carson was used to her by now.

"Our kid is half Australian. You bet your cute ass, I'll teach her how to play cricket," Carson returned, purposefully thickening his accent as he pressed a kiss to her temple.

"Are you gonna talk to Dahlia like that?" Noelle questioned, an amused smile growing on her face. She felt warm in the best of ways when the two of them just talked about their daughter. Their little girl who, even though wasn't planned, was created out of nothing but pure love, and they were going to meet in just five short months.

It was mind-blowing for Noelle to think about. She was pregnant. She and Carson were expecting their first child together. When she had first found out, Noelle had been terrified. The second she had woken up with morning sickness, she just knew.

The excitement that hit her once the shock subsided was instant and then came the nervousness and fear of telling Carson.

He was a family man; it was one of the endless things Noelle loved about him, but they hadn't planned for having a kid. They weren't engaged or married, and she just wasn't too sure how he would react.

But when Carson fell to his knees in front of her, his hands on her hips and forehead to her still flat stomach, Noelle knew they were more than okay.

"Definitely," Carson answered with a matter-of-fact scoff. "She's gonna have a proper Aussie accent."

"You barely have an accent, and I don't have one. Don't see how your plan's gonna work out, babe."

Carson's arms tightened slightly around Noelle, his curls brushing along her cheek as he dipped his head to press his lips to her bare shoulder.

"If there's a will, there's a way." With a smirk curling at his lips, he added, "'S kind of how you got pregnant, innit?"

Noelle elbowed him, though her cheeks hurt from smiling. "Shut up."

$$* \qquad * \qquad *$$

"Alright, kid. Sleep well, yeah?" Carson smiled, straightening once he finished assisting Andrea into her wheelchair. He did it effortlessly now. It was something Carson had to learn to do when it became obvious that he was going to be sticking around for a long time, and it brought Dr. Simon comfort knowing whoever was heavily involved in theirs and Andrea's lives knew how to help her into and out of her chair properly.

The younger girl smiled up at him. "You too, Car. Night, guys!" Andrea bid goodbye with Carson and Noelle returning the sentiments as she rolled herself up to the front door. Carson stood with one hand on the car door, watching until she was inside and the door shut behind her before getting back into his car.

Music was softly playing through the stereo with nothing but background noise to accompany the dull roar of the wind as they drove with the windows down. That was how most of their drive went, enjoying each other's presence as they reached their apartment building.

"It was a fun day, hmm?" Noelle hummed as she got out of the car. Her left fingers lightly played with Carson's right ones as they walked inside and to the elevators, not quite holding hands but still touching one another.

"It was," Carson easily agreed as he pressed the button for their floor. A smile twitched at his lips as he wiggled his own fingers around Noelle's lightly, returning the gesture. It was instinctive, the desire to always be touching Noelle in some way. The need for it just grew even after a few years of being together already. "Don't think I've ever seen Aiden this happy."

"Yeah," Noelle breathed out, her eyes on the mirrored ceiling of the elevator as her smile grew fond, thinking of the glow her sister had on the entire day. Noelle let out a light laugh just as the elevator opened up, and they got to their door. "Thank God it's over though. If I wasn't pregnant, I think Beverly would've been more of a bridezilla than she already was," she mused.

Carson's low chuckles joined in with Noelle's laughter while he opened the door to their apartment. Oreo was sound asleep in his bed by the couch as Noelle switched on the hallway light. Carson followed her into the kitchen as she got them both a glass of water. He then offered a single-shouldered shrug.

"When the time comes, you can go full bridezilla on her while planning our wedding."

The glasses nearly slipped out of Noelle's grasp, her eyes widening the second Carson uttered those words. What the hell? Maybe her heart picking up its pace was an overreaction, but Noelle and Carson hadn't ever discussed marriage—not when she got pregnant, not when she spent all those months helping Beverly plan her wedding. The two of them just went with the flow, took life as it came their way, and they were more than happy with that, but still . . . marriage was a big thing. While it was ridiculous how she and Carson never even talked about it, him bringing it up so casually in conversation had her eyes practically jumping out of their sockets.

"I'm sorry." Noelle cleared her throat, putting down the glasses before she dropped them as she faced her boyfriend. Carson dropped his suit jacket on the stool on the other side of the center island, the sleeves of his button-down rolled to his elbows and his tattoos deliciously on display as he raised an eyebrow at her. "I . . . what'd you just say? Our wedding?"

"Yeah." Carson shrugged, his silver bracelet tinkling as he lifted a hand to run through his curls and slowly made his way around the island. Noelle's heart jumped as Carson smiled a confused grin, not totally understanding why Noelle looked so shocked. "Come on, love. It's gonna happen eventually." His arms wound around her waist, pulling her close. He smiled at the feeling of Noelle's round belly against him as she peered up at him with gorgeous wide hazel eyes. "You're not gonna be my girlfriend forever."

Okay, so Noelle of course always thought of a bound future with Carson, but she hadn't expected it to go like this. Since she became pregnant, all their focus went on the preparation for the arrival of their baby—nothing else in the world seeming to matter. They had good jobs, ran successful businesses, and were so happy and so in love. What more could they ask for? Marriage could've been discussed later, and now that the topic was up, Noelle's heart was going into overdrive.

Before she could even hope to respond, parting her lips soundlessly, Carson continued with a boyish smirk, "Though, let's be honest, no matter what, I'm always gonna introduce you as my baby mama."

That had Noelle blinking back into reality, her mouth dropping with a scoff as she frowned in empty annoyance, smacking Carson's chest as she pouted.

"This isn't a joke, Car!" Carson laughed, the sound gorgeous and coming from the happiest place. "I need to know if you're serious about me or not," she joked as she couldn't fight off her own laugh.

Carson's jaw dropped, still laughing as his dark eyes glinted with amusement. He stared down at the woman he was so in love with, who was carrying a little girl he was already in love with. Noelle's hazel eyes glimmered under the single lamp hanging from the center of the ceiling, and Carson hoped their daughter had Noelle's eyes.

Bringing his hands up, Carson cupped Noelle's face as he kissed her then—a slow, sucking soft kiss that had her fisting the front of his shirt to pull him closer. Her response was instant. A comforting, loving warmth spread through Carson the moment their lips touched just like it always did, and sometimes, it still amazed him that kissing Noelle felt just like it did the first time. It was just as exciting, just as promising, just as always leaving him wanting more.

Now, when he felt his daughter kick in between them, Carson knew that this was a kind of happiness he had always hoped for.

He smiled against Noelle's lips, his thumbs brushing her cheekbones. "Want me to show you just how serious I am about you?" he murmured with a boyishly teasing grin.

Their lips brushed together as they pulled back a fraction of an inch, Noelle's teeth purposefully catching Carson's lower one as she giggled.

"Always."

He did just that. He took her back to their bedroom and showered her with kisses and touches and words derived from nothing but love and appreciation and warmth. Carson was serious about Noelle from the moment he laid eyes on her even if he hadn't known it at the time. He was serious about her when he threw a punch for her the first time. He was serious about her when he kissed her the first time, when they made love, when they fought, when they worked things through, when they moved in together, when she told him she was pregnant . . .

He was serious about her the day after that memorable one too, when he called his mum the next day and asked for his grandmother's ring. And every day since then, with the ring hidden in one of his boxing gloves that was hung in the living room, Carson had been serious about Noelle.

Five months later, when she gave birth to their gorgeous daughter, who introduced a whole new world of love neither of them had expected, with dark hair and chubby cheeks like her father and eyes like her mother, Carson was serious about Noelle.

A month after that, when Carson finally proposed to Noelle so they could become even more of a family than they already were, he was serious about Noelle.

Carson had never been this in love and this happy. The only person he could thank for that was Noelle. She brought him an overwhelming love he didn't think existed, and she reminded him every day that he did the same for her. They knew there was no one else for them but each other. That was all they needed . . . for now. Just them and their daughter.

Noelle would read and tell her baby all the wonderful stories that made up their life.

Carson would sugarcoat the hardships of the world for his little girl for as long as he could.

And Dahlia would be loved. With parents as in love as hers, how could she not be?

Do you like romance stories?
Here are samples of other stories
you might enjoy!

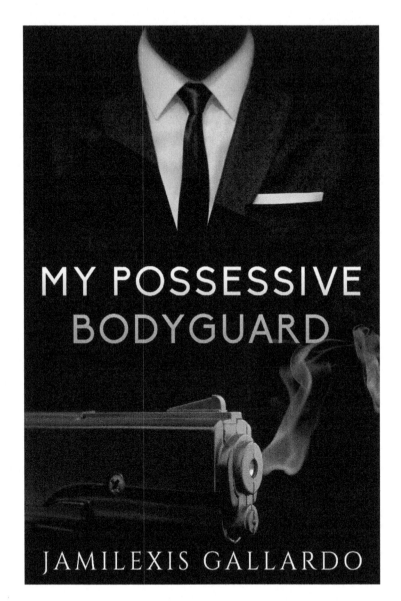

MY POSSESSIVE
BODYGUARD

JAMILEXIS GALLARDO

CHAPTER 1

The freezing cold air hit me like a pile of bricks, sweeping my long brown hair all over my face. If it were any other girl, it would look like a shampoo commercial but I was pretty sure I just looked all dorky and stupid. I pulled my hair away, cringing when my icy cold fingers touched my cheeks.

This was exactly why I didn't like having my hair down, I hated having to take care of it. My hair was wavy but it was also frizzy and those two didn't make a good combination. I usually liked to put it up in a high ponytail but my hair kept me warm, and in this freezing New York weather, I constantly had to find ways to keep myself warm. I wasn't complaining; I loved this weather. I loved wearing cozy sweaters and scarfs and sitting close to the window somewhere with a hot cup of coffee.

I walked down the stairs as people rushed past me. I had just taken my last final of the semester and it sure felt great. Being a college student kept me really busy, but I didn't mind at all. I liked having something to do. Especially after going through the worst possible break-up ever...

Don't go there, Hannah.

"Ms. Collins," Robin, my bodyguard for the day, greeted me with a nod when I made it back to the car. All of my dad's bodyguards looked pretty much the same: tall, muscular, and always in black suits with white shirts and black ties. They also wore an earpiece so they could all be in communication in case something happened. Most people would drool over them and I probably would too, if they weren't with me *all the time*.

I didn't always have bodyguards.

My dad was a famous actor. He had been acting since he was a teenager but his big break-out movie came out about five years ago, making his popularity skyrocket. Around the same time, my mom was attacked in a restaurant parking lot. The men took her purse, jewelry, and her car but not before beating her. My dad's success had put a spotlight on my family and people now knew my family had a lot of money which put us in danger. So we moved to a house with much more security and my dad hired an army of bodyguards.

It wasn't just my dad's success that put us in danger. My oldest brother, Colton, was the owner of the most famous nightclub in New York. Nicholas, my second oldest brother, had started our family's clothing brand company and he ran it as the CEO. A year ago, my youngest brother had decided he wanted to pursue a modeling career. He was currently in Paris.

Who knew success came with a cost? It cost us our safety which was what the bodyguards were for.

Unlike my brothers, I had yet to start my career. I didn't have the same talent as Nick and Colton in running a business or the flawless looks to become a model like my brother Derek. I liked to draw.

I wanted to be a wedding gown designer. I loved designing dresses and had a lot of sketch books in my room where I had started drafting a lot of dresses. Some pages just had doodles, others had the silhouette of a dress; each page had a random design that only I understood. The problem was that I had yet to finish a single whole gown; I always just stopped in the middle of it and started a new one.

I got in the car and Robin shut the door. I watched as he went around it and got in the driver's seat. I looked out the window as he began to drive.

Good-bye school, I thought happily as I watched us pass by the school.

I loved school but finals week killed me mentally and drained me physically. It was enough to make me not want to set eyes on school for a while. I had a whole month to myself. I could lie around in my room, not doing anything *and* not feel guilty about it. It was official: I had nothing to do but draw all day if I wanted…or sleep.

Robin pulled up into the driveway and I watched as he input the six-digit code so the gates could open.

My favorite part of the house was outdoors: the green grass, the big trees, and the different flowers planted in strategic places to make up the garden. The house was beautiful, of course, but I always thought it was too big. I never understood my dad's logic in moving us into a much bigger house after my mom's attack. I thought it made it easier for intruders to break in because there were more windows and more doors to break into. Of course, I knew that it was my vain mother who had a lot to do in choosing the house.

The car stopped in front of the house and I opened the door before Robin had time to reach it. "I got it." I smiled at him.

He nodded but hurried to open the front door for me. I couldn't help but roll my eyes at him. I could open my own doors, thank you very much. I wasn't the famous actress or rich businessman. I wished they wouldn't treat me like I was royalty when the only reason I needed bodyguards was because of my family's success. I was no one.

Inside, the house was warm and spotless clean, like always. The living room was the first thing you saw when you walked in, with very expensive and elegant furniture. Everything in the house was so expensive and beautiful and new. The furniture, the decorative ornaments, the expensive floor almost made this house feel like an exhibit rather than a home.

Money had cost me my parents. Especially my mom.

"Honey? Is that you?" my mom called as she hurriedly made her way into the living room. Her face fell when she saw that it was just me. My mom was a very attractive woman. She was tall with perfect hips and short blond hair with piercing blue eyes. I looked nothing like her. She was always dressed up, as if ready to meet the President of the United States. I often thought how exhausting it must be to be her but she seemed to love being Christina Collins, Richard Collins's first and only wife.

Today, she was wearing a pale pink pencil dress with white high heels, her hair was straight and she had perfect make up on. She did not look forty-five.

"Dad isn't home yet?" I asked taking off my jacket.

"He'll be here soon," she said looking annoyed by my comment.

My dad was supposed to be here last week. He was out, doing interviews or something. He was currently not working in any movie and was supposed to be here by now.

"Okay," I said as I began to make my way up the stairs.

"Dinner is almost ready," Mom called behind me.

I just nodded.

I didn't have the best relationship with my mom. It wasn't always like this but money and fame had really gotten to her. Ever since my dad became famous, she began to worry about appearances more than anything. She wasn't that motherly either, she only cared about looking good in front of the cameras. It was stupid, but I couldn't change that. She also cared more about her sons with big businesses and careers. I think she began to be even more distant with me when I refused to let her open a business to start my own brand. She didn't understand that I wanted to graduate first. She didn't understand the fact that I wasn't ready—I didn't even have a full gown finished! She found it stupid that I didn't want to be successful because of my dad, just like everyone else. I wanted to be successful on my own.

My phone began to ring just as I reached my room and I smiled when I looked at the caller ID.

"Hey, Pat," I answered taking off my scarf.

"Hannah Banana, how are you?" he said on the other end.

I used to cringe when he started calling me 'Hannah Banana' back in middle school but I began to get used to it when I realized he wasn't going to stop calling me that. Apparently, he thought he invented that nickname.

I smiled. "Good."

"What are you up to?"

"Nothing," I said as I closed my bedroom door.

"Oh come on, anything interesting? I didn't call you to be bored to death."

I laughed. "I'm done with finals?" I offered.

"Mmm… that's something I guess."

Patrick and I had been best friends since we were in middle school. He was truly my other half. I never thought a guy would understand me better than a girl but it was true. He understood me better than anyone. After we graduated from high school, he moved to Miami for school and I haven't seen him since then.

"What are you doing?" I asked throwing myself on the bed.

"Getting ready for the club, baby!" he yelled in my ear. "Hold up—I'm going to FaceTime you because I need outfit advice."

"Okay," I said rolling my eyes. He hung up and FaceTimed me a few seconds later. He was in front of a mirror, trying on different jackets.

Patrick was a fuckboy. There was no other way to describe him, maybe manwhore? He liked to sleep around. It got worse when he moved over there, just like I knew it was going to happen. Which was why, before he left three years ago, I made him take a sexual education class since high school failed to give us any useful advice.

"Now you can whore around all you want," I had told him which made him laugh.

Sometimes, I wondered how we were still friends. It had been three years since he left and we lived in different states but somehow, we had made it work. He was all I had.

I talked with him for a while, he told me about his latest hook-up and I listened like the good friend I was. After we hung up, I got in the shower and it was when I was changing that there was a knock on the door.

"Yes?" I called as I threw a blouse over my head.

"Mrs. Collins would like me to tell you that dinner is ready," Katie, one of our maids, called from the other side of the door.

"I'll be right down!" I called back as I put on some jeans.

My dad must have gotten here after all. I was excited about seeing him. I missed him whenever he was gone. I finished combing my hair and then quickly made my way out. I ran down the stairs, feeling like a little girl.

"What have I told you about running down the stairs, Hannah?" my mom asked, looking annoyed when I walked into the dining room.

I ignored her and smiled when I saw my dad. My dad was a handsome man. He was tall with broad shoulders and short brown hair with brown eyes and fair skin. I looked like him and I loved it. His smile always took me back to when I was a little girl and he would read to me while I sat on his lap. All of that was gone. He was always flying somewhere nowadays.

"Dad!" I said walking to him.

He stood up as he smiled. "Hey, sweetie," he said as he put his arms around me.

I suddenly had the urge to cry. I missed him so much. "I missed you," I mumbled.

"Me too," he said as he stroked my hair.

"Hannah, your father wants to eat," my mom said sounding annoyed.

I let him go. "Sorry, Dad."

He shook his head. "You okay?" he asked with a frown. His brown eyes studied my face as if trying to read what I had been up to for the past few months.

Oh if only he knew.

I nodded as we took our seats. "Yeah, I just missed you."

He winked at me as he squeezed my hand. I hadn't realized that Nick and his wife, Rachel, were also at the table.

"Hey." Rachel smiled across the table from me.

I smiled at her. "Hey."

I really liked Rachel. She was tall, with long blond hair, hazel eyes, and fair skin. She was not only beautiful but also modest and perfect for my brother. They had been married for about a year and they made the perfect couple. *Literally*, they were always all over the magazines as the perfect couple. Rachel was a fashion designer which was perfect because she fit right in with Nick's business. I admired and wanted to be as good as her someday.

"How was school?" she asked as my mom and dad carried a conversation. I swear she cared more about me than my own mother.

"Good. I'm done for the semester," I said as one of the maids served me pasta. "Thank you," I told her. She smiled. My mom wasn't exactly nice to the housemaids or to anyone who helped keep the house beautiful so I always tried to make up for it.

"What are we talking about?" Nick said looking at Rachel and me. Nick was the spitting image of my mom. They had the same nose, same blond hair, and blue eyes. Nick always kept himself groomed and he was always wearing suits; he fit right in with the bodyguards like camouflage.

Rachel rolled her eyes at him. "So nosy."

He smiled as he leaned in and kissed her on the lips which earned him a glare from my mom who didn't miss anything. *No kissing at the table Nick!*

I smiled at them. They always made me think that true love existed. Up to a few months ago, I thought I had found my true love but all I got was heartbreak instead. Another one added to the list. I was still in the stage where thinking about it still hurt. Thinking about him and everything that happened still made me want to crawl up in a ball and cry.

I never had luck when it came to relationships.

I fell too hard, too fast…and they ended just as fast.

I was starting to believe that maybe love wasn't for me. Maybe I was meant to be alone.

At least I wouldn't hurt that way.

If you enjoyed this sample, look for
My Possessive Bodyguard
on Amazon.

BROKEN

Hearts

S.G SONYSA

CHAPTER ONE
A Life-Changing Decision

HAILEY

I was sitting in my room near the window, reading my favorite book, which was full of mystery and thrill. I loved reading books before going to bed because they kept me from recalling all the horrible memories in my past that haunted me every night.

I shivered thinking about last week's nightmare. In it, I was crying hysterically at something my mom said, and then the world collapsed under me as I fell into darkness.

I wanted to keep reading and finish the whole book before going to bed, but it seemed impossible to continue because I was so sleepy. I closed the book and put it on my study table before I got up from my chair.

The glowing full moon outside my window caught my eye, and I stared at it. It looked beautiful, spreading light in the darkness of the night. Suddenly, the rustling of the trees in the garden made me jump. I looked outside but couldn't see anything or anyone. Before something would appear and scare me, I decided to go to bed.

I jumped on my bed and pulled the comforter up to my chin. The softness of the new sheets felt so nice, making me sigh in contentment. I snuggled my face in the pillows and drifted into a dreamless slumber.

My mother's screams woke me up. I looked around, and my eyes landed on the wall clock; it was half past twelve. I heard the shattering of glass and jumped from the bed, running out of my room to search for my parents and granddad.

The angry voices of my mom and granddad led me to my granddad's study. The door was ajar. Taking advantage of it, I silently slipped inside. I found my mom standing in the middle of the room crying and mumbling something. My dad was sitting on the couch and staring at the floor like it was the most interesting thing in the world.

I didn't know what was going on and I was scared to find out. I noticed anger and worry etched on my granddad's face while he was busy glaring at my mom. They didn't know I was standing in the corner and watching everything.

Finally, I found the courage to open my mouth. "What is happening? Mom? Dad?" I asked them.

Their heads snapped in my direction, and their eyes stared at me with terror. My mom met my gaze and I felt myself freeze. Her eyes were filled with hate, as she looked straight at me. I feared for my life at that moment.

In my sixteen years of existence, I never saw this much hate for me in my mom's eyes. I was used to her disappointed glances, but this glare felt dangerous like it promised to inflict me an unimaginable amount of pain.

My father noticed the look on my mom's face and shook his head.

"Hailey, go back to your room," my dad said.

I was about to turn around and leave the study, but my mother's angry voice stopped me dead in my tracks.

"No! She should know what is going on in this house. Emily left us because of some stupid promise your grandfather made years ago to his best friend," my mom yelled, making me freeze.

I couldn't believe my ears.

My sister left! Why would she suddenly leave the house? What happened?

I asked my mom. "Why did she leave?"

My grandfather heaved a sigh and stood up from his chair. He took long steps, and within seconds he was standing in front of me.

"Hailey, when I was young, I made a promise to my best friend. Now, he is on his deathbed. He wants me to fulfill my promise before his death," my granddad said.

I was more confused after hearing what my granddad said. I didn't understand how it was connected to my sister leaving the house.

My mother noticed my confusion and said, "Tell her the truth!"

My granddad glared at my mom then turned back to me.

"My friend and I made a promise that someday, we will unite our families by arranging a marriage between our first grandchildren. Now, that he is not well and dying in the hospital, his family contacted me. They want me to fulfill my side of the promise before my friend's death. He wants to see his grandson happily married to my granddaughter before dying," my grandfather said.

I looked at him in shock. Now, it all made sense. That was why Emily ran away in the middle of the night. She had always been against marriage, and an arranged marriage was something she would never do. She always wanted to become a model and marriage meant the end of her modeling career.

"Why did you tell them that Emily would marry their son? She is eighteen, and it's too early to get married. She has her whole life ahead of her to spend the way she likes. Please don't ruin it by forcing her to marry a man she barely knows. Please, I beg you! Stop this nonsense so she can come back home," my mom said.

"What do you want me to do, Melanie? Do you want me to refuse them or tell them that I can't fulfill my friend's last wish?"

My mother's eyebrows scrunched up at his words. A few moments later she started smiling cryptically my way. I felt nervous while staring at her. With slow predatory steps, she approached me. "I think Hailey is the better candidate to marry off. She doesn't look that young. She has good height and weight. She will look perfect as the wife of your friend's grandson," Mom said and gripped my arm.

I was shaking with fear, but her grip was so tight, making it impossible for me to move.

"If she marries your friend's grandson, you will be able to fulfill your friend's dying wish, and I will get my daughter back in this house." She suggested.

My eyes widened, and I instantly paled. My hands started shaking violently in anxiety, but she tightened her grip on my arm, digging her nails and making me hiss in pain.

"Are you out of your mind? How can you suggest something so absurd?" My dad was in a rage.

"This is the only solution. Believe me. It's best for all of us, even for Hailey," my mom said looking at me.

I felt tears brimming in my eyes, and they were ready to fall.

"She is sixteen, Melanie. She is younger than Emily if you haven't noticed," my grandfather said.

My mom's grip on my arm loosened.

"I don't care how young she is. I just know she is not Emily, my blood, my real daughter. And it's time for her to repay me for taking care of her all these years instead of making Michael leave her outside some orphanage," Mom yelled.

I went numb after her words registered in my mind.

Why was she saying this? Did it mean she was not my real mom?

"Melanie, why have you done this? It is not the right time to inform her all about the past. You promised me that we would not discuss this with her until she turns eighteen," Dad yelled.

At that moment, I forgot how to breathe. It meant whatever my mom said a few seconds ago was the truth. I was not her flesh and blood. I was not her real daughter.

Was my dad even my birth father? Was he?

"Yes, I promised that I will not tell her anything until the right time comes. But I think this is the best time to talk about your past, Michael," my mom said with nonchalance.

My dad looked at her in utter disappointment. The betrayal that he was feeling after my mom's revelation reflected on his face.

"Hailey, look at me," my father said, walking towards me and cupping my face. "I wanted to tell you this before, but then we decided to wait until you become mature enough to understand it. I am your dad. You are my own flesh and blood, but Melanie is not your real mother. Your real mother died giving birth to you."

I stopped breathing after what my dad said. My world collapsed, and I felt like falling into a dark hole.

"I was already married to Melanie and had Emily when I went to England on a business trip. There I met your mother and fell in love with her. Then one day, I found out that she was pregnant. I didn't know that the doctor informed her that there might be complications during the birth. She kept that information to herself and stayed positive. She decided to bring you into this world. The doctors tried their best to save her, but she died a minute after you were born."

I gasped and pulled away from my dad's grasp. It felt like he ripped my heart out.

He continued, "I informed Melanie about my infidelity, and about you. She was angry and hurt when she found out that I cheated on her. But after some time, she forgave me because of Emily's and your future. Melanie accepted you and me. She is just angry at the moment," he said to me.

He thought she was only angry. I wanted to tell my dad that she was not only angry but that she also hated me. No one deserved a cheating husband and his bastard child from another woman. At that moment, I understood her constant jabs and hatred towards me.

I deserved her hate and Emily's hate.

Oh, God! I destroyed their happy family by intruding.

All my life, I thought this woman was my mother. Even when she called me a freak and constantly sent me hateful glances, I never doubted that she wasn't my mom.

I remembered when I was small; she played with me, took care of me, and fed me with her own hands. But when I turned eight, she stopped doing anything for me, and I started spending more time with grandma. From that day onwards she never showed any affection to me. But I still loved her.

I was completely silent absorbing everything in. My dad looked defeated, and grandfather was deep in thought. My mom was staring straight at me still waiting for my answer.

"Michael, I forgave you a long time ago and accepted her. Now it's her turn to do something for me. I want my daughter back in this house at any cost. Emily and I cannot tolerate her presence here anymore," mom said.

And at that moment, I realized that she really wanted me to leave. Her last statement made me choose my poison, and I decided what I needed to do next. I was already standing on the edge of a cliff, but she finally made me jump and fall.

My voice was emotionless when I announced my decision.

"Mom is right. I will marry your friend's grandson instead of Emily," I said to my grandfather. "Please, ask Emily to come back home. She deserves to live here more than me," I said, turning towards my mom.

"Thank you so much, Hailey. I'll stay grateful to you for this sacrifice." She smiled at me.

I left and ran back to my room as fast as I could and locked my bedroom door. My eyes were misty from the tears pooling in them. I flung myself on the bed and hugged my pillow tightly. The tears that I had been holding back started falling from my eyes soaking the pillow.

I cried for my dead mother and for my father's infidelity. But mostly for the decision, I made a few minutes ago without thinking about the consequences. Thinking about my past and future, a sob broke out from my chest.

*   *   *

CHASE

After my last class, I decided to go to the hospital to visit my granddad. He had been preparing me for the day that he would leave me all alone in this world.

I was running towards my car when Jack called me.

"Hi, buddy. We are leaving for practice. Are you coming?" Jack asked me.

"I have already talked to coach about skipping today's practice. I need to visit Granddad."

"Okay. See you tomorrow." Jack turned to leave with the team.

I got into the car and started driving to the hospital.

I still remembered the first day my granddad taught me how to play soccer. At first, I was not able to throw the ball in the goal net, but he made me practice and told me that one day I would be able to do it. Now, I'm on the NYU soccer team and one of the best players on the team.

My granddad became my best friend as my dad had always been busy with business meetings, and my mom stayed out with her friends enjoying her life. My twin sister and I used to stay at home with Granddad, and he would make us dinner then played with us.

My mom had always been controlling. She was very specific about what I needed to do to stay on her good side. She was the one who decided where I should study and what I should choose as my major.

My twin sister, Kate, quickly turned into the girl my mother wanted her to be. She took fashion design because of Mom even though she wanted to become an artist. Her passion for painting and drawing had diminished due to the constant pressures of her studies.

I parked my car and made my way inside the hospital, taking the elevator to the second floor where my granddad had been staying for the past two weeks. Instead of recovering he had become weaker.

I opened the door to his room and slipped inside silently. My granddad was sleeping peacefully. I sat on the empty chair beside his bed and placed my hand on his fragile one. His hand used to be so tough and strong, but now, it felt soft and lifeless.

When I looked at his face, he opened his eyes and stared at me. He moved his hand up and removed the oxygen mask from his face.

"Granddad, why did you remove this?" I asked him, trying to make him put it back on his face.

"I want to talk to you, son." He stopped me from putting the oxygen mask on.

"Okay. I'm listening, Granddad," I said.

"Chase, I have this friend, and we made a promise to arrange… arrange a marriage between our first grandchildren." My granddad stared at me.

I didn't know what to say at that moment.

"I want you to marry his granddaughter. This is my last wish, son," he said, clutching my hand.

"Granddad, I…" I was about to remind him that I'm still in the last year of my bachelor in business administration but he cut me off.

"Please, Chase. Do this for me. I want to see you married before my death," he said.

At that night, I made the decision that would change my life forever.

If you enjoyed this sample, look for
Broken Hearts
on Amazon.

HER
PERFECT
REBOUND

BOOK ONE
LOVE AND LUST SERIES

E.R. KNIGHT

CHAPTER 1

Emily threw her phone on the covers of her bed. It bounced once and then lay still.

She was pissed.

Parker hadn't been answering her calls for the past hour. He was still monkeying around with the football team, hours after the end of their practice session.

Emily prided herself on not being the nagging and needy girlfriend, but this was taking things too far. Parker had promised to be early today because she really didn't want to be late for the musical this evening that was going to begin in exactly an hour.

Emily was a theatre buff. She had saved up for three entire months so that she could get not one but two tickets for the musical. She had wanted to spend time with Parker. With all the running about due to the midterm examinations, they hadn't gone out for a long time.

She had wanted today to be special, just the two of them, but it looked like Parker had other plans.

Emily turned to the mirror. She had taken efforts today. Her hair was curled up in a loose bun at the back of her head and showcased her slim neck. She had worn a sleeveless navy-blue dress with a sweetheart neckline that showed off her curves and completed the outfit with a pair of black sandals with high heels. Her makeup was minimal and consisted of a tinge of blush on her cheeks, eyeliner that highlighted her olive-green eyes, and a dab of lip gloss on her full lips.

She wrung her hands while she stared at her reflection.

This was the second time Parker had stood her up. The last time was when they had decided to go to his house to celebrate Thanksgiving with his family. More like with his uncle and guardian, Gage.

Parker was an only child. His parents owned their own company in Greece and lived there most of the time. Since they couldn't be around that much for Parker, they had sent him to America to live with his mom's younger brother.

He and Emily had met in college. She had been pursuing her medical degree at MSU and was in her second year while Parker was a third-year student.

She was an orphan and had grown under the care of her housekeeper who had chosen to look after her after she lost her dad due to cancer. Her mom hadn't survived after giving birth to her.

After six months of knowing each other, Parker asked her out, and they began dating.

They had been together for a year now. Emily still remembered her first kiss with him and also, the night she lost her virginity. It had been their eighth-month anniversary. Parker had taken her out for dinner that day and told her that he loved her. Emily had felt like the luckiest girl.

He dropped her off at home that evening. But when he kissed her goodnight, they had suddenly found themselves inside her dorm room, tearing each other's clothes off. They had slept together that night, and Emily couldn't help feeling that everything had turned out perfect for them.

The musical that she had bought the tickets for was based on a famous movie, *Mamma Mia*, and was going to be held at the Orpheum Theatre.

She glanced at her phone again, willing it to ring, but it didn't.

She couldn't believe Parker could be so inconsiderate. She had called him before she began to get ready to remind him to be there on time, but he told her off by saying that she was acting like his mom and was getting on his nerves. Emily had been hurt, but she excused him, thinking he was just tired and needed a bit of time to relax with the guys.

The clock ticked by, and Emily tried calling Parker a few more times. But he didn't answer.

The show would begin soon, and she was sure the theatre would be full today. She was starting to get frustrated when suddenly, her phone rang. Startled, she grabbed it, expecting Parker's face to flash on the screen, but it wasn't him.

Her hopes were shot down.

Trying to keep calm, she took a deep breath and answered the call. "Hello?"

"Emily?"

She had heard that voice before.

"Who's this?" she asked.

"It's Gage."

Emily stared at the floor in confusion. Why was Gage calling her? Where the hell was Parker?

If you enjoyed this sample, look for
Her Perfect Rebound
on Amazon.

ACKNOWLEDGEMENTS

The only reason I continued this story when I first started posting it was because of the readers I garnered on Tumblr; if I could name and thank every single one of them by name, I would. Every word of feedback, every comment and compliment I received gave me the motivation to finish this book, and it's thanks to them I saw it through.

My dad, who always wonder what exactly I write about but never try to push me away from my love for writing. My mom, who is the reason why I grew such a love for writing because she's the one who made me enjoy reading.

Professor Janis Hubschman, who taught me Introduction to Fiction Writing and Intermediate Fiction Writing. Her classes taught me how to read between the lines, how to edit, how to pick apart a story, how to write a good one worth telling, and these are all skills I've been pouring into my writing ever since.

My editors and publishers at Typewriter Pub. You work diligently to help me shape my story into the best version of itself and allow me to share it with everyone, and I can't ever express my gratitude enough for it.

AUTHOR'S NOTE

Thank you so much for reading *Sugarcoated Pain*! I can't express how grateful I am for reading something that was once just a thought inside my head.

Please feel free to send me an email. Just know that my publisher filters these emails. Good news is always welcome.
summer_nawaz@awesomeauthors.org

I'd love to hear your thoughts on the book. Please leave a review on Amazon or Goodreads because I just love reading your comments and getting to know you!

Can't wait to hear from you!

Summer Nawaz

ABOUT THE AUTHOR

Born and raised in Pakistan, Summer now lives in New Jersey and is currently studying to earn her Masters in English. She is an avid reader of YA and NA fantasy and romance books, and when she isn't reading, she's working on the various books she hopes to one day finish. She lives by the idea of books serving as the number one form of escapism, and strives to instill those feelings in those who read her books the same way she experiences them in reading her own favorite novels.

Made in the USA
Las Vegas, NV
04 February 2021

17230180R00233